THE TIMETRIPPERS

HAMISH ROBERTSON

Hamish Robertson Publications

Published in Great Britain by Hamish Robertson Publications
Liberton, Scotland

This first edition published 2007

1 3 5 7 9 10 8 6 4 2

Set in Jenson Pro by Zero Design, Edinburgh, Scotland

Printed and bound by Scotprint, Haddington, Scotland

A CIP catalogue record for this book is available from the British Library.

ISBN 978-0-9555555-0-3

www.thetimetrippers.co.uk

FOR MUM, DAD AND RODDY
– TIMETRIPPERS ALL

The Author

Hamish Robertson lives in Edinburgh, and allegedly was once a child, which may have helped him write this masterpiece of invention which children between 10 and 110 will love.

Decades ago, he wrote some poems and once or twice he wrote a play, but this is the first big book he's written – and there'll be another one soon so you can find out what you didn't in this one.

What else do you need to know? Well, probably nothing, but here goes anyway.

He says he plays a mean game of snooker, can pull golf clubs round a course, and used to long and triple jump for Scotland and Great Britain.

He's got a family, which includes a beautiful wife, three sons and five grandchildren he's pretty proud of. He's also got a big brother who still keeps an eye out for him.

He reads a lot, still knows who Snow Patrol are and cooks a pretty amazing curry when he's asked, and even when he's not.

Don't ask him about wine – you'd miss the time that would be better spent reading The Timetrippers.

And if you want to find out even more about Hamish – and why wouldn't you? - go to www.thetimetrippers.co.uk

Excerpt from A Drunk Man Looks at The Thistle, by Hugh MacDiarmid
used by kind permission of Carcanet Press Limited.

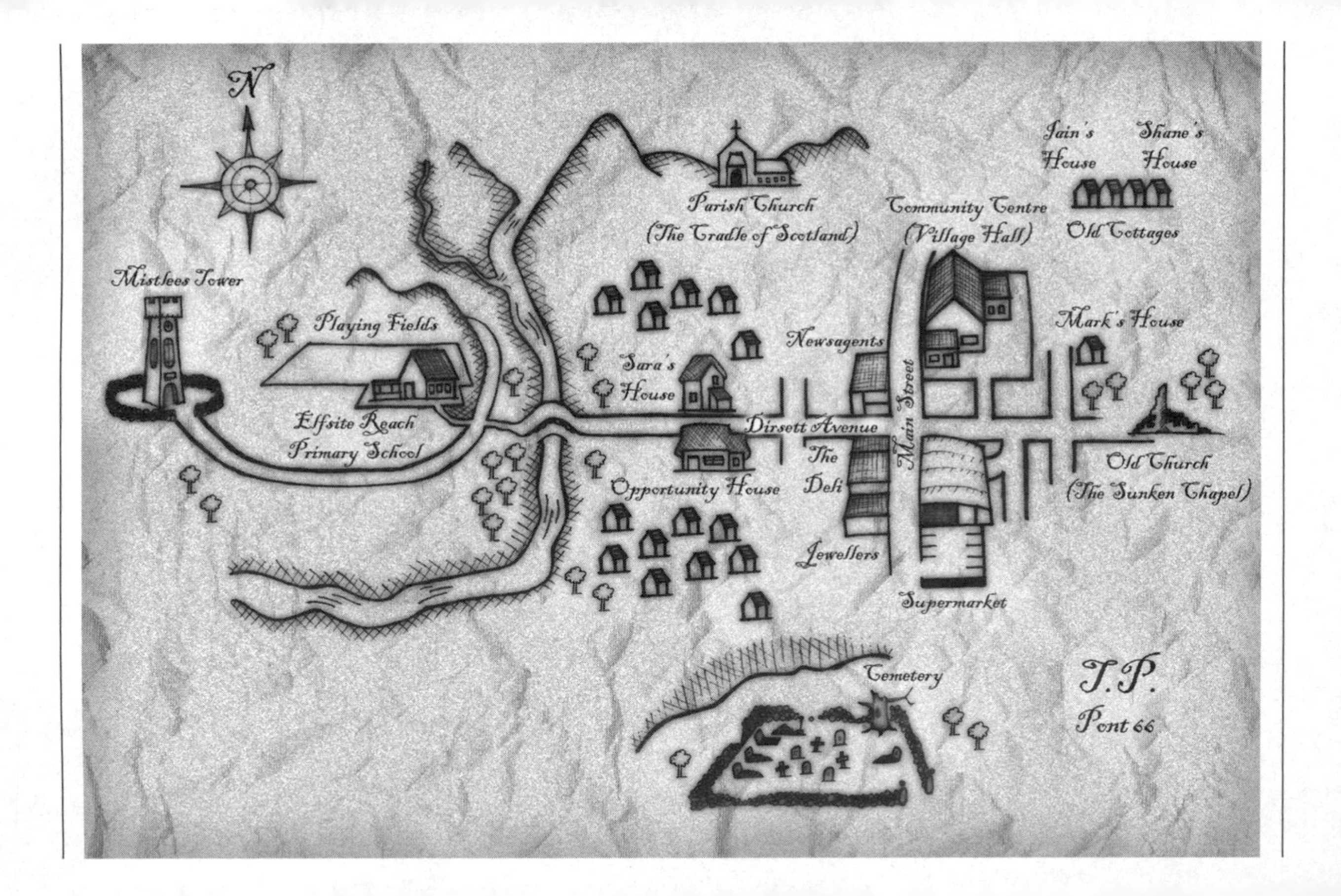
N
Iain's House
Shane's House
Parish Church
(The Cradle of Scotland)
Community Centre
(Village Hall)
Old Cottages
Mistlees Tower
Playing Fields
Mark's House
Newsagents
Sara's House
Main Street
Dirsett Avenue
Elfsite Reach
Primary School
The Deli
Old Church
(The Sunken Chapel)
Opportunity House
Jewellers
Supermarket
Cemetery
T.P.
Pont 66

Chapter 1

The icy water pulled him into its racing torrent as he twisted and tumbled and started to sink.

He struggled to turn on his back, feet pointing down-river. The current eased, but the pace was still frightening.

The water gripped him fiercely and chillingly. The roar of the river's race was bewildering. Ancient trees loomed over the bank, too high to catch and hold on to. Overhead, the sun blazed down.

There was a girl in the water beside him. She pushed closer and reached out. He grabbed her hand, and she held on as they tumbled past dark rocks, dense undergrowth and through a channel. They swept round a bend. He lost the girl's grip, and she surged ahead.

Suddenly, they were squashed between an enormous moss-covered rock and the reedy bank. He paddled to catch her.

The water roared louder, and they plunged deep down and under. They were pulled, pushed and lifted back to the surface to a waterfall of white foam ahead. They tumbled head over heels, and twisted like a crazy corkscrew down and through the torrent.

Time jumped, and he lay beside the girl on a pebbled beach, tossed there by the spin of a whirlpool.

He looked at her, stunned.

She said: "What happened? Where are we? Who are you?"

"I don't know where we are", he spluttered. "And who are you?"

"I'm Sara", she said, patting him on the back to get his breath back.

"Thanks. I'm Dan. What's going on?"

They looked round at a stunningly beautiful scene.

Behind them was the river, gurgling as the whirlpool sucked in and spat out tree roots, branches and weeds. In front was a crescent of gigantic tropical trees, tendrils trailing lazily in the brilliant sunlight. The air was humid and still.

Circling effortlessly above were three large black-winged birds, sizing them up, moving closer and closer.

"Hey, I think we need to move. Quick!" said Sara, grabbing his arm and tugging him towards the trees.

They stumbled up the pebbles to the shelter of an ancient wrinkled tree, its branches stretching up to the now hidden sun. They sat down to recover, exhausted by the effort of staying afloat.

Dan gasped; "I can't believe it! I've never swum in a river before! I've never seen anyplace like this! And it's so hot and steamy!"

Their clothes were soaked, but quickly drying in the shelter of their guardian tree.

Sara said "I was on the net, doing homework on Africa. We've to find out what animals live on the Savannah. I took some notes, closed the PC, and before I know it I'm in a crazy rushing river!"

Dan looked around. "This can't be the Savannah! These trees are like you'd see in a mangrove swamp. But there's no swamp here."

"And I hope there's no alligators", chimed Sara, laughing at his puzzled face.

"Let's check it out", he said, and stood up. A few yards away a gap in the trees caught the sun's rays, inviting them in. They looked at each other, nodded and walked forward. Dan moved without effort, and looking down, realised he was floating over the ground.

They were climbing, and glided through the trees, up a steep slope to the top of a hill, with the river far below. Its racing torrent sounded as a background murmur. They could see for miles, and the sun was again beating on their heads. The view was stunning.

For as far as the eye could see was dense forest, crowned by a ring of snow-capped mountains, and wreathed in white puffy clouds.

The evil bird trio had gone, replaced by ghostly figures flying lazily back and forth in complex patterns. The shapes and sizes of these creatures kept changing. They were about Dan's size and shape, but with see-through wings. In seconds, they grew bigger and more solid –like flying adults. Suddenly they shimmered out of view, and he wondered if the blazing sun was affecting his eyes.

The sounds of the forest were all around –insects chirruping, and birds cawing from the trees below. Monkeys chattered in the undergrowth. A small red and black snake, startled, slithered silently off, making them jump.

They glided on to reach a smooth grass meadow. In front stood a small circle of rocks, with two large stones in the centre, each about their own height. Beyond were countless vast stone buildings, with avenues leading off in all directions.

The city was made of huge blocks of grey weathered stone. Many of the structures were pyramids, and most were several storeys high, pillared and majestic, shimmering in the sun.

There was no sound at all.

Dan walked towards one building. The pillars were carved with strange symbols and shapes. He walked in wonder through the massive entrance. Inside, the walls glowed. In front were rows and rows of stone shelves, full of books sheathed in a leathery-leafed soft green substance.

"It's a library!" he cried, astonished. He picked up one of the heavy books from the nearest shelf. Sensing he wasn't alone, he looked up to see a dark skinned girl hovering above the floor, straight in front of him.

His jaw dropped, and so did the book, with a soft clump, to the paved floor. The girl, strangely dressed in a loose-fitting tunic, shimmered and gave off a soft radiance. She spoke without opening her smiling mouth. "You see our past, and come from our future. I have waited till the end to greet you".

Sara shrieked in alarm as she entered the building to see the girl flicker and disappear as quickly and quietly as she had arrived.

Dan had a feeling something dreadful was going to happen, and picked up the book, knowing it was vitally important.

Suddenly, the ground beneath his feet collapsed, and he felt himself falling, falling, falling, arms and legs flailing frantically to stop himself from somersaulting.

"Heeeeeeeelp!" He shouted.

"Dan! Dan! Wake up!"

The voice came from the end of a dense tunnel that dissolved and turned into a pile of bedclothes. His mum, Liz, lifted them gently from his head.

"Dan – it's OK! - Where were you? What happened? You were dreaming again!"

He slowly came to, the visions from his dream still vibrating in his mind. He looked round, and with a start, remembered this was the first morning in his new home. He felt for the book but held nothing in his hands.

Liz sat on the bed and put her arm round him: "Are you all right? You were thrashing around and shouting for help".

As the dream faded, he shivered and hugged her.

Chapter 2

He began to dream vividly six weeks earlier, after learning they were moving to Scotland.

The Goodwins lived in Southcoats, near Bournemouth in England, and his dad, Hugh, worked with a big American Company – GU e-Fortunes - making mobile phones. The company was moving to a new factory in Scotland, to make, he said to Dan and his young brother, Tim: "new communication devices".

"What are they, dad?" Tim asked curiously in his squeaky cheerful voice.

"Well ----- we're not sure yet, Tim, but nearly everyone's got a mobile now, so we're looking at new ways of communicating. We'll give people other ways to get in touch with each other; catch up with the news; and use different technologies."

"What are they?"

Dan laughed. "It's like the way things work, Tim. Dad's going to invent new gadgets." He asked: "Do you mean like flat-screen TV's and –what's the name of these pictures in the air ----- hieroglyphs --- I mean holograms!"

Hugh smiled. "Yes – something like that, but we haven't worked much detail out yet. I've to go to Scotland to start things off."

The boys were quiet for a moment.

"How long will you be away, dad?" Dan asked, a worried frown crinkling his forehead.

"I don't really know, but we have to move to Scotland very soon, because that's where my new job is."

Tim looked up: "Will I get new friends in Scotland?"

"Yes, Tim, you will, and you'll be going to school, not nursery.

We're going to find a nice house with a big garden".

"Will you be at home more, dad?" asked Dan, knowing what long hours he worked. Hugh hesitated for a moment: "Well, at the start, I'll be really busy, but I'd like to live closer to work so I have less driving to do".

Dan's face fell. He was upset, and thought about his friends, John and Derek, due for a sleepover on Saturday. "But dad, we've got a nice house and garden here, so why do we have to move? Will I still see my pals? And what about school?"

Dan was ten, but looked older. With dark curly hair and blue eyes, he was a cheerful and open personality, bright and doing well at school, with reading and computer games his passion. He'd read everything from Harry Potter to Rudyard Kipling's Jungle Book, which he'd devoured in two sittings.

He'd even got through dad's copy of The Celestine Prophecy, which he thought was exciting, but wasn't sure if he understood it all. He was reading Lord of the Rings, and found the action scenes riveting.

He loved playing strategy games on the computer, and got so wrapped up that he could really imagine himself in the Sahara Desert, guiding a camel train to the nearest oasis; or leading a charge of Crusaders breaking through enemy lines to capture a cliff top castle. He was a good chess player for his age, and played in the school team.

He had a huge thirst for knowledge, and really enjoyed helping others. Though he tried hard, he wasn't very good at sports, especially football.

He was in Year 5 at Bogrin Place Junior, ten minutes' walk away, though he didn't often walk, mum insisting he share lifts with next-door's spoilt daughter, Sally.

His classmates were really good fun. Even the girls were OK, except when playing games with so many rules – like tig, with extra do's and don'ts, like: "You must tig on the right shoulder; and if you put both hands up at once, you're safe; and you can't be IT more than three times", and on and on it went------.

He was daydreaming again, and wiped tears from his eyes. "Dad, I'm really sad we have to move. I love it here".

Hugh replied awkwardly: "I know, Dan, but we can't stay. My new job's a good one, and Scotland's a great place to live. It's full of history, and castles, and lovely scenery, and there are fewer people living there, so it's quieter.

I hope we'll have more time together when we move----and the schools are good. I'm really sorry, but that's the way it is".

His deep blue eyes looked at them sharply through his glasses. A tall bony man with short dark hair, thinning on top, he spoke with real concern, and obviously felt awkward about breaking the news of the move to the boys.

Dan, still upset, and a confused but chirpy Tim, dragged their heels going to bed that night. Liz read them a story about Indians in the Wild West, and the soldiers who fought and robbed them of their villages, land and hunting grounds.

As she read in her soft voice, her brown curly hair bobbed up and down, her greeny-blue eyes reflecting the bedside light. Dan thought it was like his dad's Company stealing his job, forcing them to move to a strange and distant place.

That night, he dreamed of dinosaurs.

Big dinosaurs, flying dinosaurs, swimming dinosaurs and charging dinosaurs.

He stood on a flat dusty patch of earth. The scene before him took his breath away.

Tall ferns, sprouting from palm trees, fringed a green lake stretching into the distance. Dotted over its surface were small islands, covered with trees, impossibly high, climbing towards a dull grey sky. Dark masses of scudding black clouds shadowed the earth.

Flying around the giant trees were pterodactyls – at least they looked like pterodactyls, but with feathers –red, blue, yellow and orange feathers. The birds were agitated. Bizarrely, they sounded like cows – mooing to reassure each other in an otherworldly conversation.

He realised a herd of dinosaurs had stopped eating the ferns, and was nervously pacing the beaten earth.

He had to blink hard, because what he saw was impossible.

Astride the dinosaurs- they were iguanodons- were people - men, women and children, two on each animal hanging tightly on their backs.

The dinosaurs walked on all fours. They were about ten metres long, dwarfing the riders.

A curling stinging wind hit him in gusts, dust and tiny stones peppering his skin.

A loud trumpeting sound pierced the air, and he saw two creatures like Loch Ness monsters surging through the green water. Long glistening necks and a series of humps left arrow shaped wakes. Their heads looked like giant seals.

The pterodactyl-birds got more agitated seeing these giants approach, and more lifted from the trees to take the air.

Suddenly, in front of him, stood a boy, his own age, and he turned to see a familiar looking girl standing beside him. She was slightly smaller, with blond hair cut short like a boy's. Her deep brown eyes shone brightly from her freckled face.

Though she'd been there all along, the scene had so captivated him, he'd not realised. He knew she felt the same.

The native boy spoke in a language they didn't understand. Dan asked him to repeat his words, and, like headlights cutting through a fog, he felt the meaning directly in his own mind. The boy told them his tribe were on the move because of the storm.

He pointed at one of the iguanodons, signing them to climb on its back. It stood restlessly, tossing its short scaly red and brown-speckled neck. Its rolling leathery tongue licked nervously round its mouth.

As Dan and the girl climbed up, scrabbling for hand and toe-holds on their mount's humped back, they felt a ripple of fear run through the herd. Shouts of alarm came from the tribe.

There were about twenty iguanodons, all moving quickly away from the lake. Charging towards them was a huge dinosaur, its reptilian eyes starting from its oversized head. Its long scaly-skinned tail lifted up and thumped the ground as it headed towards the nearest iguanodon.

Terrified, the smaller animal swivelled, tossing its two riders off. The woman got up quickly, and ran to Dan's iguanodon, nimbly leaping up behind him. The man fell heavily, and lay with his leg twisted under him.

Before anyone could move, the tyrannosaurus swooped, and with a fearsome crunch, caught his body in its mouth, serrated teeth snapping through bone and muscle. The man cried out briefly, then was silent as the huge carnivore settled to finish its prey.

Horrified, Dan felt the girl slump forwards in a feint, and held her firmly to stop her falling. The woman made a sharp whistling noise between her teeth. Their mount turned with the herd, and escaped the grisly scene in an uncomfortable wobbling ride. They rode in convoy for what seemed like an age, but Dan knew time had flashed past in moments, like a high-speed film.

They reached a rocky cliff, and the herd pulled up. The tribe dismounted, and he and the girl joined their strange companions. They talked quickly and nervously, pointing back at the lake in the far distance.

Dan couldn't make out the words, but in the same strange way he'd understood the boy's words, he knew what they said. They were sad about losing one of the tribe, but were terrified about the storm.

The sky was completely black, swirling with particles of soot that rained down constantly, stinging their heads and bodies. The sun had disappeared.

He knew they had to get away and instinctively held the girl's hand. She looked at him trustingly as they ran to the shelter of the cliff. An opening in the rock face gleamed brightly, and they dashed into a large circular cave.

Suddenly they were tumbling, tumbling, tumbling down, down, down in a mad gliding fall.

The last thing he saw and heard was an enormous slab of rock completely filling the sky, falling faster than the eye could blink.

It crumped with a wrenching tearing explosion into the earth.

He twisted his body round and round to keep upright. He woke up sweating, his eyes opening to the gloom of his bedroom.

It was the most powerful dream he'd ever had. Though it felt like a nightmare, he felt no fear, only a real sense of being part of the prehistoric scene.

He hurried through to his parents' room. They woke as he burst in the door, and described his dream.

His vivid account rushed forth in an excited torrent of words.

"Wow!" said Liz, "That's some dream. I wonder what it means."

"Do you think it means something?" asked Dan

"Well" she said, "Dreams often do. They can sometimes be about things you've said and done during the day, or things you're worried about. Sometimes you see things that happen in the future".

"But this was the past, not the future, mum – and it was so real I felt I was actually there!"

Hugh asked: "What was the girl like?"

"Hmm - a bit smaller than me, and the same age, but I don't know who she was, dad. I thought I knew her – she was familiar, as if she was part of me, but I've never seen her before".

They were curled together on the bed, and Tim joined them, rubbing bleary eyes: "What's all the noise?" he asked, dragging his herd of soft toy animals in a blanket, his hair dishevelled from sleep.

"Did we wake you, big boy?" said Liz, as Tim snuggled up.

This gave Dan another chance to tell his dream, and Tim's eyes popped as he dwelt gruesomely on the t-rex's attack.

"Well, boys", said Liz, "this is some start to the day, and it's not even 8 o'clock! Listen – we're going to look at a new house tomorrow, so we need to pack our stuff to drive north this afternoon. We're staying in Carlisle tonight in a hotel, so you'll need to be on your best behaviour!"

The boys were bored with the journey, but enjoyed the treat of staying in the hotel, especially Tim, as they ate in the dining room. His blue-green eyes flicked back and forth as he took it all in. A small alert boy, he had the same sharp features as Dan, with black curly hair, slightly darker than Dan's.

Liz told them the curious story of the house: "I got a phone call two days' ago from the Estate Agent. It sounds like it might suit us. It's in a lovely village in Perthshire, called Mistlees, which is only twenty minutes drive from dad's work."

"Where's Perthshire?" asked Dan.

Hugh replied: "It's in the middle of Scotland, a very pretty area, full of farms".

"It'll be good if the house doesn't need much work," said Liz.

"Will I have my own room?" asked Tim.

"Of course you will, Timmy," she said. The house is a good size, and there's a really strange big cellar which could be a den for you!"

The boys looked at each other, and Dan rolled his eyes. "Mum, it might be a den for Tim, but I'm too old for that".

"Well", said Hugh, "Tell the boys the mystery".

Liz leant over the table and lowered her tone. "The house has a peculiar history. It's bizarre, but its owner has disappeared! He was an inventor – a bit of an oddball who often spent days in the house without going out".

"An inventor! Who was he, mum?" asked Dan.

"He was called Peter Friis. I think his family were Dutch, but he came from South Africa. He'd lived in Mistlees for seven years, but disappeared completely a year ago. His family have given him up for lost, so they're selling the house. It's got a real air of mystery about it."

Dan felt the thrill of adventure.

Farms surrounded Mistlees, in the heart of Perthshire, and the village was like an oasis in a sea of green fields. The many stone buildings, built solidly to protect against the weather, gave it a strong respectable feeling, but Dan couldn't help wondering what secrets they hid.

When they saw the house, he shivered with anticipation.

It was built with grey blocks of stone with a slate roof, and squatted solidly, with a timeless air, in the centre of the village. It stood out from the other buildings with its commanding presence.

The wooden door said "OPPORTUNITY HOUSE".

It was all on one level, except for the cellar, and nestled in the peace and quiet of a large grassed garden surrounded by trees. It sat in Dirsett Avenue, a street with only a few houses, which ended at a small stream ("it's called a burn in Scotland, Tim", said Dan). A path snaked over the burn to the next street, and beyond, they could see the School.

As they wandered round, guided by the Estate Agent, they smelled its musty air and felt its curious lived-in atmosphere tinged with a faint air of hidden menace.

The boys' bedrooms were side-by-side, and Dan could see exactly where his PC would go. In the main bedroom, the bed, wardrobes, and a large dressing table were covered in white sheets.

In the middle of the room was a startling rug.

It was multi-coloured and round - about three metres in diameter - dusty and a bit tattered in places. It looked like a giant bulls-eye, though the colours were different.

The outer ring was a faded red, and seemed to bleed into the wood of the floor. The next ring was orange, and inside that were rings of yellow, green, blue and violet. The centre circle was indigo, completing the colours of a circular rainbow.

It had a faint peppery smell.

The rug was so strange, it hinted at a world of mystery and magic.

Dan loved it.

The Estate Agent coughed, embarrassed. He said: "We tried to move the rug before showing you round, but – it wouldn't let us!"

"What!!" said Hugh, "It wouldn't *let* you!"

"Eh, no – it seemed to want to stay here. We got it as far as the cellar door, but it slipped through our fingers and stayed quite firmly there – we had to carry it back here."

Hugh and Liz laughed, and the boys joined in nervously.

"Maybe it *should* be in the cellar," Dan said with a smile.

"Well, that's where it can go – I don't want that thing in our bedroom, that's for sure!" said Liz with a grimace.

The highlight of the house for the boys - even for Dan - *was* the cellar. From a door in the hall, a steep set of wooden stairs reached down into a high room stretching the length and breadth of the house.

As they opened the door, they smelt the curious aroma of burnt ash and wet animals. "Where's that coming from?" Liz asked.

"I don't know," replied the Estate Agent. "The cellar's clean enough – our surveyor gave it a clean bill of health."

The floor was crammed with shelving, boxes, packages, machines, pipes and strange contraptions.

Most curious of all were the dozens of beautifully made models strewn everywhere. The floor was packed with tiny model buildings, animals and figures. Amongst them were a flying saucer and a bubble car with stilt-like legs.

"Wow!" said Tim. "It's amazing!"

"It sure is, Timmy", said Liz. "I wonder where all this stuff came from. You and Dan will have fun clearing it out".

"It's great, mum", said Dan, "It's a treasure trove!"

As he spoke, he felt a breath of cold air sweep past him, and he ducked quickly, startled.

Nobody else seemed to notice and the Estate Agent told them

this was where Peter Friis had done his experiments.

"What are they?" asked Tim.

"It means trying different things out, Timmy", said Dan, recovering from his fright.

"What kind of experiments?" asked Hugh.

The Agent hesitated. "I've heard different opinions. Some say he was an inventor, others that he made models for a living, and some even think he was trying to make a time machine, of all things!"

Hugh shook his head in disbelief, but the cellar fascinated Dan, and Liz had to hurry him away. He looked back down the stairs, and felt a thrill of expectancy.

Their next stop was the school - a solid old slate-roofed grey-stone building with a concrete playground. In the middle was a small fenced enclosure, packed with plants, flowers and vegetables.

The sign on the front gate read: **"Elfsite Reach Primary School – 1872".**

A middle-aged woman in a long black dress was sweeping the playground with an old broom, muttering to herself. She saw them and put the broom down.

"Can I help you?" she asked in a crackly voice, sweeping her straggly grey hair aside. She peered at them over small round glasses perched on the end of her long thin nose

Liz smiled warmly: "Hello, we're the Goodwins. We've been viewing Opportunity House."

The woman's crinkled eyes lit up briefly with surprise. She rubbed her knobbly hands together: "I'm Mrs Braid, the Headmistress."

Dan and Tim took an instant dislike to this large lady, who eyed them up with a cool sharp expression on her face, which softened and became all smiles for Hugh and Liz.

She showed them the school garden: "Each term, a different class look after it, planting, weeding, and tending the crops. It encourages children to understand nature, and give them a healthy respect for living and growing plants. They get to eat the vegetables too!" she laughed in a hollow way.

Liz asked: "Why's it called Elfsite Reach?"

" Well, when the original villagers came here, they built a farm in the middle of the valley, and grew crops. However, when they were ready to harvest, the crops mysteriously disappeared, and legend has it that the elves reached up from their underground homes to pick them!"

She rubbed her hands together as if inspecting them for dirt: "The elves are one example of the village's hidden power. It's peaceful on the surface though."

Dan wanted to know more, but Mrs Braid ignored him: "It's a lovely place to live. You know, Opportunity House was built on the site of the original farm".

She looked coldly at Dan, as if unwillingly sharing a secret. Her wrinkled olive skin glistened in the sunshine, and her glasses gleamed at the end of her nose. Dan shivered.

Tim gazed at the drawings on the corridor walls.

"We like the children to express themselves in their work. Tim, you'll be starting in the middle of August, and for the first few weeks, you'll be coming in just till lunchtime".

"But what'll I do after lunch?" he asked nervously.

"Don't worry. I'll be here to walk you home, and you can help me get the house in order", Liz replied.

Tim's face fell. Mrs Braid swept back a wisp of her hair, and

Dan noticed how long her nails were. "After the first few weeks you'll stay on till three o'clock". She said to Liz and Hugh: "It gives the youngsters the chance to settle in to their new class without tiring them out too much. And Daniel – this is your class – we have seventeen children in Primary 6, and you'll bring the number to eighteen when you start".

Dan thought for a moment. No one called him Daniel, except when he was in trouble. He was puzzled by the term times. "August's early", he said. "I don't usually start till September".

"Yes," she explained, with what Dan thought was a look of triumph: "The system in England is a bit different from here, but you finish earlier for the summer – at the end of June".

Feeling a bit cheated, he looked at his new classroom. He liked it – tables and chairs were arranged in little groups, and the room was bright with class-work on the walls.

Hugh and Liz thought the school was perfect, though Dan wasn't so sure. Mrs Braid had really spooked him. He hoped his teacher would be friendlier.

Later, they walked round the village, A bright straight main-street was cheerfully decked with barrels and hanging baskets full of colourful flowers. There was a small supermarket, a newsagent, and a range of small shops, including "The Deli", a well-stocked delicatessen, and a small dingy looking jeweller's shop.

Carved on a brick at the old stone building housing the Community Centre was the inscription: "VILLAGE HALL". The little parish church in the north of the village looked very old, and Dan felt it had a haunted atmosphere.

Strangely, the cemetery was a good mile away to the south, beyond their new home and some other houses. The church and the cemetery were on slightly raised ground, with Opportunity House in the middle at the foot of the valley.

To the east were the ruins of another even older church, and about a mile from it, again with their house in between, stood a tall stone tower, topped by a broken clock-face.

"You know, mum," said Dan, back in the car: "I think I'll like it here after all, though I'm not sure about Mrs Braid".

Liz laughed: "Don't worry. She'll be fine when you get to know her."

"I like it here too," echoed Tim.

The Friis family quickly accepted their offer for the house, and six weeks later, on the first of August, they moved in.

Whilst Dan said a tearful goodbye to his friends, he was excited by the prospect of a new life and new friends in Mistlees, though he was nervous about the school.

The mysterious cellar, its strange contents, its smells and its atmosphere, and the inventor who had vanished fascinated him.

When he finally fell asleep on their first night in Opportunity House, he had his second powerful dream about the river, the book in the library, and the city hidden deep in the jungle.

Chapter 3

Every Saturday, Sara shopped at the supermarket with her mum, Diana.

She loved it. Her step dad, Bruce, worked away from home a lot, though he was with them this weekend. While he sat in the car, Diana pushed the trolley, and Sara filled it.

She was ten (and a half, as she reminded everyone), and had lived in Mistlees all her life. Slim, but with a slightly chubby freckled face, she had short blond hair, like Diana's, and deep brown challenging eyes.

She was a loner, but not by choice. She didn't share her friends' interest in pop music –she didn't care about knowing all the new singles or words of songs.

Bruce and her mum couldn't afford designer clothes, so she often felt the odd one out, wearing football tops and jeans most of the time. She wasn't very good at school, being easily distracted and quickly bored.

Boys were a big topic of conversation, and Sara liked this, but not in the same way as her friends. Her interest in boys was in playing their games, but they didn't let her, so she didn't get the chance to show she was as good as them at football and computer games.

During the week, there had been a lot of talk about the newcomers. Her classmates had seen Dan's family walking round the school and the village. She was excited by the chance to meet a boy she could bond with. She looked forward to the new family moving in to the house across the road, which had lain empty for over a year.

Sara had liked Mr Friis, though everyone thought he was a bit odd.

He had always made time for her. He was a stooped old man, dressed in faded blue overalls, with a sense of humour to make you chuckle. He wore outsize glasses that made his brown eyes seem huge. When he smiled, they wobbled and his whole face lit up. Magnified laughter lines crinkled round his eyes, and his bushy black eyebrows shot up to his long curly white hair.

He knew what the villagers thought of him, and seemed to take pride in his reputation as the local eccentric.

She often heard strange noises coming from Opportunity House.

Once, she saw him peeping round his bedroom curtains with a smile on his face, after an afternoon of loud bangs and crashes had disturbed the neighbourhood. He saw Sara watching, and gave her a little wave before silently withdrawing.

"Sara – have you got the butter yet?" asked Diana, interrupting her daydream.

"Coming, mum!" She picked up a large pack of unsalted butter and put it in the trolley.

Later, as she helped cook tea, she heard a car drive up and stop outside. She ran to the window and peered round the curtains.

Diana raised her eyebrows at Bruce, as they acknowledged her excitement.

Diana had been devastated when her first husband, Guy, had left them to live in London, and their divorce had been very upsetting and driven Sara in on herself.

When she met Bruce at a wedding three years ago, she had been swept off her feet by his sense of fun and romance. Sara had taken a while to get to know him, and Diana was still concerned at how much she missed her dad, who had lost contact with her.

Sara really needed a close friend.

"Let's hope they're a nice family," Diana said. "Sara deserves some real company".

"Maybe we'll make friends with the Goodwins", said Bruce. "They must be a better bet than potty old Peter!"

Sara's eyes widened as she watched the family unload the big hatchback. She'd never seen a car so full of bags, boxes, parcels, and people. Her gaze took in the elder of the two boys. He looked about her age, slim but taller, with dark curly hair frizzling back in closely tangled rows across his head, just reaching the collar of a blue and red sweatshirt. His face was thin and alert, and he had a way of looking around him, as if picking out and noting everything he saw. His expression was cheerful and open, and his movements quick and positive.

Suddenly, Sara realised he was looking at her, and as he waved with a smile, she blushed and ducked down below the windowsill.

"Caught in the act, were you?" laughed Bruce sarcastically. "Never mind – you'll meet them soon enough."

Sara slunk back to the kitchen, hardly noticing the appearance of the boys' parents, and his young brother leading them eagerly up the drive to the front door.

She couldn't wait to meet the curly-haired boy. She was sure she'd seen him someplace before.

Soon, a removal lorry drew up, and until darkness fell, furniture and box after box poured into the waiting house. The removal men took away most of the old furniture too.

Sara kept clear of the windows, but lingered while pulling the curtains. Opportunity House glowed with light, full of life for the first time in a year.

Diana and Bruce decided to invite the Goodwins for dinner to welcome them to the village, and Sara dropped off to sleep that night with a tingling sensation that something exciting and a little bit scary was about to start.

Chapter 4

The following morning, Diana, Bruce and Sara went over to the Goodwin's. Liz and Hugh opened the door, smiling. From the hallway, a high squeaky voice, shouted: "Who is it, mum?" and Tim rushed to join them, dragging his blanket-full of soft toys behind him. He was still flushed with excitement at Dan's dream about the river, the forest and the strange city.

He peered round Liz's legs.

"We're the Christie's from over the road. I'm Bruce; this is my wife – Diana – and this is Sara".

Bruce wore jeans, trainers and a baggy blue sweatshirt. He was small, bald and slightly plump with a round cheery face. A livid scar shone on his right cheek and he had black deep-set eyes. He smiled impishly, and winked at Tim.

Diana, in striking contrast, wore a bright red top, check trousers and suede shoes. She was tall, slim and pretty with short blonde hair swept back from her face, and soft brown eyes.

"Nice to meet you", said Liz, introducing Hugh and Tim. "Come in, come in. It's a bit chaotic this morning and we had a long drive yesterday. The house is a mess and we can't find a thing, but I'm sure we can rustle up a cup of tea!"

They settled into the lounge, while she put the kettle on.

"Where's Dan?" asked Hugh, but before Tim could reply, he walked in, an enquiring look on his face. He looked straight at Sara, and went pale. She returned his gaze with a shy grin. He knew immediately she was the girl from his two dreams – her cheery freckled face, brown eyes and short blond hair were etched firmly on his memory.

She wore faded denims, dark blue football top and old trainers.

"What's up Dan?" said Hugh,"Cat got your tongue?"

Dan felt embarrassed and confused. His mind in turmoil, he gulped, and to cover up, blurted out, "No, I'm still thinking about my dream. I'm not quite with it yet!"

Diana said: "That sounds interesting. What were you dreaming about?"

Liz looked at Dan and said: "He's had a couple of rather strange dreams recently, and last night, he found a lost city, or that's what it sounded like!"

Over their cup of tea, she told them about his dreams. "I'm sure they're caused by the excitement of the move, and all the upheaval."

Sara was fascinated, and felt they were important to her too in some way.

Hugh and Liz told the Christies about their move, their captivation with the village, their new home, and the previous day's journey.

Liz said, "We thought we'd spend the next few days sorting ourselves out, and I'm having fun organising. We've got more space here than in Southcoats, which is great, but the boys need some new furniture, and our bedroom and the lounge need some more bits and pieces. The only place we don't need anything is the cellar, and the boys haven't had the chance to rummage round there yet. Mr. Friis left everything in it, and it's crammed full of junk, so we'll probably need a big clearout".

Sensing the children's mood, she added: "Dan, why don't you and Timmy show Sara the cellar?"

"Good idea – come on guys, let's go", said Dan.

While Tim went to put on his slippers, Dan said: "I know this must sound weird, but I've seen you before – you're the girl in my dreams!"

Sara gasped: "That's bizarre! I feel I know you too! How come?"

"I don't know, but I knew it the moment I saw you!"

Sara shivered slightly at this odd sense of shared experience, and Tim trundled up scuffing his feet in slippers.

At the cellar door, Sara said: "This is where Peter did all his experiments. I've always wondered what he was up to. What a racket he used to make. Hammerings and bangings, whooshing noises and all sorts of clattering. Everyone thought he was odd, but I liked him – I think he was just a bit shy."

"What happened to him?" asked Dan, liking the look of his new friend. Whilst a bit smaller, she was confident, and spoke with a soft lilting Perthshire accent he found strange but appealing. Her whole face lit up with animation as she spoke: "Peter spent days on end in the house, and when he did come out, it was usually to the supermarket, midweek to avoid seeing people. He was a bit of a recluse ---"

"What's a recluse?" asked Tim, in his piping little voice.

Sara and Dan laughed, and Dan explained: "It means someone who keeps away from people".

"Why did he do that?" asked Tim.

Sara replied: "Well, he was an inventor – or a scientist – I'm not sure which. In fact, nobody knew much about him, because he kept pretty much to himself, which made him more curious. We didn't see him for ages, and then he would just suddenly pop up at the shops, ambling along in his half-lost sort of way. Then, last July, he just disappeared! It was really strange – the police came round, asking us all questions. His family came and searched the house. and his brother even stayed for a couple of months, hoping he would come back – but he never did, and nobody knows what happened to him.

And we haven't seen old Nigel either".

"Nigel? Who's Nigel?" asked Dan.

"Oh, Nigel was the chap who used to help him. He was like an assistant. He would come round in his old Volvo, crammed to the roof with mysterious boxes, loading them in to the house, before going off again. No one knows where he came from or where he lived".

"How strange", said Dan. "So they did their experiments down here?" He pointed down the steps, and again felt a shiver of anticipation.

"Yes! I'm dying to see! Let's go!"

Dan switched on the light and led, followed by Sara, with Tim trailing behind.

They were struck by the smell of the place. It was a mixture of old and new. Aromas of exotic spices competed with a stale dried leather smell. There were hints of wet grass, flowers, animals, paint and tea.

Sara sniffed: "What a funny smell!"

"I know", Dan replied, "We noticed it before. I don't know where it's coming from."

The room was over three metres high. Fluorescent lighting cast a strong sharp light into every corner. Around the four windowless walls metal shelves stretched from floor to ceiling, crammed full. Amongst the clutter, Sara saw the models. They were made of plaster, carved from wood and fashioned from pieces of metal, cloth and cardboard.

"These are cool", she said, picking up a wood-carved aeroplane. It had a row of clear Perspex windows on its underside. Small dart-shaped wings studded its sides and top and rotated round the main body of the craft. It looked very sleek and futuristic, but - strangest of all - they could see lifelike little figures through the Perspex, dressed in violet-blue clothes, peering back at them.

"The detail's amazing!" said Dan, his blue eyes sparkling, as he picked up a plastic moulded lion that snarled at him, its mane framing its magnificent head.

Tim was playing on the floor with two other animals, and Sara leant over to see. Dan gulped: "They're the same as the iguanodons in my dream!"

Sara said: "Oh, that's weird! I'd love to hear more about your dreams".

"OK, Sara, but let's explore some more first".

They rummaged through piles of crates and boxes without finding much of interest. They were full of bits of wood, plastic and metal, and brightly coloured scraps of fabric.

Sara said: "He must have used these to make the models".

In the centre of the floor, a sheet covered a bulky object, and they pulled it off to reveal a square metal table. Engraved on its surface were strange symbols and etchings of buildings, people and animals. In the middle was a sequence of letters.

"What an amazing table!" said Sara. "It must be something to do with his experiments".

Tim, bored, crawled underneath, and yelped as he stood up and banged his head.

"Ouch – I felt that too!" said Dan, and bent down to pull him out. A perfect circle was outlined on the floor. Through it cut two straight lines dividing it into four equal segments. The lines continued to the four walls from end to end, and side-to-side, dead straight, quartering the cellar. The rim of the circle and the lines were no more than a centimetre thick, carved into the concrete floor.

"How odd!" said Dan. "I wonder what all this is, and what Peter got up to here. Have you noticed that everything's clean and free of dust? The rest of the house is a bit grimy, but down here, it still feels lived in".

"You're right", said Sara, rubbing Tim's head.

Dan was about to speak when he felt the air swirl around him. He ducked and gasped, and Sara quickly said: "What's wrong? Are you all right?"

"Yes – yes, I think so! I just got a fright. It felt like something brushed past me!"

Sara shivered: "Ooh, I didn't see anything. Are you sure?"

"It happened once before, but it's maybe just a draught."

Bruce shouted down: "Come on Sara, time's up! We have to go now, but you'll see the boys later. We're having dinner about six o'clock".

They climbed upstairs. The adults were chatting in the hall. Sara and Dan grinned at each other. They heard Liz ask: "So how did you meet?"

Diana laughed: "Oh, it's all my mum's fault. Because I was on my own at the time, she asked me to go with her to a wedding in Glasgow. Bruce was propping up the bar, and the rest is history! How about you pair?"

Liz smiled: "Hugh and I grew up together in Kent, in Tunbridge Wells. We went to school together, got engaged, and got married fifteen years ago – all very conventional, nothing as exciting as you and Bruce."

Bruce gripped Diana's arm firmly, and said: "That's enough

chatter! We'd best get away before all our secrets come out! Come on Sara, let's go".

Hugh and Liz were dragged down to the cellar after the Christies left.

The metal table and its inscriptions fascinated them, but even Hugh couldn't make sense of what the etchings meant. The circle and the lines that criss-crossed the cellar seemed important, and it was Liz who noticed the lines pointed north, south, east and west, following the layout of the village.

"How strange", she puzzled.

Hugh spotted some drills and other tools to add to his tool-kit, and grinned his satisfaction.

Before they knew it, it was time for dinner at the Christie's. Hugh's quiet thoughtfulness was a good match for Bruce's humour and constant chat. He never stopped asking questions, often answering them himself.

Liz and Diana chuckled when Hugh, asked about his work, got no chance to say a word as Bruce told him about his own job as a consultant engineer with ASE Thorn, an American Oil Company in Aberdeen. It sounded like he had invented North Sea oil.

When he laughed, the scar on his cheek went red, and Liz couldn't help asking: "How did you get your scar, Bruce? It must have been very painful."

A brief flash of annoyance crossed his face, but cleared immediately, and he joked: "Oh, that was my tussle with a wild boar - but you should have seen what *he* looked like when I'd finished with him!"

"Bruce, that's nonsense!" Diana explained: "He was bitten by an Alsatian, Liz, one of those horrible guard dogs, but the funny thing about it was that Sara was bitten by a collie on the very same day! We had to rush her to the doctor's to get stitched up, but you can hardly see the mark now, can you, love?"

Sara blushed and stroked her cheek. "No, it's just about gone now."

"OK, OK", said Bruce, interrupting. "Why don't you kids go to the lounge and leave the grown-ups to talk about you behind your backs!"

Dan wasn't sure how to take this remark. Sara reddened, and said nothing as she and the boys left the table. The children were quite happy to be on their own, but Sara was annoyed that Bruce had cut her off. Dan could see she was upset, and to distract her, told her about his dreams.

"Mum asked me what I thought the dreams meant, but I'm not sure. I've never had dreams like these. They were so *real*. And seeing you in our lounge, after sharing these adventures was incredible!".

"But I feel the same! OK, I haven't had your dreams, but when I saw you yesterday, I *knew* we'd met before. I wonder how we both think that."

"I don't know, but I'm sure it means something."

Tim chipped in: "Can you dream some more please!"

They laughed, and Sara said, "As long as I'm in them too!"

She told them about the school, due to start in two weeks: "Tim, your class is quite small – only about ten children, I think, but Dan, I hope you'll like Primary 6. The boys are OK, but Mark's a bit of a bully, always trying to get people in trouble, chucking his weight about. He's a real oddball, you know. He's lived here for just over a year, but the way he behaves, you'd think he owns the place. The girls are mainly interested in the boys going into

Primary 7, and – and – well, I'm not really close friends with any of them!"

"Don't worry", smiled Dan in his conspiratorial way. "I'll be your best friend!"

She grinned. His easy quick wit and ready smile made him good company, and her normal shyness quickly gave way. Tim wandered back to the dining room.

"What's Southcoats like?" Sara asked

"It's much bigger than Mistlees," Dan replied, "It's got a great beach, and it's always busy with tourists. Mistlees feels tiny compared with it – what's it like to live here?"

"Well, I like it, but by the sound of it, you'll find it much quieter----" her voice tailed off, and Dan, puzzled, asked: "What's wrong, Sara? Are you OK?"

Sara's head was down, and she took a moment to reply: "I'm fine – it's just – just difficult to talk about."

Instinctively, Dan asked: "Is it Bruce?"

She blushed: "How did you know?"

"I didn't really, but you seemed a bit awkward with him just now."

"Oh, he's so annoying sometimes. I miss my real dad so much, but he never phones or writes. Bruce is all right most of the time, but he doesn't love me the same as my dad did!"

She stifled a sob, and Dan patted her reassuringly. "I understand. My dad can be a bit like that sometimes. He's always working, always late home and he never seems to have time for Tim and I. Mum keeps saying he'll do things with us, but he always finds an excuse to stay at work."

"That must be awful! What does your mum say about it?"

"Oh, she's used to it. I think she hopes it'll be different here."

"I hope so too. It's awful when you're stuck on your own."

"It's not too bad. I kind of look after Tim, and he trails after me. He had a rotten time a couple of years ago. He got measles, mumps and chicken pox all in one year!"

Sara grimaced: "That's horrible! Did you not catch them too?"

"No, but I shiver when I think of it. My grandpa was very ill at the same time, and it seemed all I was doing was visiting him, and reading to Tim to cheer him up. Illness is so unfair."

"It's like when that collie bit me. We were playing behind the couch, and suddenly, it snapped at my cheek. I got such a fright, and I yelled and jumped up. Mum came running in and she screamed. I had blood pouring down my cheek, but I didn't feel anything for a moment. When I saw the blood, I must have fainted, and the next thing I knew, I was getting stitched up at the doctor's."

Dan shuddered. He asked: "How do you feel about dogs now?"

"I get really scared. I can't bring myself to touch them, and I just freeze!"

"I know that feeling. When I was younger, we went on holiday to Blackpool, and mum took me up the big Tower. It was awful! I couldn't look down, and I froze up completely. She had to take me straight down in the lift again and I can still remember that horrible sick feeling inside!"

They were silent for a few moments, feeling the bond of shared experience.

In the dining room the adults chatted.

"How are the boys feeling about Mistlees?" Diana asked.

Liz hesitated before answering: "I think OK now, but Dan wasn't happy to start with. He had a great crowd of friends in Southcoats, and he'll miss them, but he's really quite outgoing, so I hope he'll make friends here quickly. Tim just adores him, and if Dan's all right, he will be too."

"Well, it's a friendly village, isn't it, Bruce?"

Bruce hesitated a second: "I guess so," he replied, "But it's always more difficult for newcomers to settle in, like in any village."

Diana reddened: "I know, but you're away a lot, so people don't get the same chance to know you."

"Just as well!" Grinned Bruce, breaking the awkward moment.

Liz coughed politely: "Well, we're all looking forward to settling in, aren't we, Hugh?"

"Yes, dear, of course!" He looked at his watch: "My, is that the time – we'd better get the boys off to bed."

At the door, they all thanked Diana and Bruce for dinner, and they left, Tim's eyes drooping heavily, ready for bed and a good night's rest.

Chapter 5

Reorganising the house made the next two weeks speed past as the Goodwins got curtains up, the lounge redecorated, and the children's bedrooms finished. They went shopping to Edinburgh, which Dan loved - and hated.

He hated being dragged round furniture showrooms, but loved Princes Street, with the castle sitting solidly on the rock growing from the Gardens below.

It was a good day for Liz, who bought everything they needed for Opportunity House.

They got home after 7 o'clock, and ordered a carry-in meal from The Deli. Twenty minutes later, the doorbell rang. Standing on the doorstep was a small man in crumpled clothes. At his feet was a large plastic carrier bag. He grinned at Liz, and swept his long black floppy hair back from his forehead: "Welcome to Mistlees!" He drawled in a loud American accent, "I'm Brad Maipeson from The Deli."

"Oh!" said Liz, "That was quick."

"Service with a smile and quickest by a mile!" he quipped.

As Liz paid him for the meal, he asked: "Well, how do you like this little place then?"

"Oh, we love it thanks Mr Maipeson, but we're still very new as you'll know."

Mr Maipeson peered over her shoulder: "Nice place. Are you doing much to it?"

Liz frowned, anxious to get away: "No, not really. Thank you very much."

She bent to pick up the carrier, but Mr Maipeson quickly lifted it and said: "Allow me. Just show me the way!"

An astonished Liz led him to the kitchen and he put the meal on the waiting table. Dan was at the sink and turned round.

"Well hello young man, you'll be Dan I guess. Hi, I'm Brad Maipeson. I own the Deli."

Dan shook his hand dutifully, wincing at his hot and clammy grip. Though he seemed quite young, his face was heavily lined, and he had a restless air about him, fidgeting as he took in the kitchen, eyes roaming round hungrily. Liz had to hurry him away: "Well thanks Mr Maipeson, we really need to eat now."

"Yes, of course, and I hope you enjoy the haggis – it's a Deli speciality!"

"Yes, I'm sure we will."

"Just let me know if there's anything I can do to help you feel at home here – anything at all. Nothing's too much trouble you know."

"Yes thanks. We'll let you know, "she said, weary at this constant barrage of talk from the little man. On his way out, he said:" It's an amazing village you know. It just takes time to get used to its atmosphere – and the people of course."

"Yes, thank you Mr Maipeson. Goodbye for now!" As she closed the door behind him, she said to Hugh, in the lounge: "Remind me not to answer the door when he comes around. What an obnoxious man!"

Despite this, the haggis, a first for them all, was delicious, served as the chatty Menu said, with ***"Neaps and Tatties (mashed turnip and potatoes for all non-Scots!)"***

Dan didn't get time to see much of Sara as they got the house furnished and settled in, but promised they'd explore the cellar again the weekend after school started.

On the first day, Sara walked in with him. They arrived early, and she introduced him. He took some good-natured ribbing about his English accent, but accepted it in good spirit, joking: "I can't understand any of you either!"

Dan liked Iain, a chunky gap-toothed boy, and Shane, his tall skinny curly-haired friend who both lived in a row of old cottages outside the village. They stood in a little group, Sara basking in the reflected glory of being Dan's friend.

A larger boy shouldered roughly past Iain. He stood intimidatingly beside Dan, sized him up and announced in a deep sinister tone: "So you're the new boy – not much to look at, eh?"

"Hoy, Mark – lay off", said Shane, "This is Dan, from Southcoats. He's OK. He's in our class."

Mark snorted, jutting his chin out aggressively. He stood head and shoulders above Dan. He had closely shaved black hair, and a big nose jutting out almost from his forehead, where his eyebrows met in between two beady brown eyes. He looked ferocious.

"Another blooming southerner. They can't help themselves, selling their measly little houses, and buying our village up like there's no tomorrow. I wish they'd stay where they belong".

Dan reddened, and was about to react angrily when Sara coolly interrupted. "Take no notice of Mark – he's the school bully. Mark, if you say another word we'll tell Miss Ambrose and she'll shut you up".

"Humph – Miss Ambrose – you try it and see where it'll get you, tomboy!" threatened Mark, and pushed his way past to the school door, as the bell rang.

A bit shaken, Dan followed his new friends to their classroom, to be met by Mrs Braid and a younger lady, who greeted everyone with a smile and a few welcoming words. Mrs Braid, in long black skirt and a high necked black jacket, looked Dan up and down sourly over her glasses, and coolly introduced him to his new teacher – Miss Ambrose.

Dan took to her immediately. She wore a white dress patterned with bright red roses. She was small with sharp freckled features, startling long red hair tied back from her face, and smiling blue eyes. She spoke slowly and deliberately, and her soft low voice gave her an air of timeless patience: "Hello Dan, and welcome to Elfsite Reach. We're delighted to see you, and to know Opportunity House has found itself new owners. I'll spend time with you to find out what stage you've reached in our subjects, but meantime, I've teamed you to sit with Shane and Iain".

Dan sat down, relieved at being with two friendly faces, but puzzled by her comment on the house finding them. She turned to the rest of the class, and said: "Well, I hope you've all had a good summer. Welcome back. Ali and Asha – let's see a bit more effort from you this term. Mark! No trouble please! And Sara, maybe this is the year you'll get a bit more involved!"

Ali, Asha and Sara looked embarrassed, but Mark glared back at her. She smiled sweetly, and carried on. The day passed quickly as he learned everyone's names, got used to the Scottish accents, was issued with a Homework notebook, Maths and English books, and took in the work the class would cover.

He was really interested in the project – "The Story of Mistlees".

Miss Ambrose told them to explore the history of the village: "Who first lived here, why they came to the area, and what they did. Draw a detailed map of the village, and describe the historic buildings and main points of interest".

Looking significantly at Dan, she said: "You'll find some strange and wonderful things in Mistlees, I'm sure".

She lowered her voice so only he could hear and said: "Explore the colours, Dan. There's a rich world waiting – and things only you and Sara can discover!"

Dan had no chance to ask what she meant, but thought this was a great chance to find out about the village. He quickly read the worksheet. Iain and Shane exchanged a grin at his enthusiasm. This was child's play – they knew the village inside out, and both had older brothers who'd done the same project. At lunch-break, they cornered Dan, and told him Primary 6 did the same project every year. Iain, grinning lopsidedly, boasted it would be "a skoosh case."

Dan said: "What's a skoosh case?"

They doubled up laughing, and Shane replied, in a posh accent: "Oh, I suppose you might call it a piece of cake!"

Dan grinned self-consciously: "Ah! I see! What's Miss Ambrose like?"

Shane said, "She seems to have been here forever. She taught my big brother, Iain's big brother, who's sixteen now, and Iain's dad before that too!"

Dan calculated: "She must be at least 50 odd, but she looks much younger!"

The boys shrugged, and they finished lunch with Dan getting to know some of his other classmates. The girls eyed him up, while Sara watched possessively, daring them to interfere.

Dan asked her: "What was that Miss Ambrose said about being more involved?"

Sara reddened: "Well, I get bored with some of the stuff we do, and she has this habit of spotting it."

Dan laughed and said: "She told me to explore the colours. What colours? And she said there are things only you and I can discover. What did she mean?"

Sara frowned: "I don't know. That was a bit odd. Maybe she meant we should work together on the project, but the thing about the colours I don't follow."

"OK, fair enough. Can we work together then?"

Sara smiled and her whole face lit up: "I'd like that. Yes!"

Mark interrupted with a snigger: "Well, little ones? Having a good cosy chat then?"

Dan replied: "That's our business, thanks."

He snorted and walked away, but there was no further trouble from him during the day, except for a sneering comment about how much work Dan would have to do for the project. Dan thought this was fine, and said nothing.

As they left for home at half past three, they passed Ali and Asha (Sara called them the deadly A-bomb duo, after their initials:"They're the madams of the class").

"Hope you enjoyed your day, Dan", smiled Ali, a pretty brunette, with a coy look, accompanied by a guffaw from Asha, her larger friend, whose straw coloured hair was tied in a pigtail down to the middle of her back. Asha added: "I suppose you'll be a swot, Danny boy. I saw you sooking up to Old Ambrosia. Some good that'll do you!"

Dan ignored them, but Sara felt a hint of rivalry.

Dan gushed about his day to his mum, leaving nothing out, though embarrassed about the comments from Mark, Ali and Asha.

"Don't worry about it – they're just sizing you up to see how you react to a bit of kidding".

Dan wasn't so sure.

Tim had had a great day, but was exhausted. He'd finished at 1 o'clock, and walked home with Liz, chatting away ten to the dozen about his new friends and his teacher. He was sure Miss Wade, from Norway, would have him reading and writing in a matter of days. He was fast asleep on the couch.

Over dinner, they talked about the day, and Liz and Hugh, home early, listened.

Dan and Tim were excited and tired, so had an early night, Tim having the last word when he called Elfsite Reach: "Superbrill!"

Little did they know what the next weeks had in store.

Chapter 6

It was a glorious Saturday morning. The cloudless sun blazed down on Mistlees as Dan and Sara went to explore the mysterious cellar. Tim was still asleep.

The first few days of school had passed smoothly, and Dan felt more and more accepted by his class, except for Mark, who continued to be rude to him. Even the girls, led by Ali, seemed to feel he had a role to play in the tight-knit group of Primary 6. He was emerging as a bit of a leader, and his sense of humour and good general knowledge were winning him respect. Never very sporty, however, he was last to be picked at playground football.

Tim loved Primary 1. Already, as youngest in his class, he too had become a favourite, and was good friends with Jack and Guy, the three sharing secrets and sandwiches at lunchtime. Guy was full of life and energy, and Jack had also moved from England.

Dan and Sara went downstairs to be met with the subtle aroma of burnt toasty wood.

"How come there are all these strange smells?" wondered Sara.

"Maybe it's just all the different things in here", said Dan, "Or maybe smells from the house or the street somehow get carried in"

"But how, Dan? I can't see how they get in. Is there an air vent someplace?"

They looked round, but saw nothing obvious.

Dan said: "Well, it'll just need to stay a mystery for now!"

"Hmmm" said Sara, unconvinced.

They started to work with the models, in a space cleared at one end of the basement, separating them into groups of buildings, animals, vehicles and people. Dan's favourites were the dinosaurs –a t-rex, the iguanodons, and some smaller dinosaurs. Altogether, there were about thirty, including one he thought was a brachiosaurus, and a brightly coloured feathered bird with a claw in the middle of each of its large wings. There were long-necked dinosaurs, dinosaurs with large hoods at the back of their necks, and spiny dinosaurs.

"Stegosaurs!" Declared Sara.

Together, they formed a spectacular army. The peculiar thing was the brightness of their colouring. Dan said: "I thought dinosaurs were brown and grey, but these are red, green, orange, and black as well."

The winged dinosaur had feathers of blue, yellow, red and orange. The rest of the animals included horses, lions and a snake.

They grouped the model buildings together. Several were pyramids, and one looked like the art gallery in Edinburgh's Princes Street. It was rectangular with imposing pillars, made of plaster, and painted a light tan colour. The detail of the carved statues peering over the roof was exquisite and surprising in a model only 30 centimetres long, and half that in width.

Some of the buildings were futuristic, with sweeping curves, smooth edges, and clear plastic windows. Others were of churches and houses, amongst them the Parish Church and the Community Centre.

They arranged forty little structures into sets of similar age and type.

The transport models included the futuristic plane, with captive passengers glued to its windows, chariots, and a variety of cars. One was no more than a bubble on wheels, with stilt legs, one at each corner. There was a flying saucer, like a spinning top.

It was heavy, and made of a bright shiny metal reflecting the lighting in different colours as Dan spun it round.

The models now filled a quarter of the floor.

Sara said: "It feels like we're in a museum. Look at them all lined up".

"It's like a huge Christmas morning", chuckled Dan. "You know, when you get new toys and soldiers, and spread them out on the floor to play with".

"Yeah, and dad comes in and stands on something, smashing it to bits!"

As Sara said this, her expression changed, and tears welled in her eyes.

"What's wrong, Sara? Asked Dan, concerned.

"Oh, nothing really – it's just – it made me think of dad again. I wish he was still here."

Dan sympathised in silence for a moment, wondering what to say: "I'm sure he thinks a lot about you, Sara – and Bruce seems to love you. He's always cheerful anyway."

"Sometimes I'm not so sure!" Sara sniffed. "Anyway, let's carry on."

They worked in silence for the next few minutes. Dan felt a shiver run down his spine. He gasped and quickly looked round.

"What's up?" asked Sara.

"I got a fright again! It's like someone's watching us. Don't you feel it?"

"No, but you're giving me goose bumps! Can we stop for a break now?"

"Yes, good idea!" He replied gratefully.

Over lunch, between mouthfuls of toasted cheese, Dan said: "That was a bit scary! But up here, it's like I imagined it.

I don't know what's going on with me!"

"Don't worry, Dan, it is a bit of an odd place!"

"I guess so - what a fabulous collection. It makes you wonder how long it took Peter to collect".

"To make, more like. He must've spent weeks and weeks at it"

"That'll be why you never saw him for ages."

"Yup – I'm sure you're right. You can just imagine him sitting down there, working away and losing all track of time. But when you think about it, why would he leave everything just like that? How could he have just abandoned things? "

"Don't know", said Dan thoughtfully. "He may have had an accident, or maybe he was in some sort of trouble, and had to get away. But at least we've got some idea of what he was up to!"

"Hhhmmmm ---", mused Sara. "But it doesn't explain all the noises we used to hear. Making these models wouldn't have needed all that banging and clattering, and ----". She stopped in mid-sentence as a thought struck her: "You know, I'd forgotten. One of the noises was a loud whooshing. We didn't hear it often, but it was like a rocket taking off. We would hear it twice at a time, if you know what I mean. Once was like a take-off from a space launch, with all the wheezing and blowing of steam, and a roaring sound which built up and built up until it fizzed off; and the second sound came straight after, and it sounded the same, but backwards!"

"How d'you mean backwards?"

"I mean like the noises went up a tunnel one way and then back again, so they ended with the same wheezing and blowing noises they started with".

"How odd", said Liz, joining them as they drank the last of their milk. "I just had a quick look downstairs. You've made a good job of organising things. The models are great, aren't they?"

"That's what we thought", said Dan. "Sara felt it was like a museum".

"It's as if they've come from one", replied Liz. "Peter was really good at making models".

Tim butted in, dragging his feet as he tried to stop his slippers, too big for him, falling off. "You never woke me to help in the cellar!" he accused. Dan and Sara looked away, trying not to laugh at his outrage. They'd got on much faster without him.

To make up, Dan said," We've sorted out most of the models, and if you're very careful, you can play with them".

Tim rushed through the cellar door in a flurry of excitement, thudding softly down the stairs in his socks as his feet lost their uneven battle with the slippers.

Dan and Sara followed and found him in the middle of the models. One minute he had armies of dinosaurs battling each other, and next he wandered round with the mysterious plane in one hand, flying saucer in the other. He completed a circuit before landing them both with a loud crrrumping noise.

Dan and Sara finished sorting out the models, by grouping the human figures - about fifty of them. These too came from different time periods. There were men, women and children, in normal everyday clothing; futuristic figures in bright coloured clothes; artists with paint pallets; and people who looked like Native Americans. All were beautifully coloured and detailed. Some wore Roman togas, one clutching a scroll of parchment in his outstretched hand.

The tallest figure was no more than ten or eleven centimetres tall, which made the detail even more fascinating. They were the same scale as the dinosaurs, but out of proportion with the buildings and vehicles.

Among the electrical gadgets was an old radio, a set of jump leads (identified by Sara, who had helped Bruce start the car after a flat battery), a food mixer, toaster and an old whistling kettle, half full of water. Dan laid it on a shelf, and said to Sara. "Let's look at the table."

She wiped it, but there was no dust. It sparkled under the fluorescent lighting.

The surface was like a dartboard, but instead of twenty sections, there were seven.

The central circle consisted of letters and numbers. These were perfectly etched, and formed a central ring, so they had to walk round the table to read them. Each segment was marked. They read TERC; AYAM; ARAT; EMOR; NOEL; and AMOF; and the seventh was a number - 1922.

There were etchings in each segment, and a good few matched the models, including a lion, a t-rex, a pyramid, the museum, a flying saucer, and one or two of the human figures. Some of the symbols were hieroglyphs.

They had forgotten Tim who was sitting on the old multi-coloured rug Liz had dumped in a corner of the cellar as she had promised.

"This is really comfortable", said Tim, "And it likes me too. It's heating me up!"

"Don't be silly", Dan replied. "It's only a rug".

"Well, *I* think it's cosy and warm!" He stalked back to the models, leaving Dan grinning.

There was something strange about the rug. It seemed to softly pulse, its colours fading and glowing. It no longer looked sad and shabby – the dusty tattered look was replaced with brighter sharper colours and a feeling of energy.

It was like an optical illusion Sara had seen - a black circle you stared at, till eventually it appeared to go round and round.

This was similar, but it didn't so much go round and round as subtly change colour. Fascinated, Dan moved closer, but forgot the table was in his way, and bumped it with his hip.

"Ouch!" he yelped, and the impact shifted the table a little.

On impulse, they looked under the table at the circle, and Dan asked: "Are you thinking what I'm thinking?"

"Yes, I am! But how did you know?"

"I'm not sure, but it seems obvious somehow. The Estate Agent told us the rug wouldn't leave the house, and here it is, quite at home. Look – it's the same size as the circle!"

"I think you're right! Let's check and see!"

They moved the heavy table aside, and pulled the rug along the floor towards the circle.

Suddenly, the air in the cellar grew cold, and they both felt a whistling sound behind them.

The rug started to pull them along, and they were also pushed from behind. Quickly and firmly the rug planted itself in the middle of the circle.

They tumbled and landed with their hands on its green ring, which pulsed and glowed brightly like a traffic light.

The last thing they heard in the cellar was a loud *whoosh* like a rocket's take-off trail.

Chapter 7

Clad in nothing but torn scraps of leathery old animal skin, wrapped round their legs, waists and chests, they stood on a dusty patch of earth.

Dan knew immediately this was the scene of his dinosaur dream.

In front of them were the giant ferns, the green lake, and the iguanodons with their riders. On their right, framed against a dull grey sky was a volcano.

Dark masses of scudding black clouds shadowed the earth. The atmosphere felt hot, clammy and oppressive. The air smelt of burnt toasty wood.

They looked at each other, amazed.

"What's happened, Dan?"

"Don't you see? This is what I told you about! This is my dream!"

"But this is real – we're both here. I can see you and touch you," said Sara, squeezing his hand.

"I know, I know, but I told you it felt so real. No wonder I could remember so much about it – it was a premonition! The rug's taken us through time. We're back in prehistoric times!"

"And the smell's come with us!"

Stunned, they took in their new surroundings. They saw the pterodactyls with the multi-coloured feathers, and the Loch Ness monster look-a-likes swept majestically across the lake.

There was consternation all around them.

The patch of earth he and Sara stood on topped a small round hill partly covered in shrubs and flowers. Scattered over the dusty earth were dark green crystals, like lumps of wet coal, shining in the leaden air.

An iguanodon lumbered towards them, creating dust devils with its tail. The boy from the dream slid off its back, and walked quickly towards them. He was light-skinned and slightly taller and broader than Dan. He was clad, like themselves, in scraps of animal skins, and carried a staff in his right hand. His long blond hair was tied back from his forehead. He put his hand on his heart and greeted them in a strong lilting voice, but they didn't understand; and only when Dan asked him to repeat himself did they feel the meaning directly in their minds.

He told them they had to leave as the storm was coming. He signed for them to mount an iguanodon, and Dan felt a hidden hand lift him up. He turned but there was nothing there.

Suddenly the T-rex charged, just as in Dan's dream. The man and woman fell off their animal, and whilst the woman leapt up behind Dan, the man was quickly killed. Horrified, Sara fainted, and Dan held her to stop her falling off. The woman whistled, and their mount made off with the rest of the herd.

Sara recovered quickly, and they headed towards the volcano.

After about an hour, they started to ache, and were relieved when the boy, heading up the iguanodons, whistled sharply to call a halt at a rocky cliff. He jumped off, and helped a striking looking woman down. She was tall and golden haired with piercing blue eyes that flashed with spirit as she spoke.

They approached Dan and Sara who were stretching their stiff legs.

The rest of the tribe gathered round, but neither felt threatened. The boy introduced himself as Phaelar, and the woman – the tribe's leader – as Jafyre. He told them in mind-to-mind communication that their small tribe had been travelling for days to reach the volcano.

He called it Akaela-hal.

Phaelar and Jafyre looked expectantly at them, and Dan felt he should say something, but couldn't think how to describe where they'd come from.

Jafyre laughed, and nodded, and Dan realised she'd read his thoughts.

As he pictured the cellar and the rug in his mind, she picked up the images, and beamed them telepathically to the rest of the tribe.

Dan saw this cause some commotion and framed a question in his mind about the tribe and where they'd come from.

Phaelar said: "We are the last of our kind. We have lived for many generations in the forests, gathering and eating berries, fruits, plants, and leaves, but now we are prey to the dinosaurs".

Dan and Sara saw in their minds' eye the events he described.

"Our tribe are now only this small group of survivors. People from another age came and caused much fighting amongst us."

Before the children could ask about this, Phaelar and Jafyre talked quickly and agitatedly, looking back towards the lake in the distance. Dan couldn't make out the words, but knew what they meant. Apprehensive about the air thickening, as the wind blustered and gathered force, they moved fully into the shelter of the cliff.

Jafyre gave instructions for camp to be set up for the night. They were amazed to watch Phaelar start a fire by using a contraption made from a block of tree bark and some fibrous material. He set a pointed stick spinning within the bark. The friction sparked a handful of dry grass in the hollow of the bark, and he used this to light small pieces of timber and branches the tribe had piled up in the shelter of the rocks.

Sara said: "I didn't know fire was invented millions of years ago!"

Phaelar heard her, and beamed them mind pictures, showing how they had learned to make fire. They saw sun baking the earth, almost feeling its scorching heat. A green quartz crystal with a red tip started to glow, reflecting the sun's rays. This created a beam of intense light, which made the surrounding grass smoulder and burst into flame.

They had mastered this technique, and later learned how to use bark with a stick and dry grass when there was no sun.

While they settled round the fire, the tribe collected berries and leaves they wrapped round a knobbly root vegetable. They pushed this mixture into hollowed tree branches, roughly sealed with moistened red clay and set these on top of a layer of stones at the heart of the fire. Gradually, the hollowed tree branches started to smoke.

Sara said, "They're steaming the food!"

Dan smiled, and looked beyond the sheltering rocks to the plain. He watched as a succession of dinosaurs passed, driven by the storm. He saw the stegosaurs from the cellar troop by, their unmistakeable bulky shapes defined by two rows of spines running along their backs. Elephant-like legs carried them at a fast pace, spiky tails sweeping the ground behind, as if to eliminate their tracks. Their purple-brown bodies were covered in grey spots and the plate-like spikes on their backs flapped gently up and down in a rippling motion, to cool them while they moved. Their small heads had lipless mouths lifted high to sense the air. They grunted like giant pigs.

The atmosphere was sharp with the smell of their wet skin and fear.

Behind them came a succession of smaller brightly coloured dinosaurs, some with long clubbed tails, and others with crocodile skin and hooded necks. A small group with bony crested heads and sharp roving eyes walked two-legged.

Dan's jaw dropped as four enormous creatures swung placidly past. They were bigger than double-decker buses, with huge elegant necks, bulky bodies set low to the ground, and tails as long as their necks. Dan knew they were brachiosaurs, one of the largest animals ever to have lived. Their green and red scaly skin rippled as they moved, their huge feet thumping the earth with bone-shuddering force.

All the dinosaurs were heading for the volcano.

Sara stood silently beside him, watching the incredible caravan of legendary animals move past. She spoke quietly and nervously: "This feels so real. It's like being in a film. I'm worried - how are we going to get away?"

"I've been wondering the same, Sara. In my dream, we escaped through a cave, but there's nothing like that here".

She bit her lip agitatedly: "Maybe there's a cave at the volcano".

"I hope so, but how long will it take us to get there in this storm?"

She clenched her fists: "So what *are* we going to do then!" She burst out, "Dan, I'm scared! We're stuck here and something awful's going to happen. I can feel it! Do something for goodness sake!"

"Calm down Sara, I don't know what to do right now, but it turned out all right in my dream. You just need to trust me."

"That's all very well, but what if you're wrong!"

They were interrupted by one of the tribe walking slowly past them to Phaelar. The injured woman, with long red hair, and a face that looked vaguely familiar, pointed at her shoulder where an open wound bled profusely. Phaelar sat her down, while he cleaned the wound with water. He prepared a mixture of dried herbs which he folded into a large leaf and bound this round the wound. Sara smelt the soothing fragrance of jasmine and lavender, which calmed her down a little. "I'm just frightened, Dan!"

"I know. So am I! Let's just hold our nerve and see what happens, shall we?"

She nodded doubtfully and he squeezed her hand in reassurance.

The tribeswoman smiled in relief as Phaelar's cure took effect, and rejoined her companions, moving much more confidently.

Phaelar grinned, and beckoned them to sit by the fire. Nervously, they ate their meal of steamed vegetables, washed down by clear cold water from the nearby stream.

As the dim light of day began to fade, the acrid air began to crackle with fire and pressed down on them making breathing difficult. The storm grew wilder, the roars and grunts of panicked dinosaurs grew closer and louder, and once more Sara's heart began to race.

Chapter 8

"Keeping calm's the key, Sara! I know this place feels scary, but I'm sure we'll be OK!" Dan said convincingly.

Sara said: "But Dan, this is unbelievable! We're in deep trouble. This storm is ferocious, and what happens if the dinosaurs attack us? Listen to them. They're getting closer!"

"I know, I know, but Phaelar and Jafyre feel like they'll protect us."

"But what about getting home again? How can we possibly get back? There's no rug here! Will we be safe in the middle of all this?"

"Sara, all I *do* know is that my dream turned out OK, so I think we'll just need to trust that everything will be all right! We can't do much anyway, so let's find our balance and sit with the others".

Jafyre motioned them to be comfortable round the fire, and looked at them unblinkingly. She wore a necklace of amber coloured stones glittering brightly in the firelight, and radiated calming and soothing power. She sat curled up in a long cloak of hide and falcon feathers. She spoke with an accent like Phaelar's, an attractive lilt: "We cannot imagine fully the time and place you come from, but we know you will be safe. You are here to learn".

Immediately, Dan framed the question in his mind: "To learn what?"

In reply, she told them about her tribe, graphic pictures illustrating her story.

"Peace has always been at the heart of our existence, and love and mutual care give us common purpose. However, the dinosaurs have killed many of us." She conjured the image of the attacking t-rex.

"Two strangers, from another age - strangers with the power of knowledge - came. The man and woman were friendly and encouraged us to defend ourselves; and some of the tribe, led by Dion, made spears from tree branches to attack the dinosaurs, killing some of the mighty animals. They cooked and ate the flesh, the first time any of our kind had eaten meat.

It caused madness!

Some fought their friends for food, jealously guarding their own store of meat. Others fell ill, becoming withdrawn, bitter and angry.

Then the strangers disappeared, taking with them Dion's young son. I argued with Dion about whether to follow and capture them.

Half the tribe, like Phaelar and I, did not wish to change our peaceful way of life, and we left, splitting the tribe. We travelled from the cold of home to this now terrible place."

Dan asked: "What happened to Dion?"

"Half of the tribe, under his leadership, went in search of the strangers and are now all dead. Some were attacked and eaten by the tyrannosaurs; the meat poisoned others; and the rest died quarrelling over food. The strangers and Dion's son have not been seen again".

She gazed sadly into the fire as she relayed these cruel images to Dan and Sara, who said: "That must have been terrible for you all. Do you know who the strangers were and why they took Dion's son?"

Jafyre looked steadily at them, and said: "We hope that is something *you* will learn".

Surprised, Dan said: "Us? How can *we* find that out?"

Jafyre gazed back at him and her eyes clouded as she replied: "You will find the answers – answers *we* will never know."

Dan gulped, not understanding, and silence fell.

After a while, Sara's curiosity got the better of her, and she said "We've always believed mankind developed *after* the dinosaurs all died. In a project, we learned the earliest humans came thousands of years later!"

Jafyre looked thoughtful, and smiled. She said: "It is hard to believe the dinosaurs can ever die. They are masters of this world".

To help them understand, she again conjured the image of the t-rex attacking, and extended this picture so they saw the tribesman being eaten by the t-rex.

It made them shiver.

Dan said quietly to Sara: "I understand now. The saliva of the t-rex is like acid. It dissolves everything, bones and all! No wonder archaeologists have found no human remains from this time!"

"Yes, I get it! That makes sense. It wouldn't be surprising then that so many died from eating the meat. The acid would poison them."

"But why wouldn't *their* bones remain? Dan asked.

In reply, Jafyre relayed an image of small dinosaurs eating human remains, bones and all. Phaelar added: "When our tribesmen die, these scavengers are ferocious in finding our sacred burial places. They leave nothing!"

"Yuck!" groaned Sara.

Dan said: "Phaelar, you seem to be the tribe's healer."

"I am their healer *and* their guide".

"But you're so young!".

Phaelar grinned infectiously: "Our leader always bears the name of Jafyre, and our guide and healer always Phaelar. When they die, successors trained from birth take over. Dion killed my predecessor trying to cure some of the men poisoned by contaminated meat. I took over from him".

Phaelar painted pictures of their long journey to reach the emerald green lake a few days earlier. The storm had come just before Dan and Sara arrived.

Jafyre told them: "Our way of life is ending now. When the tribe split, there could be no future. We lived in harmony and peace. Balance and compassion were our strength. The strangers and Dion ended this forever."

She placed her hand over her heart, saying "anahata" clearly as she sent the children these images, and they felt a charge of energy in their hearts, as they understood the impact of her words.

Dan framed their thoughts:" You're telling us that people shouldn't fight".

"Yes, but more than that". She spoke passionately, the importance of her words springing from a well of deep feeling: "Those who split us failed to understand what made us happy. The strangers made them think they could change the way everyone lived, by force. They stopped being true to themselves. They lost their identity in a futile search for another."

Dan thought this through, and said: "So we need to be true to ourselves, Jafyre?"

"Above all else – and if you are, you will be true to others too".

"But sometimes our parents tell us to do things we don't want to, or friends dare us to take risks and act stupidly, so we do things we shouldn't or don't like doing".

"You must see the difference between doing things you truly *know* in your heart to be wrong, and doing things you simply do not like."

Dan, embarrassed, saw the difference.

The wind continued to rise, and Phaelar said: "We must rest.

We will set off early in the morning".

Dan and Sara found space near the fire, and stretched out on a bed of ferns and leaves the tribe had gathered. As they settled down, the leaves rustled as if disturbed, and Dan felt a rush of cool air ruffle his hair like a spider crawling through it. He shuddered and swept his fingers over his head and the feeling passed.

His last memory before sleep was a genuinely magical one of Jafyre sweeping her long cloak over the dying embers of the fire. The fire rekindled and burnt brightly in full flame again, giving them back its warmth.

Chapter 9

Opening their eyes, they awoke to the howl of the wind. The fire was completely scattered.

Dan and Sara looked at each other in dismay, sensing something terrible was happening. The storm raged ferociously round them, whipping their bodies and tugging at their thin clothes. The sun had disappeared as if an eclipse was happening. The air smelt scorched and burnt their throats. The sky was completely black, swirling with particles of soot, which stung their heads and bodies.

A small stone struck Dan on the forehead, and he cried out in pain, clinging to Sara. He shouted: "Watch out! This is really dangerous!"

"I know, Dan!" She shouted back, particles of dust and dirt hurting her face.

"Are you OK?"

Dan sniffed back tears, and nodded as Sara pointed: "Look! Everyone's on the move again!"

The tribe mounted the iguanodons, and riders and animals were terrified.

Phaelar and Jafyre were calm in the midst of chaos as they motioned Dan and Sara to straddle their animal.

"Fafa!" Phaelar shouted, and it seemed to recognise its name. It approached and let them pull up on to its broad back. They sensed its fear and bewilderment, and Phaelar gently stroked its neck to settle it. Several of the tribe were without mounts as some animals had fled in the night.

Phaelar pointed his staff to the horizon, dark with menace, and they saw the mental image of the volcano, felt the word Akaela-hal ring through their minds, and sensed the ripple of anticipation sweeping through the tribe as they set off.

Dan gently squeezed the iguanodon's neck with his knees: "Come on Fafa! Let's go!"

Small groups of dinosaurs were moving in the same direction as the tribe, and overhead, the pterodactyl-birds from the lake swooped past in a tight-knit group, making their deep mooing sounds to each other, for support and encouragement. They flew in formation like geese migrating, first one leading, and then another as the lead reptile dropped to the back of the group.

They made good pace across the swirling plain, but the horizon was so low they couldn't make out Akaela-hal, and Sara tugged Dan's arm. She shouted above the wind: "I'm really worried. How can we get out of here? It's like the world's coming to an end!"

"I don't know, Sara, but we've got to keep moving! We have to trust Phaelar and Jafyre!"

They looked ahead, and saw the tribe hunched on the backs of their iguanodons. The proud animals moved with certainty under Phaelar and Jafyre's leadership.

Every so often, a fierce swirl of rushing air brought with it clouds of volcanic dust and ash, which stung their arms and legs, and got into their eyes, mouths and noses, but still the group made steady progress towards the volcano. Dan's forehead hurt, and he gripped Fafa's neck. Sara clung even tighter as the ground started to rise, and she felt, for an instant, as if her waist was being tugged. She looked round quickly and saw nothing, and realised it must have been the force of the wind, now approaching gale force.

Phaelar and Jafyre were directly ahead, and with a start, they saw they were within reach of Akaela-hal. They passed through an uneven field of black lava, the outflow from some previous volcanic eruption, and Fafa picked his way carefully.

The volcano radiated a powerful presence, dominating the landscape. Smoke and flames spewed from its mouth, mixing with the dark overhang of clouds.

For miles around, lava had formed amazing shapes on the surrounding plain. Strangely curved arches, roughly hewn pillars, and unevenly tumbled heaps of lava formed weird contours and structures. There was no dense vegetation, but brightly blooming flowers, straining against the wind, provided bright splashes of colour.

The base of the volcano was enormous and ringed with thousands of dinosaurs, jostling for position, trying to get as high up the slope as possible, all seeking shelter from the howling storm that raised ever more violent clouds of dust and ash across the unprotected plain. As they climbed, however, panic set in, as fresh flows of lava began to pour down from the volcano's crater, trapping them, and beginning to bury those closest to the top. The horrifying roars and bellows of dying animals filled their ears, and the acrid stench of burning filled their nostrils, and made their eyes stream.

Phaelar urged everyone on.

The iguanodons were exhausted, some carrying three or four riders. Dan knew they had to escape, and instinctively clutched Sara's hand. This reassured her, and they both felt calmer. When they next looked up, Phaelar and Jafyre were dismounting where the lava formed a rough square.

The tribe did likewise, and looked upwards as one, squinting their eyes against the rising tempest. Dan and Sara joined them, and saw to their horror the sky had cleared, but in its place an enormous dark shape hurtled towards them.

In seconds, it grew larger and larger, till it virtually filled the sky.

Sara shrieked in terror, and Dan looked desperately around.

There was no place big enough or close enough to hide or shelter.

The dinosaurs scattered, making frightened roars, cries, screeches and high keening sounds of terror that were quickly drowned by the awesome power of the howling earth-bound projectile.

They felt an intense burst of energy hit them, and tore their eyes from the scene to see Jafyre and Phaelar in front of them.

Jafyre drew a picture in their minds - of both ending and beginning – an end to the life of the tribe and the dinosaurs, but a beginning for Dan and Sara. She turned to the volcano, and Phaelar pointed his staff at a huge mound of lava.

He clearly said: "HOME" and a beam of light and flame jetted from the end of his staff, splitting the rock.

Dan shouted: "Thank you for everything!" and grabbed Sara's hand.

They pelted towards the opening Phaelar's staff had blasted in the lava. A gap in the rock face gleamed brightly, and they raced into a large circular cave.

Before they had a chance to see anything inside, they were tumbling, tumbling, tumbling down, down, down in a somersaulting fall.

The last thing Dan saw and heard was the sight, outside the cave, of the enormous slab of rock falling faster than the eye could blink, crumping into the earth with a wrenching tearing crash that turned black day into black night.

Chapter 10

Falling back on the rug, they were clad again in t-shirts and jeans.

The green circle pulsed with energy in a warm and friendly way, then returned to its normal colour. They heard the fading sound of a loud wheezing and blasting, disappearing into the air round them as if being sucked into a vacuum cleaner.

They looked at each other, bewildered, Dan rubbing his forehead where the stone had hit him.

To their surprise, Tim was sitting playing as if nothing had happened. He looked up at them: "What's all that noise?" he asked curiously as the din died down.

They looked blankly at him, thinking how long they'd been away, but Tim carried on, "All that whooshing and whizzing – what was it?"

Sara tugged Dan's sleeve, and quietly said: "He hasn't noticed we've been gone. Time has stood still!" Out loud, she replied: "I'm not sure, Tim – what do you think?" But Tim was already distracted by the flying saucer beside him – it lifted straight up in the air and flew round his head, landing beside him with a bump.

"Wow! How did it do that?" He cried, clapping his hands in excitement.

Dan gaped, and picked up the toy. He examined it, but couldn't see how it had flown on its own. He threw it up in the air, but it fell to the floor. Dan felt decidedly spooked and said to Sara: "This gets weirder and weirder. What's going on?"

"I don't know, but we need to think what we're going to say about all this".

Dan looked at Sara. "Ah! What *will* we tell mum and dad?"

Sara said immediately: "The truth of course – we must tell them the truth. Remember what Jafyre said – we must be true to ourselves, and in telling the truth, we'll do that."

"But what if they don't believe us?"

"They will, Dan – they will", she replied determinedly, "And you can show them where that stone hit you -----". Her voice tailed off as she saw Dan's cut had healed completely.

He rubbed his forehead and said: "So time stood still when we were away, and my cut has magically healed!"

Sara shook her head, and said: "Well I suppose that's good, isn't it? Anyway, not to worry, come on, let's go!"

Liz and Hugh listened to the excited children, puzzled, disbelieving, and astonished, as they told their story. They exchanged concerned looks as Dan described their talk with the tribe leaders, and the horror of the giant object crashing into the earth.

Liz, while desperately proud of Dan, found it too much to take in. She knew he'd discussed his dreams with Sara, but now she felt they had gone too far. "Dan, I've never heard anything like this. It's a great story, but you're just telling us what happened in your dream!"

Hugh, alarmed at how the dream had grown arms and legs, said: "Children, I don't mind you making up stories. When I was a kid, we did that too, but you can't expect us to believe all this. You've talked about being away for days, but you've only been downstairs for an hour or two!"

"But, dad – this really happened!" exclaimed Dan.

"Listen" said Hugh, "We've enjoyed the story, and you've had great fun telling us, but that's enough for today. Time travel is off the agenda!"

Liz chimed in: "Sara, it's probably time for your lunch anyway. Why don't you nip back home, and we'll see you later."

Sara's face reddened in disappointment as she heard their reaction. There were so many things she wanted to say, but somehow couldn't find the right words. She said goodbye and ran across the road, hoping her mum and Bruce wouldn't react in the same way.

Diana and Bruce – at home after a week away on the oilrig – were watching TV, and were only half listening when Sara started to speak. This changed quickly when she told them she and Dan had travelled through time from the cellar.

"You what?" asked Bruce.

"We left the cellar! The rug worked like a gateway to the time of the dinosaurs!"

"What?" repeated Bruce.

"Shut up, Bruce!" said Diana, curiosity roused.

All the same, as Sara told them what had happened, he kept asking questions: "What were you wearing? How did that happen? What did they look like?"

He had an amused look on his face, and his scar grew redder and redder. Sara knew this was a danger sign, and slowed down in her rush to explain everything.

Diana was curious, brushing her fingers through her hair as she followed events. She asked what the tribe ate, and how they hunted.

"They were vegetarian, but the tribe split up because some of them killed and ate dinosaur meat".

When she finished, Bruce persisted: "What did Dan's parents think of all this?" he asked, suppressing a laugh, the scar on his face now glowing.

"They didn't believe us. They thought we'd made it up".

Bruce slapped his thigh and grinned in a forced way: "Well, I'll give you ten out of ten for imagination - but nothing out of ten for reality!"

His face grew darker as he said firmly: "That's enough, Sara. What a ridiculous story. This is all about Dan's stupid dream. What on earth made you think we'd believe that stuff and nonsense?"

Sara gritted her teeth, having lost the battle to convince them. She felt her cheek stinging suddenly, and flinched. Diana, concerned at seeing her tears well up, said: "It's OK, darling. I know you've been looking for more adventure, but dreams don't come true like this!"

"I know what a dream is, mum!" said Sara, and stomped off.

Across the road, the doorbell rang, and Hugh answered it.

A tall black man with a shock of white curly hair stood there, calm and relaxed. He smiled broadly and warmly, the edges of his mouth crinkling under a greying beard and moustache. The whites of his eyes were startling against his deep black skin, and his whole face radiated happiness. He was dressed smartly in a dark suit, white shirt and purple tie

"Perhaps I can help you", he said in a deep booming voice.

"I beg your pardon", said Hugh: "Who are you?"

"I'm Nigel, Peter Friis's helper. I believe the children have just had a little trip".

Hugh's jaw dropped: "What?"

"If it's all right with you, I'd like to see Dan".

"Hang on! Hang on!" declared Hugh, " ----- the Nigel who used to work with Peter?"

"Yes – Peter's helper. I would very much like a word with Dan."

"Well – all right – why don't you come in for a moment"?

"Thanks." Nigel spoke with no accent, but his tone was warmly reassuring. Hugh showed him into the lounge, where he seemed to fill the room with his presence.

"Hello, Mrs Goodwin - I'm Nigel," he said, smiling at Dan and Tim arguing over which TV channel to watch. "Hello, Dan. Hello, Tim."

Liz said: "Nigel! What a surprise! We've heard a lot about you, but nobody's seen you for a long time. Where have you been? And whatever happened to Peter?"

Nigel looked calmly and intently at Liz, and she immediately forgot what she'd just said. It was as if he had taken her words and swallowed them like they never existed. Hugh, who had turned off the television in the meantime, didn't seem to notice, and Nigel said: "I can't stay for long, I'm afraid, but I know the children have been travelling, and I just popped in to say I'm glad".

"What do you mean?" asked Liz.

He looked at Dan, saying: "I'm glad you're using the cellar, and glad you came back OK, and glad you've told your mum and dad. This is only the start. There is much to find".

Hugh butted in: "What do you mean? How do you know all this? What's going on, Nigel?" As he spoke, his words seemed to be completely absorbed by Nigel, sinking in like footsteps in quicksand. Hugh shook his head, trying to recall what he'd asked.

"Everything's fine", replied Nigel, handing Dan a business card. "The great path has no gates; thousands of roads enter it. Call me when the time's right. You'll know when."

With that, he left smiling, leaving a thousand questions unanswered.

Dan looked at the card, which simply said:

Nigel d'Arguana
Mistlees 393939

Nobody knew what to say, but Dan smiled to himself.

Later on, Sara came back, and they shared the disappointment of everyone's disbelief. Sara was excited however by Nigel's visit, and looked at his card: "What did he mean when he said you'd know when to call him?"

"I don't know, but he seemed very sure."

"What d'you think about it all?" she asked. "Why has Nigel suddenly reappeared? It's a bit of a coincidence, isn't it?"

"I know, " said Dan, smiling. "He's got amazing power. Mum and dad asked him questions, and he just ignored them, but they didn't even seem to notice!"

Sara was quiet for a while, and then said: "We need to talk about our trip and what happened. I was terrified at the end. That rock was like a mountain!"

"It sure was! You know, I think we saw the end of the dinosaurs. I think the volcano and that meteorite wiped them out."

Silence greeted this, and then Sara said: "That makes sense. People have always wondered what happened to the dinosaurs. Somehow, we've seen what happened, and come back to tell the tale".

"Yes, but nobody believes us!" said Dan.

"Not yet, but they will!" replied Sara determinedly. She continued: "What did you make of the tribe splitting up? And what about the strangers?"

"I don't know, but it was quite a story, wasn't it? I'm sure Jafyre meant us to think more about it. She said the tribesmen who killed the t-rex's weren't acting normally - they weren't being true to themselves. She meant it's really important to be true to ourselves – to trust in our sense of right and wrong".

"Well - mum always tells me to be myself, but Bruce often pulls me up if I do something wrong, and then I feel bad. But mostly the things I get a row for are things I shouldn't have done anyway, so I suppose that's me not being true to myself".

Dan thought about this. When he was tired and had homework to do, or was asked to help round the house, he often stomped off in a mood. He realised, when he was annoyed at his teacher or his dad, he was really annoyed at himself, not them, and was just seeking attention for himself.

He felt guilty, and Sara smiled. "I think we should learn to understand ourselves better, so we can understand other people better too. Maybe I need to make more effort with Bruce".

"Yeah", said Dan. "Me too, with dad!"

"So what do we do now?"

"Trust our instincts about what's right and wrong, and think more about things when we're asked to do them – not just moan because they don't suit us".

"OK, fair enough, but we should be careful we don't go *too* far to please other people"

"Fair comment. I'll think about what's best for me first, and *then* think about what's best for the other person. If I can please them while doing what's right for me, at least I'll be being true to myself".

"And what about when Miss Ambrose gives you homework you don't like!" said Sara.

Dan grinned. "Yes, but that's different - we have lots to learn.

There'll be loads of stuff we'll have to do we won't like, but at least we'll know why, won't we?"

"I think you're right, and for a start, I'm not joining the A-bomb duo, just because they want everyone to act like them!"

They laughed, and then Sara went quiet. "Dan, who were the strangers, and where do they fit in?"

"I haven't a clue, but they obviously influenced Dion and his crew."

"Yes, for the worst – and how awful they went off with his little boy".

She suddenly burst out: "Oh, Dan, everyone was killed!"

"I know, Sara, but we saw what happened millions of years ago, so we shouldn't be too sad, because we can't change that".

"I know that really, but those poor people – and the dinosaurs - and Fafa – how terrible it must have been!"

Dan nodded, laughed quietly and said: "Pity Mark hadn't been there!"

They grinned, thinking about Mark and the others in the class.

Chapter 11

They walked to school on Monday morning, with Tim lagging behind, scuffing his feet on the path. They were still disappointed nobody believed them, but assumed somehow everyone at school would know about their adventure, but of course, no one did, so it turned out a normal school day.

At least most of it did. Sara thought Miss Ambrose was giving her knowing looks, but must been mistaken. She felt she should make more effort to pay attention.

Miss Ambrose was discussing old books and how important they were to society. Something about her was puzzling Dan. She kept rubbing her shoulder as if in pain, though it didn't stop her writing on the board, her red hair swinging from side to side. Dan gulped and went white.

She was the woman from the tribe whom Phaelar had healed!

As this realisation came into his head, she turned round and spoke to the class, though Dan was sure her words were aimed directly at him: "So you see, long before we had all the modern techniques for printing, people recorded their stories – on tablets of stone, on wood and on materials like the Egyptians' papyrus, where our word paper comes from. We have learned many important secrets from the past from the scribes of ancient civilisations."

Immediately, Dan thought about the book from the library in his dream, and smiled to himself. He suddenly felt uncomfortable, and turned round to see Mark looking intently at him as if trying to guess what was in his mind. He held his gaze for a few seconds, before they both looked back at Miss Ambrose.

Over a lunch of tuna and cheese rolls with Sara, Dan said,

"That was weird! Mark kept looking at me, and Miss Ambrose looks just like the woman Phaelar healed! Did you see her rubbing her shoulder?"

"Oh, don't be silly, Dan. That's impossible! She may *look* like her, but that's all – it's just a coincidence."

Dan chewed silently for a moment and said: "Well, I suppose you're right, but it *is* a bit odd – and that stuff about old books. I'm sure she was talking about the book I dreamed about!"

"Dan, stop it! You're imagining things. Settle down, for goodness sake!"

Before he could reply, Mark interrupted them, as if on cue, "Well well, what's the plot today then? Having a lovely time, eh?"

"Mind your own business, Mark", said Sara, turning away.

Left only with Dan to talk to, Mark kept on:" Can't speak for yourself, Danny boy? Have to get the girls to talk for you? Enjoy old Ambrosia's lecture on books did you? Not that you'd understand much of that."

Dan bristled inside, but his adventure had given him new confidence. Mindful of Jafyre's words, he looked coolly back at Mark, and grinned, his eyes levelling straight at him. After a heart-stopping moment, Mark flushed under the intensity of his stare, and pretended to look at his watch, saying:"Can't waste my day on the likes of you, can I?"

He stalked off, muttering under his breath.

One or two of the class saw this, and, unused to seeing anyone get the better of Mark, gave a quiet cheer. His ears reddened, but he didn't turn round, and Dan felt elated by his own self-confidence.

As they left school, Mrs Braid appeared and asked Dan in a clipped tone: "Well, Daniel, settling in all right?"

"Yes thank you," he replied surprised by the venom in her voice.

Her face clouded briefly, as if disappointed. She scrunched up her eyes, peered at him over her glasses, sighed and said: "You'll have to work very hard here. We set high standards in Elfsite Reach!"

She swirled away, and Sara said: "Don't worry Dan, she's always like that. She just wants you to know who's boss!"

"But that was nasty! I feel really shaky now."

Sara aimed a playful punch at him: "Come on! Don't go all soft on me!"

He couldn't help but grin at her infectious smile. They crossed the bridge over the burn to start work on the village project, going first to the old ruined church along the valley. Sara led the way, and after twenty minutes or so, they approached the ruins. Dan had the feeling they were being followed and kept looking over his shoulder. On the way, they saw lots of brightly coloured little birds on the path and in the trees, but as the church came into view, all they saw were crows.

The air seemed to thicken and fall like a cloak around them. The leaves on the trees were perfectly still, and it was completely silent. The crows flew off as the two reached the ruined gateway. The only bird inside the church grounds was a beautiful little red robin, which cocked its head at them, twittered cheerfully and flew off with a twitch of its wings, leaving them alone outside the silent place of worship.

The atmosphere was brooding, and the old stonework oozed an air of mystery and hidden secrets. The air smelled of decaying vegetation. They both shivered as they absorbed the powerful feel of the old building. Dan still felt they were being watched, but could see no one.

Sara said: "It's called the Sunken Chapel".

"What an odd name! Why's it called that?"

Just then the village minister appeared. Dan had the feeling he had been rushing, but when he arrived at the churchyard, he walked in a slow stooped manner. Mr Dewbury had been in Mistlees for at least two generations. He was dressed in ancient baggy trousers and a faded brown shirt, which had seen better days. He peered at them through horn-rimmed glasses, looking intently at Dan. "Hello, Sara - good to see you"; he said in a dry voice, "It must be school project time again!"

"Yes, you're right, Mr Dewbury. Dan and I are checking out the history of the village, and we thought we'd start at the Sunken Chapel".

Mr Dewbury looked curiously at Dan: "So you're Daniel then. I've heard a lot about you".

Dan was puzzled, but smiled politely as he returned his rather limp handshake.

"Pleased to meet you", he said. "Sara was telling me the church is called the Sunken Chapel."

Mr Dewbury paused as if he hadn't heard, and looked into the middle distance.

"Yes, and the story of how it got its name will interest you."

He led them through a gap in the stones, which at one time marked the entry to the church. They could see remnants of the old building, and one half-ruined wall stood proudly on its own, with tumbled stonework at its foot. The ground fell away sharply from the wall into a dip, which looked as if it had been the centre of the church. Scattered all around were blocks of stone.

"I still find this place a puzzle", he said, as if talking to himself, "You'll see the mound to the right over there. That's where they used to bury the villagers in olden days. Apparently, there was great controversy about where to build the church in the village, and the minister at the time was determined it should be on this site. They say there used to be an underground lake here, and many people felt it was unsafe to have a church built here, but the minister prevailed by insisting it was a site of great spiritual power.

Anyway, they went ahead and built it, but still the villagers weren't convinced. They made sure it had very solid foundations, and, because of the underground lake, used large bars of iron forged here in the village to support its weight. It took two years to build, and when it came to the first Sunday it was to be used, many of the villagers sat on the burial mound, refusing to step inside.

The minister and a few worshippers went ahead, and the church bells tolled long and loud to celebrate the opening sermon."

Mr Dewbury paused for effect at this point, gazing into space, and the children hung on his every word.

"Legend has it that the sermon was never finished, because the church sank into the lake, and the congregation were never seen again".

Dan gasped:"Is that true?"

Mr Dewbury didn't reply for a moment and his eyes clouded over. Dan repeated his question, somewhat nervously. He felt the minister was hardly aware they were with him. Slowly, he turned to look at Dan and Sara as if seeing them for the first time. "We don't know, but they say that every year afterwards, on the anniversary of the day, you could hear the church bells ringing out over the village. People refused to come here for fear they would suffer the same fate as the congregation that disappeared. They didn't even come to visit the old burial ground in case it sank into the lake.

Whether the foundations collapsed under the weight of the people inside or whether the bell ringing unsettled the structure, we'll never know, but the chapel was never used again, and it was left to fall into rack and ruin!"

"So that's why there are two churches here!" Dan exclaimed.

"Yes. After a time, they decided to build a new church, a new minister was appointed, and the present church was built, this time on a more secure site – where it still is now. However, because of what had happened, the superstitious villagers didn't want to bury their dead in the same place as the church, so they made space for a new graveyard at the opposite end of the village from the new church".

Dan was fascinated by the story, and was about to ask more when Mr Dewbury abruptly strode off towards the village without another word.

"What a strange man!" Dan said.

Sara replied: "Yes, he's always a bit like that, though he seemed even more distracted today. But what a great start to the project!"

They drew the Sunken Chapel in their notebooks and walked home. As they neared Dirsett Avenue, Dan turned round quickly, once again sensing a hidden presence. He spotted a figure disappearing round a corner, moving so fast he couldn't make out whom it was.

Dan pointed and said: "Look! I was *sure* we were being followed!"

Sara was too late to see anything, and frowned. Before she could say anything, Dan said: "Yes! I *am* sure!"

As the days passed, Dan and Sara felt excitement mount. They planned to revisit the cellar at the weekend.

On the way out of school on Friday, Miss Ambrose greeted

them, with a smile. Twisting a copper ring round and round her finger, she said: "It's important to understand the way we live is shaped by how we see things. Take advantage of the coincidences and you'll learn so much more".

Dan and Sara gaped, as she winked and left the playground.

"What does she mean? Asked Sara.

Dan looked thoughtful, his alert gaze still following her departing back: "It's as if she knows what's been happening, Sara. She talked about coincidences – well, we've already had a few, haven't we?"

"You mean like how we met, and already seemed to know each other?"

"Yes, and how I dreamed about the dinosaurs, and then we lived out the dream --- and then old Nigel's appearance----and how we were thinking about the history of the Sunken Chapel when suddenly Mr Dewbury arrived".

"You're right, and think about how we managed to get back home when we thought the world was coming to an end. Suddenly Phaelar and Jafyre seemed to sense it, and showed us the way!"

"Well, it must mean something, so we'd better watch out for them as she said".

Sara mused: "But how come she knew what to say to us?"

"Coincidence!" he said, and they both laughed.

That night, Dan dreamed again.

He and Sara stood at the edge of a forest of ancient broad-leafed trees. It was raining, and the rain heightened the green of the meadow before him. Beyond, the ground formed the shape of a hill round which clustered groups of tall red-haired men and women in woollen cloaks, fastened with ornate iron brooches. He wore a similar cloak, and underneath it a plain linen tunic. His shoes were made of animal hide.

The people greeted a warrior who stood head and shoulders above them. He carried a shield of leather, and a fearsome-looking sword, and at his side rested a long gleaming spear. The most striking feature of this bearded figure was his right hand, which was made of silver.

The crowd roared their approval of the awesome character, who motioned them to be still. He started to speak in a lilting, deep and resonant voice. He roused their spirits, urging them to be ready for the battle ahead. When he finished, Dan heard the beautiful strains of a rippling harp, playing a delicate and complex tune, creating an atmosphere of great joy.

Time passed quickly, and the scene changed. He was watching a game of chess, played on a magnificent silver chessboard. The pieces were made of gold studded with precious jewels. The two players, dressed like warriors, played a series of games, and one player won game after game, only to lose the last in the series.

The scene changed again to show a stone tower, exactly like the one in Mistlees. The people from the first scene were saying farewell to the silver-handed giant who strode purposefully towards the forest.

Dan felt they were part of the scene, sharing this moment of great passion.

He woke with his hands clasped together, as if in prayer, the dream filling him with great energy. He felt a sense of completeness, and the image of the silver-handed warrior was like a photo in his mind.

He got slowly out of bed, and walked to his parents' bedroom, stopping at their door. He felt foolish, wondering what to tell them. As he puzzled, Liz opened the bedroom door: "What's up, Dan? We heard you coming along the hall!"

"I'm not sure, mum. I've just had a strange dream about a man with a silver hand, but it was a bit jumbled up."

As he saw Liz's face wrinkle up with that "Oh no, not again!" look, Dan decided to say no more. "It doesn't matter mum, I can't remember much anyway." She looked relieved, and Dan went to the kitchen for his cornflakes.

In the meantime, Sara had been dreaming too, but everything was a bit misty.

She saw a tent with a procession of solid wooden carriages go past, and someone sat on a huge stone. People cheered and the dream faded.

There was much more, but she couldn't remember it.

At breakfast, she hesitantly told mum and Bruce.

"So Dan's got himself some real competition in dream-world then", said Bruce, smiling as she blushed.

"Oh, Bruce – it's not like that. I just can't remember much of my dream, but it was so real".

"I know, Sara, dreams are like that. When you're in them, they seem so real, but when you wake up they often don't come back to you at all, unless something happens which reminds you. Oops – watch out for that t-rex behind you!" He snarled sarcastically, his scar glowing.

Sara jumped, and squirmed, scratching her cheek.

"Bruce!" said Diana, "Leave her alone!" She ruffled Sara's hair and said: "At least your dream's a great start to the weekend. Let's hope it's a good one for you!"

Chapter 12

Having breakfast, she tried hard to recall more of her dream to share with Dan, but could only remember the tent, the stone and the wooden carriages.

Diana said: "Don't worry, it'll maybe come back later when the time is right. Are you remembering your homework?"

Sara had forgotten, and hurriedly switched on the PC to check some information for her essay on Africa. It was only when she went over to Dan's house she realised how much she'd been looking forward to the cellar and its secrets.

"You'll never guess what! I had a dream last night!"

"Brilliant!" Replied Dan, "So did I. What was yours about?"

"Well, I can't remember much, but there was a tent with some wooden carriages going past, and someone sat on a huge stone while people cheered ----- and that's about it!"

"Do you know where it was?"

"Em, no, it was misty – but this is the first time I've ever remembered a dream! How good is that!"

"Terrific! Well done, Sara!"

"Well, come on then, tell me about your dream, smarty!"

Dan grinned and told her. She listened, fascinated, and said, "What an odd mixture. I like the sound of the guy with the silver hand. He sounds a real warrior."

"Yes, but I don't remember any fighting".

"I wonder what it's all about."

"I'm not sure, but never mind, let's go!"

Tim had gone with Liz to his weekly swimming lesson in Perth, so they had peace and quiet as they switched on the cellar lights.

They felt a thrill of anticipation, remembering their adventure the previous weekend, and Dan led the way down the steps.

The tangy aroma of freshly cut oranges and lemons crept towards them and wrapped them in its folds. Dan laughed: "Well, we're getting the full range of smells, that's for sure."

Sara laughed too, and pointed: "I see you've reorganised things. When did you do that?"

"No, I haven't been down here since we were together. Oh, my goodness!" he exclaimed, seeing all the models lined up like soldiers on top of the long straight lines quartering the cellar, "Who on earth did that?"

"Wow, it's spectacular!" Sara said, and it was.

One line started at the far end of the cellar, with the tallest buildings – the pyramids – and ended at the opposite end of the floor with the smallest vehicle – the little bubble car. The other line began at one end with the tallest figures and finished with the smallest animals – the snakes.

Sara said: "This must have taken Tim ages to do. Everything's in perfect lines, biggest to smallest! Amazing!"

Dan didn't reply for a moment: "Tim's not been here, Sara, and I don't think mum and dad have either. They'd have said."

Sara's eyes widened: "How, then -----?"

"I don't know," said Dan his mouth dry.

"Let's have another look at the table", he suggested weakly.

They studied the symbols on its surface, intrigued by the shapes and lettering, though unable to work out what everything meant. One of the seven segments, with the letters TERC, had the t-rex etched on it. Sara saw what she thought was Phaelar's staff, pointing at a conical mountain.

"That's Akaela-hal!" she said, and they realised this section showed pictures from their adventure. The dinosaurs, the volcano, Phaelar, and Jafyre were all there, immaculate in tiny detail.

"But how can that be?" she said.

"I don't know, Sara, but what about the other segments? What are they all about?"

Before she could answer, they felt warmth from the rug, and moved the table back. The lines of models stopped neatly at the edges of the rug.

Its bright yellow ring pulsed warmly, and they were drawn towards it. As they stepped on the ring, it seemed to suck them in to its orbit. They felt the irresistible pull of the rug, and once more heard a loud whooshing noise rising to a crescendo as they disappeared from the cellar.

They stood on a circular outcrop of rock, and, still reacting as if standing on the rug, stepped backwards only to feel a dreadful falling sensation as they toppled into the rushing river below. They plunged under the surface, and struggling for air, kicked out to escape the whirling sucking pull of the depths. They gasped as they re-emerged on the surface, but the icy water pulled them into its racing torrent.

Dan struggled to turn his body so he lay on his back with his feet pointing down-river, like a torpedo. The current eased slightly, though the pace was still frightening.

He realised that, for the second time, he was reliving his dream.

They swept past rocks, through the narrow channel, and were separated and reunited as they were pushed under the water and plunged over the waterfall.

The river opened out into a ravine bounded by vast cliffs. They paddled furiously towards the outer reach of the bend, and suddenly he was lying side-by-side with Sara on a pebble beach, tossed there by the spin of the whirlpool.

"What happened?" Sara said. "Where are we?"

"I don't know where we are", he spluttered in between gasps, choking and coughing up some of the water he had swallowed, "But we're in my dream again!"

Sara patted him firmly on the back to get his breath back. They looked round at the stunningly beautiful backdrop to the small area of beach. Behind them was the river, and in front of them the gigantic tropical trees.

Three ominous looking black-winged birds with hooked beaks circled above, their shadows criss-crossing over them.

"Eh, Dan - we'd better move from here!" said Sara, grabbing his arm and tugging him towards the trees. They half-ran and half-stumbled to the relative shelter of a gnarled but friendly tree stretching imposingly towards the now hidden sun.

They sat down and recovered their energy. Their clothes were sopping wet, but quickly drying out, steaming in the humid shelter of their guardian tree. They wore leather sandals with hide lacings, and bleached grey cloth garments, with an odd grainy texture. These wrapped round them from their shoulders to just above their knees.

Dan said: "Well, at least there's something more to these than last time!"

Sara laughed and said: "Just like your dream said – I was doing my African homework---"

"But we're not in the Savannah – these trees are like the ones you see in a Mangrove swamp. But there's no swamp here."

"And I hope there's no alligators either", chimed Sara.

Dan laughed as they spoke the words from his dream.

"Let's explore", she said, "And see where that rug's taken us this time!"

A few yards away, a gap between the trees caught the rays of the sun, inviting them in. The ground was hard underfoot, and they walked carefully to avoid tripping over roots and tendrils stretching from the gigantic jungle trees.

They were climbing, though it was hard at times to be sure because the trail was bumpy. It wound its way through the trees, and up a gradual incline till they stood at the top of a hill, looking back at the river far below, its racing torrent now a background murmur. The humid smell of wet vegetation hung in the air.

They could see over the tops of the trees for miles around, and the sun beat hard on their heads. The view was stunning. For as far as the eye could see, was dense forest, crowned by a ring of snow-capped mountains, and white puffy clouds.

The evil looking bird trio had disappeared to be replaced by small ghost-like beings flying lazily backwards and forwards in fascinatingly complex patterns.

At first, Dan thought they were about his own size and shape, but with transparent wings, but then he realised they were much bigger and more solid looking – almost like flying adults.

As he thought this, the creatures shimmered out of vision, and he wondered if the blazing sun had affected his eyesight. He looked down and shook his head, to rid himself of the dazzling glare of the sun and think about what he'd seen. When he looked up, Sara pointed. The flying beings were back, and a few circled closer.

They had an air of absolute grace and serenity.

As they took in this amazing otherworldly sight, one figure hovered right in front of them.

Sara gasped: "Dan!" she cried, gripping his arm fiercely, "It can't be what I think it is!"

It looked exactly like an angel, white flowing robes covering its body and limbs except for its magnificent wings. Dan's jaw dropped in astonishment. The ethereal being hung in mid-air.

"Welcome", it said in a trilling voice which seemed to come from the air around it. "I am Zuphlas, protector of the trees and the forest".

"But---but---you're an angel!" exclaimed Dan. "How can we see you? We're not dead, are we?"

Zuphlas replied: "No, you are not dead! You see me because you believe you see me, and that is sufficient in our realm. My role is to watch over you, and ensure you come to no harm while you journey to your destination".

"What destination?" asked Sara nervously.

"That will become clear to you shortly, and you will meet others whose task is to guide and protect you. As long as you hold your trust in what you see, you will see us. If you cease to believe, we will have no place in your minds, and will not be a presence in your vision".

"But angels don't really exist!" Dan cried.

Zuphlas shimmered softly and vanished. So did the others.

"Dan – you've made them disappear!" protested Sara.

Dan groaned in despair and confusion, realising he had done exactly that.

They were aware of the sounds of the forest – an incessant

chirruping of unseen insects, and the cawing of birds from the trees. In the undergrowth that crawled, spread, and wrapped itself round the base of the huge trees, they heard a soft insistent chatter, like an animal commentary on their presence. The dampness of the vegetation smelt like stale mown grass.

Nerve ends jangling, they hesitantly moved forward, minds in turmoil at the strange meeting with the angel. Dan wondered if anyone lived in this strange and beautiful place, as they walked as quickly as they could along the narrow winding trail. He had that now familiar feeling of being followed, and kept peering over his shoulder, but they were alone.

In places where the ground was soft, they saw paw marks like a giant cat's. Sara shivered, her sense of adventure crushed as she realised this was a dangerous place. She felt their winged protector had abandoned them, but suddenly they saw Zuphlas again through a gap in the trees ahead.

"We're sorry!" Dan shouted, and the angel hovered in front of them.

"I understand," Zuphlas said. "We can only help when humans truly wish us to."

A small red and black snake, startled by the intrusion on its coiled resting place, darted towards Sara, who jumped in alarm. As she squealed, Zuphlas turned round faster than the eye could see, and his rapidly whirring wings created a draft of air that blew the snake away. It slithered off silently into the undergrowth.

Sara shivered and said: "Thank you, Zuphlas."

Another angel joined Zuphlas and floated in front of them. In a deep voice, it said: "I can help you hold the visions – in other words, see us - for longer. My name is Metatron, and my worldly role is to assist you to communicate with – in other words, talk to - the Third Sphere. When you relax your minds and open them to their infinite possibilities – in other words, think freely - we will always be there, for so it is ordained – or supposed to be".

They grinned at his strange way of speaking and his funny habit of explaining things twice. He appeared not to notice their amusement, and it seemed he was poking fun at himself.

"What do you mean, Metatron?" asked Dan, "And what's the Third Sphere?"

"I mean that if you open your hearts, and ask for help, you will receive our guidance, our assistance, and our help when it is appropriate – or when you require it. Our inspiration is all around – in other words, we are here when you want us. There will be darker days, times of trouble and periods of strife ahead when you will need us and seek our support and aid."

Dan and Sara looked at each other as the angel continued.

"We are the Divine Messengers from the Third Sphere. Some call us Angels or Muses, and others still, the Dakinis. We are the link between the earthly realm, or world, and the higher realms of teachers and leaders. All of us have a part to play in assisting – or helping - mankind to grow and develop. We are those who deal with you."

"But that's fantastic!" said Dan. "I always thought angels were to do with religion and Christmas carols and that people turn into angels when they die."

"We are all of these things, but we are far far more, as you will learn in your travels and on your journeys".

Metatron finished and then seemed to address the air around them: "Hide and seek, and follow and find, but first know the mission in your mind." Dan felt something brush against his arm, and drew back instantly, clutching it. There was nothing there.

He replied shakily: "I don't understand. What mission?"

His question was met with silence, and the two angels hovered in harmony before silently and gracefully soaring into the trees ahead. The children looked at each other in the baking sunshine, and sat down on a tree root.

"Well, I never thought I'd meet an angel, but they seem so – so – real – so human!" said Dan, a note of wonder in his voice.

"Human - apart from the wings, you mean!"

"Fair enough", laughed Dan. "But I got a real fright there. Something landed on me, but it was gone before I could see it. Must have been an insect. But their message was clear, wasn't it? – except for that stuff about the mission, which made no sense - so we must believe in the angels. They seem to know what's going on anyway!"

This made Sara smile, and after a few minutes' rest, they got up and carried on walking, excited by the magic of the surroundings. Every step they took, the undergrowth thinned and the trees grew further apart.

Suddenly, the path opened on to a smooth grass clearing, surrounded by vast stone structures with broad avenues leading off in all four directions.

It was a city, hidden deep in the jungle wilderness.

Chapter 13

Each avenue which quartered this amazingly beautiful city was dominated by giant pillared buildings and massive pyramids, made from huge blocks of bright red stone.

In front was a small circle of low irregular shaped granite stones, with two larger hunks, about Dan's height, in the centre.

There was no sound at all.

Dan felt shivers run down his spine as they took it all in. The ancient city was completely intact. Sara's eyes were wide as she pointed ahead. Gathered in a large square was a market. Hundreds of people bustled about their business, and row upon row of traders displayed their wares.

The aromatic smell of exotic spices wafted past them.

Dan asked: "What should we do?"

Sara shrugged and said: "It's your dream – what do you think?"

"I don't know what to think. It feels like we've tumbled into a history book, but everything looks new, doesn't it?"

"I think it's an Aztec or Mayan place. They were supposed to have built pyramids like the Egyptians. We must find out! Shall we go to the market?"

Dan wasn't sure, and felt really nervous. His knowledge of the Aztecs and Mayans was limited, but he knew they had a reputation for human sacrifice.

He thought for a moment, looked at Sara for confidence, took a deep breath and led them forward.

The hubbub of the market started to wash over them.

People were dressed simply, like themselves, with strips of fabric wrapped round their bodies. Many had cloth bands round their heads, stretching down to support bundles on their backs. The bewildering aroma of spices was sharpened by the tang of lemons, limes and oranges. "That smell's come with us again," Sara grinned.

They stopped at the fringe of the market. A few people looked curiously at them, smiling welcomingly. They nervously grinned back, embarrassed by the attention.

The crowd parted to let two tall natives through, carrying a hammock. Sitting in this portable bed was an impressive figure in a brightly coloured padded tunic, and linen headdress. The bearers set him down, and spread blankets for him to walk the short distance to the nearest stall where he had a lively conversation with a woman selling maize and vegetables.

She looked uncannily like Miss Ambrose, her red hair shining in the sun.

After a few moments, she handed him some tomatoes and two huge corn-on-the-cobs, in exchange for some beans. This was the first time Dan and Sara had seen bartering in action. All around them was a frantic chorus of pleading, shouting, demanding and wheedling voices.

They couldn't make out words, and Sara asked: "How will we understand them? Will it be like last time?"

Before Dan could answer, a small slim teenage girl, her dark hair tied back with a colourful headband, appeared beside them and said something. They were flustered and Sara muttered "Hi".

The girl's eyes widened, and she spoke hurriedly. This time, they understood perfectly, as the meaning of her words automatically translated into their minds.

She said, "You are the ones we are expecting".

"What do you mean?" Dan replied.

"My father said two children would come from another time to see the end".

"The end?" asked Sara, puzzled.

"We cannot talk here", the girl said, and led them through the market to a wide avenue. Dan stopped to marvel at one particular building, built, pyramid style, on five massive levels, each with a windowed terrace on which the next level sat. The terraces narrowed towards the top and a wide steep stone staircase formed most of the front of the building.

At either side were identical statues showing an enormous serpent swallowing a man. All he could see of the man was his face framed in the serpent's gaping mouth. He shivered, feeling uncertain and vulnerable, and jumped as the girl gripped his arm to lead him on.

They walked past more pyramids, and several open spaces where people played a ball game with hand rackets. The girl stopped at a row of small red-painted mud buildings, with thatched roofs.

"These are the scribes' homes".

She led them inside the first and largest house. It was gloomy, except for patches of light streaming from two windows in the opposite wall. It took them a few moments to refocus. A figure sat cross-legged between the windows, stooped over some writing materials. Without looking up, he greeted them. "You have come as I hoped. Come in. I have much to tell you."

As their eyes adjusted to the dim light, Dan saw that the man was old, his face wizened and wrinkled. His long curved nose stretched from a broad lined forehead, almost meeting his pursed lips. His dark hair was streaked with white.

The girl said: "This is Parimanu, my father. He is the chief scribe to our ruler, Ramona."

Parimanu at last looked up, and Dan and Sara were startled by the power glowing from his eyes. They were clear and piercing, pools of light with black centres like magnets, swirling centres of intense energy cutting through the faint light to focus on them.

It was impossible to hold his gaze, and Dan looked down. The pages on his knee were folded like an accordion, and the cover was made from a soft green substance. Ornate pictures of ceremonial figures, with plumed and feathered headdresses, adorned the pages, with picture-symbols and hieroglyphs round the borders. Stylised writing formed neat rows of squares, each containing a small number of symbols. Dan recognised some from the table in the cellar.

His mind buzzing, he looked up from the manuscript to meet Parimanu's eyes again. He immediately felt a rush of energy to his stomach, and his nervousness disappeared. Sara felt this boost to her energy too, and experienced a whole flood of emotions that made her reel. She felt strong, brave, powerful, confident and cheerful all at once.

"Don't be afraid", said Parimanu, in a gravelly voice, "You must stabilise your energies before we talk".

Dan and Sara sensed images of swirling mist whirlpooling slowly to a settled steady flow. They felt calm and stable once more, their energies rebalanced.

Parimanu asked his daughter to fetch water. Her name was

Kaimi, and when she returned with pitchers, Sara said: "Thanks, we're really thirsty."

Kaimi blushed and said: "I'm glad I found you. I've waited for several days."

Dan asked, "But how can you have been expecting us? How did you know we were coming? Where are we? What's going on?"

Kaimi laughed, and Parimanu motioned them to sit. He said: "You have followed the false prophets who came before, and are now long gone. We expected you, because our ancient texts foretold it. You have been chosen to save our knowledge and protect mankind's future.

We are the Mayans.

Our people are ready to move on, but our disappearance has been misunderstood. We need messengers from the future to see the truth. We had hoped the ones who came before you would tell our story but they cannot. You are the ones to safeguard the Mayans' ancient knowledge and use it for the good of all."

Sara's thoughts were in turmoil as she remembered about the Mayans. Images of war and disease and sacrifices jumbled up with pictures of ruined cities and jungles.

Parimanu nodded, and said: "All of these are true, but only tell part of our story. As chief scribe, my role is to record important events. This is done on fig tree bark in our language of hieroglyphics and symbols."

Their eyes were drawn to the book he was inscribing, and he smiled. "This is the last book we will write – it contains the secrets of the ages. Your people call them codices".

They saw images of scribes writing codices, and setting them on shelves in a huge vaulted building, like a library.

"For generations, the scribes have passed on knowledge through their writings. In the ancient texts, it is said our world will end when tomorrow's sun sets. It is also foretold that our secrets will be lost, but that two will come from a future time to discover them for all mankind.

You are the ones.

This is your personal mission. It will drive you and give you energy and purpose. You must not fail!"

Sara and Dan looked at each other, feeling nervous, extremely confused and suddenly burdened with something they did not yet understand.

Dan broke the silence that followed. "How can this be true? How can we be the ones for a mission like this? How can *we* do what you're asking?"

He shivered again, and Sara asked: "Is this why we're here? And how is it we understand you?"

"We understand each other because we read minds and create a common language. I will try to answer your questions. Do not be afraid".

Kaimi brought them a hot dish of thin gruel served in pottery bowls, and, smelling its spicy aroma, they realised they were starving. While they ate, Parimanu continued. "Our nation and our culture have been here for hundreds of years. Our ancestors came from the land you call Egypt, travelling like Gods, through space and time."

The children looked at each other, while he went on. "We have long devoted ourselves to following our ancestors, and now everyone from our city of Tikal will move on together to our future beyond this life".

Sara said: "I don't understand what you mean by moving on to your future. How can there be a future if your world ends?"

"Our physical life will end, but our spiritual life will continue. We have dedicated all our energies to our spiritual selves so we may exist in the world beyond time. We are preparing for our final ceremony tomorrow."

The pictures they felt him create in their minds were amazing. They saw a series of different scenes showing the Mayan way of life. People cultivated the land, growing maize, corn, and cocoa trees. They used irrigation channels to water the crops, and hillsides were neatly terraced to maximise the harvests. Agriculture was their lifeblood, and images of the market showed people bartering for food.

They saw thousands of people building the incredible city of Tikal. Planned in meticulous detail, its large open square sat at the heart of pyramids, temples and a number of raised round buildings Parimanu called observatories.

"We study the stars, the sun and moon. They are important to our lives and to measure time. We have three calendars – each for a different purpose.

Our daily life is in years of 260 days, with 13 cycles of 20. Our farmers' calendar however is based on the sun and the seasons. It is like your modern year with 365 days, but divided into 18 periods of 20 days. There are then five days of uncertainty and doubt, before the New Year begins. After every 52 years, our two calendars end on the same day, and that day is tomorrow.

We have a third calendar, of 584 days, to calculate our festivals, and for the first time in several generations, tomorrow is also the end of this calendar. This is why we choose tomorrow to fulfil our spiritual lives."

Kaimi saw they were struggling to understand, so resumed the story, showing them startling pictures. A small group of people stood, relaxed and smiling. Their bodies began to shimmer and sparkle softly till the outline of their shapes started to blur.

They then disappeared completely.

"We have reached the stage where we can live without our physical bodies. Tonight our people celebrate their last night on this plane, for tomorrow we will raise our energy levels so the atoms making up our bodies vibrate so fast we turn into pure energy".

Sara could see Dan's confusion, and asked: "How's that possible?"

Parimanu explained: "We have followed the teachings of our Egyptian ancestors in developing a deep bond with nature and with each other. We are all connected through the power of our minds, and can read each other's thoughts and wishes. We are all part of the same deep well of energy, indivisible from each other."

The image of the people vibrating out of existence hovered in the air before them. Parimanu said many cultures had practised this skill over the centuries, including the Egyptians, and the Tibetans.

"But we thought you sacrificed people!" Dan blurted out.

"All you know about us is what you see in engravings and in the codices you have discovered over the centuries. Whilst they seem to show acts of sacrifice, they simply depict those who have given up their physical lives for an everlasting spiritual one".

"You mean these people weren't sacrificed?"

"These ceremonies allowed the priests to show there is nothing to fear in physical death. All those you believe were sacrificed were ready to move on to the spiritual world and no longer needed their physical bodies."

Kaimi smiled "This is what tomorrow brings".

"Are you going to sacrifice everybody?" asked Dan.

"No – we no longer need to destroy our bodies. We can now rejoin that vast energy source you call the Universal Consciousness or the Universal Mind."

"I've read about that", said Dan, startling Sara. "It's about seeing the world full of great beauty and energy. The more we see that beauty, the more we evolve, and the higher our energy levels make our atoms vibrate. That's how we've developed!"

"Yes, and also how all mammals, animals, birds and fish have evolved over the centuries. As each species develops, it learns new skills, and as it masters its environment is able to change its physical appearance and develop new mental abilities to continue its evolution and face new challenges. The powerhouse of our mind will lead us to a spiritual world."

Sara asked: "Do you mean like heaven? Like dying and going to heaven?"

"Yes, like that, but with all our conscious powers intact."

Dan thought this was too fantastic, and the doubt in his mind returned. He felt anxious and scared. Parimanu looked deeply into his eyes, and again Dan felt a huge surge of energy in the pit of his stomach. He felt light headed and dizzy, and had to steady himself.

"You are feeling a small sample of the energy which allows us to control the vibrations within our bodies. I am recharging one of your energy centres to dismiss your fears."

Sara asked: "What happens tomorrow?"

Kaimi replied: "Ramona will lead the ceremony in our largest temple – Kormanjiali. Everyone will be there before dawn when proceedings start. It will last all day"

Dan asked: "But what about our mission? What do we have to do?"

Parimanu held up a hand: "You will find out tomorrow. Now you should rest to be fresh for the morning."

Kaimi laid out blankets for them to sleep on, and she and Parimanu went to a neighbour's home to give Dan and Sara privacy and time to think through what was about to happen in Tikal.

Chapter 14

Getting ready for bed, they discussed the amazing day. Neither felt tired, despite their adventure. Sara said," This is a whole new world!"

Dan, feeling confident again, laughed and said: "Two actually – the Mayans and their future".

"Is what they said possible, Dan?"

"I don't know, but they sure do believe it. Those pictures of people disappearing were really cool."

"They were, but what did you make of Parimanu saying we've been chosen to bring back their knowledge? He said this was our personal mission. He made it sound like we're going to save mankind!"

Dan laughed: "Yeah, right! I can hardly see that, can you?"

"Not really, I must admit. He did say we'd find out more tomorrow, so maybe it'll be clearer then. Anyway, I'm worried about you - you've been anxious today."

"I don't know what it is, but it's like when I couldn't believe about the angels – remember? When I doubted, they disappeared."

"Maybe you just need to trust more in what we're seeing".

They felt a change in the air around them, and heard a soft rustle. Their eyes widened as Metatron appeared with a new angel, taller and slimmer, beside him.

"I felt your need for help, your desire to believe, your wish for understanding", Metatron said in his deep voice.

Dan couldn't help grinning. "We're glad to see you. We've had an unbelievable day since we saw you".

"I know. I see. I hear. And I bring Vohumanah who will help you, assist you wisely, and let you believe more. He will communicate with you – speak to you and tell you what you need or require to know".

Vohumanah looked steadily at them.

They felt his power and presence before he said anything. He didn't move at all, yet gazed directly into both their eyes at the same time with deep intensity. He seemed to see through them in a way that relaxed them. It was hard to make out his features as they shimmered constantly. When he spoke it was in soft measured tones with a slight echo.

"It is hard for you to understand all you have seen and heard. You have grown up in a world where time to contemplate and meditate has been forgotten. You live in a world of conflict and competition. Few people follow a spiritual path. The pursuit of material things is everything.

This is changing now as people discover there is more to life than the physical level. Throughout time, many have discovered this truth. You need only open your hearts to receive the guidance which is all around you".

His words felt as if they were still hovering in the air after he stopped speaking. They felt as if all he told them was replaying in their minds, lending meaning and understanding to his message.

"How do we open our hearts?" asked Dan.

"You can create what you want by believing it will happen. Trust your instincts to lead you. Listen to all you hear. Keep a positive mind. Learn."

Again his words rolled around them as their impact struck.

"Vohumanah", said Sara, "How come you've appeared to us now?"

"There is a time in life when we need to know more about why we are on this earth. Your time is now. You have been given a purpose. My role is to let you see life as the constant energy flow we are all part of. There is no separation of life from death.

The spirit lives within you, through and beyond time".

"You mean like going to heaven? Is that where the Mayans are going?"

"Their heaven is here on earth. They will vanish but they will be here, and they will see you - as you will see them in time".

"That's like you guys – angels!" exclaimed Dan.

"Or ghosts!" added Sara.

"Yes" Said Vohumanah in his soft echoing tone, looking just beyond them both.

"That's mind-blowing!" said Dan, wondering what he was focussing on.

"That's mind power", said Vohumanah.

Metatron fluttered his wings softly, and the two angels melted into the air around them. A soft lingering rustle remained and swept through their hair. Dan and Sara looked at each other for a moment, stunned, and brushed fingers through their hair as if to shake loose a lingering cobweb.

She broke the silence. "Wow! That was powerful! You know, I've always wanted to believe in ghosts and angels, but I've been too frightened. People laugh at you if you talk about them. But from now on, they can laugh all they want to! What Vohumanah said is brilliant. Imagine that – the Mayans are joining the angels!"

"And he talked about us being given a purpose – that must mean the mission Parimanu talked about. Well, tomorrow's going to be some day!"

Dan fidgeted with his sleeping blanket, a coarse orange cloth: "You know, something else's been bothering me, and I've just put my finger on it. Do you remember when we arrived outside the city we saw a stone circle with two big boulders in the middle?"

"Yes – you mean the two knobbly stones".

"Uh huh. Well, they looked quite different from the stones the buildings here are made of. These stones looked – looked – Scottish!"

Sara laughed, but Dan said, "No, I'm serious, and I know why it's been on my mind. I've seen that circle before!"

"Oh come on, Dan. How can you possibly have seen it before?"

"Well, when we got the project to do about Mistlees, Dad got me a book about Perthshire, and there was loads in it about the history of the area. There's a photo in the book of the circle. I'm sure it's the same one. They're standing stones!"

"You're kidding me!"

"No, no I'm not. I wouldn't – not about something like that. The circle's the same as the one in the book – I'm really sure about it".

"But there must be loads of stone circles around".

"Not like this one with those two big stones in the middle, there aren't!"

"Well, I don't understand that".

"Nor me, but there must be an answer".

"Yup," said Sara distractedly.

"What's up, Sara" asked Dan.

"I've had something bothering me too – Parimanu talked about people who had come before us. What was it he called them – false ----"

"Prophets!" Dan finished.

"Yes, but who were they? What did he mean?"

"I don't know. I'd forgotten he said that".

"Yes, he did. He said they'd hoped they would tell their story, but couldn't now".

"Maybe he meant the angels?"

"You might be right, but I'm not up to wrestling with that tonight", said Sara. "My brain hurts already, and I think I'm ready for sleep now".

"Yes, me too. I wonder what tomorrow will bring. I'm feeling excited, but I'm worried about how we'll get home again, and what our mission holds".

As they settled to sleep, Sara replied, yawning, "Do what Vohumanah said – be positive – believe everything'll be OK and it will!"

Chapter 15

After what seemed only moments, Kaimi woke them, shaking their shoulders gently. Blearily they struggled from under their blankets. It was still dark, and she carried a burning torch, which threw flickering shadows on the walls.

"Hi, Kaimi", greeted Sara, while Dan stretched and yawned.

"I hope you slept well", said Kaimi. "Our people are gathering now at the Kormanjiali temple. When you are ready, we must join them".

She set down pitchers of water and a plate of tortillas. It took only a few minutes to finish them. They were hungry, and even the unaccustomed dry taste of the tortillas was welcome. Dan said they had slept soundly, and were ready for the day. "What do we have to do, Kaimi?"

"You may come to the temple whenever you wish. The ceremony will last most of the day, as our people must all be ready at the same time to cross over to our future."

"How many will be there?"

"In your thousands, twelve."

"Twelve thousand! Wow! That's a huge number!" exclaimed Sara.

Kaimi explained this was the entire remaining Mayan population. People had travelled from many other towns and cities to join those in Tikal.

Dan thought for a moment, and said, "If they've come from lots of other places, twelve thousand doesn't seem that many after all".

"There were many many more than this – hundreds of thousands of our people, but disease and war have taken a heavy toll".

She conjured up images of the Mayans defending their land from invaders from the North. They fought with swords and spears, and their skills with these weapons were clear as they cut down vastly superior forces, though their armies suffered huge losses. The pictures rolled forward to show thousands dying in great pain. Plague had swept through the countryside, leaving only the fittest and strongest unharmed.

She explained that this was part of the great design for their people. Without these recent disasters, they would have been unable to cross over into their future with many of the children and weaker old people.

"Come", she said, "We must go to Kormanjiali".

Light gently filtered through the forest beyond the city as they walked to the temple. The air smelt so clean and pure, it made them feel giddy. It was eerily quiet.

Thousands of people were gathered outside Kormanjiali, all dressed in white, and Dan was surprised to see this was the building he had stopped at the previous day. So many folk stood silently before them that they could only see the tops of the two huge statues. On each side of the vast staircase, the mouths of the serpents swallowing the men were now lit by the blazing dawn sun, which stretched up and over the horizon. The heat warmed them immediately, and the atmosphere outside the temple was charged with electric anticipation.

"Where's your dad?" asked Sara.

"He is inside the temple – he will record today's events. This is the day he has worked and planned for since he began studying the ancient manuscripts."

As she spoke, a ripple of excitement ran through the crowd, and all heads turned. They witnessed an amazing sight. At first they thought it was a vast thick red carpet being rolled out, but quickly realised it was an unending stream of red-painted Mayans who lay on their fronts in a long continuous line.

Eight tall natives carrying a ceremonial litter walked over the backs of the chain of red bodies. As the litter passed, people shook themselves free of dust, ran forwards, and lay down again as part of the human carpet.

Dan and Sara absorbed the scene silently. This was Ramona, the Mayan leader's arrival.

His litter was fashioned from snakeskin. It was an astonishingly bright tapestry of kaleidoscopic colour. He sat upright, his face impassive, completely covered by the skin of a jaguar, its proud head sitting above his face.

The procession stopped at the foot of the steep temple steps, the crowd parting to allow the human carpet to roll right up to the base of the vast pyramid.

Seven natives, dressed in shimmering silver costumes, blew long golden trumpets to still the crowd.

The bearers set the litter down, and Ramona alighted, jaguar skin glistening in the sunlight. The animal had been a magnificent specimen, its fawn coat beautifully patterned with distinctive clusters of dark brown spots. It had been tailored to Ramona's figure and he wore it like a vast cloak, its paws stretching over his hands. Its teeth and bright yellow eyes glowed as if still alive.

As the tall impressive ruler started to climb the steep narrow steps, the crowd began a steady chant: "Ra-mo-na! Ra-mo-na! Ra-mo-na!"

He turned to face the crowd, and quietened them by raising his arms. On his forehead gleamed a bright yellow stone, like a tiger's eye. He wore a necklace of precious stones - amber, citrine and topaz. His chest glistened with oil.

For a moment, he looked straight at Dan and Sara. They were sure a flicker of recognition crossed his face, and were stunned to see images of his life flash before their eyes.

They saw him as a small child being taught by the scribes in an observatory; as a teenager practising his sword skills with a weapons teacher; as an adult hunting and killing the jaguar with one throw of his battle spear; and as a ruler presiding over the headsmen of the different cities with Parimanu at his side.

He spoke in a loud clear voice: "My people, we have awaited this day with patience and dedication. You have all earned this rich reward. We go with our ancestors. We join our parents and their parents too. We have wrestled with our daily toil for long enough. Many months and years of supporting each other, of giving strength and energy to our friends and to our neighbours have brought us here today. Our minds are open. Our spirits are prepared. There will be an end to sacrifice and suffering, and the start of a new eternal kingdom at the time of the end.

Our people are ready. We cross over to our future now."

A huge cheer rang out and he shrugged off the jaguar skin, continuing his ascent. He entered the temple through a doorway at its second level.

Anticipation heightened, and Kaimi explained that Ramona would preside over a series of identical ceremonies, allowing everyone to participate. They could observe whenever they wished. She would be among the last to go through the ritual.

Dan and Sara debated what to do, while a large group from the crowd followed Ramona into the temple. They sat down in the sun.

"How long does the ceremony take?" asked Dan.

"It will be short for some and longer for others. Some will need support and energy from their close ones to be prepared, but all will come back here ready for the crossover".

Soon, people began to re-emerge, and it was extraordinary to watch. Faces glowed with an inner light. Bodies seemed buoyant, almost floating down the steps. With a shock, Dan realised there were moments when he could see straight through them to the temple behind. They all gave off a field of vibrant energy, which clearly affected those now climbing the steps to take part in the next ceremony.

"Come on Sara, let's go now!" exclaimed Dan, and they followed the group of several hundred people up the steps into the temple. As they walked through the huge open doorway, the first thing they were aware of was the atmosphere.

It was electric.

The air inside crackled with energy. The pure delicate scent of carnations was smothered by an intense smell of burning incense, the smoke stinging their eyes.

As they adjusted to the dimmer light, they found themselves at the top of stairs leading down to a vast amphitheatre. The crowd filled this open space, walking towards a raised platform at the far end. Seven large bowls sat ranged along the front of this stage. They followed the stragglers, and stood at the back of the throng.

Parimanu sat to one side of the stage, engraving a tablet of stone. He looked over, and even across this huge crowd of people, they felt his energy lift theirs.

Silence fell, and on the raised stage, two half-naked men very gently struck two round metallic objects with bronze hammers. The sound they created was a soft insistent metallic tinging.

The two circles vibrated softly, making slightly different tones.

The end result was a strangely satisfying "mi" note, which echoed round the temple.

The sound was very quiet, yet filled the vast room.

Two women appeared and began to dance together slowly with the musicians. Both circles disintegrated and inside each was a white flame burning fiercely. The dancers tipped a small amount of liquid from each of the seven bowls, and as the liquids spilled into each other, a chemical reaction created bursts of fire and smoke.

People began to move in perfect rhythm with the dancers. The tinging sound continued even though the circles had gone, and the tension in the air increased to the point where people reached an ecstatic state, eyes and faces glowing with a fire reflecting the flames.

Dan and Sara felt the insistent "mi mi" sound resonate in the pits of their stomachs. They saw the shape of individuals in the crowd begin to soften and blur, and realised everybody was achieving some form of vastly heightened perception, enabling them to glide up the stairs to the outside of the temple and allow the many still to come to take their place.

The children felt heady, as they followed people outside. The last sight they had was of Parimanu chiselling his tablet. Sara guessed he was counting the numbers going through the intense ritual.

The pair sat down in the sun again. Kaimi appeared with water to quench their thirst.

"That was so amazing," Sara said. "Everyone has changed. They even *look* different from before".

Kaimi told them the heightened energy levels would continue to rise as the day wore on. By the time everyone went through the ceremony, all would reach the same energy level, the cumulative effect allowing them to move into their new world.

They spent the next few hours exploring the city, marvelling at the architecture, the splendid buildings, carved pillars and statues. Some engravings showed groups of people dancing, singing, eating and drinking. Some were of battle scenes, with plumed warriors spearing the enemy. Many showed images of snakes coiled round trees and human heads. Others depicted grotesque faces with huge noses, bulbous eyes, and thick-lipped mouths. The pair shivered at the severity of some of these monsters.

Dan walked towards a building supported by pillars, carved with symbols and shapes, supporting the roof soaring high above. The two pillars flanking the entrance were covered in intertwined dolphins and hieroglyphs.

He stopped in his tracks. This was the building from his dream!

He walked through the massive portal into a shaded interior glowing from within.

Rows and rows of stone shelves were full of what, at first sight, looked like books, but in place of book-covers, they were sheathed in a leathery-leafed soft green coloured substance.

They were codices.

This was a library.

Drawn to a codex on the nearest shelf, he picked it up, and as he opened it, the pages turned of their own accord, making a soft whistling sound.

Startled, he almost let it go, and suddenly sensed he was no longer alone. He looked up to see a duskily skinned girl hovering about a foot from the floor, directly in front of him. His jaw dropped, and he gasped, dropping the book with a soft clump, to the paved floor.

The girl, dressed in a loose-fitting tunic, which shimmered and gave off a soft radiance, spoke without opening her smiling mouth: "You see our past, and come from our future. I am Theena, the keeper of our records".

"I've seen you in a dream!" Exclaimed Dan. "Where have you come from"?

"I have been to the temple and wait to cross with the others, but I felt your vibrations here. Your presence has a purpose. You must take back with you our knowledge and our secrets."

Theena pointed at the codex, and he picked it up nervously. It fell open at a page, and, startled, Dan recognised it. It was the codex Parimanu had been working on.

This was their mission.

They had to take this codex back.

"I must return to the others. I cannot stay long without my people's energy".

Sara shrieked in alarm as she came into the building in time to see the girl flicker and disappear as quickly and quietly as she had arrived.

"What was that?" She asked breathlessly.

"It was a girl called Theena who's the keeper of all these codices".

Sara's gaze took in the surroundings, and she took the book from Dan's trembling fingers.

"She said we must take this back with us. It's our mission! It's Parimanu's codex!"

"Oh, that's brilliant! People will have to believe we've really been here now, won't they?"

"I'm not so sure", Dan said hesitantly, and Sara frowned at him.

"OK, I know, I know – be positive".

"We'd better get back. It's getting late, and we mustn't miss the end of the day".

They walked back through the deserted city to Kormanjiali, Dan clutching the precious codex tightly, as the last group of Mayans reassembled at the base of the pyramid. They saw Parimanu, Kaimi and Ramona, and at their side a still glowing Theena. From this small group of four came a clear message – an image of peace, harmony, and of hope for their future. Ramona saw the codex in Dan's grasp and smiled faintly. Parimanu nodded his satisfaction.

The air stilled around the huge crowd, and Dan and Sara sensed the atmosphere heighten further. A soft haze surrounded everyone. They all stood silently. Gradually the haze developed into a bright sparkling light, which enveloped them all. It shimmered and glowed for some moments with increasing brilliance.

Gradually, the intense brightness faded, and Dan and Sara were left standing alone, open-mouthed, in an empty city.

Neither could speak for a moment, until Dan weakly said, "They've done it. They've gone!"

Sara was deeply moved. A feeling of calm filled her. She looked at Dan and saw he was pale and anxious, and she knew what to do. Her warm penetrating gaze allowed her own strong energy to reach and strengthen him. He felt his confidence grow, and his mind unfroze.

"Thanks Sara, I felt that!"

She smiled.

Darkness fell quickly, and Dan wondered out loud how they would get home. He felt no nervousness now, and his blue eyes sparkled with enthusiasm.

After a few moments, the air around them changed, softened and radiated energy. Their three angel friends hovered in front of them.

"Hi", greeted Dan, and Sara said, "It's good to see you. You knew we might need you, didn't you?"

Metatron replied "We watched and saw you, and waited until we knew you were ready, until you reached out in your minds for us – to connect with us, to join us, to feel the need for our help, to use our knowledge".

They laughed at his long-windedness, and he looked back with a twinkle in his eye: "You have learned much today. You know more than before. You are richer and wiser, your minds have grown".

"Yes, we know, Metatron", said Dan, "We've had an amazing day, and it looks like the Mayans have succeeded in their mission".

Vohumanah spoke. "They are all safe. We see them now. Their energies are strong enough to connect with the universe, and to stay within the timeless world. Your friends wish you well, and Theena wishes you to care for your message". The soft echo of his words pattered around them like raindrops.

Dan looked down at the codex and nodded thoughtfully.

"It's just amazing", said Sara, "It must be wonderful to have their strength of belief".

"You can join their path, in time", Vohumanah replied.

"I think, for now, we'd be happy to get home", said Sara.

Zuphlas moved closer, and his tingly voice told them he would lead them through the city. It was now dark, and the only illumination was the soft glow around the angels.

Dan asked, "Where do we go?" and Zuphlas replied, "You will know the place".

Without another word, he moved ahead, and they followed his

shimmering figure. Vohumanah and Metatron had disappeared.

After a few minutes walk, they were disorientated by the darkness, but confident in Zuphlas, they followed on. They reached the standing stone circle they had seen when first arriving at Tikal.

Dan said, "I *knew* it was important".

"But what do we do?" Asked Sara.

This time it was Dan who was confident.

They thanked Zuphlas for his guidance, and entered the circle. It was pitch black, but the two central stones gave off a slight radiance, allowing them to walk towards them. They were about the same shape and size as themselves.

Dan told Sara to put her arms round the smaller stone, and simultaneously did the same with the larger one. They felt a light breeze around them, the ground beneath their feet vibrated, and a rushing roaring sound filled the air and disintegrated the circle.

Chapter 16

Moments later, they landed together on the rug in the cellar. The yellow circle pulsed and glowed for a second before losing its vitality and fading to its previous dull tone.

Dan looked round, gulped, and patted Sara on the back. "We made it – I knew we would!"

"You didn't seem so confident some of the time".

"No, no, that's true, but *they* gave us confidence, didn't they?"

"Yes, they did. That was incredible. What a beautiful place, great people, and an *amazing* experience. It feels like we've been away for days".

"I'm sure it'll be like last time when we were away for only moments. Are you tired?"

"No, I'm still full of energy. Let's look at the codex."

They opened it up. It was folded like a concertina, so they each held an end.

It felt like tree bark, fragile to the touch, but strong enough to open out and show its colourful contents. It was a record of the Mayans' life, showing scenes of farmers sowing seed, of the Tikal market, and of people wearing fancy headdresses, and ceremonial costumes. Dozens of colourful scenes were crammed into the pages.

Spread throughout were hieroglyphs and symbols they couldn't understand.

In silence, Sara pointed to the last of the several hundred illustrations.

It took up the whole of the final section, and showed Kormanjiali temple with a huge crowd outside. A white mist partly obscured the detail of the people, but the figures were transparent.

They could see the temple through them.

"That's what we saw!" exclaimed Dan.

"This is the proof we need to show mum and Bruce!" Sara said.

Dan thought for a moment and said. "I don't know, Sara. Something tells me we'll need more than this. They'll probably say we borrowed it from the library".

"No way Dan. It's obviously very old".

"Well, maybe you're right", said Dan. "But we need to think what we do with it. They've trusted us to bring it back, so we'll have to be very careful. I know! Why don't we give Nigel a phone? He did tell us to get in touch, and that we'd know when the time was right."

"That's a good idea. When?"

"Well, let's work out how long we've been away first, and show our faces upstairs. Don't say anything for now though. We'll leave the codex here".

He carefully placed it behind a cardboard box, and they went upstairs.

Hugh was reading the paper in the lounge. "Hello!" he said cheerfully. "Lots of whooshing noises downstairs. I suppose you've been boiling that old kettle, have you?"

Taken aback, Dan stammered, "Eh, yes. Yes, dad. We fancied a cup of tea, but there are no teabags down there, so we've come up for some".

Hugh looked curiously at them from behind his paper. The TV was on in the background: "Everything OK? You seem a bit jumpy".

"No - I mean yes. Yes, everything's fine. We're just in the middle of listing the models downstairs, and I guess my mind's still on that. You and mum haven't been in the cellar this week have you?"

He asked, thinking about the rearranged models.

"No. Why?"

"Oh, nothing. I just wondered, that's all."

Hugh frowned, looked at his watch and said: "Ah – that time already. Mum and Tim'll be home soon, I expect, so I'd better get back to my chores!"

He folded his paper, the Mistlees Post, and Dan saw the headline:

"FAT COW MYSTERY!"

Hugh shook his head in amusement: "It's incredible what counts as news here. The local farmer has a problem with cows overfeeding. Some are so bloated they can hardly walk. They don't understand what's causing it, so the local vet's been called in to investigate."

"How odd!" said Sara.

Hugh went through to the kitchen and handed them a pile of teabags from the jar. He crossed to the dishes in the sink. Dan and Sara went back to the hall, and he motioned her into the lounge. She said, "Phew! That was a close shave! Thank goodness he thought we were boiling the kettle."

"I know. And he was obviously amused by the fat cows – how bizarre. Tell you what, though – it proves we've not been away long, otherwise he'd have said something. Why don't we phone Nigel now while Dad's busy?"

He went to his room and picked up Nigel's card from his computer desk. He rushed to rejoin Sara who kept watch while he dialled 393939. The phone rang for the briefest of moments, and Dan heard Nigel say, "I'm glad you've called. I'll be right over".

Before an astonished Dan could react, the line went dead.

"What's happened?" asked Sara. "That was quick. You never said a word".

"I didn't need to. He knew it was me, and he's coming here now".

Somehow, Hugh missed hearing the doorbell, and they smuggled Nigel down to the cellar.

"How did you know it was me on the phone, Nigel?"

"I knew it was time", he answered in his velvety tones, "and I think you have something to show me, haven't you?"

His mouth crinkled into a huge smile that quite relaxed the nervous pair, and Sara picked up the codex. She silently handed it to him.

His eyes lit up. He opened it and his fingers lovingly followed the beautiful pictures. At one point he started to say something, but stopped suddenly as if giving away a confidence. He stayed quiet till he'd looked right through the contents of the codex. "This is priceless – a very rare find. Do you realise how important it is?"

Dan and Sara exchanged a quick glance, and Sara said: "Well, we know it must be precious. We were told it contained the secrets of the Mayans. Is that what you mean?"

Nigel fingered the pages. "*This* is what we sought, but could not find. It holds secrets lost to mankind for centuries. It is indeed very special."

He hesitated, as if holding something back, and his tone became lighter. "It's splendid, isn't it? You know, the Spanish destroyed many of the Mayans' codices, and most of the rest have simply disintegrated. You've done very well to bring this back, and we must be very careful, *very* careful indeed with it".

He stared into the middle distance for a moment, and added, "When you are full of doubt, hundreds of books are sometimes not enough. When you are sure, often one word is too much".

Dan looked confused and said, "Nigel, when you say you sought this, but couldn't find it, what do you mean?"

As Nigel looked steadily back at them both, he suddenly forgot his question, Sara looked confused, and Dan stammered instead: "We called because we don't know what to do. We were told it was our mission to bring the codex back. But you seem to know where we've been, and it's like - like you already know about the codex".

"That is true, Dan. Peter will be delighted."

"But how can he be delighted? Where is he? I thought he was gone!"

Nigel again looked intently at them, and Dan couldn't remember what he'd just said.

Nigel continued: "For now, this must be our little secret. I'll take it to a friend of mine and think about what we should do next. I'm sure we'll be seeing a bit of each other over the next while".

Without further ado, he picked up the codex, and walked purposefully upstairs with Dan and Sara trailing in his wake. Hugh was whistling over the dishes in the kitchen, so Nigel's visit went unnoticed.

Sara heaved a sigh of relief, and Dan smiled and raised his eyebrows heavenwards: "Yes, phew is right! How incredible. He seemed to know all about it!"

"And he didn't even ask about where we were, or what happened!"

"Like he knew anyway!"

"But how?" asked Sara.

"I've no idea, but thank goodness he's doing something.

I guess we'll just have to wait till we see him again before we say anything."

Before long, Tim and Liz were back from swimming, and Sara went home for lunch. The rest of the weekend passed uneventfully, but Dan thought a lot about what he'd learned and decided, after school on Monday, to put his newfound knowledge to the test.

Chapter 17

Earlier than usual, Dan and Tim left for school and Sara joined them. Tim's incessant chatter kept them amused. He told them his class were finding out about Julius Cheeser.

Dan said: "Do you mean Julius Caesar?"

"That's right. The man who bossed all of Rome. He was killed by a brute, you know".

Dan kept a straight face. "His name was Brutus".

None of this stopped him from continuing. "They all came together in a big meeting, and Brutus stabbed him. It's like a murder mystery, isn't it?"

They reached school, Tim running to join his mates.

In class, Miss Ambrose carried on her lesson about old books. She clapped her hands: "Right! Who can remember one of the oldest types of writing materials?"

"Papyrus!" replied Mark in his deep flat voice.

Astonished, the class all looked at him. Mark never volunteered replies in class.

"Very good, Mark. And who used papyrus?"

"The Egyptians and the Mayans were two of the main civilisations, Miss, but they perish quite quickly if they're not preserved properly."

As he finished, he glared directly at Dan, who flinched at the intensity of his stare.

Miss Ambrose continued: "Yes, that's true. There are very few examples of complete works that have survived the ages, which makes them very valuable. Several codices are thought to contain secret codes, placed there by the ancient scribes, able only to be deciphered by those with special knowledge."

Sara sat on the edge of her seat, and Miss Ambrose said to her: "Ah, Sara, is this a topic you're interested in?"

She flushed: "Eh, yes, Miss, it's very interesting."

"Excellent! Well, with Mark *and* you paying attention, there must be something for us all to treasure!"

Monday was football practice, and Dan was determined to improve his game by being more positive about the way he tackled and passed the ball. After school, the Primary 6 and 7 classes went to the sports ground at the back of Elfsite Reach. Dan had played football since joining the school, but wasn't very good. He hung back a lot, and always got to the ball after everyone else.

Today would be different.

They played five a side, and held a mini-tournament with four teams. Dan was last to be picked, as usual, and he joined Iain, Shane, Struan and Hamish. The other four weren't expecting much help from him, and were disappointed he was in their team, but they all liked him, so put a good face on it.

They were astonished.

He made several saving tackles, passed the ball perfectly, and put two right foot strikes past Mark, in goal for the other team.

They took great heart from Dan's play, and the five went on to beat the other two teams as well. The talking point afterwards was his amazing improvement from being a poor player to the inspiration behind the best team.

Dan glowed with energy, and this lifted his teammates to a real high.

Mark was not happy at all, having let in several goals in his three matches. As they walked off the pitch, he towered over Dan.

With a start, he realised Mark had grown taller.

Though the highest scorer with five, Dan reacted modestly, and told the others he had decided to "go for broke", fed up with never helping his team.

Iain said he would definitely get into the school side. Dan was thrilled, and couldn't wait to tell his mum and dad. Hugh was puzzled at the transformation, but Dan grinned widely, winked and said: "You know what it's like, dad. You just need to do what you're always telling us – be positive".

Hugh laughed and Liz fussed around getting tea. Tim basked in the reflected glory of Dan's great football day.

The week passed slowly, and Dan and Sara walked through the village on Thursday, picking up a snack at The Deli. Brad Maipeson served them, his long black floppy hair tied back in a pigtail. He swept round the counter to greet them with an over-enthusiastic attempt at a high five, which Dan and Sara ducked. He seemed hardly to notice and rushed on in his loud grating accent: "So how are you guys all doing with the project work on Mistlees?"

Sara asked: "How do you know about that, Mr Maipeson?"

"Hey, the other kids are talking about it. It seems to be the in thing. Young Mark's in here all the time telling me about it."

"Really?" asked Dan, surprised.

"Oh, yeah, he's really keen, wandering round the village, taking notes on all sorts of things. So how's it for you?"

Dan and Sara exchanged a look, and Dan said: "Well, we're enjoying the project too. Mr Dewbury's been a great help."

"Really?" Mr Maipeson queried.

"Yes, but you sound surprised, "Sara replied.

"No, no, not at all," the American quickly answered, "Not at all.

He's been here a long time – must know loads about the history of the place." In an aside, he said to himself, "And the rest!"

"Pardon?" asked Dan.

Mr Maipeson flustered: "Nothing. Nothing. No, nothing at all. Crisps and orange juice – can I get you something else?"

"No thanks," answered Sara, keen to get away.

They left, feeling his gaze follow them. Dan said: "That was weird, hearing that Mark's been talking about the project."

Sara shivered: "Mr Maipeson's a creep. He's always asking nosey questions. I don't like him at all!"

In mock horror, Dan replied: "Really? I thought he was your best friend!"

She punched his arm: "You know what I mean. He's always on about stuff which is none of his business."

Dan munched his crisps: "Maybe, but their haggis is delicious."

"Yes, I know, it's their speciality."

"It's a bit odd, though about Mark. On Monday, he was the one talking about papyrus, wasn't he?"

"Yes, and Miss Ambrose gave *me* a right look too. It's like she knows something about our codex."

"No way, she can't possibly!"

"Well, how come she seems to home in on what's in our minds?"

"I don't know."

Dan was thinking, and Sara asked, "What's up?"

He grinned: "I'm probably wrong, but at football, I thought Mark was taller than last week!"

"Really! Are you sure?"

"Well, have a good look and see what *you* think."

"OK, I will."

They walked on and Dan continued: "Since we came here, I've been puzzled about the layout of the village".

"What's the puzzle?"

"There's something just too neat about it. Our house is right slap-bang in the middle of everything".

"What's wrong with that?"

"There's nothing *wrong* with it, but I'm wondering why. See how the old church and our house line up with the clock tower. And the graveyard's in a straight line through our house to the proper church"

"Yes, I see what you mean. I wonder why too!"

Dan sensed a whoosh of air swirl round him, and felt his sleeve twitch.

"Hey!" he yelled, "What was that?"

"What was what?" said Sara, picking a leaf from his arm.

Embarrassed, Dan said: "I felt something touch me."

"Of course you did, silly, but it's only a leaf!"

Just at that, Mr Dewbury appeared, dressed in brown check trousers and an old anorak. He gave them an irritated look, which passed quickly, and said.

"Finished the project yet?"

"No, not yet, Mr Dewbury. We're still researching. We've been curious about the position of Dan's house".

"Ah! Yes. Yes. A powerful spot."

Dan asked, "Why's it powerful, Mr Dewbury?"

The minister looked distractedly around, and switched to a tone like a tour guide, reciting a familiar story. "They used to carry the dead from one end of the village to the other.

From the church to the graveyard. Had to be space between them, you know, in case of disease spreading".

"When did they do that?" asked Dan.

"A long time ago, Daniel."

"Why's it a powerful site?" Dan persisted.

"Obvious really", Mr Dewbury mused. Sunk deep in thought, he meandered off towards the church.

"How frustrating!" exclaimed Sara, "Just when I thought he was going to tell us something interesting".

"He's like that, isn't he? But he did say the house is in a powerful place, even if he didn't say what gives it power."

On the way home, Sara said: "What on earth does then, I wonder?"

Chapter 18

The week finished with Hugh getting home early. He asked Dan to join him in the lounge.

"Well, Dan – didn't see much of you yesterday. Did you work on the project?"

"Yes, we did," replied Dan cautiously, wondering if he was in trouble: "I went out with Sara, and we bumped into old Mr Dewbury. We asked him more about the village. You know how we're bang in the middle of it? Well, we wondered why, and he seemed to know but didn't tell us."

"He seems a bit of a strange character. I'm sure if you catch him again, he'll tell you what he thinks. You're right about the position of this place though – it's right in the middle of Mistlees. Probably means we're the most important people here!"

Relaxing at his dad's light tone, Dan said: "Yeah, right dad! Anyway, the project's fine, but we've still got loads to do on it".

"When's it to be handed in?"

"Sometime in October, I think".

"So you've still got a good few weeks to go then."

"I suppose so, but I really want to do a good job on it, and so does Sara."

"You seem to be getting on well with her".

"Yes, I am. She's a good friend".

"Well, I've got a little something that may help", said Hugh, with a grin.

He put his hand in his jacket pocket, and brought out a small flat rectangular object, a bit bigger than a credit card. It was black and colourfully striped. "Remember I said we've been working on new types of communication? This is a test version of our new model. It's a Rainbow Catcher."

"Rainbow Catcher! Why? What does it do?" Asked Dan, desperate to get his hands on it.

Hugh laughed softly. "We called it Rainbow Catcher, meaning something very elusive. You can't catch a rainbow because it keeps moving away from you, and dissolves into thin air. We wanted to produce something tiny which could do all you want from one piece of kit – something that seems so impossible, you could never do it. Well – we have, and this is it!"

He handed it to Dan. The Rainbow Catcher fitted snugly in his hand. It was warm after being in Hugh's pocket. The upper face was like a mobile phone with the usual keypad buttons, but there were another six buttons above a small split-screen, and a further two buttons on either side.

The underside of the device had four screens quartering it, each with four keypad controls underneath.

"What on earth does it do, dad? Asked Dan, excited.

"It's a mobile phone, television, radio, and PC all wrapped into one. It has a scanner, built in camera with video, torch, and infrared viewer too. The refractive optics we've designed have miniaturised its telescope too!"

Dan's jaw dropped. "No way!"

"Oh, and it's a very sophisticated music player too. We've updated the technology so you can do the usual stuff like loading your CD's and internet downloads, but this has a seeking device. You can tune in to Radio and TV channels, programme for the type of music you want, and it'll pick them up and playback for you on or off screen."

Hugh was triumphant as he smiled. "Yes, we've done what everyone's been trying to do, and we're years ahead of the competition, but we must test it thoroughly, so we've produced a dozen of these to try out. This is yours for a month!"

"Oh dad, that's fantastic. How does it work?"

Hugh showed him. One of the two front screens was the same as a normal mobile phone, the other the sight for the camera, telescope, scanner and infrared viewer. The mobile phone screen doubled as a miniature PC screen, and Dan said: "Dad, there's no way you can see that screen – it's way too small".

"I know, but look at this".

He clicked one of the buttons to the side of the screen and pointed the Rainbow Catcher at the wall. A beam of light shot out and the PC screen lit up on the wall.

"That's brilliant – it's so clear".

"The screens on the other side do the same kind of job – there's one for the camera, one for the telescope and one for the infra-red viewer. The fourth's your TV screen. It means you don't need to screw up your eyes to see anything, and you can use it on a flat surface too, by using the hinge".

Hugh put it on the table, pushed another button, and the device split almost in two, the back of the Rainbow Catcher tilting upright to keep the PC screen beaming on the wall.

"It's really important you keep this to yourself, Dan. I don't even want Tim to play with it yet. Use it yourself, and share it with Sara, but that's all for now till we're more confident about how it works."

"Dad, I don't know what to say. This is just incredible! I'll have great fun with it!"

They spent some time running through the controls till Hugh was sure Dan could work everything, and he went to his room to try it. It took a while getting the hang of the TV and PC controls, as they were so small, but the images were clear on his wall – the beaming device was brilliant. It could magnify to focus on small detail, and he could change the colours to soften or sharpen them.

The camera was easy to use, sighting through the front of the Rainbow Catcher, and the photos he took of the room were crystal clear. It could take photos from the TV screen too, and record programmes to play back later.

The telescope was a bit awkward to start with till he realised the best position for sighting was with the Catcher set slightly away from his eye - the magnified view then showed up well on the front screen.

Liz had to drag him through for tea. While Tim was carefully inspecting his pizza to make sure no one had tried to poison him with hidden carrots, Dan whispered excitedly to Hugh, "It's just amazing. Still to try the phone, the music player and the infrared, but it all works great."

"What's that?" said Tim, ears like wings.

"Just checking what's on this weekend," replied Dan quickly.

"What?" Tim asked.

Liz interrupted. "I'm taking you swimming in the morning, and we thought we'd go for a run in the car on Sunday".

The boys groaned, but Dan was excited about Saturday. He would show Sara his new toy, and have peace from Tim. He stayed up late, loaded some of his CD's, used the torch, and phoned Sara to check when to meet in the morning. He turned off the light and opened the curtains. It was getting dark, but he could still see reasonably well. He clicked on the infrared viewer, and everything was fuzzy on the screen, but as he waited and watched, the picture sharpened with darkness. Everything looked greeny grey, but the trees and shrubs gradually came into focus, and he saw the neighbour's cat stalk across the grass in the dark.

"Yes!!" He exclaimed.

Getting to sleep was difficult. He couldn't stop thinking about the Rainbow Catcher, and was itching to show Sara his new device.

Chapter 19

A rainy morning greeted them on Saturday.

Liz said: "Very wet, this Perthshire rain. It's the kind of day you just want to curl up in bed with a good book."

Dan looked out, and saw the drizzle slanting across the garden. The wind tugged furiously at the bushes and trees, whose colours were already starting to change shade from green to autumnal brown. Hugh was reading his paper when Sara arrived, and Dan opened the door. She didn't look happy.

"Hey! What's up? You look miserable".

This made her look even more miserable. "I've got to go back in an hour – for the shopping"

"I thought you liked shopping?"

"I do, or I did, but not on a Saturday morning when we've got stuff to do!"

Dan pulled her in conspiratorially, and pointed to the cellar: "Wait till you see what I got from Dad!"

An hour later, Sara was her usual cheerful self, having shared the fun of the Rainbow Catcher: "This is just so cool. You feel it could make the tea too! Anyway, I'd better go", she said, climbing the stairs. "Can I come back after lunch? We said we'd do a bit of tidying in the cellar". She winked at Dan so that Hugh, in earshot, didn't see.

"Yup. Come across when you're ready. I'll be here".

As she ran across the road, Hugh asked, "What did she think of it?"

"She was blown away! I think she wanted to take it with her!

She asked how you power it up, dad, because you can't see any connections for a charger or anything."

Hugh knowingly tapped his forehead with his forefinger: "Ah-ha. Forgot to tell you. It's wire-less. Doesn't need charged up. It works by taking energy from any available light source. In daylight, it'll power up from the sun, or inside just by being in the light, but quicker next to an electric light."

"That's why I haven't needed to recharge it, because I've used it lots since yesterday. The cellar lights kept its energy going".

"Yes – all that lighting would keep it at full power. Look, there's a small gauge you can key up".

As he pressed a button, a little battery indicator showed three full segments.

When Liz and Tim arrived, Dan tucked the Rainbow Catcher in his jeans' pocket. Tim came in like a whirlwind: "Dad, dad, I swam with no wings! The whole way across the pool. Faster than anyone!"

He flung himself at Hugh who staggered back with the force of his charge. He pretended to trip, and rolled on his back, cuddling Tim tightly so he didn't get hurt.

"Fantastic, Tim. Well done. I'm so proud of you. You'll soon be swimming with the dolphins."

"Will I dad? Will I really?" His face was bright with excitement as Liz pulled him up: "Dad's only teasing, darling. But maybe you will when you're older. You did very well this morning. You'll soon be swimming all the time without wings. Well done!"

She ruffled his tousled hair as he rushed off to his bedroom to find his "All the Fish of the Sea" book to look at dolphin pictures.

After lunch, Sara reappeared.

"I suppose you're off to the cellar again?" Asked Hugh.

"Yes dad. We're going to play for a while".

"OK. See you later. Try to include Tim, will you?"

But Tim still had his nose in his book, so they sneaked off quietly.

"What should we do this time, Sara? Do you reckon the rug will work again for us?"

"I don't see why not. We've got that dream of yours to check out, haven't we?" She was right. He was sure his dream about the warrior with the silver hand and the mysterious chess players would come true.

"Sara, when I have my dreams, we live them out. I hope today will be the same, and if it is, I'm wondering something else."

"What, Dan? What are you on about?"

"Well, I've been thinking really positively most of the time since we left Vohumanah, and my football last week was great. Do you think I could plan my dreams by thinking positively so we can go to times and places we'd love to see?"

"What a blast that would be!" She chuckled. "How about the French Revolution – or the sinking of the Titanic?"

"Ho ho ho. Very funny."

They opened up the cellar to the smell of fresh paint, and looked at each other puzzled.

"It must be something to do with the kitchen fan," said Dan, "Though how that happens I've no idea".

"But you haven't been doing any painting, have you?"

"No. No, we haven't. How come we can smell paint?"

Sara clutched Dan's arm: "You've moved them! What a good idea!"

The models sat in their straight lines, but now there were some gaps. In one corner, all the dinosaurs stood together, and in another sat the pyramids and buildings from their Mayan adventure, with the red and black snake, which had startled Sara, coiled in front.

Dan just stared: "I didn't touch them!"

"You must have!" laughed Sara.

"I didn't! Honestly!"

"Well, there must be a ghost at work!"

As she said this, she felt her hair rise, and a shiver ran down her spine.

The rug, under the table again, rippled and the orange ring glared and pulsed, appearing to suck all the colour from the other circles. As they walked towards it, it began to pull them in like a gravity field. They moved the table aside, and the rug responded with a twitch, the orange ring now dominating the other colours.

They stepped on to it, and felt the intense thrill of whipping through time, their ears buffeted by the shock.

Chapter 20

Ears still tingling, they landed beside a giant oak tree at the edge of a forest of ancient trees, amongst them yew, rowan, ash and willow. They felt gentle cool drizzle on their faces.

The wet paint smell was replaced with the softer aromas of wet grass and soaked vegetation.

They wore drab gray woollen cloaks and sandals, Sara sporting a brown ribbon tied round her forehead. Under their cloaks were long plain linen tunics. Dan felt the weight of an iron brooch on his shoulder fastening his cloak. It was a shape he recognised from the table.

The meadow in front was an incredibly bright green, and it sloped gently down from the forest to a large raised oval section of land. A low hill rose in the middle, and criss-crossing the lower slopes were long banks on which stood groups of tall red-haired men and women. They all wore cloaks similar to the children's though some were woven with designs of swirling spirals.

The sight of the figure towering above the crowd transfixed them. Standing at the top of the hill, his silhouette was amazing. His clothing was emerald green, his face lit up like lightning, his eyes shone with fire, and his arms and feet were burnished bronze in colour. He carried a shield of leather, and from his cloak protruded a long sharp bladed sword with an ornate handle. At his side rested a bronze spear with a golden point.

The most striking feature of this awesome giant was his right hand, which was made of silver.

"He's the man from your dream, isn't he? Asked Sara.

Dan nodded, "Yup. We're definitely in dreamland again!"

It was clear the warrior was about to address the crowd, but when he saw Dan and Sara, he motioned to a woman in the crowd to bring them forward.

"Oh no!" exclaimed Sara. "What's all this?"

"It looks like we're being taken to the front."

The woman strode between them, gently pulling them by the arm. She smiled reassuringly and spoke words in a gentle lilting voice. They didn't understand her, but she repeated herself, and their senses recorded the meaning.

"Don't worry. Nuada knows you are here. He's going to meet the Firbolgs and is ready to speak".

She led them to a small group of people distinguished by their proud bearing and brightly coloured cloaks of red and green.

Sara tugged urgently at Dan's sleeve. "Look, Dan, look – it's Miss Ambrose!"

"What?" said Dan. "What d'you mean?"

"Look at her face – it's her!"

Dan turned to look more closely, and his jaw dropped. Their guide was exactly like their teacher, but younger, with softer features. Her red hair was longer too, reaching down to her waist. She showed no sign of recognising them, but it was Miss Ambrose's double!

While this sank in, Nuada of the silver hand began to speak. His voice was utterly compelling, his words strong and proud, and his tone deep and resonant: "My people of Dana, you know our sovereignty and our right to this land. From Falias, from Gorias, from Finias and from Murias, our ancestors came. With music and magic, with knowledge and craft, with wisdom and skill, sowing and reaping, they made this land our heritage.

We are one with it, and it is one with us. We feel its very birth, we sense its every move, and we grow with its seasons and wither with its storms. We worship the sun as it nourishes us, and we welcome each new birth as it strengthens our everlasting soul. We live in peace, but we wait for war."

The crowd roared their support, faces radiant with the power of his words.

"These invaders, these sailors from the sea, these exiles from the lands whose very rulers we have taught, have come too far. They must be stopped, by words or weapons. The Firbolgs are strong, their weapons heavy, but their wisdom light.

I will meet with them after one day's march, and we will talk. Their listening will be short. Sreng knows not peace. When I return, be ready for war!"

Nuada finished, lifted his spear with his silver hand, and with unbelievable power threw it, straight as a die, at the forest. It thrummed in flight, and pierced the air as fast as the eye could follow. It struck a huge oak tree at head height, and the impact reverberated back to the crowd. The tree shook. The crowd roared and roared again, on fire with the mood and magic of the moment.

Nuada strode down the hill, crossed the meadow with long purposeful strides, pulled the spear from the tree in one quick motion, and disappeared through the forest.

There was an unnatural silence for a second before everyone burst into speech, voices raised and excited.

Dan struggled for words. "That – that – was incredible. Did you hear that? He's going to try to head off the enemy on his own! And did you see that spear throw? It's over 200 metres to the trees! I can't believe he did that!"

Sara was still tingling from Nuada's words. "I think I'm ready to fight myself!"

"Hoi, come on, don't be silly. This is serious stuff".

"I know, I know, but what a leader, what an inspiration".

The crowd started to disperse slowly, and they realised their guide was watching them expectantly.

"You will be safe with me", she said softly. "Come".

Dan felt like saying something to her, as if she really was their teacher, but bit his tongue, feeling foolish. She carefully picked her way through the crowd, which parted respectfully for her. They attracted more than a few curious, though friendly, looks. Dan didn't know which language everyone spoke, but understood the words and meaning of the buzz created by Nuada's speech.

"*When will we know?*"

"The children will go to the water".

"*Goban will have his busiest days*".

"Have we enough spears?"

"*Aye, Credne and Luchta will not sleep tonight!*"

Through the melee, the woman steered them till they had manoeuvred all the way round the hill, to open countryside sloping gently down to a lake. They followed a well-worn track.

Sara caught up with the woman and, catching her arm, asked, "Where are we and where are you taking us?"

She gently shrugged Sara off, and carried on at the swift pace she had set.

Sara's jaw set. She wasn't going any further till she knew what was going on.

"Stop now!" She shouted, doing so herself. Dan nearly ran into her and pulled up. The woman took a few more steps, and, realising they were no longer following, turned back.

Sara said, "Look, you know we're new here. We haven't a clue about where we are, who you are or what was going on back there. You must tell us, talk to us."

The woman's face, set in irritation, softened. She sighed. "Yes. Of course - I should". She collected her thoughts, and introduced herself. "I am Sorbema, Nuada's wife. You are in Ireland, at a place we call Tara".

Dan spoke. "Tara?"

"It is the heart and spiritual centre of our people, a wonderful and mystical place."

Sara chipped in, "Is Nuada your leader?"

"He has led us for a short while, since Ecne's time. He is a great warrior."

Dan and Sara were full of questions, but Sorbema held up her hand. "Stop now. I will tell you more, but we have much to do, and we have to get back to the village".

Dan challenged, "Do you know our names? Do you know what we're doing here?"

Sorbema simply said, "Yes. Come".

She led off again, the children trailing in her wake.

"She's something else, isn't she?" said Dan.

"And she speaks the same way as Miss Ambrose, as well as having her look. Where's she taking us? What's going on? What do *you* think?"

Dan felt surprisingly confident, and sensed Sara's nervousness. He took her hand, and as they walked on, looked across at her to get her full attention, grinning in his captivating way. He asked, "What am I doing?"

"I know, I know. You're making me feel the same as you. You're giving me your energy!"

They both felt the adrenalin rush of the moment, and began to appreciate more of their surroundings. The path was wide enough for two or three to walk abreast, and was well worn. All around was green, different shades and hues of grass and meadow, with a treasure store of shrubs and plants giving bright splashes of colour.

Dan said, "I wish I knew more about flowers and plants. What are they all called?"

The air softened and shimmered ahead of them, and from this haze came a familiar trill. "These are foxgloves, there bell heather and there orris root. Sundew by the track and yellow fleabane in that patch!"

"Zuphlas!!" they both exclaimed.

"Why, of course it's me. Who else would it be?"

"It's brilliant to see you again", said Dan. "Does that mean we're safe here?"

Zuphlas floated along with them, as they kept close behind Sorbema who didn't seem to notice the winged visitor.

"Safe? Safe? What is safe?" He appeared to be asking himself the question. "Yes, safe, but beware the rebels."

"Who are the rebels?" Dan asked.

"Those who would pull you from the path. And there." He pointed. "Orchids!"

The fragile bright orange flowers peeped out from behind a bank of bell heather.

Dan and Sara felt their spirits rise as Zuphlas stayed with them for a few more minutes, telling them more about their Irish surroundings.

"What about animals, and what about snakes?" asked Dan. "Remember that one you saved us from?"

"There are no snakes in this fair land," Zuphlas announced, and a moment later he dissolved into the air as Sorbema stopped ahead of them.

"We are nearly there", she said, pointing.

Ahead lay the village, spread along the bank of the lake. The houses were a curious mixture of shapes, sizes and materials. There was no logical layout, with small brick built dwellings jostling next to structures built with dried and hardened mud. There were tree houses, wooden houses, and stone houses. There were new houses, old houses, ancient houses and ruined houses.

And everywhere, people.

The village was an incredible hive of activity. Cooking over fires, talking in doorways, grooming horses, mending roofs, and walking the narrow twisted lanes.

And preparing for war.

Blacksmiths hammered anvils, carpenters fashioned staves, sword smiths sharpened blades, and women polished shields.

The acrid smell of burnt metal mingled with appetising aromas of roasting meat.

Dan and Sara soaked in the scene, their eyes alive with its vibrancy.

Sorbema took them up a twisting alley of wooden buildings, which tilted towards each other across the passageway.

She stopped at an impressively ornate iron gateway, promptly opened by a young boy who bowed. He stared curiously at the children but did not return Dan's greeting.

The house at the end of the driveway was unlike any they had seen.

Four storeys tall, it formed a long curve from a centre point that housed a wide wooden door carved with symbols of primitive boats. The windows were bay shaped and all tightly shuttered, and the roof a flat structure of huge slate tiles. Extraordinarily, the thick stone walls were iron clad.

Without comment, Sorbema approached the door, which was raised like a castle portcullis, straight upward.

"This is a real fortress!" said Dan.

Beyond the door was a large open central area, paved and overlooked from all four sides by the inner building, clearly designed as a defensive structure with long narrow windows protected by metal shutters. One side of the quadrangle housed stabling, and a multitude of boys and girls groomed dozens of tall black horses. Armour plating for them was being beaten, polished and laid out by a small team of blacksmiths. Smoke and sparks drifted across the courtyard carrying the smell of molten metal. The horses whinnied their disapproval.

The rest of the open area was filled with men wrestling, sword fighting, exercising and talking animatedly.

This was a courtyard going to war.

Sorbema wove her way through the busy scene. All around, people bowed as she moved purposefully toward a studded wooden door. A tall guard, with raised spear opened it and they passed through to a cool stone corridor. The passageway to left and right had doors evenly spaced along its length.

She turned left and opened the second door to the delicious aroma of home baking. The room was a large kitchen. An open fire burned, and a long trestle table and chairs filled much of the space.

Dan and Sara were tired and hungry from the brisk walk, and she motioned them to sit at the table.

A maid brought water and a platter of still warm oatcakes, which they gratefully devoured, Sorbema busying away at the cooking grill over the fire.

When they'd finished, Dan, feeling drowsy but full of questions, asked, "So tell us, Sorbema, what's happening?"

She sat down beside them, took a deep breath, and started to talk. "Our tribe are the Danaans. We have lived here for many years. We are of timeless ancestry."

Dan and Sara shivered as they felt and saw the now familiar sensation of images conjured up by her words. They saw rolling clouds sweep over the countryside, and from them stepped a race of warriors that swept like a tidal wave over the earth, defeating all in their path. They moved with amazing grace and power. Camp followers built towns and villages, farms and fortresses, houses and homes.

"We have made this land our own."

"How long ago was this?" Asked Dan, "I mean, when – what time period – which century are we in?"

"Time has no force, no measure of import for us. We are, now and always, when you would like us to be! We lead and others follow".

"What do you mean?"

"You join those who come to learn. Our lessons are eternal. Our people are here and everywhere, our influence felt through time and forever, but our memory dissolves with the spread of our word".

Sara, listening intently, was frowning. "I don't know what you mean. What are you teaching? Who are you teaching? Where do they come from?"

Sorbema held her hand up and for the first time, smiled. Her whole face lit up, her eyes sparkled, and they saw, with a jolt, a hazy shimmer of light surround her whole body, her face framed by a rainbow of colour.

"You can now see what was always there. If you focus your energies, and nurture your strength, you will feel the flow".

She stopped abruptly, and the aura surrounding her faded.

"We will talk more tomorrow. Nuada will be gone for two days, and we must be ready for his return. We will not then have time to talk."

She showed the children to a small room at the end of the corridor. It was like a dormitory with low beds lined along the far wall under small port-holed windows.

Sorbema left them to choose their beds and sleep.

As Dan sat down, he heard a wheezing sound, like a whoopee cushion, underneath him. He leapt up, startled: "What was that?"

Sara laughed, and said: "I don't know, but I've never seen you move so fast!"

"I got a real fright. I sat on something!"

"But there's nothing there, Dan. Look! Don't be silly."

Distracted, he examined the bed, but found nothing. As he settled gently back down, Sara asked: "What d'you make of this place, Dan? Is it like your dream?"

"Part of it is. I remember Nuada and his speech - and the hill, which Sorbema called Tara, was in it too. I don't remember her, though, and there was other stuff, like someone playing a harp, and a funny kind of game of chess."

Sara thought for a moment, and said, "This place is kind of weird. It's like it doesn't fit in to time properly. Did you notice the houses? They were all sorts of different shapes and sizes, and some of them were absolutely ancient, but others brand new".

"And the way Sorbema spoke - like she didn't want to be pinned down. Did you see the haze all round her?"

"That was a bit spooky. But she said it was there all along. How can that be right?"

"Don't know", said Dan, "But I do know I'm going to sleep now. I'm knackered!

Maybe it'll all be a bit clearer in the morning".

"Yeah, maybe! Sorbema said we'd talk some more tomorrow. I wonder if Nuada will stop a war."

"If he doesn't, will we see them fight?"

"I don't know, but if they do, I hope we're not involved!"

Dan replied earnestly: "And so do I!"

Chapter 21

Sounds of bustling activity woke them up. Voices in the corridor drifted past them, one way and then the other. Sharp hammering noises from the courtyard competed with heavy thumps from above. The air smelt of wood smoke, a lovely tangy aroma that curled round the room.

It was still only half light outside, but already the world was ready to go.

There was a gentle knock on the door.

"Come in!" Sara said loudly,

Two young girls carrying pitchers of water entered, shyly avoiding eye contact. They left them on bedside tables and left quickly. Dan and Sara splashed their faces, gasping with the shock of the cold water.

"Oh no!" exclaimed Dan, "No hot water!"

"How do they keep clean, I wonder?" Said Sara. "It must be really hard when you can't just switch on a tap and get hot water".

"You're assuming they *do* keep clean. I'm not so sure about that. Didn't you smell the people in the streets?"

"Oh, that's not fair, Dan! Poor folk. As if they haven't enough to think about without worrying about hot showers and stuff".

"Well, we've got a lot to think about too. What happens next?"

"Well, Sorbema said Nuada would be away for two days, but it sounded like they'll be at war straight after that".

"So that might be tomorrow! The courtyard was full of hustle. They must expect war."

"I guess so. Weren't the black horses fantastic? So tall and proud – so strong, so----"

There was a loud knocking on the door, and Sorbema swept in, her red hair tied behind her neck in tight pigtails, showing off a magnificent coral necklace. She looked tired, but smiled in a bright pinched way. "How did you sleep?" She asked.

"Well, thanks", said Dan, "I hadn't realised how tired we were. We slept right through till the noise woke us".

"Ah yes – so much to prepare, and so little time! Would you like to see what we're doing?"

"That would be brilliant!" said Dan, his curiosity fully roused. He was still feeling really positive, and his enthusiasm swept Sara along as well, a half smile on her lips.

The day passed in a blur as Sorbema escorted them round the building, the courtyard and the village. The horses whinnied and snorted, excited by the bustle of activity around them. The stable boys and girls polished their shining coats, and the blacksmiths, sweating profusely from their labour, carefully tested the fit of the close-linked chain mail on each horse.

Sara reached up to pat one of the tallest animals, towering above her, and it stilled completely, bending its forelegs to let her stroke its proud mane.

Dan was impressed. "How did you do that?"

"It's like Fafa. Don't you feel that sense of connection, the power of its feelings? It makes me quiver!"

Dan tried for himself, and the horse reacted in the same way. The men around them drew back, and bowed deeply and reverently. Sorbema spoke to the men quietly, and they moved away, leaving the trio standing beside the horse. "This is Pan, Nuada's mount. He senses you are different, and the men respect your connection with him. This is rare, as Pan bows to no man except Nuada, and to no woman but me. You have the energy within you. Gaia has her flow."

The children were silent as they absorbed her words as mind thoughts.

Sara shivered and asked, "Who's Gaia"?

"I will tell you when we finish our walk", she said intriguingly.

As they started off again, the noise in the courtyard picked up with renewed vigour. There were teams of wrestlers exercising on the far side of the yard. A small elite of the strongest and tallest wore bright orange loincloths. Their movements were extraordinarily quick and graceful. They seemed to anticipate their opponents' every move, and counter them with lightning speed.

Each bout they fought ended rapidly and decisively.

The same was true of the sword fighters wearing orange loincloths. The speed of their movements was incredible. Fighting with wooden batons to avoid injury, they moved with a sensitive poise and grace. Never making the first move, their responses were thrilling and devastatingly effective.

One fighter attacked a tall orange clad warrior at great speed, swinging his baton in a fast murderous arc. The air seemed to breathe a fraction quicker around the still defender, they heard a "swoosh", and the attacker pitched forward on his face, his baton split in two and torn from his hand.

Dan was fascinated. "How fast was that? Fantastic!"

Immediately, the warrior turned around and swept his baton through the air as if fending off an invisible attacker. As the weapon stopped suddenly, they heard a loud gasp coming from thin air.

Sorbema didn't seem to notice and said, "The ones who wear

the tribal colours are Nuada's guard. The Vashad Thains are undefeated in many battles, always tasting the sweetness of victory. They are immortal and bring the chill of cold fear to our enemies. The Firbolgs have not yet seen them fight, but will live to regret the day they came to Tara!"

Dan asked, "Who are the Firbolgs, Sorbema? Nuada talked about them yesterday. And how come the orange guys are immortal? That's not possible surely?"

Sorbema held up her hand, smiling. "So many questions. So many things to know. So much to say! Hold, and we will talk tonight."

After their tour of the courtyard, Sorbema showed them the rest of the house, and they understood why they had been woken by all the early morning noise. Every room teemed with people preparing for the battle.

Women washed and dried tunics and orange loincloths; polished spears, swords, bows and arrows; cooked bread and cakes; dried and cured meat; and filled leather water bottles.

Boys and girls fetched and carried cleaning and cooking materials; sped off with prepared food; replenished water jugs; and assembled weapon packs.

Sorbema watched for a while with Dan and Sara, and they snatched a bite to eat in the huge kitchen, a welcome plate of fresh baked bread, with a bowl of thick vegetable soup eaten with wooden spoons.

After lunch, they toured the village, watching with amazement the furious pace at which the villagers prepared for war. The streets straggled round the houses and barns of the village, and every inch of space was full of people pushing hurriedly this way and that, carrying weapons, food, clothes and household goods – brushes, bales of cloth, baskets and sacks, all bursting with mysterious contents.

Beside the lake, which Sorbema called Lake Rury, was an open space where three men, stripped to the waist, worked at bewildering speed.

"These are our proud craftsmen", said Sorbema, "Men no other can match".

She pointed. "There is Credne the Gold and Silversmith, there Luchta the Carpenter, and Goban the Blacksmith".

Goban, an enormous giant of a man, worked in a haze of smoke from his red-hot fire. He wielded a hammer with a head as big as Dan's, yet it seemed no heavier than a paperweight. He hammered so quickly the air blurred around his arm, and the light reflected rainbows from his anvil each time he struck it. Three blows from his hammer made a sword.

Luchta, Goban's equal in stature, but darker skinned, worked beside him, with knives singing from the wood he carved. Tree branches were chopped, split, shaped and smoothed in seconds, and as each sword left Goban's anvil, he threw a handle and it wedged around the blade.

At the end of the line worked Credne, much smaller than his giant friends. A little wizened old man, his grey hair spun round his head and shoulders, entwining with his beard, which reached his waist. As each newly fashioned weapon whipped down the line, Credne pulled red-hot rivets with his tongs from the open fire before him, and banged them at speed into the sword, securing the join of blade to handle.

This production line fashioned dozens of swords as they

watched, and spears and arrows followed with the same amazing grace and speed.

"It's magical!" Said Dan, his deep blue eyes reflecting the glare from the two fires worked by the craftsmen.

Further along the shore of the lake, past a line of rickety wooden buildings, tipping drunkenly towards the water, was a small rough square of land. In the centre of it, standing on wooden trestles around a cooking fire was a massive iron cauldron, being stirred by three women standing on a platform that encircled it. The enticing aroma of cooking meat washed over them.

Sorbema said, "This is the Cauldron of the Dagda. The women are preparing the food for the battle".

"Where's the battle going to be?" Asked Sara.

"Nuada will decide, but the Plain of Moytura is his chosen site."

"Where's that?" Dan asked.

"Beyond the Hill of Tara".

"So how do they get this huge cauldron up there? It's massive!"

"You will see".

Without another word, Sorbema led them back to the heart of the village.

The weak sun was low on the horizon as they saw dozens and dozens of children scampering past them, each carrying a bag or sack.

"Where are they off to?" Sara asked, frowning.

"They go to safety. During the battle, we must be sure our children are secure. At the far side of Lake Rury they will find shelter. When we have triumphed, they will return".

Dan said to Sara; "That's what I heard someone say as we left Tara – "the children will go to the water"."

"I remember that too", said Sara, "And we heard the names

of these sword makers too – Credne, Goban and Luchta. They were like a whirlwind. Whoosh, whoosh, whoosh, and out pops a spear. Did we really see that?"

"We sure did. No wonder Sorbema says no one can match them. I'm glad they're on our side!"

Sara was quiet for a second. "I hadn't thought about that. Will we have to fight? Or should we be with the other kids?"

Sorbema heard this brief exchange, smiled and said, "You have little cause to fear. You will watch the battle from afar."

"Well that's a relief", Sara sighed.

They walked back to the huge house as activity in the village died with the fading light.

"Nuada will return tomorrow, and then we fight", Sorbema told them.

"How are you so sure he won't talk the Firbolgs out of fighting? Dan asked.

"This is how it is foretold. The battle will decide our future. The Firbolgs sailed for one hundred days to reach our fair land, and they will not live in peace with us. They have conquered many people, lived in many lands, and always slay those they conquer. Nuada knows this, but he must try to change their path. He will not succeed, but will learn about their numbers and their weapons".

"So he's on a scouting trip!" said Dan.

Sorbema smiled. "You may call it that, but he would say it is a trip of honour he makes, a trip which could save the Firbolgs".

"How are you so sure you'll win?" asked Dan.

"The Vashad Thains will never lose in battle, no matter the odds, and Nuada is invincible with sword and spear. We will win, and win well."

Sara looked at Dan, as they reached the portcullis gate of the house. "That's confidence for you!"

"Sure is, but when you see the Vashad Thains, you can understand it. I wonder if the Firbolgs have soldiers to match."

Chapter 22

Towards the end of the day, over a bowl of meat stew, Sorbema spoke about the Danaans. "We live now in Tara but have lived in many different places, always moving, always learning, and always teaching".

Dan made to ask a question, but she held her hand up: "Let me tell our story, and you may judge if your questions are answered. We are a simple people, with timeless beliefs, which carry us through wars, in different lands and different times.

Our truths are unchanged and unchanging, and many come to learn from us. You asked me about Gaia. We are of Gaia. We are part of Gaia. We are Gaia."

As she spoke, clouds showing her thoughts swirled around her. They saw the four seasons - winter's snows chasing autumn's leaves, and summer's sun growing spring's budding plants. Rain filled rivers and lakes, animals stalked and fed in meadows and woods, birds flew and sang in hedges and from treetops, and fish swam and swarmed in oceans, all in a wonderful hazy swirl.

This kaleidoscope of images faded and in their place came the Danaans in a series of different settings; living in caves in sandstone cliffs by a desert; in tree houses above a swamp; in wooden huts on a snow-clad mountain; and finally in Tara.

Sorbema watched their reaction, smiling faintly: "We hold eternal truths, and share them with those who wish to grow. To the Danaans come the Pharaohs from Egypt, the leaders and scribes of the Mayans, Tibetan monks, the Romans and the Greeks. Many others too come to share our ways and their beliefs; and return with our knowledge and faith".

"What is your knowledge? What is your faith?" Asked Dan.

"We are all connected. We ebb and flow with Nature. We are energy. All that you do, all that you think affects you and all you connect with. In your time, people say you are an environorganism – indivisible from everything outside you in the material world".

"I don't think I understand", said Dan, "But I know what you mean about energy – we've been using our energy to help each other and be really positive about things".

"Yes. Everything has a field of energy. You can project your energy by focussing your attention on what you want to happen, to help it do so. Where attention goes, energy flows."

Sara said, "That's what we've been trying to do, and it seems to work."

"Continue with this and you will feel the benefit in your lives. Focus on the things you wish to happen, fill your whole being with these thoughts, and energy will flow through you to create the result you want. This is positive energy - for your personal growth. Your energy will seep away and drain you if you focus on negative things."

Sorbema saw they were tired and said: "We must sleep now. Tomorrow Nuada returns from meeting Sreng, the Firbolg's ambassador, and tomorrow we fight."

"Why do you fight? Surely fighting is negative energy?" Asked Sara. "It can't be right if you believe we're all part of the same energy. You'll be destroying part of yourselves if you fight".

"If you are ill, your body has defences to help you battle the illness and make you better. The principles of Gaia are the same. There are always those who will try to defeat the good, or poison the positive. In this land, we will defend, as we always do when there is an attack on Gaia. The Danaans are her defences which heal and repair."

Dan and Sara went back to their room, silent as they thought about what Sorbema had said. They sat for a moment before Dan sighed loudly, stretched, and said,"Well! What d'you make of that?"

"I understand a fair amount, but it's so much to take in that I'm a bit overwhelmed".

"Yeah, I feel the same. I wish I had a magic wand to make it all clearer."

Suddenly, they felt a rush of cold air. In seconds, the temperature dropped and the air clouded. They shivered violently, and Sara shrieked.

In front of them were two dark shapes, flickering and sparking as if not fully formed. Their bodies were swathed in grey cloths, tattered and torn, and where there should have been hands were grizzled stumps. These apparitions filled the air with menace, and their eyes glowed like coals in the thickened air. The stench was awful, and Sara covered her nose, disgusted.

Dan gripped her hand, and he shouted: "Who are you? Get out of here!"

The smaller of the two laughed, a hollow echoing rasping sound, grating on their ears. The other figure faded in and out of the light like an old film, and declared, in a croaky rattle: "*Do not meddle with the forces of old. This is not your place!*"

The smaller figure raised his arms, and said: "*Samahazai! Beware!*"

Both of the horrible apparitions doubled up as if struck, and hazily vanished into thin air. The temperature returned to normal, and the horrid smell vanished, leaving Dan and Sara to look at each other dumbstruck.

"Oh, Dan! What on earth were they?"

"I – I –don't know, but they were fearsome! Horrible things!"

The air rippled and in a soft haze before them were Metatron and Vohumanah.

"Thank goodness you're here!" exclaimed Sara, "We've just had a terrifying time! Two dreadful------"

Metatron held his hand up. "We know – we are aware. We sensed the rebel angels, felt their presence, but came too late and arrived when they were gone!"

Dan said: "But you scared them away, didn't you? It was as if someone punched them – they keeled over and vanished!"

"That was not us," said Vohumanah in his all-enveloping tone. "Your companion was strong in your defence."

"What companion?" asked Sara.

"You will soon see," Vohumanah replied mysteriously.

In his deep tones, Metatron continued: "We have followed and gone after you today, and seen with our own eyes the scenes, the places, the countries, and the things you too have viewed and seen as well"

Dan relieved the tension by cracking a forced smile, and said to Sara, "Why use two words when twenty will do!"

She laughed, relieved too that the terror of a few moments ago had gone, and Metatron's eyes screwed up slightly and twinkled back at them.

"Well, Metatron", Dan replied. "Before these two monsters arrived, we were talking about the day. What do *you* make of what Sorbema told us?"

Without moving an inch, Vohumana's presence suddenly became more obvious. It was as if Metatron had faded slightly to allow his taller angel friend to shine brighter. His voice surrounded them with its soft clarity: "The Danaans are a mythical race.

They live in all places at all times, and yet in no place or time. Their teachings are real, and their message is true. Their influence is a dawning day, waking a world ready to be filled with light and warmth."

"Hang on, Vohumanah!" Exclaimed Dan, "You're making it sound like they're immortal".

"And timeless", Vohumanah added, his words gently surrounding them.

"So they're like you and Metatron!" Said Sara.

"And like you", the angel finished as the two white visions faded into the air.

Sara said, "I can't get my head round this. The Danaans teaching the Egyptians. Timeless people, living here, there and everywhere – including us, it seems. It's not real, surely? And what about these – these – Metatron called them "rebel angels." Who were they and where did they come from?"

"And where did they go? I hope we've seen the last of them. Scary! What did he mean about our companion? What companion?"

"Oh, Dan, I don't know – so many questions. I was feeling OK until they came along. And tomorrow's the battle. What will that be like?"

"I'm sure it'll be fantastic - as long as we don't get too close to it!" Dan replied.

"Well, Sorbema *said* we'll be safe, so we should be."

They thought quietly about the incredible battle they were about to watch.

Chapter 23

After Nuada's return early the next morning, Sorbema stood with them outside the village watching the army go to battle.

The Vashad Thains led the way, with Nuada riding Pan at their head, their orange banner fluttering in the breeze. They moved as one, silent and purposeful, swords and shields glittering in the early morning sun. Behind them came the troop of black horses, lightly armour clad like their riders, spears resting along saddles. Dan sensed the horses' excitement, barely contained by gentle prompts and soft reassuring words.

Next marched the foot soldiers – hundreds of tall red haired men and women. Some carried swords, and all had bows and arrows. They had two quivers, cross-slung over their shoulders, each full of orange and black-feathered arrows.

Dan gasped as he saw the final regiment of this impressive army. He couldn't speak, and instead gripped Sara's arm and pointed. A hundred elks, like giant moose, loped elegantly along, five abreast, their hooves raising soft clouds of dust from the trail. Each elk's antlers formed a massive single sheet, up to four metres across, from which sprung a series of pointed horns. The spread of their antlers formed a solid wall across the track.

These magnificent animals were over three metres tall.

Astride them were warriors very different from the Danaans – small wiry men with curled dark hair, wizened features and bright piercing eyes. Their tiny bare-soled feet spurred the elks, but their arms were astonishing. Twice the length of their short legs, and thick with sinewy muscle, they curved and stretched around their mounts' antlers, guiding and steering them. Long strong fingers gripped and interlaced their horns. All carried a huge bow with a small clutch of long curved arrows.

"I wouldn't want to get in their way, that's for sure!" Said Dan. He asked Sorbema about them.

"They are the Coegloamers, men born to ride the elks, raised from childhood to run with them, fight with them, and trained to scatter all before them in war."

"They're truly amazing. What an army! How will the Firbolgs cope with them?"

"We will watch and see", said Sorbema.

Following the elks, pulled on wooden rollers by six strong men, came the Cauldron of Dagda, to feed the army. Sorbema and the children walked behind, past the field at Tara to a hill overlooking the battlefield – the plain of Moytura.

They looked in awe at the scene before them.

The Firbolgs were drawn up at the widest part of the plain. Their front line was almost two miles wide – thousands upon thousands of warriors, massed in line abreast, with leather shields, swords and spears at the ready. Dressed in fir skins, with gaudy painted faces and bodies, they presented a staggering sight.

Behind the front line, they were at least twenty men deep, a solid army of over fifty thousand.

Sara was pale as she watched the Danaans line up: "Dan, they're completely outnumbered. They'll have no chance against them. Just look at their force – and listen!"

They heard the Firbolgs chant their war cry: "Re! Re! Re! Re! Re! Re!"

Their throaty roar washed over them, and Dan shivered. He took in the rest of the scene. Behind the Firbolgs the ground was stony and deeply ridged, and to their left was a winding river, fast flowing and rock strewn. In a line stretching up their right was a row of part ruined towers, behind which sheltered a small group of archers.

Dan frowned, and nudged Sara. "Look! It can't be, but it's the Mistlees Clock Tower".

"What? So it is – but there's no clock!"

The tower stood proudly, tallest in the line, its stonework undamaged, its shape perfectly silhouetted in the sun, which broke through the grey clouds above the battlefield.

Sorbema said, "Nuada has a plan which will win the day. The Firbolgs are lined up to defend. They know we will attack, and in their strategy lies defeat".

"But you can't possibly beat them!" Said Dan, "They've got fifty times your number, and they've got a really strong position. Look - they've got the river over there to stop you outflanking them, and the towers are a pretty solid defence on the other side. You can't go around them, so you'll *have* to attack from the front, and there's far too many of them!"

Sorbema smiled faintly as Nuada walked Pan along the front of his army. He spoke fast and urgently to the Vashad Thains, and to the archers behind them.

"Re! Re! Re!" Roared the Firbolgs, spears now thumping the earth in a fast paced rhythm.

The Danaans were completely still and quiet in the calm before the storm.

Nuada raised his spear hand, and the Vashad Thains trotted line abreast towards the centre of the enemy line, followed by the horse troops.

As they drew closer, the front line of the Firbolgs knelt, shields up, with their spears angled to stop the advance. A hail of arrows was released from the ranks behind.

Suddenly, the Vashad Thains broke to the right, and as they did so, the black horses overtook them at the gallop, all heading directly for the troops gathered at the riverbank.

The main body of the Danaans behind, stopped, formed two lines, and as one, let loose a flight of arrows at the Firbolgs' centre.

Confused by the Vashad Thains' sudden switch of direction, the defending troops in the centre of the line tried to follow their charge, but were hemmed in by the huge press of their own men. Chaos reigned, and the first hail of arrows struck this tangled mess of men. Flight after flight followed at amazing speed from the Danaan archers.

The black horses charged full tilt towards the riverbank defenders. The whole of the Firbolgs' line started to dissolve as the men in the centre tried to push towards the Danaans, but there were simply too many warriors blocking the way, all trying to move to the river. Shouts of command from the Firbolgs' leaders went unanswered.

In the meantime, the Danaan archers continued their flow of arrows directed at the logjam of struggling Firbolgs. Hundreds of men had been hit and their bodies made the confusion in the centre of the defence even worse.

At a signal from the leader of the Danaan archers, they split quickly to left and right, now forming two columns instead of two lines. They began to fire their arrows at the ranks of men to left and right of the chaotic centre of the battlefield.

As they did so, Dan and Sara heard a blood curdling battle

cry, and through the centre of the Danaan archers swept the elks, now in one long sweeping line, galloping at full speed, forming a solid line of impenetrable horns. The Coegloamers shrieked their war cry, and let loose their terrible curved arrows. As they left their bows, they straightened and seemed to lengthen, glittering in the light of the sun. The first flight went high in the air, hovered above the ranks of the Firbolgs, and swooped down like angry wasps to strike the rear line of defence. Distracted by the cries of the men hit, those directly in front turned to see what attack they were under, and the thundering herd hit the centre of the enemy ranks, splitting them completely and causing the whole length of the front line to buckle and collapse in chaos. At the same time, the black horses, formed now into an attacking wedge, struck the Firbolgs' flank, sweeping men aside left and right, pressing the crush of defenders back towards the river.

The Vashad Thains followed this furious onslaught, Nuada leading. The children saw his magnificent tall figure, emerald green cloak flying behind him, spear poised to throw in his left hand, sword raised in his silver handed right.

He hurled his spear deep into enemy ranks, and it struck three men in its one travel. Magically, it flew back into his hand, and he threw again. The enemy around him were beginning to scream, and try to escape, but were pushed back by those at the riverbank trying to avoid being flung into the water. Nuada seemed to be in the air, above his horse, his legs bent under him, turning round and round amid a hail of sword blows aimed at him.

He thrust at lightning speed, time and time again, his silver hand glistening.

His sword arm moved so fast, it seemed like ten, each blow and thrust telescoping into the next, his speed incredible, and his force irresistible.

The Vashad Thains swiftly followed his crushing advance. Every move they made was perfect, coordinated and graceful, as they fought their way through the enemy ranks. Hundreds of men were pushed or jumped into the river as the unstoppable force of the horses and the Vashad Thains swept all before them.

They fought their way along the riverbank, crowded with thousands of Firbolgs, but just as Dan and Sara thought there was no way they could continue to advance, the sky above changed.

As the elks swept through to the rear of the enemy lines; as the horse troops and the Vashad Thains pushed deeper into the Firbolgs' flank; and as the Danaan archers reformed into two lines and charged; the sky began to boil.

At first the patterns of cloud seemed random, swift scudding shapes fleeting across the sun's rays, but sparks of lightning energised them, whipping like snakes, crackling faster and faster till the rolling thunder which crashed from the air around them forced the sparks of lightning into one huge electrical charge which exploded in the sky.

From beneath this heart stopping avalanche of sound and light swept the clouds.

A boiling mass of rolling black cloud filled the sky, and changed shape rapidly to become an enormous winged warrior, bushy beard and horned helmet clear as day. In each hand, this monster held an enormous sword thrusting straight at the Firbolgs' ranks.

The energy from this apparition burst over their heads, and sucked the life from the already battered troops. With one voice, the enemy wailed, dropped their weapons and ran. Many jumped into the river, more turned tail and hundreds were crushed in the retreat through the deep crests and troughs of the ground behind their battle lines. The archers behind the towers, who had been too far from the action to make an impression on the battle, escaped in terror.

The Danaans stopped their ferocious advance and watched them flee.

As they did so, the air cleared, the sky brightened, the mysterious rushing cloud no more than an illusion left fluttering in the minds of the children, stunned by what they had seen. Dan was speechless. He pointed at the largest clock tower.

It now had a clock face, its hands frozen at the time - 11 o'clock, exactly the same as the Mistlees tower.

Sara nodded, also dumbstruck. How had that happened?

Sorbema broke the spell. She quietly spoke: "I must look to the wounded. You will be safe here".

Off she went, and the children watched the scene. The Vashad Thains were unharmed, as were the elks and the Coegloamers. Some of the horses had been injured and their riders too, and a dozen or so of the Danaan archers lay still on the battlefield, struck by enemy arrows.

As Sorbema went to tend to the horses and riders, the children watched in amazement as tiny old men popped up all around the fallen warriors. They had wrinkled faces, and wore cocked hats and leather aprons.

They fussed over the bodies, muttering between themselves, their toothless mouths twisting and curling as they examined the fallen. They carried little hammers and tongs, and used them to prise loose the arrows. They then dressed the wounds with some form of animal skin, and one by one, the men recovered, dazedly shaking their heads, and stretching their limbs as if they could hardly believe what had happened.

The little men gathered in a tight group in the middle of the battlefield, and as if to celebrate the Danaans' return from the dead, a beautiful rainbow appeared in the sky, stretching from the horizon beyond the river to end just in front of these curious people. Dan and Sara distinctly heard them cackle, look furtively around, and slide one by one down the rainbow into the ground. As the last one disappeared, so too did the rainbow.

"I don't believe it!" Exclaimed Sara.

Dan couldn't help himself. He chuckled – and heard an answering chuckle behind him. It was Metatron: "These little people, the tiny ones, the small men, have gone back to their homes, returned to their dwellings, and now are no longer here!"

"Yes, we can see that. But who are they? How did they heal everyone?" Dan asked.

"They are the leprechauns, the Irish miniature folk. They have vanished and disappeared and are now hidden in the earth, unseen underground. They repair the wounds, make well the fallen, cure the warriors with their magic pigskin, their secret healing remedy".

Sara said, "They're the ones who're supposed to be rich and know where there's a crock of gold!"

"Well, that's the rainbow then, isn't it?" Said Dan. "This is just amazing!"

"What a battle! What an incredible morning!" Sara added, as Metatron dissolved as if by magic.

Chapter 24

Roaring fires provided never-ending supplies of stew from the cauldron of Dagda. It refilled itself as fast as the Danaans could eat.

A makeshift tent was set up in the middle of the battlefield, and Nuada and Sorbema entertained the leaders of the victorious army. The mood was lively, and a slim young girl played cheerful rippling tunes on her golden harp.

Dan and Sara sat quietly at the back of the tent, watching proceedings.

"Well, we stayed safely out the way, Sara".

"I know. Thank goodness! I was a bit worried earlier, but Sorbema made sure we were out of range. Where d'you reckon the Firbolgs have gone?"

"Not sure, but they raced off quick enough when the clouds chased them!"

"I don't blame them. Did you feel the force of that charge? All the elks, the Vashad Thains, the horses, Nuada, and then to crown it all, that enormous rushing cloud. It was just amazing. What a victory".

As they spoke, there was a stir at the entrance to the tent. The buzz of noise died quickly and they saw, to their amazement, one of the Firbolgs, in perfect silence, stand in front of Nuada.

Sorbema said: "Welcome, Sreng".

Dan nudged Sara excitedly. "It's their ambassador, the guy Nuada met before the battle. What's he up to? Oh! I know – he's come to play chess, just as I dreamed!"

After a rapid series of words between Nuada and Sreng, a space was cleared and a magnificent chessboard was brought in and placed on the table in front of them. Sorbema quietly came up to the children and explained, "Sreng has come to negotiate land for his men".

Dan said, "But they were beaten. Surely they can't come back and get land from you?"

"Our traditions have a proud place for the game of chess. This is rarely done, but we must play a series of games when challenged by a defeated foe. For them, it is to save face. For us, it is a matter of honour".

As they watched, the board was set up. It was huge, double the size of any they had seen, and made of silver. On it, a steward set up the pieces, representing fierce warrior figures. They were beautifully carved in gold, studded with jewels and shards of coral, which glittered in the beam of light from the entrance to the tent.

Dan said to Sara, "This is the chess game from my dream!"

"Who wins then?" asked Sara nervously.

"I can't remember".

In silence, the two men started to play. Dan was fascinated. He had studied tactics, and knew many of the popular openings to the game as well as some of the ways experts played. He was astonished to see Sreng win the first game with a fool's mate – Nuada lost in four swift moves.

"Oh no!" said Sara.

"He must have done that deliberately", replied Dan. "There's no way he should have fallen for that one. Just as well they're playing a series".

Sreng won game after game, and the children were depressed, wondering what this would mean for their hosts.

Sorbema seemed untroubled, even though the scribe beside the board, map in hand, drew an ever widening circle of land which would be the Firbolgs if Sreng won all the games. From time to time, the scribe angrily brushed the air around him, as if a troublesome fly was bothering him. He swatted several times, once almost knocking his map to the floor.

At the end of one long game, which Nuada lost narrowly, he talked in a low tone to Sreng, who thought carefully and nodded decisively. The two shook hands, and Dan said: "It's like this is a decider. Nuada's gambling everything on this one game!"

The two played their opening moves. Unusually, it was a four-knight opener, with all the pawns left unmoved. Both players then cautiously developed their centrepieces, with Nuada also opening up the way for his rooks to get into the game. Sreng countered by swapping bishops.

Nuada then attacked Sreng's king with his Queen's knight, backed by his two centre pawns and queen. Sreng defended fiercely, capturing Nuada's queen.

Dan groaned, but swiftly, Nuada closed in on the now undefended king with his other knight and king's rook. There was no escape for Sreng.

"Checkmate", breathed Dan. "That was Anastasia's mate".

"What's that?" Asked Sara.

"Anastasia's mate", said Dan, "It's a checkmate using your knight and rook. Brilliant play!"

Sreng paled, stood up without a word, and stalked out of the tent. The stunned watchers cheered Nuada who smiled broadly, and winked at the children.

"He could have won anytime," Dan exclaimed. "He was fooling

him all the time, getting him to commit everything before he whopped him in that last game. Fantastic!"

"Does that mean he's saved Ireland from the Firbolgs'?" asked Sara.

The answer came from Metatron who appeared again beside them: "Sreng will go and return to his men, his army. They will make off, escape and go from here, and sail in boats and ships they call barks. Thirty men in each or three times ten will sail to other lands and different countries".

Sara asked, "How do you know this, Metatron?"

"They go, travel and journey through many times and many places. We see and observe them. We know".

He faded away as the tent filled with activity. The chessboard was moved and a huge heavy stone was manhandled into the centre of the tent, its bearers staggering under its obvious weight. Outside they saw and heard the trundle of wooden carriages from which stepped a succession of finely dressed men and women, tall and elegant in purple robes. Several carried sceptres and one a simple crown set on a satin tray.

Sara swayed against Dan and said, "Dan! Dan! *This is what I dreamed!* This is the same tent, the same carriages and that's the stone I saw. I know what's going to happen! They're going to crown Nuada king!"

Dan looked at her, realisation dawning. "That means we've both dreamed some of this!"

They shared a moment when their energies surged with excitement, the feeling surrounding them with a shivering tingle. Nuada sat on the stone, with Sorbema at his side, and as he was crowned, he rose, raised his silver hand, and the onlookers cheered.

Outside, the entire army echoed the rousing applause, and their ears rang with the incredible racket.

Sorbema looked round the tent, acknowledging the children with her gaze, and Nuada's eyes followed hers to rest on them. They sensed this was their time to leave.

"What's going to happen to us now?" Dan asked nervously.

Vohumanah rippled into view, his presence creating a feeling of peace around them: "Children, you will be well. Hold your energies in a positive way. Focus on your inner self. Know it and be it".

Dan and Sara were reassured, and remembering how they had managed before to keep calm, breathed deeply, and became less agitated. Sara grinned and said to Dan: "Right, we have to get back home and we have to do it now!"

Sorbema came over to them, her eyes shining. She seemed not to notice Vohumanah: "We had a good and wise ruler. We *have* a good and wise king. Your stay with us is at an end. Follow your instincts and return home. Remember what you have seen and learned".

"Thanks Sorbema", said Sara and impulsively leant forward and kissed her cheek. Dan muttered his thanks and escaped before he had to kiss her too.

They stood outside amidst the incredible scene of the army celebrating Nuada's victory and coronation. Men danced and capered wildly, women cheered, harpists played uplifting melodies, and the former battlefield was awash with waving banners.

Sara led Dan round the tent where it was quieter, and as she had sensed, there waited Zuphlas. Sara said, "Hello Zuphlas, I know where we're going this time, but lead on if you like!"

Dan frowned, but as they started off towards the line of towers on Moytura plain, he grinned: "Of course – the Mistlees Tower".

They soon reached the tower, its clock face proudly reading 11o'clock.

Dan asked, "How do we do it this time, Zuphlas. How do we get back?"

Zuphlas shimmered through the door at the base of the tower, and it slowly swung open to reveal a set of stairs winding upwards. In the semi gloom, they climbed, and just before the top of the tower, the steps stopped at the level of the clock face. They stood in a circular room with the works of the clock and Zuphlas for company. The air swirled round their heads and they instinctively ducked.

Suddenly, the clock came to life, metal levers clanking, gears shifting and ratcheted wheels turning, grinding the clock face into action. A large bronze hammer struck the bell that sat over the clockwork. As it tolled out its eleven hours, the children stood quietly. On the exact stroke of eleven, their surroundings dissolved into the twilight.

Chapter 25

The rug's orange circle slowly pulsed to a stop and they stepped back on to the cellar floor. Everything was as they'd left it, including the smell of paint.

Dan said, "Time's stood still again".

"It's bizarre, isn't it? You'd think we'd missed days and days, but we come back with no gap at all. Amazing! How's your energy?"

"It's great. I'm feeling really excited and still all charged up!"

"So am I! So what did you make of Tara?"

Dan found two old chairs to sit on. "That battle was fantastic. Nuada seemed to have no chance at the start, but the way he fought and got the Firbolgs to try to chase him and the Vashad Thains was amazing. They couldn't get at him because they were so tightly packed".

"I must admit I was worried. Even though we were a long way from the action, what if they'd lost? What would have happened to us?"

"We'd probably have been grabbed by the rebel angels!"

"That's not funny!"

"Yes, I know! But surely Zuphlas would have saved us. He has the knack of turning up at just the right moment".

"I suppose so. We'd have certainly had to practise using our positive energy then."

"What Sorbema said about Gaia was fascinating".

"Did you understand it all?"

"Haven't had much time to think about it really, but it's obvious that loads of different peoples came to Tara to learn from the Danaans. She said we're all part of one big energy source".

"Gaia", Said Sara.

"Yes, but on the other hand they still had to fight a huge battle, so Gaia's not all good, is it?"

"Is it not like having an infection in your body? You know, like the red blood cells battling the white ones".

"I like that," Dan chuckled. "It's just like today really. There's always wars and fights, and struggles for power. Why do people do that all the time?"

"Don't ask me! If it was up to me, we'd never have a war or anything".

They sat in silence for a while, and then they heard a beeping sound.

"What's that?" asked Sara.

"Oh, it's my Rainbow Catcher! I'd forgotten about it".

He took it out of his jeans' pocket, still beeping. "I've got my first text. It's from Dad. Look!"

Sara leant over. The screen read: "wair r u wot up 2 dad".

They laughed, Dan's face a study as he read Dad's message. "He's trying to be all trendy with his words. I'll text back."

He keyed: "in selr y funi words".

Sara laughed as Dan sent the reply, and two minutes later, Hugh came down the steps: "I thought you'd like my style", he said.

"Dad! No! Just text like you'd type. The Rainbow Catcher has predictive text, but I had to turn it off to text you back."

"OK. How are you getting on anyway?"

"Fine thanks," said Dan, surprised at his interest. "We're just chilling out. How's Tim?"

"He fell asleep over his book. He's still dozing".

Sara said, "I'll need to get back home now. Dan, I'll catch up with you tomorrow".

"We're going for a run in the car, Sara", said Dan, arching his eyebrows in despair.

"OK. I'll see you Monday then". And off she went.

The Goodwins toured the towns and villages around Mistlees on Sunday.

They liked Braco, with its long straight main street, and quiet churchyard, a haven of peace with birds chirping in the sunshine. The air smelt sharp, fresh and clean in Comrie, where Hugh said a lot of retired people lived. They stood on the bridge watching the river gurgle past. Dan was reminded of his trip to the Mayans, though the flow of the current was gentle and the water shallow. There was something about the sound of the water swishing through the rocks.

Lost in thought, he realised his mum was shouting on him. "Come on Dan, we're off for lunch!"

He gave himself a mental shake and joined the family in the local tearoom.

Tim was restless, and Dan found himself exercising his positive energy, focussing on getting him to sit still. Amazingly, he did, and Dan wondered if it was just coincidence, but after lunch, he continued to practise his skills. The main street was busy with traffic, and as they walked along, looking for a place to cross over, he concentrated on willing for a gap in the stream of cars and buses.

Just then, a car slowed down and waved them across the road.

"Wow!" he thought, "That seemed to work!"

Later in the day when they had trouble parking in Crieff, he focussed on finding a space, and a van suddenly pulled out in front of them.

"That was lucky!" said Hugh as he parked. Dan smiled quietly to himself.

When they got home, he had some homework to do. Miss Ambrose had asked them to find out all they could about Leonardo da Vinci, the famous Italian painter. Dan used the PC on his Rainbow Catcher, and clicked the "Search" button. Dozens of websites were listed, and he clicked on one.

Da Vinci lived from 1452 to 1519. Dan was staggered at the incredible range of his work.

He wasn't just noted for his paintings, like the Mona Lisa and The Last Supper, but for designs of aeroplanes, giant catapults and all sorts of amazing instruments, hundreds of years ahead of his time. Dan wondered how anybody could possibly be as forward-looking as that.

He once had described himself as painter, architect, philosopher, poet, composer, sculptor, athlete, mathematician, inventor and anatomist.

Dan was fascinated, and took some notes for his 300-word essay. He saved the website in his "Favourites" folder, and typed his homework, his head buzzing with Leonardo da Vinci.

Chapter 26

After breakfast, Dan met Sara at the bridge over the burn before school. Tim was grumpy. He'd slept in and Liz had woken him three times. He kept muttering about the day ahead. His class were finally going to present their very own version of Julius Caesar, with Tim playing Brutus. He was obviously nervous, but excited as he repeated his lines: "I loved Caesar, but loved Rome more. That's why we killed him and now you know the score!"

It was all Dan and Sara could do to keep straight faces.

When he sprinted off at the school gates, Dan said, "Poor Timmy. He's so wound up about this. It's the first big thing he's done at school. It's asking a lot of him to remember so much".

"He'll be fine", Sara replied. "When I did it in Primary 1, I was Calpurnia, Caesar's wife, and all I had to do was wail and wring my hands. Tim's only got a few lines, and of course the song."

"What song?"

"Do you know the nursery rhyme, "Old Macdonald had a farm"?"

"'Course I do".

"Well, to welcome Caesar to the Forum, they sing, "Julius Caesar is our king – hip hip hip hooray!"

Sara sung the words to the old tune, while Dan cringed. "Well", he said, "Let's hope he does all right today". They focussed on Tim, picturing him delivering his speeches in a loud clear voice.

Over the past few weeks, everyone had noticed a difference in Sara's work. Her concentration was better, her marks had improved, and she was now giving the best in the class, including Dan, a run for their money.

Sara knew it was because of their timetripping travels.

She was determined to keep improving, and Sorbema's words and what they'd seen helped her too. Miss Ambrose looked at her thoughtfully at the start of class, and Sara realised with a jolt that she really *was* an older double of Sorbema, except for her red hair, which was shorter. She grinned at Sara and asked, "Nice weekend? Did you go anyplace interesting?"

Sara gulped before replying, "Er, no. Not really Miss. Just around the village."

"No real dramas then? No big excitements?"

Sara looked confused, and Miss Ambrose turned to Dan. "And what about you, Dan? Any developments at the weekend? Any revelations?"

Dan replied, "Yes actually. We went to Crieff and Comrie".

"How nice", Miss Ambrose said with a smile and a knowing look.

Mark snorted quietly, and muttered, "Teacher's pet".

"What was that, Mark?" Miss Ambrose asked sharply.

"Nothing Miss, just saying it was a bit wet yesterday".

"Hmmm", Miss Ambrose said.

She said: "Every country has its history and its traditions. We've talked a bit about the Egyptians and the Mayans, and their writings. The Celtic nations too have a proud history. There is a great affinity between the Irish and the Scots, and parallels in their literature and spoken language too."

Her gaze flicked from Dan to Sara, and Dan felt the back of his neck burn. He glanced round to see Mark staring intently at him, his eyebrows bunched angrily.

Miss Ambrose interrupted: "Who can tell me the names of any famous Scottish writers?"

Quick as a flash, Sara said: "Robert Burns, miss!"

"Good, Sara. Who else?"

"Sir Walter Scott!" announced Ali, with an embarrassed grin.

"Yes, Ali – well done! Any others?"

"Hugh MacDiarmid, miss!" said Iain.

"Ah, yes, Iain, famous for his epic: "A Drunk Man Looks at the Thistle". Now that was a wonderful poem:

"What's in a name? From pole to pole
Our interlinked mentality spins.
I know that you are Deosil, and suppose
That therefore I am Widdershins."

The class looked puzzled, and Dan asked: "What do Deosil and Widdershins mean, miss?"

"They mean clockwise and anti-clockwise – one way and the other way, Dan. Anyway, let's not get sidetracked. Yes, Scotland has a rich vein of literature – one we should all be very proud of." She looked distracted for a moment and concluded: "Well, how's the village project getting on?"

There was a bit of discomfort among the pupils, and it was clear that Dan and Sara were ahead of most of the others. Mark was obviously embarrassed when Miss Ambrose found out he had actually done some research. Dan and Sara nodded to each other, remembering Brad Maipeson's comments.

"You all need to spend more time on it. A little work done each week will make it much easier!" She said meaningfully.

Dan and Sara planned to meet on Wednesday to go to the old tower and the graveyard.

School passed quickly, and Sara's energy was high. She was feeling very confident about her schoolwork, and less distracted than normal. After class, Dan said to her: "I'm glad we seem to be

OK with the project but Mark wasn't very happy, was he?"

"No, and you're right by the way! I think he *is* growing taller, and his voice is deeper too."

"It's a bit odd, isn't it?"

Just at that, they saw Mark at the end of the corridor knock on Mrs Braid's door and go straight in. They looked at each other: "Oh, dear," Dan said, "I wonder if he's in trouble."

"I don't know, but I think she's got a soft spot for him."

"Really! You mean the old battle axe is human after all?"

Sara thought for a second: "Yes, I wonder why, especially since he's hardly Brain of Britain!"

Dan chuckled on his way to football practice. It was even better than last time, and he scored goal after goal. Mark turned up late and was not happy. Dan had even started to think about being captain of the team, and was sure he'd make a better job of it than Hamish, who was a bit quiet and slow to decide on things.

Mrs Braid spoke to him after the practice, clenching and unclenching her long fingers. She was clearly uncomfortable, and didn't look him in the eye once: "There's an inter-school five-a-side tournament coming up, Dan, and the team have asked for you to be Captain of Elfsite Reach. I'm not sure. I think it might be a bit much for you, so shall I tell them you don't want to do it?"

"Actually, Mrs Braid, I'd be thrilled", replied Dan, flushing slightly.

"Ah well, only if you're sure!" she said, disappointed

He rushed home with his news, only to find Tim waiting at the front gate, excited and gushing with the story of the Julius Caesar performance. "I was *so good*", he exclaimed. "Everyone said so, even Miss Wade. And *this* is how I got Caesar". He lunged at Dan, his right arm raised.

"Hey. Hang on, Tim! Don't murder me!" Dan picked him up and carried him inside, kicking and struggling. Liz chuckled: "I gather you've been stabbed too then!"

"'Fraid so, mum, but I've come back from the dead to get Brutus, so it serves him right!"

He set Tim down, but he continued to act like Brutus till Dan said, "OK, OK, enough, enough! I give in. I'm dead!"

Tim looked suspiciously up at him, snorted and walked off with his nose in the air, singing: "Julius Caesar *was* our king. Hip hip hip hooray!"

Liz gave Dan a hug. "How was *your* day?"

"I've been chosen as Captain of the Football team!"

"Oh that's great! Well done Dan. When? What for?"

"We've got an inter-school competition sometime soon, and Mrs Braid's asked me to be Captain, though she seemed a bit reluctant about it".

"Well, even so, Dad will be thrilled for you. He used to be captain of his school team too, you know. Like father, like son!"

Hugh was delighted, and the week had got off to a flying start.

On Wednesday, Sara and Dan walked west to the old tower at the edge of the village. Dan felt a little shiver of anticipation, thinking about the tower from Tara at the battlefield of Moytura.

It took about ten minutes to reach it, walking leisurely past the school and the playing fields beyond. It stood in a low-walled stone enclosure, its clock facing the village. It was about ten metres tall, with a battlement like a castle's, and its square sides were six paces wide. On each face were long oval windows, stretching half the height of the structure, and the doorway was beautifully arched.

A plaque above the door was faded with time but they could

make out: "WHERE TWO OR THREE ARE GATHERED TOGETHER", followed by several more words they couldn't read. They sketched the tower showing the clock stuck at 11 o'clock, and Dan photographed it with his Rainbow Catcher.

He wondered if Mr Dewbury would appear when, as if on cue, he wandered from the village towards them.

"Well, children! I suppose the project's still going then?"

Dan replied, "Yes, Mr Dewbury. It's going pretty well really. We've still got a fair bit to do though".

Sara said, "I'm glad you're here, Mr Dewbury. Can you tell us anything about the old tower?"

"Well," he said after a long pause, "I've researched its history, but can't find any record of it being built. I'm sure it's very old, and you can see the old inscription above the door is fading away. It used to say, "Where two or three are gathered together in my name, there am I in the midst of them". It's from the gospel of Matthew, you know."

"Did this used to be a church then?" Asked Dan.

"I don't think so. You can see there's hardly any space inside".

Sara asked, "Can we get inside to have a look?"

"Certainly not, Sara. The Council say it's not safe. The stairs are quite worn and they worry about people tripping in the dark".

"What a pity" Sara continued, "We'd really like to get a closer look for our project".

Mr Dewbury looked thoughtful for a moment and said, "Two or three. Three. That's all we need".

"Pardon?" asked Dan.

"Nothing, my boy, nothing, just thinking out loud".

There was silence for a minute before Dan asked, "Mr Dewbury, when we saw you last time, you seemed to know why Mistlees seems a powerful kind of place".

"Yes, that's right." He replied.

"Well, can you tell us why?"

"It's to do with ley lines. Very powerful".

"But what are ley lines? Dan asked.

Mr Dewbury said, "Well, I'm sure if you find out, that'll help your project, won't it?" He glared at them as if he'd said too much, turned round, and walked slowly off, head down.

Sara spoke first, "Oh he's so frustrating! Why can't he just come out and tell us stuff?"

"I don't know Sara. He always seems to resent telling us anything, but he's obviously full of information. Anyway, we can check out these ley lines on the Rainbow Catcher later on".

"OK, let's do that. What have we got left to do for the project do you reckon"?

"Well, we've looked at the Sunken Chapel and the old Clock Tower, so we've still to go to the graveyard, the village church and the Community Centre, but they're all the main features. We need to write a bit about the village history, and that's about it".

"So there's still a lot to do."

"Yup, so let's get back now, and see if we can research ley lines."

He set up the Rainbow Catcher in his bedroom, projecting its screen on the wall. He clicked on the Internet, put "ley lines" into Search, and was surprised when there were 24,920 results. He skimmed down the list with Sara looking over his shoulder: "Here's stuff about Glastonbury, Earth mysteries, and cult archaeology. Let's check them out."

He clicked on a site that looked interesting, and then another and another.

The information was fascinating. In the 1920's, an Englishman called Alfred Watkins had noticed that various prehistoric sites, like standing stones, burial mounds, and earthworked hills often fell into straight lines across the countryside. He believed that old straight tracks, running from mountain to mountain, and hilltop to hilltop, had been made by surveyors in ancient times to join up the sites. Most of the tracks had disappeared over time.

People began to believe that the ley lines, as they were called, were lines of energy or magnetism, and many thought they attracted UFO's – "that's Unidentified Flying Objects", Dan explained to Sara. Many strange events had been recorded where ley lines crossed each other.

Sara said, "Dan, this is spooky. These articles talk about standing stones, old churches, and burial grounds. We've seen *all* of these here and on our travels!"

"I know! Isn't this pretty cool?"

"I'm not sure about cool, but it's quite a coincidence."

"Coincidence again!" said Dan.

He folded up the Rainbow Catcher, and Sara went home, puzzling about these strange powerful lines criss-crossing the earth.

Chapter 27

That night in his room, Dan couldn't stop thinking about ley lines and Leonardo da Vinci. He took ages to fall asleep, and kept waking up.

At one stage, he dreamed.

A young man grabbed something of his, and he tried desperately to hold on to it, but the man took it away, studying it intensely. Dan felt a sense of great loss. He knew he was in a strange town, the houses stone built, and the place was baking hot, the sun blinding in its intensity.

He was in an artist's studio crammed with paintings, casts of statues and uniforms. It was a darkly forbidding place, and he shivered violently.

Suddenly he was awake, shaking, with his duvet tumbled on the floor. He pulled it back on his bed, but could sleep no more.

Sara fell asleep excited by the day's events, and she dreamed too.

She was looking at an unfinished painting of an ancient baptism, with one man pouring water over the head of another dressed in a loincloth. The baptised figure had his hands clasped in prayer.

There was huge activity around her in what felt like an artist's studio.

People laughed, talked, sculpted, drew and painted in a central space full of their work. One wall had a large mirror hanging on it with a desk underneath.

All the other walls were covered in tapestries and paintings.

A man with long curled hair spoke softly to her but she couldn't make out his words. He repeated them louder and again louder--------

"Come on Sara! Time to get up!"

It was Bruce, home on holiday for a week. Annoyed, he said: "What was all that about? You were snoring and grunting, tossing and turning and yakking away about paintings!"

Sara was embarrassed. "Oh Bruce, leave me alone. I was dreaming."

"Ah ha!" said Bruce, quick as a flash, his scar glowing, and a triumphant gleam in his eye: "Tell me about it then! Happy dream? Sad dream?"

Reluctantly, Sara replied, "Actually it was quite an interesting dream – about artists and sculptors and paintings and things".

"Quite the little highbrow, eh? Get any good tips for my paintbrush for the kitchen?"

"Ha ha ha! Why don't you get on with your painting and let me wake up in my own time?"

"Can't do that, my girl. It's school time nearly. Come on, up you get!"

Sara surfaced, scratching her cheek, showered and got ready for school, recalling her vivid dream. Over breakfast of tea and toast, Diana quizzed her.

"You don't often remember your dreams. This one must have been a bit special, was it?"

"Yes, it was fascinating. Someone was half way through this painting of a man being baptised, and there were loads of people around, working on other paintings and sculptures and things".

"Sounds good", Diana replied, and then fell silent as she looked over Sara's shoulder: "Bruce! What *are* you doing?"

He was half way up a ladder in the corner of the kitchen, watching something.

"Look at this! It's a spider weaving its web. It's stuck though. It's swinging madly all over the place trying to get away from me. Ooops! There it goes – its seventh swing – into the corner and gone!"

Sara muttered, "Not the only one trying to get away from you this morning!"

"What was that, Sara?" he asked, brushing the cobweb away and decisively starting his repaint of the kitchen with a bright yellow brush.

"Nothing Bruce. Have to go now. Byee!"

She met up with Dan, and was excited relaying her dream. He was quiet for a while and gave her a strange look. "You're winding me up aren't you?"

"Winding you up? Why d'you say that? 'Course I'm not!"

"It sounds really like my dream, except my artist's studio felt kind of threatening. It was stuffed full of paintings and sculptures though, like yours, but someone was stealing something from me, and I don't know what it was".

Sara laughed. "Maybe it was me pinching your dream!"

"Eh no, not unless you've turned into a man overnight".

They both laughed and finished the walk to school in pleasant silence.

The day went quickly, and on the way home, they agreed to meet on Friday night to review their project work.

When Dan got home, Liz was hanging out some washing: "Oh, there you are! You've had a visitor today".

"Who? Who would come to see me?"

"Nigel. He dropped by at lunchtime to ask if we'd all like to go to the Edinburgh Museum on Saturday. He says he's got somebody he wants us to meet".

"You're joking, mum!"

"I am not. I'm serious. I said that you and dad would go, because Tim's got swimming."

"Can Sara come too?"

"I don't see why not, as long as her mum and Bruce don't mind".

"I'll ask her", said Dan.

He phoned on his Rainbow Catcher, and, excited at the prospect, Sara got permission from Diana.

On Friday night, they went to the cellar to compare notes. Again, the models had been rearranged, and they both felt goose bumps run down their skin. A small section of models contained what clearly represented their visit to Tara – the Cauldron of Dagda in miniature, an elk with huge antlers, a harp and a chessboard.

Sara looked around. "How is this happening, Dan? It's scaring me!"

"I really don't know! It's as if we've got a ghost down here!"

He yelled as a gust of air whistled past his ears: "That was freaky! Something just brushed past me!"

"Right!" said Sara, "That's enough! Let's get out of here!"

"No, no! Wait! We need to work this out. Whatever it is, it's not harming us. It seems to know where we've been, laying out the models like that, and I don't think it's evil or anything."

"How can you say that?"

"It keeps giving me a fright, but I feel it's looking for us to recognise it!"

"How can we recognise it if it's a ghost?"

"I don't know, but let's give it a few more days, and maybe we'll find out."

Sara grudgingly agreed, and they looked at their project. Dan had written a bit more than Sara, but Sara's drawings were neater and clearer. They felt a hint of competition as they looked at each other's work.

The cellar began to smell of tea and toast, and Dan couldn't understand it.

"We've not had toast since this morning! Where's the smell coming from?"

They walked round the cellar sniffing for the source of the aroma. Dan stopped short of the table with a jolt: "Sara! The lines!"

He pointed and it dawned on them at the same time.

"Ley lines!" They chorused.

Dan felt a shiver run down his spine. The rug seemed to respond, twitching slightly, and the red circle began to softly pulse. They moved the table and stepped forward. They heard the familiar swoosh and were off as soon as they touched the red circle!

Chapter 28

He took one look at Sara and laughed, despite the noise in the street around them.

"What's so funny? You don't look so brilliant yourself!" Sara replied, laughing too. They were dressed in white togas. Dan's reached below his knees at the front, and was longer at the back, Sara's to her ankles. They were constantly jostled and pushed by the throng of passers-by in a street crammed with activity.

The atmosphere was electric, and the air sticky with the crush of people. The tangy smell of frying sausages mingled with burnt copper and the press of sweating bodies pushing in both directions.

The street was defined by two rows of brick buildings, rickety wooden balconies almost touching each other above their heads. They counted at least six storeys in height before a thin blue skyline appeared.

Women draped washing and gossiped in raised tones to make themselves heard above the din in the street below. Roars of laughter and loud cries came from the arched doorway of an inn beside them. Men drinking from pottery cups spilled into the street, where a barber shaved a large fat man on whose belly sat a flagon of wine. At his feet crouched a young girl begging.

Next to the inn was a butcher's shop with joints of meat hanging from two poles. The butcher chopped meat, weighing it in a large pan, while his customer sat waiting. Across the way a shop owner shouted loudly while tossing sausages in a saucepan.

A schoolmaster bellowed at three pupils, separated from the noise and smells of the street by a screen of grey cloth.

The master sat on a chair, faced by three boys on a wooden bench. Beside them was a scrawled upon blackboard.

A succession of tables stretched down the street. At one, a metalworker pounded his hammer, fashioning sheets of copper; next to him, a money changer rang his coins; a trader shouted loudly the merits of his glass ornaments; and opposite, a customer bartered in a strident voice for a pair of gaily patterned cushions.

A flute player competed with a young girl plucking delicate notes from her lyre.

Men and women waved their hands and talked animatedly. Most wore tunics and togas in varying shades of white, but some men wore hooded leather cloaks with strips of cloth wrapped round their legs.

Dan and Sara stood amazed at the scene.

"Where are we?" shouted Sara.

"I think this is ancient Rome!" came Dan's reply.

"What a nightmare! What a din!"

"Let's get out of here and find someplace a bit quieter!"

They joined the crowd pushing past the tables. So far, they hadn't made out any of the words being shouted, but as they focussed, their amazing translation mechanism took over, allowing them to hear what was going on.

"Come on you old bat!" shouted the cushion merchant, face red with effort, "Twenty denarii, and that's my final word!"

"I'll give you eighteen and not one more!" The old woman shouted back.

"Nineteen!" roared the trader.

"Done!" cried the woman, a smile on her lips.

Muttering under his breath, the exchange was made.

"Silk from beyond the Empire!" The trader began his sales pitch again, "Finest spun cloth you'll ever see. Cotton died with onionskin, wool steeped in cedar wood. Step right up!"

Dan and Sara struggled past him, and continued along a line of traders' stalls laden with fruit, melons, fish, pastry, confectionery, oils and wine; sellers of rings, ivory tusks, robes, cloaks and boots; dyers, goldsmiths, rope makers, metal workers, carpenters and embroiderers all shared the crammed space between the tall houses.

"What an incredible place!" shouted Sara in Dan's ear, as they reached the end of the street, which opened on to a marble paved square. They took in their new surroundings in awe.

The square was massive, surrounded by vast pillared temples, marble statues and monuments. Soaring archways sheltered yet more traders; and farmers sold crops and livestock, sheep bellowing, goats bleating, cocks crowing and oxen lowing. The racket and its accompanying farmyard smells didn't seem to put off hundreds of citizens browsing market stalls, talking in groups, and walking through the square.

"The forum", said Dan. "I can't believe the number of people here!"

Sara said, "Isn't it amazing! The atmosphere's fantastic! What do you think we should do?"

As she spoke, a small man dressed in a tunic approached them, his gaze direct but respectful: "Greetings", he said clearly, bowing slightly, and looking round to avoid being overheard: "I wish to escort you to your host".

"Host?" said Dan, "Who is our host?"

In a quiet tone, the man said: "Marcus Antonius invites the pleasure of your company on this auspicious day."

"Marcus Antonius?" replied Dan, "Is that Mark Anthony?"

"Indeed the same", replied the man, "And I am Antonidus, the consul's ab admissione".

Sara asked, "What does that mean, Antonidus?"

"I am the slave who escorts guests. Mark Anthony is consul to Gaius Julius Caesar - his chief magistrate".

Dan gritted his teeth, and said quietly to Sara, "Julius Caesar. This is all down to Tim!"

"Didn't you ever wish you'd go to Rome? - think about it, dream about it maybe?"

He shrugged, "I guess it crossed my mind".

"Me too, so we've wished it on ourselves, Dan!"

Antonidus led them through the forum, Dan admiring one particular statue, inscribed to Auriel, carved with dolphins perched on large conch shells, themselves supported by two elephants at the base.

Their pace was brisk, and as they walked, they felt the air change rapidly, blue sky giving way to grey. A breeze sprang up, and spits of rain hit them. All round the square, traders began packing up, and people dispersed quickly. They both felt a change of atmosphere, more than that caused by the weather. An air of menace and danger filled the city, and they kept looking round, feeling someone was following them. Antonidus led them through two short streets, like the first one they had seen. He called the houses "insulae" in answer to Sara's question. Many were nine or ten storeys high.

"Like flats. In fact, almost like skyscrapers", Sara said.

They reached a long blank walled building, windowless and featureless in the now fast gathering gloom of early evening. The street was deserted as Antonidus rapped on a narrow door.

He looked apprehensively up and down the street, before a shutter opened slightly. It was rapidly closed, and a series of bolts released, allowing them in to a short passageway to an open courtyard, tiled beautifully with multi-coloured mosaics of flowers, animals, and stunningly intricate designs.

As the door closed behind them, they saw the size of the doorman. A gigantic man with the glistening muscles of a wrestler, he wore an armoured breastplate and carried a short sword. He looked impassively at them down the nose plate of his bronze helmet.

From around the pool filling the centre space of the courtyard scurried several slaves who escorted them into a large covered room. There was very little furniture, a few couches and desks, and again the mosaic tiled floor, surrounded by marble fluted pillars.

Antonidus bowed to the lady sitting in the centre of the room. "As you thought, ma'am, they were in the Forum".

He withdrew, followed by the other slaves, and both the children felt very alone and vulnerable. Far from being welcoming, the middle-aged woman stood up, ignored them for a moment as she adjusted her purple robes, and fixed her steely gaze on them: "There are enough things to do today of all days", she said in a haughty tone: "However, let's get on with it!"

Sara stuttered, "Get on with what, ma'am?"

"Names?" She barked.

Dan gathered his confidence while she looked sternly at them. He breathed deeply, and focussed on keeping his voice steady and firm: "I'm Dan, and this is my friend Sara".

"Ah, 'tis good to claim friends. How many can do that?"

Her voice softened and she relaxed, a slight smile curling the sides of her mouth. She wore bright red lipstick, smudged below her wide lips. Her cheeks were ghostly pale, obviously powdered, and her curling eyelashes were accentuated by purple eye shadow. She was not a pretty woman, tall, with a broad hooked nose, hard brown eyes and long black hair swept around her head into a point above her brow.

"I am Fulvia, wife to Mark Anthony. You come at a difficult time, and your stay with us will not be easy. We have many things to do, and many people to see. You will be looked after by Mur-A-Halad. Stay with him".

She swept out of the room, leaving them feeling foolish and depressed.

"Oh Dan, I don't like this! What a horrible woman. It doesn't feel safe here."

Dan nodded, "I agree. And listen to the storm".

The wind howled round the courtyard outside, and rain battered the tiled roof.

Three slaves appeared and lit lamps around the room, lifting the gloom, but creating ghostly shadows on pillars and walls.

"What have we got ourselves into?" asked Sara.

"Let's think about this logically", replied Dan.

"Logically!" shrieked Sara. "Logically! How can you think logically about this? We've been lifted up and dumped in Rome, led to this horrible mansion, and abandoned by a woman who looks and acts like a witch. There's a raging storm outside, we're hundreds of years and thousands of miles from home, and you expect me to think logically!"

"I do actually", said Dan quietly but with authority. "We *must* - for all the reasons you've mentioned".

"Right! Right! I'll just put my logical thinking hat on, look around, find an escape hatch and get out of here. Fast!"

"Sara. We need to focus on what's going on here. If it's like the other places we've been to, something's going to happen and we should be ready for it ----".

He stopped speaking suddenly, paled, and said, "Sara! Sara! Your aura! The colours around you!"

"What colours? What d'you mean about my aura?"

"You're lit up like a firework! All round your head – it's --- it's --- grey and brown, and there's red and yellow too! And wait, it's changing now, and there's green coming in. The brown and grey are fading!"

"What is it, Dan?" said Sara, calming down after her outburst.

"Do you remember that time with Sorbema when we saw her aura, with all the colours round her? That's what you're like now – it's incredible, there's a whole energy field around you, pulsing away, and radiating colour".

"I can't see anything!" Sara complained.

"Well maybe you're not able to see your own aura, but it's fantastic. As you got angry and shouted, I saw it suddenly surround you, flickering in the lamplight!"

"What's happening now then?"

Dan screwed up his eyes. "It's fading now, and I can't see it clearly, but it was radiating all round you – stretching for nearly a metre, especially round your head".

"It must have been my temper that made it appear. Sorry Dan, I got really upset for a moment".

"I know, I know. We'll have to think this through a bit, and work out what to do. Do you hear the storm?"

The rain was pelting down, and ripples of thunder rolled round the villa. Through the doorway to the courtyard, jagged sheets of lightning pierced the darkness like an unearthly stroboscope.

The lamps flickered as the wind howled in and round the room.

They both shivered. Dan looked round quickly, sensing something, and jumped in surprise. An Arabian man, in flowing pink robes stood directly in front of them. His light brown face was clear and shining in the flickering light. His grey beard curled under his chin. He bowed deeply, and with a start, Dan saw a yellow haze round his head.

The man spoke in a deep clear voice: "Greetings, Dan and Sara. I am Mur–A-Halad, soothsayer and guide, at your service".

Sara clenched her fists, gathering her strength, and pulled herself up to full height: "Well Mr Murray Hullad, can you explain what's going on? That Fulvia woman said we'd to stay with you, but how do we know we can believe her or trust you, or – or – or anything!"

The man bowed again: "I am Mur–A-Halad, soothsayer and guide," he repeated. "Come with me".

He swirled round and led them into a small tiled room. A wall painting showed a tall elegant Roman reclining on a couch, talking to a slave who poured wine into his cup. Mur-A-Halad motioned them to sit on the open-backed bench facing the painting. He sat opposite in a beautifully carved armchair. The children propped themselves up with cushions.

Mur-A-Halad adjusted his robe, clasped his hands firmly together, rested them on his knees, and spoke: "This is a time of strife in Rome, a time when no man can say who his friends are, and be sure the same is true tomorrow. The storm gathers, and the storm will pass but leave no calm here. My master wishes you to be in my care. He has much on his mind and many things to do before the day is done. Tonight, he will try to see you, but he has many people to meet, and the lamps will burn through the night."

"What's going on then?" Asked Sara. "Why is there so much trouble?"

"Many fear the power of Caesar, young lady. He has done much for Rome. He has spread the Empire's power and influence through many lands, won many battles and gathered great tributes to Rome.

He is revered by many, but there is growing concern in the senate and beyond, that he now demands too much, listens to no man, and will destroy the good works he and his forebears have fought and died for."

"So what's going to happen?" Dan asked in a hushed voice.

"March is wasted fourteen days. Tomorrow, the Ides will tell," came the ominous reply.

Dan muttered, "The Ides of March". He and Sara both knew enough about the Julius Caesar play to guess what Mur-A-Halad meant, and Dan was worried. He took Sara's hand and squeezed it, sensing her alarm. Mur-A-Halad nodded. "You should value each others' company and be reassured by it".

All of a sudden, there was a loud fizzing noise and they felt a rush of heat.

A huge ball of flame and fire hurtled past, crashed into the far wall of the neighbouring room, throwing off a hissing cloud of blazing sparks. It bounced back in its tracks and disappeared, spitting cascades of glittering fire.

Sara said, "What on earth was that?"

Mur-A-Halad seemed unconcerned. He replied, "The gods are angry. They vent their wrath on this house."

The children looked at each other and felt the same wave of concern. Sara squeezed Dan's hand tighter. The sparks of flame and fire had fizzled out, but they still felt the heat of the fireball.

In the light of the lamps from the other room, they saw Antonidus lead a guest to a door in the far corner. He ushered the man through and returned quickly, head down.

Over the next ten minutes, he led in six more visitors, all heavily cloaked.

The last two came together, and Antonidus motioned for them to wait. The children heard one say, -- "a tempest dropping fire".

The man, face concealed by his cloak, continued; "A slave you might know held up his left hand, and it seemed to burst into flame, but the fire didn't burn him. I also saw a huge lion, which snarled angrily at me, but thankfully passed me by. It's so unsafe out there."

His companion replied, "And it's not going to get any better either, considering our meeting tonight---"

Their voices faded as Antonidus led them through the door.

Mur-A-Halad said, "I think it is time to get some rest. This night will be a long one. Come with me".

He led them to a bedroom at the far end of the house. Again there were only a few furnishings – two short cushioned beds, a table and chair and an open shelved unit. "You will be undisturbed here. I will call for water and some food. You may sleep in peace. I will guard you till morning".

"Are we in danger?" Asked Sara.

"You are not the focus of attention here, but it is wise to be aware of danger."

He withdrew, leaving them alone in the flickering torchlight. Sara sat on one of the beds, and Dan collapsed with a sigh on the chair. "Do you remember what happened in the play, Sara?"

"I do a bit – from school - the stuff about the slave with the flaming hand, and the lion wandering around – that rings a bell."

"It does with me too. I'm sure those who killed Caesar met the night before to plan how they'd do it, and there were all sorts of weird happenings in the streets".

"That's right. I think these last two were Casca and Cicero. But why are they meeting here? Wasn't Brutus the ringleader? I thought Mark Anthony was a good guy".

"I did too, but it doesn't look like that now, does it?"

A slave came in with a jug of water, two cups and a plate with a small loaf of bread, which he set on the table.

"Well that just about does it", Sara said. "Prison food! Bread and water and that's our lot!"

Dan chuckled, and Sara's serious face creased in a smile. As if in reaction to all they'd been through, they released their tension in fits of laughter. They ate all the bread, and sat in silence for a while drinking the water.

Dan spoke first: "Well, I feel a bit better now. I was really hungry."

"I was ready for that too – and I'm ready to sleep now".

"Me too. Let's get ready. I'll take the other bed and you can stay there".

"Oh that's kind of you!" she said sarcastically, ducking as Dan aimed a playful punch.

All tension gone, they settled into bed. Dan, lying on his back, stretched his arms above his head, and with a start, realised he could see, against the white ceiling, a faint blue haze between his hands. It rippled gently as he moved them together, and just before his palms met, he felt a slight pressure between them, a sort of bounciness in the space between.

He separated his hands slowly, and felt the pressure release. Fascinated, he moved his hands backwards and forwards, enjoying the odd sensation.

Sara saw him waving his hands around: "What on earth are you doing?"

"I'm not sure, but I think I'm seeing my own energy field. When I put my hands together, it feels like a magnet. There's a kind of rubbery pressure between them – and I could see a haze between my fingers too, but that's gone now".

"What did you do?"

"Put your hands up with your arms straight, and keep your palms facing each other", Dan instructed.

Sara pulled her arms from under the cover, and shook them as she followed Dan's lead.

"Now bring your arms in to meet each other – ever so gently, till your hands are almost touching, but not quite. Now pull them slowly away from each other and bring them back again. Slowly! Slowly! Can you feel it?"

Sara shivered with excitement. "I can! I feel it! It's like suction between my palms. How weird. But I can't see anything. How did you see it?"

"I don't know, but I was all ready to go to sleep and my eyes were kind of scrunched up, not fully open, and as I stretched, there it was! It soon faded though, but I can still get that funny wobbly feeling between my hands".

Their arms soon grew tired, and within minutes sleep overtook them both.

Chapter 29

After what seemed no time at all, Dan was woken up by the sound of a chair scraping on the marble floor outside. He sat up quickly, and seeing Sara was still asleep, swung his legs over the edge of the bed. He shuffled his feet into his sandals and crept to the door in the dim light of the wall-mounted torches.

Mur-A-Halad was nowhere to be seen, but Dan spotted a ghostly figure, clad in black, moving swiftly away from the bedroom. Curious, he followed, rubbing sleep from his eyes. He realised the storm had died away, leaving a flat calm atmosphere.

He muttered to himself, "It's so quiet - must be why I heard that noise."

The figure turned slowly and signalled for him to follow. It looked like a minister, wearing a white collar and with a flowing black robe, but it was indistinct, not firm and solid. It glided through the villa and out the front door. There was no guard and no bolts were drawn to allow the shadowy form through.

Dan felt a thrill of anticipation, breathed deeply, and followed into the darkened street. He knew he should not be out on his own, but the urge to find out who the mysterious figure was, was overwhelming. He chuckled, thinking of Sara's reaction when he told her later.

At the end of the street, he looked left and right, but the ghostly form had disappeared. He concentrated hard, closing his eyes to hear better. A faint noise in the distance to his left rewarded his patience, and he quickly strode towards the sound.

In minutes, however, all was again silent, and no matter how hard he tried, he could not hear any steps. To make matters worse, the thin cloud cover that had given him moonlight to see by, was replaced by the thick black of night.

At another crossroads, he felt the curve of a wall and followed it round, tripping on the uneven street surface. He fell and rolled over, getting tangled in his toga, and was desperately struggling to release his arms when he heard heavy footsteps marching towards him.

"Thank goodness!" he exclaimed.

The flames of several torches lit up a small group of soldiers, carrying round shields and short swords. As soon as they saw him, they rushed to surround him, and stood menacingly.

"I'm glad you're here, to be honest", he said breathlessly, tugging the toga from under him. He stood up and grinned hesitantly, but was met with hard stares and cold looks.

The officer in charge addressed him: "Who are you, and why have you broken the curfew? Nobody is allowed out of doors after darkness!"

"I've j-just arrived in R-Rome", Dan stuttered. "I'm really s-sorry but I didn't know I shouldn't be outside. I've b-been at M-Mark Anthony's villa with my friend Sara, and----"

He broke off as one of the men muttered, "A likely story – Mark Anthony's villa indeed!"

The officer sized him up, and barked: "Name, child! What is your name?"

"I-I'm Dan G-Goodwin".

"Where are you from, boy?"

Dan felt very scared, realising this was going to be difficult to explain. He took a deep breath, calming himself: "Well, I'm actually from Scotland. That's in Britain. I live in Perthshire in a village called Mistlees. I'm only here for a few days, and then I'll be going home again".

The officer looked startled: "Britannia? You're from Britannia? Going home in a few days? I think not! Take him to the cells!"

It took a second or two for his words to sink in, and Dan panicked: "No! No! You don't understand. You can't lock me up. I'm not really supposed to be here!

I can't stay – it's not possible! You must get Sara, and tell Mur-A-Halad what's happened!"

One of the men gripped Dan's arm firmly, and said, "Mur-A-Halad. That bag of bones! That about settles it, my lad! Arms behind your back, and quick about it!"

They tied his arms tightly with rope and dragged him through the darkened streets. Dan stopped resisting, his mind in turmoil.

What was going to happen to him? Where was the ghostly figure? What about Sara? What about his mum and dad? What about Mistlees?

This adventure had turned into a nightmare, and he was right in the middle of it.

Chapter 30

Moments after Sara woke, she sensed quickly something was wrong.

She felt her heart wrench, and a sudden pain coursed from the pit of her stomach to the base of her spine. She looked over at Dan's bed, saw it was empty, and jumped up in panic: "Dan! Dan! Where are you?"

Mur-A-Halad raced in, skidded to a stop beside her, and looked desperately round the room.

"He's gone!" Sara shrieked.

Mur-A-Halad's face went ashen, and he fell to his knees: "This is a calamity! The boy has disappeared in the night. How could this be?"

His reaction astonished Sara: "Hang on – Fulvia said we'd be safe with you! You were supposed to be guarding us. This is all your fault. Where is Dan? You must find him, and fast!"

Mur-A-Halad got to his feet, and, bowing deeply, retreated from the room, leaving Sara confused and angry. "Right!" She declared. "I need to find Dan. Let's see who'll help!"

She swept through the villa, deserted except for a few slaves, who avoided her studiously, until she stopped by a woman sweeping the floor. "Where is everyone?" Sara demanded. Where is Fulvia, and where's Mark Anthony?"

"Ah! Madam, everyone has gone to the games. Before the Senate meet today, the people celebrate at Circus Maximus. Mark Anthony and Fulvia will open the proceedings".

"Where's Circus Maximus? Quick! I need to get there. I need help to find my friend!" Said Sara, determined to succeed.

The woman looked nervously around, and replied, "It is in front of the Aventine Hill, overlooking the Tiber".

"But where's that?" said Sara impatiently, "I don't know my way around. You'll have to take me there!"

She tugged the woman's sleeve, but the slave pulled free and ran inside.

"Blast it all!" Sara exclaimed, "What now? I need help!"

As if in response to her heartfelt plea, Mur-A-Halad appeared, looking calmer and composed: "I have knowledge of Dan. You must come with me now!"

"Where? Where is he? What's happened to him?"

"We go to the games!" he replied.

They walked briskly through the streets, the heat from the rising sun baking the paving slabs under their feet and thickening the atmosphere. Early morning aromas of fresh baked bread mingled with the now familiar smell of sweating bodies. Crowds flocked in the same direction, voices raised in cheerful chatter. They squeezed their way through the throng, past several magnificent pillared temples.

In other circumstances, Sara would have lingered to study the beautiful statues lining the wide streets, and the fine fluted pillars supporting the marbled buildings.

Even in her rush, however, she was startled to see a huge ivory statue of a Roman nobleman, clutching the end of his toga in one hand, and a rolled parchment in the other. His manner indicated he was about to address an audience. His gaze was clear, his expression open and he radiated an air of command.

It was the figure in Dan's cellar, thousands of miles and years away.

On they rushed, and as they rounded a corner, Sara was amazed at the huge amphitheatre in front of them. Circus Maximus soared into the sky, an incredible stone and marble structure several stories high and hundreds of metres in length. Thousands of people clustered through the massive entry gates.

"This is the people's day", Mur-A-Halad announced. "Today there are chariot races, gladiator battles, and a feast of entertainment with lions and elephants".

"That's all very well, but what about Dan?"

Mur-A-Halad looked embarrassed, and tried to pretend he hadn't heard. He took her arm, and started to guide her through the crowds into the amphitheatre.

Sara held her ground, and repeated herself: "I said – what about Dan?"

He replied in a rush: "Dan has been taken by the guards. He is imprisoned".

"What!" Sara shrieked, "What do you mean? How can he have been imprisoned? Where is he? Take me to him! We must rescue him!"

Mur-A-Halad flushed and said in a low voice: "We will try, but I think it will be difficult".

Sara gave herself a mental shake, realising she had to stay calm. She breathed deeply for a moment and felt her energy levels rise. This calmed Mur-A-Halad too.

She said: "Right!" Let's go get him!"

They went into Circus Maximus. Inside the entry were dozens of trading stalls spread along the inner walls, bustling with trade. Pastry and bread stalls, with delicious baking aromas, competed for trade with stalls selling appetising roast chickens and sausages. Fortune-tellers, wine merchants and citrus smelling fruit stalls were doing a roaring trade, and around them and in the open spaces under the magnificent marble of the tiered seating above, were jugglers, acrobats and the inevitable beggars.

Mur-A-Halad moved determinedly through the throng to stairs through an archway, and they followed these up several levels in the cool shade of the marble.

Suddenly, they reached the top and Sara gasped in surprise. They were in the middle of one end of the stadium, as high as they could get.

The place was almost full – tens of thousands of people sat in steep tiers round a gigantic area the size of at least four football pitches. A moat filled with water and small boats formed an outer ring to a sandy track sparkling with bright mineral specks. Gleaming white statues marked the boundaries of the track.

At the far end, under an awning were twelve stables, with chariots and horses being readied to race, and in the middle of the arena a protective tarpaulin covered a large sunken area.

Sara took everything in, hugely impressed by the scale of the scene. She tugged Mur-A-Halad's sleeve. "Where will we find Dan?"

She paled as he pointed at the middle of the arena. The excited chatter of the crowd began to quieten, and Sara saw below, a balcony, covered in flowers and garlands and draped with purple fabric. Two figures rose from their thrones. She immediately recognised Fulvia so guessed the other was Mark Anthony.

Silence washed over the crowd and in a loud clear voice, Mark Anthony exclaimed: "People of Rome – let the games begin!"

The acoustics within the amphitheatre were amazing. His voice rolled clearly around the stadium, and an express train of a roar followed it as the crowd stood up to echo their approval.

Mark Anthony and Fulvia waved to all parts of the crowd,

which responded like a tidal Mexican Wave. It took Sara's breath away, but before she could even think, a line of trumpeters stood up in front of the purple swathed balcony, and loudly blasted a fanfare that well and truly set the crowd alight.

Their pent up excitement erupted into cheer after cheer.

Sara's attention was drawn to the centre of the arena. She saw the tarpaulin slowly being pulled back to reveal an underground row of covered cages, the outline of their bars under thin covers clear in the blazing sunshine. The crowd swelled with anticipation, and then gradually the noise abated, till there was complete silence.

All eyes focused on the cage in the middle, which rose up on a platform. Agonisingly slowly, it crept up to ground level. A gladiator stood in front of it, holding a short sword in one hand and an edge of the cover in the other.

The crowd began to cheer again as the cage reached the level of the arena, sliding to a stop to a communal roar. The gladiator dramatically waved his sword, and tugged the cover free.

Inside were four figures standing at the back of the cage. In front of them paced an enormous snarling lion. The crowd clapped louder as the gladiator rolled away the stone holding the metal gate closed. Through the bars of the cage, Sara saw three of the people inside were much taller than the fourth.

As the small person moved towards the gate past the lion, Sara felt a ripple like an electric shock run through her body.

It was Dan, roared on by the crowd.

Chapter 31

Even as he was captured, Dan realised there was no point in struggling.

The soldiers were grim faced as they marched him through the deserted streets. They took him to a large blank walled building where he was handed over to a tall imposing guard who frowned silently at him.

Dan was terrified, but tried desperately to appear calm by breathing deeply and summoning his reserves of inner strength. He knew if he could keep his energy high and think positively, things would turn out well, but had to work hard to stop thinking the worst.

The guard barked at him in a stern commanding voice: "Boy! What were you doing breaking the curfew?"

"I didn't know there was a curfew. I was following someone from Mark Anthony's villa and got lost. I tripped and fell, and your soldiers caught me trying to get up".

"You were in Mark Anthony's villa, were you?"

"Yes. You see, Sara and I are here for a few days from Britain, and I wanted to explore Rome. I've never been here before and wanted to see the city at night".

"So if we speak to Mark Anthony, boy, will he confirm your story?"

Dan hesitated, realising he hadn't seen Mark Anthony. His heart sank as he took in the fact this was serious: "Well, we didn't actually meet him, but we were going to. You see, he was busy seeing people all through the evening, and he didn't have enough time to come to us."

The guard laughed: "You say you're from Britain, boy. We don't get many visitors from Britain. How did you travel here?"

"Well, that's a bit difficult to explain. You see, I live in a little village in Scotland, and in the cellar, there's this rug, and----"

His voice tailed off as he realised how silly he sounded.

The guard roared with laughter again, and shouted over his shoulder: "Dominter! We've got a right one here. Let's add him to the list for tomorrow. Put him in with the silent threesome. That'll sort him out. Maybe he'll talk sense then."

A small wiry soldier joined them, and hustled Dan through a passageway to a cell. He unlocked it, pushed Dan to the floor inside, and slammed the door closed.

Dan looked up to see three tall proud looking men gazing curiously at him. They were longhaired and heavily bearded. Their robes were worn and dirty, and all were barefoot. There was an embarrassed silence, which Dan broke.

"Em. Hello. I'm Dan."

One of the men spoke softly. "Dan. That's a very strange name. Have you no more name?"

"Well, it's Dan Goodwin actually. I'm from Britain – Scotland, from a place called Mistlees in Perthshire."

As he spoke and saw the men's puzzled reaction, he realised how hard it was to explain where he was from and how he had got here. Every time he tried, he seemed to get deeper and deeper in trouble. He gritted his teeth and asked, "Who are you then?"

The men conferred briefly with each other, and Dan sensed they were worried he had been sent to spy on them. They seemed to agree on a course of action, and the tallest man turned back to Dan and bowed: "We are political prisoners. I am Chad-Eb, and my friends are Darsheg and Nechasha-Om."

The two others bowed as they were introduced.

Dan couldn't help but grin, and said: "And you thought my name was strange!"

The trio looked at each other, and Dan, realising he may have upset them, quickly rushed on: "Why are you locked up here? And where are we?"

Chad-Eb said they had been arrested the previous day, and held for questioning, as they were new to the city, and suspected of being agitators.

"We merely wish to go about our business, but believe we will be sport for the lions at the games in the morning."

"Sport for the lions? Games? Oh no, surely not!"

They nodded as one, and as if there was no more to say, sat down cross-legged on the floor. Dan himself slumped down in despair. He knew he was in desperate trouble now, and frantically wondered how he could escape. He wished hard for help, concentrating as he'd learned over the past weeks, clearing his mind of his panic and concerns as best as he could.

After a few moments, he heard a gentle rustle beside him, and breathed a sigh of relief as Vohumanah appeared. The three men seemed not to notice, sunk in their own thoughts.

"Oh Vohumanah. Thank goodness. I'm at my wits end. I know I shouldn't have gone out on my own, but I've been locked up. These men say we're going to be sport for the lions tomorrow. This can't be happening. I must get out!"

The angel relaxed Dan with his presence, and as he spoke, Dan felt his words surround him like a protective cloak: "There is no gain in dwelling on what has been. That has passed and cannot be changed. You must trust in your energy, and your life force.

Your strength is great. Your mind is the key to unlock this prison cell. Remain positive. Know that you will triumph over what is now. It will pass, but you will continue."

Dan felt himself fill with an incredible certainty that he would come through unscathed. He felt at once strong, positive and purposeful, and instinctively knew he must also conserve his energy for the morning. As these feelings washed through him, he felt Vohumanah dissolve into the gloom of the cell, leaving him with his three new companions.

He lay down and slept for a while. The clanking of keys in the door woke him, and all four got to their feet. Three guards left a large basin of water and some thin gruel in pottery cups. Darsheg, Chad-Eb and Nechasha-Om drank deeply from the water, and motioned Dan to do the same. They all splashed their bleary eyes and faces. The three men formed a circle, closed their eyes and began to pray softly.

Oddly, Dan felt his spirits rise with the excitement of events. As he looked round the cell, he saw a black fuzzy shape slouched in the corner, indistinct in the gloom. With a start, he saw it was the figure he had followed from Mark Anthony's villa.

"Who are you?" He exclaimed.

The figure stood up, and its outline sharpened to reveal a tall thin elegant man, dressed like a picture from an old book. He wore a black robe with a white collar, and from the thick leather belt round his waist hung a set of keys and a sheaf of papers. His hair was grey and his eyes hooded, his serious face long and angular.

He spoke in a deep clear tone: "At last, young Daniel, you see me!"

Dan stepped back instinctively: "What!" He declared.

"I have tried many times to reveal myself, but your eyes have been veiled. I am Timothy, your friend from the cellar!"

"From the cellar!" Dan exclaimed, "How can you be from the cellar?"

Timothy replied: "I have lived in your cellar for many many years. When Peter left, I was alone until you came, but you could not see me."

Dan gasped: "You're the ghost!"

Timothy laughed, an echoing rolling sound. He bowed: "The very same!"

"So it was you who moved all the models around!"

"Yes!"

"And you who's been brushing against me, and following us round the village."

Timothy frowned: "I have tried to make you aware of my presence, but cannot go beyond the cellar's earthly bounds."

Dan looked puzzled: "Well, who are you, and how are you here?"

"I am Timothy Pont, minister and mapmaker. You may call me T.P., my mapmaking signature. When you and Sara travel, I travel with you."

Dan thought for a moment: "That explains a lot! You helped us on to Fafa's back, didn't you?"

"Indeed!"

"And did you turn the pages of our codex?"

"Ah, what a wondrous find!"

Dan thought: "You're a mapmaker. Were you in the tent at Tara – annoying the man doing his map?"

"Pah! A primitive scribe with no talent!"

"And was it you who helped us escape from those horrible rebel angels?"

T.P.'s face clouded: "The forces of evil must not prevail. I did what a man of the cloth must do!"

"You punched them!"

They both laughed.

Dan thought for a second: "Did you practise with the Vashad Thains?"

T.P. looked sheepish: "I was not ready when he hit me."

Dan laughed: "We heard you gasp! But why did you lead me out of Mark Anthony's villa?"

"That was not meant to occur. I went to map the city, and did not know you followed."

"How do you mean, map the city?"

"I am a mapmaker. I sketch towns and villages, and in my own time, travelled the country to chart its mountains, rivers, coastlines and all between". He patted the papers at his waist, and Dan saw the front sheet was a rough sketch of streets and buildings.

"That's incredible," he said, "But now we're both stuck in this cell. We need to get out!"

Dan felt another surge of confidence, boosted by T.P.'s presence. He looked at each of his three cellmates, who stopped praying. Dan felt his energy wash over them. They looked surprised and grateful, and Dan was astonished at how calm he felt.

The guards came back to the cell, and one barked: "Well, you lot – anything you want to say? Any confessions to make maybe?"

Even as he spoke, giving them no time to reply, he motioned his fellow soldiers to take them out of the cell. They were blindfolded and led down the corridor and outside. Dan felt the humidity of the early morning air, and breathed deep lungfuls of air much fresher than in the cell.

They were marched for a long time, in silence, and Dan felt the atmosphere change as if they were entering another building, but still in the open air.

They were halted, blindfolds removed and pushed one by one into a metal cage. As Dan's eyes refocused, he saw to his horror an enormous lion slumbering against the bars at the far end of the cage. He realised it couldn't reach them as there was a metal barrier penning it in and separating them from it, but the size of the beast made him wince.

The guards exchanged looks, cracked a joke, threw a thin cover over the whole cage and left them. The three men and Dan, in the semi gloom, exchanged glances, and Dan could see that, whilst the others were clearly frightened, they were resigned to their fate. T.P. stood silently looking at the lion.

Noise came from all around the cage. He heard swords clashing, voices raised in anger and protest, horses whinnying, and shouts of encouragement. He smelt the steam from the horses' exertion and the lion's foul breath.

Nechasha-Om, standing next to him, told him they were in the underground holding area for the stadium above - Circus Maximus: "The sounds are those who practise for the games. Some will live and others die. We will be the first", he said. "Caesar begins always with the lions."

"When do the games start?" asked Dan.

Chad-Eb said thoughtfully, "I think we will not be long. Listen!"

The rising murmur of voices reached them through the immediate sounds. The volume of noise grew and grew, and for the next twenty minutes or so, Dan listened intently, absorbing everything, as the atmosphere intensified.

Worryingly, the lion had awoken with the hubbub around it, and was snarling, tossing its golden brown mane angrily as it paced backwards and forwards fretfully.

Suddenly the sounds from the stadium reached a crescendo, and wave after wave of cheering reached their ears. Dan was prepared mentally, but was still very nervous, and just as his positive thoughts wavered, and he thought about Vohumanah's words, the cage began to rise, pushed from below by some unseen mechanism.

All of them stumbled slightly, thrown off balance, and the lion roared loudly, its yellowed teeth dripping saliva, its putrid breath washing over them. T.P. stood in front of it, arms raised as if to block its view of the four others.

Dan tightened up and suddenly saw the air in front of him solidify into the fluttering shape of Metatron. His three companions talked together in low voices, not seeing his arrival.

"This is your time, when your moment is nigh, and the minutes arrive", he intoned. "You must show no fear – be not afraid. You will lead your friends to safety, guide them without harm, and free them from the lion's wrath. You will know what to do, the action to take, and all will be well and everything good".

He disappeared quietly, and Dan *did* know what to do.

As the cage rose to ground level, and the level of light increased, he looked carefully at Chad-Eb, Darsheg and Nechasha-Om and saw their energy fields glowing dimly around their heads and shoulders. With a conscious and sustained effort, he became fully aware of his own intense energy, felt his confidence soar, and saw the bubble of his energy field enveloping all three men.

Their auras brightened, and began to glow with warmth and colour. The atmosphere between them became a bond that created an invincible energy field. T.P. waved his arms at the lion, and Dan even raised a smile at the comical picture this ghostly figure presented.

The cage stopped rising, the cover pulled away, the barrier between them and the lion was raised, and they were in the middle of Circus Maximus' roaring atmosphere.

Chapter 32

The four of them, led by Dan, walked right past the roaring lion, confident no harm would come to them. T.P. continued to wave his arms at the lion, which seemed completely disorientated by the incredible volume of noise from the crowd which stood clapping, cheering and shouting, amazed by the staggering spectacle of one small boy leading three men past a man-eating lion.

Dan walked confidently into the huge arena, looked carefully around and headed for the purple balcony where Mark Anthony and Fulvia sat.

The lion came cautiously out of the cage, whisked its tail busily and sat down. T.P. sat beside it.

The crowd began to jeer, their anticipation of a one-sided fight spoiled.

The jeering quickly turned to thunderous applause however when the small group of four stopped below the balcony. As Mark Anthony rose to his feet, the crowd could see he now wore the bright red toga of the victorious competitor. He wore a wreath of golden leaves.

Slowly, the crowd grew quiet, and he raised an ivory baton topped with a golden flying eagle. He raised it horizontally, and the crowd held its breath, aware that life or death for Dan and the three men now depended on his decision.

He held the baton for what seemed like an eternity to Sara watching from above, heart in mouth. Suddenly, he lifted it high above his head to signify release, and the stadium exploded with joy for the heroes from the lion's cage.

In the arena, Dan faced Chad-Eb, Darsheg and Nechasha-Om.

One by one, they bowed proudly to Dan, who grinned infectiously, relief at their incredible escape obvious. The men thanked Dan.

"We owe you our lives", said Chad-Eb.

"We did it together," replied Dan. "And we had some help from above!"

"I think our salvation came from within", said Nechasha-Om.

Through the cheers of the crowd, Dan felt rather than heard a thin piercing cry from the crowd: "Dan! Dan! Up here!"

He looked above the balcony and saw Sara waving frantically, Mur-A-Halad at her side. He waved back, and Fulvia tugged Mark Anthony's sleeve. They conferred for a second before he signalled two of his guards.

While the arena was cleared, Dan and his companions were escorted to the stables, where the guards met them. Charioteers were readying their horses and chariots for the races while Dan said farewell to his three friends.

Within minutes, he was reunited with Sara, and they hugged each other in delight. All round them, citizens patted him on the back. The atmosphere was buzzing.

Sara was desperate to hear Dan's story, and during the day's games, Dan told her everything.

However, before they could talk to each other, the first chariot race began, and it was like nothing they had ever seen. The chariot drivers wore white, green, blue and red tunics. The chariots gleamed in the sunshine, their trim and wheels sparkling with the colours of their drivers.

Everyone was talking about the fierce rivalry between the competitors. The favourite for the race, steering the red chariot was called Dorius. The track was a long oval.

Mark Anthony dropped a white napkin, triggering a loud trumpet blast to start the race, and the four chariots, each drawn by four horses in line abreast, were off.

The red chariot edged in front on the first lap, nearly toppling over as it veered round the wooden post marking the turning point, the blue chariot pushing it hard. The white and green chariots locked wheels as they entered the turn, and the drivers frantically tried to keep their chariots upright, all eight horses packed tightly together, straining to get in front. They somehow managed to stay on course, but lost ground to the leading two.

Up ahead, the red driver, whip in hand, urged his magnificent team of horses on, tightly braided tails waving high above their gleaming black coats. The crowd urged him on, chanting: "Do-Do-Do-Do-Do-Do-Dorius! Do-Do-Do-Do-Do-Do-Dorius!"

Dorius responded, his mounts leaping further ahead. The blue driver, head tightly helmeted, leggings wrapped all the way up his legs for protection, whipped his horses on in pursuit, their breastplates studded with bloodstones and rubies.

The crowd roared on their favourites, and booed their rivals. The noise was deafening, the excitement almost unbearable. As they chased round the track, dust flying from the charging wheels, the red chariot gradually increased its lead despite the best efforts of the blue driver, himself pursued closer and closer by the other two teams, still neck and neck.

Seven large wooden eggs in front of the stables were moved, one by one, to mark the passage of the laps. With one egg left in place, and six laps gone, Dorius in the red chariot whipped round the second last turning post, the two outside horses visibly foaming and streaked with sweat, straining inwards to keep the other two from pushing the chariot over.

Dorius stood tall, reins wrapped around his body, and cracked his whip above the horses' straining necks. They pulled further away from the blue team.

The white team drew level with the blues and pushed them out to the edge of the track. At the same time, the green team pulled level on the inside, and the three teams hurtled down the straight together, dust from the reds blinding them.

Dorius coaxed his horses round the final post to a soaring cheer from the crowd, and he pulled off towards the finishing post twenty yards clear of his pursuers.

The three other teams pulled in to the final bend locked together.

The blue team on the outside crowded the other two and they careered, seemingly out of control, round the final post, the green team's horses bumping it as they swivelled round. The driver grabbed the pole and used it as a lever to accelerate the turn, and the greens shot into the last straight ahead.

The four dappled brown horses positively soared down the straight, almost catching the red team as they crossed the finishing line victorious, Dorius already waving to the cheering crowd.

The blue team horses were nudged further out by the whites, and suddenly their wheels locked. After an agonising few seconds, there was a loud crack, and the inner wheel of the blue chariot split apart, the chariot rocked wildly and its driver was hurled over the heads of the horses. His reins broke with the strain and the crowd gasped as he rolled under the wheels of the white chariot as it crossed the line in third place.

Miraculously, the horses stayed upright, but the chariot

upended and splintered as they reached the finish, the blue driver trampled underfoot.

All round them, people jumped up and down, cheered themselves hoarse and hugged. Sara and Dan were breathless with the excitement and the drama.

On the track, the red chariot skidded to a stop in a swirl of dust. Dorius cut himself free of his reins with his dagger and jumped down. Before he could reach his horses, stable boys, trainers, grooms, and a host of other supporters swamped him.

Despite their shock at the fate of the blue driver, Dan and Sara couldn't help but be gripped by the incredible atmosphere.

In between the chariot races, the huge crowd was entertained by trick riders who galloped bare backed, standing up, lying down, sitting backwards and straddling underneath their horses at full tilt. They jumped over fences, zig zagged round a course of gaily-coloured poles, and ran mock races for the crowd.

In mid afternoon, Mark Anthony and Fulvia left Circus Maximus. Dan overheard people talking about the vital Senate meeting he had to attend, and wondered what would happen. Sara picked up his thought and nodded silently in agreement. She was desperate to hear more about T.P., their friendly ghost: "Where is he anyway?" She asked. Dan scanned the arena and the stadium, but couldn't see him.

Mur-A-Halad told them they had to leave, and the disappointed pair were led off, their upset tempered by the fact that the gladiator fights were about to begin. Sara said, "I really don't want to see them killing each other".

Dan agreed as they battled through the crowd, down the stairs, past the bustling trading stalls, and back into the street.

The atmosphere was strangely calm, but Dan sensed an ominous tension in the air. "What's happening, Mur-A-Halad?"

He looked serious as he replied: "The Senate meet to make important resolutions. My master will lead the debate. All the Senators will be there. This is a unique occasion. May the Gods decree a good outcome".

"What will we do now then?" asked Sara as they strolled back to Mark Anthony's villa.

Unexpectedly, Mur-A-Halad grinned and said, "We will have our own games!"

When they arrived home, he ushered them into a small room at the back of the villa perfumed with the delightful aroma of cedar. He produced a black chessboard, eight squares by twelve, and taught them to play latrunculi, the Roman version of chess.

Dan quickly got the hang of the movements of the twelve men, called latro, which captured their opponents by enclosing them on two sides, vertical or horizontal. He lured Mur-A-Halad's king behind his squadron of advancing latro, and captured him to win the game.

Mur-A-Halad was clearly surprised by Dan getting the better of him.

Sara preferred micatio, played by two people simultaneously raising fingers on their right hands, keeping them hidden till the last moment. The players had to guess aloud the total number of fingers raised between them.

She beat Mur-A-Halad, who was astonished: "I am a soothsayer, and have never been bettered at micatio!"

Sara grinned hugely, but soon found Dan her match, neither gaining any advantage over the other, and both together guessing correctly in an extraordinary number of rounds. Mur-A-Halad was fascinated: "You seem to think the other's thoughts – to see the other's moves and to know your end results."

Dan and Sara exchanged a conspiratorial look as the door burst open.

A slave burst in, her toga fluttering in disarray: "Caesar is dead! Murdered in the Senate!"

It was Miss Ambrose.

Chapter 33

A loud gasp escaped Sara's lips, and Dan paled, but Mur-A-Halad seemed perfectly calm.

"The Ides of March have come, but they have not yet gone", he said in a low voice, and then, much louder, addressed the slave: "Where is our master?"

"He is coming home. The senate has collapsed. Rome is in chaos!"

Dan asked tentatively: "Miss Ambrose?"

Sara elbowed him and said: "Don't be silly, it can't be – it just looks like her."

The woman looked straight at Dan without a hint of recognition, and he studied her features. The shape of her face was similar to Miss Ambrose, but she wore heavy black eye make up which shrouded her eyes, and her eyebrows were heavily pencilled in dark lines which gave her a more sinister appearance. Her face was caked in white makeup, so he couldn't see if she had freckles. She had red hair, but it was curly and short.

Dan said: "No, you're right, but it's very like her."

Suddenly, Mark Anthony appeared, looking pale but with a faint smile on his lips.

"Master", said Mur-A-Halad, "The deed is done?"

"The deed is done, soothsayer. But not complete. We will meet tomorrow to arrange matters further."

Dan realised this was an amazing opportunity to find out about events at the Senate, and he plucked up courage to ask: "What happened today, Mark Anthony?"

Mark Anthony's distant gaze vanished and he focussed on Dan and Sara.

"Ah! Our brave lion conqueror! I am sorry we did not meet before now, but this has been a busy time. Yes –a busy time."

He sat down on the couch opposite them, and said, "It is good for you to hear the story of the day's proceedings for this is a new beginning for Rome. Caesar has been a leader standing head and shoulders above others. He has fashioned our State with great foresight. However, in recent times, he has ruled without the will of the people. He believes himself capable of no fault, and will hear no man's voice raised against him. This was never his right, never his privilege."

He looked thoughtfully at them, and said: "Now Rome will begin again. We will erase from the statutes the acts of Caesar, and the Senate will rule again!"

Sara looked at him, sensing the pride with which he spoke. "YOU planned his murder!" She exclaimed.

"Brutus, Casca and my other faithfuls have blood on their hands, young lady, but it will wash away the grasp of Caesar".

Sara shook her head in dismay: "You can never justify taking a life", she said defiantly.

Mark Anthony did not acknowledge her words, instead gripping the edge of the couch to stand up: "I think your time here is over, young ones. Mur-A-Halad will see you are safe".

He swept out of the room, leaving an unsettled atmosphere behind. Mur-A-Halad and the slave who had brought the news from the Senate gazed after him. Dan said quietly to Sara: "That was a pretty brave thing to say, considering what he's just done!"

"I guess so, but I had to say it. It was important to me. Part of being true to myself." She nodded gently as she spoke, as if further convincing herself.

Dan stood up and stretched. He smiled at Sara, and said:"Well done, Sara. I'm really proud of you!"

He turned to Mur-A-Halad. "Well then. You heard what your master said. How are you going to get us home?"

The soothsayer flushed, and looked bewildered: "Home! Yes – home! I must get you home. I must see the route is clear". He spoke in an aside to the slave, who quickly left the room.

They waited patiently for ten minutes, Mur-A-Halad pacing up and down, sunk in thought, while Dan and Sara reflected together on the day's momentous events. Mur-A-Halad muttered something under his breath about the slave, and went to find her. In his place, in the doorway, T.P. appeared, and before Dan could say anything, Sara exclaimed: "Dan! Dan! I can see him! He's all in black! Look!"

T.P. bowed to Sara, clicking his heels noiselessly.

"Dan, how can we see him now?"

It was T.P. who replied: "You have now succeeded in seeing your own energy fields, so my world is open to you!"

"You mean if we can see our auras, we can see you too?" Asked Sara.

"Indeed!"

"Oh, wow, this is scary!"

T.P. looked offended.

"No, no, I don't mean *you're* scary, I mean it's scary we can see a ghost!"

"I am no ordinary ghost!" T.P. huffed.

Dan grinned, and asked: "Where have you been?"

"Hither and thither, here and there," he replied airily, fingering the bulging mass of papers at his waist.

"Ah! Mapmaking!" said Dan.

Mur-A-Halad reappeared with the Miss Ambrose look-alike, and nodded at the children. They led them through the villa, past the now heavily guarded front door. The slave stayed behind while Mur-A-Halad looked left and right before walking briskly up the street.

Rome was deserted. The slap of their sandaled footsteps echoed from the high walls. T.P. trailed behind, still sketching furiously. Sara knew intuitively where they were heading: "We're going to Circus Maximus!" She told Dan.

"That makes sense! As long as we can figure out how to get back from there". They heard a companionable humming from the air beside them as Zuphlas appeared and kept up with them as they scurried through the streets.

Mur-A-Halad abruptly stopped and said, "You are with one who will protect you well. My job is done. The Ides rush on. Good fortune to you both!"

He bowed and walked back without a second glance.

T.P. had disappeared.

"Well!" Said Dan, "That's us then! Sorted!"

Sara snorted. "Come on Dan! Get your energies going! We're nearly there!"

Zuphlas shimmered ahead of them, his voice quavering from the air around him: "We must be swift. Before the evening falls is your time to go".

They entered the massive gates of the stadium, and negotiated past empty stalls and through deserted passageways. Zuphlas led them down a ramp along a covered tunnel marked with a marble sign - INNIUS MOAT. They passed under the moat, and entered the stadium at the base of a statue of a woman scattering seeds from a basket. Beautifully carved birds perched on her shoulders.

The name on the plinth under the statue read: GAIA. Dan and Sara looked at each other meaningfully as they passed the Nature Goddess.

Zuphlas hovered at a point halfway along the east side of the vast stadium, and they saw a circle chalked with Roman numerals, for all the world like a giant sundial. The sun created a dark shadow stretching from the central stone marker. It was creeping up on the numeral VII.

"That's our gateway!" Gasped Dan.

Zuphlas left them silently, and Dan and Sara walked towards the circle.

Suddenly, the air blackened, and they found it hard to breathe. In front of them were the two rebel angels, two dark figures, more solid than before, and with a thin film of flame around their heads. They approached Dan and Sara slowly, their glowing eyes piercing the gloom they had created. Their ragged grey clothes covered them and dragged along the ground. The air smelt foul.

The larger of the two cackled loudly, filling the air with an even viler stench: "*See, Azazel! Their pathetic angel guide has deserted them. Shall we show them a darker realm?*"

Azazel raised his grizzly arms and shook them wildly: "*Oh yes, Samahazai, to the River, to the ferryman! Ha! Ha! Ha!*"

They separated, and moved closer. Dan stood protectively in front of Sara. He was surprisingly calm, though Sara was visibly trembling.

"Get out of our road!" He demanded, and took a step forward.

The rebel angels doubled up with laughter, and Azazel declared: "*You puny human, you have no idea of the power we wield.*

You will come with us, prisoners for the nether world."

Sara shrieked with terror, and Dan's resolve began to give way.

Samahazai was within a metre of them, and he stretched out his wizened stump of an arm.

It was grasped immediately by T.P., who materialised between them. With a face like thunder, and in a voice of huge authority, he bellowed: "Begone, you vile scum, you parasites of the earth. How dare you meddle with these innocents, these children of this earth!"

"*We will take you too, preacher!*" Screeched Azazel, as he reached for T.P.

Like a flash, T.P. grabbed Azazel's arm with his own free hand, and with one rebel angel gripped firmly in each arm, he spun round like a hammer thrower, completing two full turns before letting them go. They spun off into Circus Maximus, Samahazai yelling: "*Your time will come, preacher man!*"

T.P. collapsed, gasping, and Dan realised they had to move fast. Daylight was fading quickly, and there was no time to lose.

They ran together into the circle of Roman numerals, Dan and Sara dragging T.P. between them, as the sun's setting shadow reached seven o'clock. Their world span as they were sucked forwards in time, still catching their breath.

Chapter 34

Even as they watched, the circle's vivid red colour assumed its normal dullness.

T.P. sat up and smiled a thin smile.

Sara said: "Thank you T.P., you were just in time!"

He inclined his head: "It was indeed my pleasure! But now I must recover."

He walked away from them and vanished between the rows of shelving. Dan shook his head in disbelief: "That was close!"

"It sure was! These rebel angels are horrible!"

"And dangerous!"

"We were lucky T.P. was with us."

"He told me he's been here all along, but said he's tied to the cellar here."

"How can he travel with us then?

"I don't know, but I'm glad he can!"

"Me too!" Sara replied, "I feel like we're living two lives – one's kind of normal, here in the village, and the other's like an extended dream, travelling through time."

"And they somehow squeeze themselves into the same days and weeks. We've been in Rome for what seems like ages, but time hasn't budged again here".

"How do you know it hasn't moved?"

"I'll check my Rainbow Catcher". He did, and grinned: "We've been away for only moments. We leave here one moment and come back the next, but days have gone by in our other life. It's fantastic!"

"If we could do that in our normal lives, we could add days on to the weekend, couldn't we?"

They laughed, but Sara quickly stopped as she thought about their experiences in Rome: "I'd thought Mark Anthony was a good character, but he was the worst of the lot!" She said.

"Yes, I know. Shakespeare says Brutus led the conspirators, but Mark Anthony was the ringleader after all."

Sara nodded and said, "You were amazing in the stadium! I thought I'd lost you, and then when I saw you in that cage, I really believed something awful would happen. You were so calm, so confident. I wish I had been as certain as you that things would be OK".

"I realised I *had* to get through the trial I was in – there was no other option. Inside myself, I was worried, but I was pretty positive things would turn out OK."

"But you didn't know that for absolute certain".

"I had to in that lion's cage!" Dan exclaimed, grinning.

"I suppose that's true – your belief was so strong and intense it became a self-fulfilling prophecy".

"Hmm - a good way of putting it. When I felt positive, my energy field just filled up and out to wrap round the others. It felt amazing!"

They sat in companionable silence for a while. Sara broke it: "We're going to the museum in the morning!"

"Oh! So we are. I'd forgotten. Nigel's picking us up isn't he?"

"Yes, around 9 o'clock – and your dad's coming too!"

"Do you think it's about the codex?"

"Well, I can't think of anything else. Remember Nigel said he'd show it to a friend. Maybe the friend works at the Museum".

"I'm dying to find out what the secrets of the codex are. It's obviously very special."

Hugh appeared at the top of the steps, and climbed down to join them.

Dan took deep breaths to calm himself: "Hi dad! We've been looking at our project. Only a few weeks left to get it finished".

"Good, good", said Hugh, obviously distracted. "I gather I've been organised for the morning! Where are we off to?"

Dan replied cautiously, "Nigel's taking us to the museum in Edinburgh".

"Why's that?"

"Well, we're not exactly sure, but we think it's to do with a kind of book we found a while back. We gave it to Nigel who said he'd get a friend to check it out".

"What book? Where did you find it?"

Sara came to the rescue, saying: "It's an unusual book we stumbled across when we were doing our project, and we think it's pretty old, so we thought Nigel would be the best person to investigate".

"OK. Fair enough. What time are we off?"

"He's picking us up about 9, dad".

"That's fine. Right, I'm off to read the paper – haven't had time today at all.

How's the Rainbow Catcher, Dan?"

"It's brilliant! We've used it for all sorts of research, and we've tested all the functions. It is a bit fiddly to work the controls, because they're so small, but that's the only drawback so far".

"Good! Make sure you use it well in the next ten days or so. I want to do a report to the Company, and I'll tell them what you say about it. And look after it! It's very valuable and mustn't fall into the wrong hands."

"OK, dad. We'll see you later".

The children stayed in the cellar for a while. They looked at the ley lines, and Dan shivered with excitement: "These lines must run between the church and the graveyard, and from the sunken chapel to the old tower!"

"And we're in the middle of it all – the centre of the energy the lines create!"

"But there's still lots to work out, Sara. This table for instance. What's it all about? There are things on it we've seen on our travels – the dinosaurs, Phaelar with his staff, and is that not Nuada with his silver hand?"

Sara looked closely and replied: "Yes, it is! Well spotted!"

Dan continued: "And look – that statue's from Rome, isn't it?"

"The guy with the scroll – you saw it too then?"

"Of course I did -----." His voice tailed off suddenly. "I don't think I did see it Sara, but I somehow knew you had, and remembered it through your eyes."

"Oh wow! How did that happen?"

"I've no idea, but it feels a bit like that dream we had the other night, when you seemed to dream one part of it, and I dreamed the other."

Sara shivered as Dan had.

Chapter 35

Picking them up on Saturday morning, Nigel tooted his old Volvo's horn.

He was wreathed in smiles, his face a beacon of happiness. Even Hugh could not stop smiling at his infectious manner. "Good morning, Nigel. What are we up to this morning?"

"Good morning yourself, Mr Goodwin. Hello Dan. Hello Sara. There's an exhibition in the Royal Museum I thought Dan and Sara might enjoy. It's been running for a week or two, and I've heard it's very good – very interesting".

"What's it about?" Hugh asked.

"Ah! Let's surprise ourselves!" Nigel replied as he drove off. Dan and Sara sat in the back seat, excited by the morning ahead. As they left the village, they saw Mrs Braid wave at somebody, but what they didn't notice was a dark car following, keeping its distance behind them.

Nigel said, "The only trouble with Edinburgh on a Saturday is parking. It can be a nightmare!"

Dan said, "Come on Nigel – think positive. We'll get parked OK!"

Hugh gave Dan a puzzled look over his shoulder, as Nigel replied, "I'm sure you're right. We'll be fine".

The trip was quick, with no queues on the Forth Road Bridge, and as they drove through the city centre, Dan began to focus on parking. As they turned into Chambers Street with its central row of parking meters, there were two buses unloading parties of schoolchildren. Nigel crawled slowly along, looking for a space, and Dan willed for one too. The dark car followed a few cars behind.

As they passed the museum, a car began to reverse out, and Dan and Sara shouted: "There's one!"

Nigel glided the old car in, fed the meter, and they walked past the modern building of the Museum of Scotland to the steps of the old Royal Museum.

Nigel explained that the Museum of Scotland had been built a few years ago, and it housed a tremendous range of exhibits and items of historical note telling the history of Scotland. This had allowed the original museum more space to house exhibitions and display its collection of millions of items.

The old building was hugely impressive, its broad imposing Victorian frontage and pillars forming a striking centrepiece to Chambers Street. They walked up the steps behind the schoolchildren, past the museum attendants, and into the huge entrance hall.

The children were stunned.

Above them swirled stars and planets, twinkling in the reflected light of the Sun, which sat huge and glowing at the centre of an amazing revolving display.

Nigel's beam echoed the Sun's as he proudly announced: "Welcome to our Solar System!"

The floor of the museum was packed with children gazing upwards, awestruck by the massive scale of the exhibition. Closest to the Sun but dwarfed by its giant mass, were Mercury, Venus, the Earth and Mars, each hardly more than half a metre in diameter, compared to the Sun, which was half the size of a football pitch hanging in the centre of the open gallery. Jupiter, the beautiful ringed Saturn and the curiously green Uranus were also much bigger than Earth. The planets slowly orbited the Sun, flashing and glowing like an oversized spotlight. Through the display were thousands of twinkling stars.

It was breathtaking.

Dan couldn't believe the difference in size between the Earth and the Sun. The sign in the middle of the room told him the Sun was 109 times the diameter of the Earth. Its temperatures varied from seething surface gases at 5,500 degrees Centigrade to an estimated 15 million degrees at the Sun's core.

He was interrupted by Nigel who said, "Why don't you both have a wander round. Your dad and I are going for a coffee, and I've got someone to meet. We'll catch you up later".

They needed little persuasion. There was so much to see. The rear of the first floor was in sections, and they wandered from one to the next for over an hour.

Each of the planets had an area devoted to it. There were displays showing the history of astronomy; models of various space ships, which brought back information about the planets they had visited; and a film showed how the Earth had been formed over 5 billion years ago.

They learned an incredible amount using the interactive displays.

The Babylonians, from around 3000BC, were the first known astronomers, and the Greeks were very important because they analysed and measured the sky, the stars and the planets.

The Chinese, Egyptian and Mayan people (Sara nudged Dan at this) all studied the skies and advanced knowledge and understanding of the Universe.

Dan liked the section on the brightest stars. He read that astronomers use a system of "magnitude" to tell the different brightness of the stars. The higher the magnitude number, the dimmer the star. Sara felt this was the wrong way around. "Why's 6 not brighter than 2?" she asked.

"Because they've done it the other way - so a star of magnitude 2 is much brighter than a star of magnitude 5, which isn't very bright at all," he explained to Sara. She looked unconvinced.

The museum showed a league table of the top 20 brightest stars, and apart from the Sun –brightest in the sky –Sirius was top. The table was fascinating. It listed interesting facts about the stars, including which constellation they belong to. They learned that a constellation is a group of stars, like Canis Major - the Latin name for The Greater Dog - and Orion – The Hunter. Alpha Centauri was third brightest, from the Centaurus Constellation, representing a centaur, the mythical beast that was half man and half horse.

Sara nudged Dan again and pointed to the star in tenth place – Betelgeux in the Constellation of Orion: "That's Beetlejuice from the Hitchhiker's Guide to the Galaxy!" she exclaimed, "You know, the mad guy with two heads!"

Dan laughed, as did several other children nearby. "Em, I think that's Beeblebrox – Zaphod Beeblebrox", he said.

An older boy said: "Beetlejuice was some wacky old film by Tim Burton!"

Sara was embarrassed. "Well – same kind of name anyway".

Dan replied: "If you say so, which makes the answer 42!"

Sara recovered and said: "That's if you like riddles!"

Dan was interested in the star ranked at 18. It was called Fomalhaut.

There was an asterisk beside the name, and they read the paragraph that explained:

***"Fomalhaut (pronounced "foh'-mah-low") is the 18th brightest star in the sky. It is about twice the diameter of the Sun, and is a first magnitude star.**

It is part of the Piscis Austrinus, or Southern Fish, Constellation, which has been known since ancient times.

Fomalhaut – meaning "the fish's mouth", is a blue-white star 25 light years away. It is surrounded by a huge disc of cold dust which strongly suggests there is an orbiting giant planet, as yet undiscovered, shaping the dust we see".

Dan's face screwed up with concentration as he read.

Sara said: "I like the name – it sounds like "home alone" – foh'-mah-low!"

"Yes, it does a bit. How far away is a light year?" He asked Sara.

"I don't know, but there must be something here about that".

They searched and found a sign giving the answer. It read:

"A light year is an important measure of distance. It represents the distance light travels in a year: 9.5 trillion kilometres".

Dan gasped: "Light travels faster than anything. Look at that! 9.5 trillion kilometres in a year, and Fomalhaut's 25 times further away than that!

That means that light takes 25 years to get here from there! Amazing!

Did you see there may be a planet hiding in its dust ring, Sara?"

"I know. It sounds really interesting".

"How come they've never found any life anyplace except here on Earth?"

"Yes, it's weird." She put on a high-pitched voice: *"Is there anyone out there?"*

They laughed, and Dan turned on his Rainbow Catcher to check the time.

"Oops! It's nearly half eleven. We'd better find Dad and Nigel".

As they wove their way back to the main entrance, Sara said: "What about the codex? We thought Nigel was going to tell us all about it –with his friend – remember?"

"Oh! I wonder about that. We haven't seen Dad or Nigel since we arrived".

They looked at each other, and Dan added: "If you're thinking what I'm thinking, then Dad knows about the codex!"

"And does that mean Nigel's told him about our time travels?"

"Shh!" Said Dan, as people walked past them. "Not so loud! What are we going to say if Nigel's spilled the beans?"

Sara frowned for a moment, but quickly answered: "Dan, we said – right from the start – that we'd tell the truth – and we've tried, but nobody really believes us."

"Well, if Nigel's told Dad what's been going on, will he believe it any more coming from him than from us?"

"Don't know, but we'll soon find out", replied Sara as they rounded a corner to reach the Museum entrance.

Suddenly, there was a commotion, and a figure dressed all in black burst past them, clutching a package, sprinting for the door. Behind, came Nigel and Hugh, his glasses askew. Nigel yelled in his big deep voice: "Stop! Thief! He's got the codex! Stop him!"

The figure pushed its way through the crowd, elbowing and shoving to create a path, and children shrieked as they were jostled aside. The museum security guard pulled himself up and blocked the way, but the figure shoulder charged him and swept through the door. Nigel and Hugh followed, and Nigel shouted: "Stop!" but the figure was too far ahead.

At the foot of the steps, a dark car sat, its engine running. The figure dived in the open passenger door and the car shot off, leaving Nigel and Hugh gasping on the pavement. Dan and Sara joined them as the car shot round the corner.

They were just in time to see the number plate: 669 NGL.

Chapter 36

Looking shaken and weary, Nigel slumped on the steps of the museum in the pale September sunshine. Hugh consoled him: "There was nothing you could do. He was too fast for us!"

Dan and Sara sat beside them. "What happened?" asked Dan.

Before anyone could reply, the museum guard, looking dazed, came towards them. "What did he get away with?" he asked, mobile phone in hand: "I need to phone the police!"

Nigel stared coolly at him, and the guard looked flustered. He dusted himself down, took one look at all the children crowding out of the museum to find out what was happening, and said confidently: "Right, have to sort out these kids. No discipline these days!"

He ushered them back up the steps, ignoring their clamour and questions, and gradually got control. "Everything's fine! Just settle down now and enjoy the exhibition!"

Hugh looked extremely puzzled, and Nigel said to Dan and Sara: "We all need to talk. I was telling your dad about Opportunity House and the work Peter Friis was doing".

Hugh rubbed his eyes: "Codices and time travel. It's too much to take in!"

"What about the codex?" asked Dan.

Hugh interrupted:"How did you get a hold of it? Professor Magnus Esian says it's priceless."

"Who's Professor Magnus Esian?" Sara asked.

Nigel replied: "He's an expert on Mayan and Aztec civilisations, an old friend of mine. We took the codex to show him."

Hugh butted in again: "Where did you find it, Dan?"

"In the only place you can, Dad – in their time, in their land – in Tikal".

Hugh shook his head, bewildered.

"Dad! Remember I told you about my trip to the time of the dinosaurs? That was *real* – it wasn't a dream. I know it sounds fantastic, but we've found a way of travelling through time! It works, Dad! Honestly, it works!"

"That's what Nigel said too. He says Peter used to travel through time, but that's just not possible!"

Dan and Sara looked at each other. Hugh had spoken out loud what they had both thought, but never voiced.

"So much makes sense now", Dan declared. "Peter travelled through time too! The models, the table, the markings on it----"

"Hey! Hang on!" Hugh interrupted again. "What do you mean?"

"Dad, we've travelled through time four times now – to the dinosaurs, to the Mayans, to ancient Ireland and to Rome. Each time we've been someplace, we've come back and recognised the models and the etchings on the table from the places we've been to! And we think Peter was there before us!"

"Yes, Dan," said Nigel, "And that's why your trips are so important. We must get Peter back. He's lost somewhere in time!"

There was a long stunned silence.

"And now the codex is gone," Nigel said.

"What happened?" exclaimed Dan.

Hugh said: "The Professor examined the codex for a long time. He was very impressed by it, but said he needed more time to examine the hidden codes. We didn't have time for that today, so Nigel told him he'd bring it back, but when we left his office, this thug pushed Nigel, grabbed the codex from him and ran for it!"

Sara asked: "But who else knew about the codex?"

Nigel hesitated awkwardly: "There are some in the village who know, but I can't be sure who they are and who now has the codex."

Dan persisted: "But you *must* know, Nigel. We must get it back!"

Nigel replied: "Dan, these may be dangerous people."

Hugh said: "I'm not having Dan and Sara exposed to any more danger. This time travel thing's bad enough, but if there's danger for them in the village, I'll call in the police myself!"

Dan and Sara were stunned, but Nigel calmly gazed at Hugh, who coughed, and said: "Quite right! Leave it to Nigel!"

The crackling of a walkie-talkie interrupted them. They looked up and saw a traffic warden about to write a parking ticket for Nigel's car. Dan focused hard on the tall warden, and felt a surge of energy drawn from the force of his thoughts. "NO! NO!" His mind shrieked. The warden hesitated, looked a bit confused, checked Nigel's windscreen and his watch, shrugged and walked back to the pavement, whistling tunelessly.

Dan shuddered with the effort, and Nigel burst out laughing.

"What's so funny?" Dan asked.

"We've still got another ten minutes on the meter!" He said, still rocking with amusement. Sara patted Dan on the back. "Well, never mind. You might have stopped him if we *were* going to be booked".

Hugh looked on blankly, and Dan rushed to say: "Dad. About our time travels! You must have wondered about that strange table, the rug, the models, and all these things?"

"Yes, of course I have----"

"Well! Now can you see how it all makes sense?"

Hugh sighed deeply: "In all my days, I've never had serious

doubts about anything. My work relies on logic and research. I make real products for real people. This is beyond my reason. I can see how convinced you all are about this time travel stuff, but I can't see how it's possible. I can't make sense of it, but I don't know why you're spinning this yarn."

Nigel said: "When you make sense of something, it often seems to fade and become less important --- only the adventure of mystery keeps things alive. Dan and Sara have gone beyond making sense of it. They're in the adventure of the mystery. What will convince you?"

"I'm not sure there's anything to be convinced of". He thought for a moment: "The codex is obviously important, and I don't see where or how you could have got a hold of it .The fact that it's been stolen proves it's valuable, and it would be nice to believe you, but it's pretty tough to believe my own son and Sara are travelling through time!"

"But dad, what about what Nigel said about Peter. We must find him! What happened, Nigel?"

Nigel explained: "He always believed he could find a way of travelling through time, and thought that if he found the right place, he could use its natural powers to help him. Mistlees was that place. It is a natural vortex of energy, a powerhouse of mysterious forces – a perfect place to work for what he had in mind."

Sara asked, "How did he find Mistlees?"

"In the sixteenth century, a young scholar from St Andrews called Timothy Pont travelled extensively, sketching the countryside, and making the very first detailed maps of Scotland".

Dan paled and gripped Sara's arm: "Did you say Timothy – Timothy Pont – a mapmaker?"

"Yes, why? Have you heard of him?"

Dan gulped and Sara rescued him: "Oh, I think Miss Ambrose might have mentioned him." She dug Dan in the ribs to keep him quiet.

Nigel went on: "All sorts of people used his maps as the basis for atlases through the years, but Peter loved the original manuscripts. He studied them in the National Library, and found one– Pont 23, I think it was – they were all numbered, you know –with a piece missing. He stumbled across the missing piece of manuscript – which was never published – in the ruins of an old farmhouse near here, stuck between two crumbling stone blocks.

Perfectly preserved, it was, locked up in an old tin box. He never told me exactly what he found on that map, but there was something Timothy Pont wanted to hide from the world. Peter was sure that's why he hid it.

He had discovered the power of Mistlees.

He was the one who gave the village its name, you know. Peter came to Mistlees, researched some more and bought Opportunity House from the owners".

"Who were they, Nigel?" asked Dan, extremely interested.

"Well, funnily enough, their name was Pont too. Christopher and Eve.

Anyway, Peter soon found out how to use the energy and power of the area, and started to travel to different times and places. He had some trouble during his first two trips but thought he had ironed that out. He always kept a record of his travels, and made the models you've seen in the cellar."

"And the table?" Sara asked.

"And the table", Nigel replied.

"We haven't quite worked the table out", Sara said.

"No. That was Peter's pride and joy. He wanted it to hide his secret travels, and unfortunately it's done just that. I can't unravel it. I'm desperately hoping you'll keep travelling and find him, and through him, the codex. He may be able to help you find it."

The children shared a look before they got back in the car, but Hugh just shook his head.

On their way back to Mistlees, Nigel told them more of Professor Magnus Esian's reaction: "He said there have been no finds like this for centuries. The work is intact and in perfect condition. All the pages, the drawings and the writing are just as if they'd been completed a few weeks ago! He was over the moon. It's only the fifth codex that has ever been found. The Spaniards destroyed nearly all of them.

Those that are left are called Dresden, Paris, Madrid and the Grolier Codex. They all deal mainly with rituals and astronomical calculations, but this one is unique. It tells the Mayan story, and he thinks it contains much more. The existence of this codex has long been rumoured, and he could hardly believe it has been found.

The Professor has called it the Mistlees Codex."

Dan and Sara were delighted.

Hugh sunk deeper in thought.

"What's up dad?"

"I'm not happy about you going on about this – and what on earth am I going to tell your mum?"

When they got home, Nigel, clearly disappointed by Hugh's reaction, waved farewell, and they walked in to the house. Tim rushed up, making wide swimming motions with his arms: "I've passed! I've passed! Come and see!"

He tugged Dan's arm and pulled him towards the kitchen.

"What is it?" asked Dan.

"My certificate silly – you know - the one you get when you can swim!"

Liz called from the kitchen, "It's in here!"

There was much oohing and aahing to celebrate Tim's certificate, which said he had passed his Beginner's class with merit. Liz told Hugh, "I've signed him up for the next level of classes. They're an hour later on Saturdays, and start in November."

"Good, good" said Hugh distractedly.

Liz looked up sharply: "Everything all right, love? You don't seem quite right."

Sara and Dan quietly withdrew, taking Tim with them, complete with his certificate. Dan said: "I think we're as well out of it for a while. Let's go over to your place."

Tim was delighted. He had a new audience to show his certificate, and Diana and Bruce were suitably impressed. Sara shook her head slowly as she sensed Dan about to ask whether to talk about what had happened.

"How was your morning, then?" asked Bruce, playfully tickling Tim.

Whilst Tim pummelled Bruce's tummy, Sara said, "It was really good, Bruce. They had a terrific exhibition, called "Planet Exploration".

You should have seen the size of the Solar System model. As soon as you came in the museum door, the planets were right there above your head."

"Ah ha! Stars in your eyes then", joked Bruce, now pushed back against a door by Tim. As she gently pulled him back,

Diana asked, "Why did Nigel take you there?"

"I don't know, mum. I suppose he thought we'd be interested. It was packed too – loads of other school kids were there. They had model space ships – there were rooms about all the planets – lots of games to play and interactive stuff too. We had a great time, didn't we Dan?"

"We sure did. I wish we were doing something at school about the planets, because we learned so much in a couple of hours".

"Makes a change", muttered Bruce under his breath, his scar reddening.

Sara felt her own cheek sting.

"Bruce – that's enough! Leave them alone. They've had a good outing, and it sounds very interesting".

Bruce began to sing in a mock accent, "Fly me to the moon---", but quickly stopped as Diana advanced, hand raised threateningly.

"OK! OK! I give in. No more jokes!"

As he went into the lounge, he spoke over his shoulder, "Any Mars bars, then?"

He slammed the door shut, and held the handle to stop Diana chasing him in.

"Sorry about that, Dan. He thinks he's so funny, he can't stop himself".

"No problem, Mrs Christie, but Tim and I'll get back now. See you later, Sara – do you want to come over tomorrow?"

"That'd be good, after I do my da Vinci homework".

"I've done mine, but we can compare notes maybe".

"OK. See you".

Chapter 37

Unlocking the front door, they met total and utter silence.

Opportunity House was deserted.

"Mum! Dad!" Dan shouted, as they went from room to room. The house was completely still – no radio or TV and no noise from the kitchen.

Dan walked quickly, with Tim chattering at his heels: "Where's mum? Where's dad? Why aren't they here?"

They weren't in any of the rooms, so Dan followed his initial instinct. He opened the cellar door. There was silence, but the lights were on.

"Mum! Dad!" Dan called.

He heard a muffled thump, and heard his dad cry out.

Liz exclaimed, "Oh, Hugh – that sounded sore. Are you all right?"

Dan breathed a deep sigh of relief as Tim swept him aside and trotted downstairs. Dan followed. Hugh and Liz were on their knees on the rug under the table. Hugh had banged his head when he heard Dan shout. He was rubbing it, while Liz had her arm round him for support. T.P. drifted round the cellar, grinning and tapping his index finger against his forehead: "Nutty as fruitcakes!" he said, shrugging his shoulders. It was all Dan could do to keep his face straight.

Tim pushed his way between them: "We couldn't find you! What are you doing?"

Liz looked embarrassed. "Oh nothing much, Tim – Dad dropped his – his –"

"I dropped my glasses Timmy, and we were looking for them."

Tim giggled. "Da-a-d! Don't be silly – you've got them on!"

Hugh put his hand to his face, and said,"Oh! So that's where they are!"

He ruffled Tim's hair, dusted himself down and stood up clear of the table.

Dan watched, amused. They had been examining the rug and the table to find out about their time travels.

Hugh said quickly, "Right, let's go, shall we?" T.P. sighed his relief, and on his way out Dan wagged his finger at him in mock annoyance. T.P. bowed deeply.

Dan sensed the tension in the house as the day wore on. He knew mum and dad wanted to talk to him, but couldn't because of Tim, who was being a nuisance He had picked up the plane and flying saucer from the cellar and was having a field day with them, dive bombing Liz, Hugh and Dan.

"Put them down, Tim", insisted Liz. Tim frowned, and grumbled under his breath, but a warning look from Dan was enough to settle him.

Hugh said: I notice that poor farmer's still having problems with his cows. Some of them have got so big and heavy they can hardly move."

"How awful," Liz replied.

"Yes, and they haven't a clue what's causing the problem. The vet's called in the local police and they're all mystified."

"But surely they can check what the cows are eating?"

"You would think so, but the farmer's locking them in the barn overnight to protect them."

"Why? Do they think someone's interfering with them?

"Well, the vet must think so. He can't find any other explanation for them all putting on so much beef!"

After dinner, they spoke to him in the lounge. Tim was in bed asleep, his certificate beside him.

Liz began, "Dad's been telling me about your adventures. I knew something odd was happening, but not this!"

Dan asked, "Mum, do you believe it?"

"I'm not sure I can. You must admit, Dan, it's a little far-fetched. I know there's a strange feeling in the cellar, and obviously it's been a mystery about Peter, but to think you and Sara have been through time – well, I just don't know!"

"Mum, I understand, but how else do you explain things – like the codex we found?"

She shook her head slowly: "I know, I know! It's just too – too-difficult! Your dad says the Professor thought it was priceless." A thought occurred to her: "Why did Nigel tell you everything today? Why not weeks ago, or when we moved in? And why hasn't he told the police about Peter?"

Hugh thought for a moment: "I don't really know".

Dan thought too. He'd seen the power of Nigel's gaze, and his ability to make people not remember what they'd just heard. Perhaps he had told them, but made them forget.

At that moment, Dan felt the gentle vibration of the Rainbow Catcher in his pocket. He pulled it out. It was an e-mail from Nigel.

"Mum. Dad. Look!"

He beamed the e-mail on the wall, and they read:

"Hello, Dan,

I trust you and Sara enjoyed the exhibition. I'm sorry it ended the way it did. There was a purpose to the day. For you and Sara much more will soon be known. Part of the purpose was to inform your parents. The time had come to tell them, and it had to come from me.

Without all your help, Peter will not be found.

Without proof, who would believe an old man who said his friend was lost in time?

Till now, I could say nothing. The codex was my sign, my proof, and now it's gone too.

Peter will help you find it. If its secrets fall into the wrong hands, it would be a disaster for us all.

You have travelled four times, and will journey three times more.

Follow the path of Peter and open for him the door.

Bon voyage,

Nigel d'Arguana

There was silence as they absorbed this. Liz was first to speak: "How can he say you'll travel three times more? Can he see the future?"

"And how does he know we'll let you go", added Hugh.

"Yes! Absolutely," nodded Liz.

Dan looked at them, and a broad grin spread across his face: "You're starting to believe, aren't you?"

Hugh and Liz looked at each other. Hugh said, "Well, I must admit, there's something going on which is pretty hard to understand. And the codex does seem to be good evidence."

Liz continued, "But if it's true, how can we tell you'll be safe. It could be very dangerous. If Peter got lost, so might you!"

Dan felt the tide was turning in his favour, and said: "I feel really sure we'll be all right, mum. It's like we're being watched over".

Hugh said, "I wonder about the Rainbow Catcher. Would it work in another time zone?"

Liz said sharply: "Hugh! What ARE you thinking of?"

"Well, when you think about it, this is a great opportunity to test our technology. And – we could use it to keep in touch!"

"Mum?" asked Dan eagerly.

"Well, if your dad's really sure. And nothing bad's happened so far, has it?"

Dan thought: "Thank goodness she doesn't know about the lion's cage, or the t-rex!" He crossed his fingers. Out loud, he said, "Thanks mum. Thanks dad," silently thanking his lucky stars too.

Chapter 38

Cold, wet and windy weather on Sunday forced Liz into cancelling plans for a run in the car. Instead, she got everyone to help in the house. Dan hoovered, while Tim rushed around dangerously with a feather duster. Hugh and Liz cleaned the kitchen, and were tidying the lounge when Sara arrived.

Dan had texted her about his chat, so she was prepared for a reaction. She wasn't prepared for the big hug Liz gave her as they wordlessly acknowledged the situation.

Sara asked, "What should I say to mum and Bruce?"

Liz drew her breath in: "Ah! That's a good point – we haven't talked about that at all. What do you think?"

"Well, Dan texted me last night about what you feel. I know it's really hard, but I think you're beginning to believe, and that's what we need right now. We've got our minds set on finding Peter, and the codex, and I feel we can do it much easier with you knowing what's going on."

Liz nodded understandingly, and Sara rushed on: "I think mum will be the same as you. She knows I wouldn't lie about something as big as this, but I'm worried about Bruce. You know what he's like – he can't take anything seriously, and he'll just tease me endlessly."

"Isn't that better than not believing you?"

"Well, I suppose so, but underneath the jokes, I don't think he'll believe it deep down".

"Let me and Dan's dad discuss it and see what we can come up with."

"Thanks, Mrs Goodwin, I don't want to hide things any more from them. It doesn't feel right."

"Yes, I understand that. Dan said you're going to swap notes about your homework."

"Yes, and I think we'll stay away from the cellar today!"

"Good idea, Sara – see you later".

She found Dan in his room, studying something on the Rainbow Catcher. He turned round: "Hiya - just looking at some stuff on Fomalhaut. It's fascinating. They're saying there could be a big planet hidden up there, but the technology's not yet advanced enough to be sure. There's some equipment being developed now, called----." He checked the website – "an ALMA interferometer, which will give more sensitive readings. For now, it's guess work – well, I suppose pretty clever guess work - that makes them think it's a planet".

"OK – seems good! How are you anyway?"

"Good, thanks – what d'you think about my texts?"

"I've already talked to your mum. I think she and your dad will speak to my mum and Bruce".

"Oh, right! You haven't wasted any time then!"

"No, I haven't. I want them to know now".

"Quite right! I tell you what, Sara, I feel a lot better, but I'm nervous again – you know, like at the start of our trips."

"Well, I'm nervous too, but that's because I've still to face mum and Bruce!"

She touched her face, and Dan said: "What's that mark?"

Her cheek was slightly red, and there was a thin white scratch.

Sara flushed and said: "I don't know, but it started to appear a few days ago. It's where that dog bit me. I noticed it myself the other day. I must have scratched myself."

"How odd. Does it hurt?"

"No, not really, it's just irritating."

"Well, best to keep an eye on it, just in case."

"I will, but it's not sore, just a bit itchy. Anyway, what do you think about Nigel's e-mail? He says we'll make three more trips, doesn't he?"

"Yes. Here – look for yourself."

He scrolled his Rainbow Catcher to retrieve the e-mail. Sara read it and asked, "Hmm, where do you think we'll go?"

Dan replied, "I don't know, but it's fantastic, isn't it? I'm desperate to find out where Peter is. How amazing that he's lost someplace in time! And Nigel seems to think he'll be able to help us find the codex!"

"That's a bit scary though! Who knew about it in the first place? I mean, Nigel won't even give us a hint. Who could it be?"

"And who'd have the nerve to steal it from right under his nose? They must be desperate for it!"

"Why though?"

"If we find it, we'll find out, won't we?"

"Yes, but how?"

"Well, I think we need to keep time travelling. You know how I said we might be able to wish ourselves someplace?"

"Yes, I do".

"I've been thinking a lot about da Vinci. Wouldn't it be fantastic to see him at work?"

"Phew!! That's some thought!" Sara replied.

"Think how brilliant our homework would be if we were like eyewitnesses!"

"Do you think we could pull it off?"

"I don't see why not. It just seems to fit."

No more was said while they compared notes on Leonardo da Vinci. Dan had written about some of his amazing inventions, while Sara had researched his painting: "He only did 17 paintings you know. I thought he'd done loads! There were a few though that may have disappeared, and one or two never got finished. He had apprentices too, and worked very closely with them – so much so, that nobody can agree who painted some things".

"Hey, that sounds really good! I've looked at his inventions. Lots were hundreds of years ahead of his time. He studied birds so closely he was convinced that man could fly too. He drew diagrams of flying machines, and even a parachute! Think about it – a parachute designed nearly 500 years before man actually flew for the first time! How did he do that?"

"Incredible! It's as if he lived years ahead of his time."

"Yes, or somehow got knowledge from the future!"

"You mean, like us – a timetripper!"

They laughed. Sara continued: "Sounds like you've got some good stuff to hand in next week".

"When's the deadline?"

Sara checked her homework notebook: "A week tomorrow", she said. "And after that we've only got three weeks to go before the Mistlees project gets handed in".

"Right! We'd better think what we've got left to do."

"Well, we've done the Sunken Chapel, and the stone tower---"

" – and we know what it looks like inside even though we're not supposed to!"

They grinned at the memory of their return from Tara.

"We know about the power of the village", continued Dan.

"Yes. True. But what can we write about that without going too far?"

"OK. Strike that then! We know a fair bit about the history, but we've still to visit Mr Dewbury's church, the graveyard---"

----"And the Community Centre", completed Sara.

"And we've got four weeks to go! Let's go on Tuesday, shall we? I've got football practice tomorrow."

"Let me check my diary" joked Sara, as they agreed on Tuesday.

When they emerged from Dan's room, Liz and Hugh met them.

"Why don't we all talk to your mum and Bruce?" asked Liz. The children looked at each other, and nodded as one. "Right! I'll see if they fancy a coffee. Tim's having a nap so we should stay here."

Ten minutes later, they sat in the lounge, Bruce and Diana easy in the Goodwin's company. Bruce told them that last time he'd been on the oilrig, he'd been advising on a complicated drill repair. A new employee had asked him for help, telling him his drill had broken: "I told him to get a new drill bit from the stores, get the riggers to fit it, and test it down to sixty fathoms on a stormy day. He passed out at my feet, and I couldn't understand why, till someone told me he was the new dentist".

He roared with laughter, and the others joined in half-heartedly. "Not funny?" he asked.

"No, no, it was funny all right," said Hugh. "It's just that we wanted to talk to you about some adventures Dan and Sara have had". Diana suddenly looked pale: "They're not in trouble are they?" "No, that's not what Hugh meant", interrupted Liz and told them everything.

At the start, Bruce kept interrupting until the more serious Diana shushed him.

By the time Liz finished, with Dan, Sara and Hugh occasionally adding comments, Diana was full of interest, belief and excitement. Bruce was silent for a change, and his scar glowed bright red. Sara instinctively scratched her cheek.

After a while he said, "Well, I knew about *time* flying, but this is something else isn't it?"

"Yes, Bruce, it is. What do you think?" replied Liz.

He shook his head ever so slightly, and with a sly look at Sara, said: "Well, the proof of the pudding's in the eating. Let's go with Hugh's suggestion that we watch and wonder on the next trip, and take it from there".

He looked at Diana for confirmation and she slowly grinned. "I wish it was me!" she said. Sara hugged them both, and Dan, who had been watching their auras sink almost in to their shoulders, and then gradually swell outward, felt a huge surge of relief.

"This is vital for getting Peter back, isn't it?" asked Diana.

"And to find the codex," added Dan.

"Yes, but will we manage to put up with *two* mad people if you find Peter", said Bruce, looking at Sara.

"Well, kids", Diana said, "When's lift-off?"

"Oh! Don't know yet. Sara?" Quizzed Dan.

"Em, how about we try on Friday night?"

"What do we need to do?" Liz asked.

"And where do you think you'll go?" Hugh added.

Dan looked at Sara, and said: "Well, we hope it might be to the time of Leonardo da Vinci".

Bruce could contain himself no longer, and guffawed with laughter: "Leonardo da Vinci – very funny!"

Nobody laughed with him, and for a second his face glowed with anger. Sara scratched her cheek furiously.

Liz broke the awkward silence: "Friday night it is then".

Sara was clearly uncomfortable, but as Dan looked at her, excitement began to fill them both.

Chapter 39

Keeping focussed in class on Monday was almost impossible, and Dan couldn't help noticing how full of smiles Mark was. At break, he smugly said: "Well, Danny boy – everything all right?" Dan did his best to ignore him, but felt really uneasy. Why was Mark asking him that? And was it his imagination or had he grown another inch or two?

Miss Ambrose also seemed more cheerful than normal, and Dan studied her face, as if this would tell him whether she had been the slave from Mark Anthony's villa, but felt silly as she asked: "Is something wrong, Dan?"

"Eh, no Miss, I was just thinking, that's all."

Mark laughed out loud, and Miss Ambrose said: "That's enough Mark, keep quiet. You should try harder to be a bit more like everyone else, and at least think more and say less. When in Rome, do as the Romans do."

Dan gasped, but she simply carried on with the lesson.

After lunch, a tired but cheerful looking Mrs Braid interrupted the class and spoke privately to Miss Ambrose. Dan couldn't hear what was said, but Miss Ambrose kept nodding and smiling, at one stage looking quickly first at him then Sara. After a few minutes, Mrs Braid left, with a satisfied grin on her face.

Eventually the day passed, and with a sigh of relief, Dan went to football practice, which proved eventful.

Mrs Braid introduced them to Graham Esson, a large fat man dressed in a saggy brown tracksuit. His greying hair hung in straggly tangles over his forehead and down to his shoulders, his face was red and spotty, and his huge glasses were steamed up as he panted his greeting: "Hi guys. I'm Graham "Pele" Esson, your new coach!"

The boys were puzzled. Mrs Braid explained, with a look of smug satisfaction aimed at Dan: "We've got the inter-school tournament in a month, and we want to give you the best chance of winning, so Graham has volunteered to help us.

He's got years of experience playing at the highest level, and is in Scotland to find a job managing a professional football team." She smiled at the boys' reaction as their puzzled looks turned to nervous grins.

"I'll leave you in good hands!" She said as she went back to the school.

Graham faced the boys, hitching his trousers up: "Right boys, let's see what talent we've got! We'll start with the biggest. That's what'll win us games, you know".

Mark puffed out his chest as Graham pointed to him:"Right lad, you'll be captain, so pick yourself a side and we'll get going!"

Dan was devastated.

Barely concealing a big grin, Mark chose Liam, Eddie, Sandy and Will, three of them, from Primary 7, new to Monday's practice session.

"They're all his mates", whispered Iain.

Shane replied, "But they're all defenders too!"

Dan recovered enough to allow a slow grin to spread over his face. "So they are!"

The new coach walked to the middle of the pitch, adding as an afterthought: "You boys who are left – sort yourselves into a team if you can and we'll get going!"

Dan, Shane, Iain, Hamish and Struan lined up, and were

dwarfed by Mark's team. Mark put himself in attack, with Will in his place in goal.

Graham dragged a whistle on a ragged string from deep in his tracksuit bottom's recesses, and blew into it. Nothing happened, so he gave it a shake, and bits of grass and earth sprayed out. He blew it again and it released a two toned blast.

Mark kicked off, passing to Eddie who immediately passed the ball to Liam.

Liam moved the ball sideways to Sandy, and Graham shouted, "Good play boys! Possession's everything in this game!"

Dan looked at Iain and Shane, and they moved in on Sandy. Under threat, he passed back to Will, who gave the ball a huge hoof up the pitch. Hamish missed it, the ball bounced at Mark's feet, and he took a swipe, heaving it into the net past a diving Struan.

"Great play! Great Play!" Cheered Graham. "What a team we've got here!"

Dan took the kick-off, and was shoulder charged by Mark. He was pleased to hear Graham blow his whistle as he picked himself up, but Graham gave the foul to Mark's team, and they quickly scored again.

"Right!" called Graham, "I think we've seen enough to know where the strength of our side is! Let me tell you a few of the tricks of the trade I've learned during my successful career".

Dan's bewildered team followed Mark's triumphant side to sit down to listen to Graham explain switch passes, quick throw-ins, dummy runs and defensive blocks. He spoke for fully half an hour, and even Mark and friends were losing interest as he droned on. Suddenly he looked at his watch and said, "OK. That's enough for the day. We'll see you next Monday - keep in shape."

Off he rolled, his feet squelching in the mud beside the pitch.

"What a disaster", said Struan loudly.

"You mean your goalkeeping?" Guffawed Will.

Struan reddened and Dan interjected:"No, he means "Pele." He hasn't a clue."

"He knows how to pick a good team though," smirked Mark, and his mates nudged each other and roared with laughter at the reaction of the beaten team.

Dan resolved they would fight back.

On his way home, Miss Ambrose gave him a wave as she got into her car in the school car park. She drove off, and he was stunned when he saw the number plate.

It was 669 NGL.

His mind in turmoil, he said out loud: "No! It can't be!" But it was definitely the car he'd seen zooming away from the Museum on Saturday. He walked home in a daze, desperate to talk to Sara.

When he got home, he said nothing about the car, but told mum and dad about the new coach and how Mark was now captain.

Liz said: "That's so unfair!"

Hugh had trouble containing his frustration, and Dan said: "Don't worry dad, justice will be done!"

He went to his room and phoned Sara on the Rainbow Catcher: "You'll never believe it! It was Miss Ambrose who stole the codex!"

"What! That's impossible! It can't be! Why do you say that?"

"I've just seen her car. It's the same one that the thief jumped into on Saturday!"

"Surely not!"

"Sara, it is – honestly! 669 NGL. It's not a number you'd easily forget".

There was silence at the other end of the phone. Dan said: "So that's why she always seems to know what's been going on. She's been following us! She's the one who's got the codex!"

"But who was with her then? She must have been driving, because the thief wasn't a woman! Oh Dan, this is awful!"

"I know! But if she's got it, we surely don't need Peter's help. We must tell Nigel, and see if he can get it back!"

"Right! Will you talk to him then?"

"Yes. I'll do it now!"

Nigel picked up the phone almost before it had rung: "Hello Dan. What's wrong?"

He listened in silence while Dan told him. "Have you told anyone about this?" he asked.

"No, only Sara."

"Good! I think, for now, you need to keep this to yourselves. There are dark forces at work here. Leave it with me."

"But what about Peter? You said we needed to find him first, and he'd help us find the codex. Surely we can get it back somehow from Miss Ambrose?"

"It's not as easy as that, Dan. We need Peter even more now."

"But why?"

"Just leave things with me. We *must* find Peter!"

Reluctantly Dan put the phone down, and spoke again to Sara. She said: "Well, Nigel must know what he's doing. We need to trust his judgement."

"I suppose you're right. But how will we face her, knowing what we know?"

"Just act naturally."

That was easier said than done, and Tuesday in class was a nightmare for them both. Miss Ambrose was her normal self, bright and breezy, but every time she asked Dan a question, he was tongue-tied. Sara was more confident, and twice helped Dan out by answering on his behalf. Mark couldn't keep a grin off his face, and Dan felt everyone looking at him.

Miss Ambrose asked him to stay behind at the end of the day, and asked him: "What's wrong, Dan? You're not yourself today."

"I – I – know, Miss, I'm sorry. I'm really disappointed that I'm not captain of the football team any more."

She looked relieved. "So that's all that's bothering you! Don't worry, it'll turn out all right in the end! Off you go, and try to keep your mind busy with the project and ----." Her voice tailed off, and Dan left to meet Sara. They made the short walk to Mr Dewbury's church, Dan updating her on their conversation.

"You did much better than me," he said. "I nearly said something, but bit my tongue and told her I was disappointed at losing the captaincy."

"Well, that would make sense to her!" reassured Sara. "I can still hardly believe she's the thief."

Dan stopped suddenly: "Hang on! She drove the car, that's for sure, but what if it was *Mark* who ran off with the codex?"

"Mark!" exclaimed Sara, "Why do you say that?"

Excitedly, Dan rushed on: "You must have seen him grinning in class, as if he knew something we didn't. What if he's working with Miss Ambrose?"

Sara went pale.

He continued: "We always seem to see her, or someone who

looks like her, on our trips. That would explain how she knows so much. And Mark's growing taller. He'd be big enough to push the security guard out the way. What if he's somehow travelling through time, and growing when he's away?"

"But that's silly. We're not growing or anything."

"I know that, but we're only away for a few days at a time. He could be away for *weeks* at a time and he'd still be coming back to Mistlees as if no time had passed."

Sara looked astonished, but realisation crossed her face: "That would explain everything. The two of them have been tailing us, and Mark stays for longer-----"

"----- to find out more about the places we've been to-----"

"---- and to be sure it's us who have the codex!"

"What a nightmare!" said Sara. "What will we do?"

"I'm not sure, but this must be why Nigel says we need help and to leave things with him."

They arrived at the church sunk deep in thought.

It was set back slightly from the road, with a small car park in front. A lovely stone archway framed the entrance to the gravel path, which cut through a stretch of bumpy grass to the church entrance. As they walked under the archway, Mr Dewbury came round the corner of the building, studying a bible.

They saw his lips move soundlessly as he came towards them, and he smiled at something before stopping, sighing and lifting his eyes. He seemed much more cheerful than normal.

"Ah! Daniel – and Sara, how nice to see you, and how opportune. You know, I've just been checking, and the church took 2,300 days to build. Funny the way they used to record things, isn't it? All of this was pastureland, you know, and there was a herd of goats they had to move before starting to build. The parish records say that when they came to move them there was a fight between the ram that led the herd and a large goat. The goat broke the ram's two horns – must have been an old animal – and the herd were scattered north, south, east and west. Don't you love stories like that?"

"Em, yes, Mr Dewbury, very interesting", said Sara. "Did the story mean something?"

"Not sure, must've been some reason for recording it! What do you think, Daniel?"

"I wonder if it was a symbol of the old church being replaced by the new."

"Outstanding, Daniel! Of course, that's it. That would be why. Anyway, off they went and built this place. Come and I'll show you round."

Dan and Sara exchanged a glance, amazed at the transformation in the minister. He ambled through the open wood door, and led them into a rather plain interior. Twenty or so rows of pews stretched to the pulpit, and a central aisle split the simple rectangular space in two.

There were small but ornate stained glass windows at either side, but the highlight and the clear focus inside the building was the beautiful circular window at the far end. It showed Jesus in his crib, with Mary and Joseph and the wise men looking on admiringly. The stars shone brightly from above, and three angels hovered attentively. Intriguingly, snowflakes drifted down on the figures, dressed warmly in furs. The colours were startling in their intensity, which made the window really compelling. Bright yellow straw, red painted stable, various hues of brown fur, pure white angels in blue and green patterned silks, and purple robes swathing the baby.

That wasn't what drew Dan and Sara's attention however. It was the large halo round Jesus' head, which helped to light the pretty scene. It was a perfect circular rainbow.

His aura.

Mr Dewbury stood rocking back and forth on his heels, hands behind his back.

"Striking, isn't it?"

Dan said, "It's stunning! So strong and bold!"

"Yes, I think it was quite unusual for its time. In fact, unusual enough now. The snow's a nice touch isn't it? I think they wanted to make it seem a bit more Scottish. That's why the church is nicknamed "The Cradle of Scotland". You know, like the centre of Scotland, the symbolism for ancient beginnings, that kind of thing".

"How fascinating", replied Sara who couldn't tear her eyes off the halo.

"I suppose you'll be writing about this in your project".

"Yes we will", Sara said.

"Don't suppose you could mention that the repair fund's a bit low, could you?

Hmm, no, maybe not," He added as he saw their puzzled reaction.

"Anyway, I'd better go. Things to read, places to go", and off he wandered.

Dan said: "What's going on? He's like a changed man!"

"I know, that was weird, but isn't this interesting?"

Dan and Sara studied the unusual window. The setting looked vaguely familiar.

Dan pointed wordlessly to the ground under the stable and Jesus' crib.

Two thin perfectly straight lines intersected at right angles under the centre of the crib, and stretched off to the four horizons.

"Ley lines!" They spoke together.

The architect of the window had etched his name on the bottom right hand corner: DANIEL VICO.

"Look Dan, you've got the same name as him!"

"Just a coincidence," muttered Dan.

"Do you really think so?"

"Well, what else could it be?"

Dan took several photos with the Rainbow Catcher, and they sketched the outside of the building. Sara, sucking her pencil, mused: "You know, the village has far more going for it than I ever realised. I've lived here all my life, but only now is it starting to come alive."

"It must be the company you're keeping now then!"

"Cheeky!" She aimed a blow at Dan who dodged back. He tripped over something sticking up from the border of the uncut grass, buried under a small gorse bush.

"Ouch!" he cried, "What was that?"

They pulled back the gorse and saw a rusty piece of metal curling up from the earth, concealed by a tangle of old roots and dead branches. They peeled the debris aside to reveal an old hatchway with a worn handle squashed flat against the metal. Under the handle was the outline of two crossed bones.

"What on earth?" Quizzed Sara.

"It's a trapdoor. I wonder what's underneath."

Sara shivered. "I'm not sure I want to know. Look at the bones – maybe it's an old grave."

"I don't think so. Mr Dewbury said they kept the graveyard separated from the church. Shall we lift it up?"

"Dan, we've no idea what we might find. What if it *is* an old grave? There might be a skeleton inside!" She shivered.

Dan laughed: "Don't be such a scaredy-cat!"

He slipped his fingers under the battered handle, and heaved. Nothing happened, so they cleared all the tangled grass and earth away to free the edges. This time they both lifted. They tugged hard, panting with exertion, and suddenly the hatch pulled free from the ground. They stumbled backwards, dropping it.

They brushed themselves down, and walked forward. An old wooden ladder stretched down into the darkness.

"Oh no, Dan! I'm not going down there. No way!"

"Oh, come on, Sara. We must find out where it goes!"

"But it'll be dark, and there'll be all sorts of horrible things down there!"

"It can't be worse than some of the things we've come across!"

"I thought you said you were afraid of heights?"

"Well, I am, but it's dark, so I can't see whether we're high up!"

Sara peered hesitantly over the edge. They could see two or three metres of ladder, and then nothing. The air smelled stale and damp.

"Right! Well, I'm going in! You can stay here if you like!"

"I'm not staying here on my own!"

"Come on then!"

He led the way, cautiously feeling for the rungs of the ladder below. "You wait till I reach the bottom!"

"Be careful then!"

Dan took deep breaths and climbed down slowly, hoping the

ladder was short. He counted twenty-one rungs. The darkness closed in around him, and he heard Sara shout: "Are you OK?"

"Yes, fine, it's quite safe!"

He felt for the next step, and suddenly the rung he was gripping gave way. He felt the wood snap and before he could do anything, fell, frantically flailing for a handhold.

"Help!" he yelled and tumbled downwards.

Sara shrieked: "Dan! Dan! Are you OK?"

She was met by silence. Panicked, she turned to run for help, but realised she must go after Dan. What if he'd broken a leg? What if he'd banged his head?

She gritted her teeth, her resolve to find Dan outweighing her fear. She swung herself on to the ladder, and began to descend, rung-by-rung, hand over hand. Her foot swayed in thin air as she reached the rung that had snapped, and she cautiously stretched her leg down to find the rung underneath. It was pitch black.

As she shouted, "Dan?" her voice echoed back at her from the depths.

She grimaced and kept on down the ladder. After what seemed like ages, her feet found solid ground. There was a moist smell, like decaying vegetation.

She heard a groan, and with a huge sigh of relief, felt round her feet in the blackness. Suddenly, a hand grabbed her ankle.

"Help!" She yelled. "Help!"

"Sshhhh! It's OK! It's only me!" Dan said.

She burst into tears of relief, as Dan stood up beside her. She clung to him: "Are you all right?"

"I'm fine. Just got a fright. The ladder broke and I fell, but I managed to grab a handhold before I reached the bottom.

I must have blacked out for a moment though!"

"Oh, thank goodness you're OK! Let's get out of here now!"

"Oh, come on Sara, we must have a look around first!"

"How can we? It's pitch dark!"

Their eyes were gradually adjusting to the gloom however. They stood in a small cave. The stone walls glistened slightly, and smelt damp. Dan reached out to touch the wall, and felt his way around it, Sara clutching his free hand. It was mossy and slippy, and cold to the touch. They inched round the cave till Dan said excitedly: "There's a tunnel! Look! The cave opens up here!"

Their eyes refocused, and they could just make out the outline of a tunnel, carved roughly into the rock, about two metres in height, stretching into blackness.

"Right!" said Sara firmly, "No more! We need torches. I'm not going in there, and you're not either!"

Dan thought for a moment and replied, "No, I guess you're right. We need to come back with torches to see what we're doing."

Sara groaned with relief, and they carefully climbed the ladder. They pulled themselves out the hatch, and scrunched up their eyes as they returned to broad daylight.

"When will we come back?" asked Sara.

Dan thought for a moment: "We may need a fair bit of time to explore. How about the weekend?"

"That's fine by me. It'll give me a few days to recover!"

"You're not chicken are you?"

Sara reddened, and the mark on her cheek showed up white: "No way! I'm just more sensible than you!"

"Ha ha ha!" Dan replied.

Before they returned home, they carefully replaced the cover, leaving the scene as they had found it by pulling back the tangled gorse and grass.

Chapter 40

The next day in class, Miss Ambrose probed how everyone was getting on with the Mistlees project. Dan kept his head down, but Sara frowned at him and he tried harder to act naturally. She was pleased to learn that several children had already finished, and congratulated them: "However", she said, "it's very important that the work you submit is all your own. I can assure you I remember very well all the projects completed by older brothers or sisters!"

Several pupils shifted uncomfortably in their seats, and Sara winked at Dan.

Ali noticed and smirked, much to her discomfort. Miss Ambrose asked Sara what stage she was at.

"More than half way through, Miss, and it's going well".

"Good! Excellent! Dan? How about you?"

"I'm about the same stage as Sara, Miss".

Mark muttered, "You would be, wouldn't you?"

Miss Ambrose appeared not to hear, and said softly to Dan: "Continue to trust your instincts, but be careful".

As Dan puzzled over this, she asked Iain what the most interesting part of his project was.

"Crops, Miss. Crops. Way back in time, they used to grow all sorts of crops. They practised crop rotation you know. Barley, wheat, corn, and vegetables like you wouldn't believe – turnips, cabbage, potatoes, and carrots. Even beetroot and brussel sprouts, Miss. It's a shame, because all that's grown round here now is rapeseed, potatoes and hay."

The class were stunned at this revelation from Iain, not noted for his academic ability.

"That's excellent, Iain! Very good indeed! Now remember, children, originality's the thing. Focus on one or two different aspects of the village, as Iain has done, and it'll make for most interesting reading. Don't forget, there's a prize for the most original project".

She clapped her hands: "Right! Break time. Back in fifteen minutes!"

There was a buzz amongst the children as they left class. Dan was thoughtful: "What did she mean about trusting my instincts? My instincts say she's a thief!"

"I know. She's got this knack of homing in on what's in our minds, hasn't she?"

"Yes, she does. Does that mean she knows we know?"

"Oh, I hope not! That would be awful!"

They thought for a moment, till Dan brightened and said: "Hey – a prize! Bet you I win it!"

"No way! I'll stun her with my brilliance. You've no chance!"

Ali and Asha wandered by, and grinned knowingly at them.

"Yes?" Sara said through her teeth.

"Why, nothing at all, Sara dear", replied Ali.

Asha bit her lip to keep from laughing, and Sara aimed a sarcastic remark at them as they went back to the classroom: "Pains in the neck", she said.

Dan shrugged his shoulders.

On Friday night, after Tim went to bed, the Christies came over. Bruce rubbed his hands, his face gleaming. Sarcastically, he raised his hands in a Karate stance and said: "Right, kids! Up and at 'em! What do we do?"

Diana elbowed him: "Keep your Kung Foo stuff for Tuesdays".

Hugh asked: "What happens on Tuesdays?"

"Oh, Bruce runs a self-defence class when he's not on the rigs."

"How interesting," Liz said, but Bruce was clearly uncomfortable.

Liz smiled patiently: "I think we need to go downstairs, but after that, Dan and Sara will have to take the lead. Dan? What do you say?"

"Well, funnily enough mum, I'm not sure. We don't really know how it works.

The rug just seems to glow and we step on to it, and that's it!"

"Sounds a bit dodgy to me", said Bruce.

Diana elbowed him again: "Just ignore him, Dan. I'm fascinated. Can we go and look downstairs?"

"Of course" said Liz.

There was an uncomfortable smell of stale sweat in the cellar. Liz said embarrassedly: "Oh dear. We'll need to get the air freshener to work here!"

Hugh said, "I don't understand how this place can smell of sweat. It's only the children who come down here. How strange!"

"It *is* odd, dad. We've noticed all sorts of different smells, and we don't know where they come from."

Bruce looked at Sara: "Sure it's not you, sweaty socks?"

"Ha ha!" Sara retorted, bunching her fists. They approached the rug, and Dan saw that T.P. was sitting on it under the table. He grinned and waved leisurely at Dan who gasped in surprise. Sara gripped his arm.

"What's wrong?" Liz asked.

Realising only he and Sara could see T.P., he recovered and said: "Oh, nothing, mum, I just feel a bit worried about this."

She nodded: "Yes, I think we all are! You don't need to do this if you're concerned."

"No no mum, we'll be fine thanks!"

Dan and Sara moved the table slightly, and T.P. tried to help, but they had to conceal a laugh as his shape went straight through it, leaving his legs beneath and his body above it. He looked ludicrous, and Dan burst out laughing.

"Dan!" declared Hugh, "What on earth are you laughing at? This is serious business!"

"I know, Dad, I'm sorry, I'm just nervous."

Hugh had brought his Rainbow Catcher to record events, and Liz clutched his hand tightly, concerned about the danger which might be involved. The atmosphere was tense, and they watched the rug in silence.

Nothing happened.

They stood for fifteen minutes or so, fidgeting and talking quietly, Bruce cracking an occasional joke, and teasing Sara, much to her embarrassment.

Her cheek was itchy.

T.P. wandered round the cellar, whistling to himself. Still nothing happened.

Dan said, "I don't think it's going to work. You can usually feel something change in the air, and I can't tell any difference."

Sara added, "It's like it doesn't know the adults. I think Dan's right. It's not going to happen tonight!"

T.P. now stood to one side, shaking his head.

Dan checked the time on his Rainbow Catcher: "Let's give it five more minutes".

They did, and there was no change except that the smell of sweat faded.

"Right!" Bruce said, "It doesn't work, so that's that!"

Diana said, "We'll have to come back another time, I suppose".

Liz said, "Well, let's go back upstairs and have a drink, shall we?"

T.P. rubbed his hands and nodded in a satisfied way. The four adults went upstairs and left a dejected Dan and Sara standing by the table.

Dan spoke first: "I guess it wasn't meant to be tonight. T.P., you knew it wouldn't work, didn't you? You were really putting us off!"

"Ah! I am indeed sorry about that, young Dan, but the rug will take you no place when the adults are present. You need to be alone."

"Typical!" echoed Sara. "Just when we were all geared up too – and wait till you hear Bruce later. He'll not let me forget this!"

"I know. I know------"said Dan, but his voice tailed off as the rug began to pulse gently, the blue circle increasing in intensity, drawing the three of them on to its outline.

With a howl of rushing energy, they were off, as T.P. shouted: "I told you---!"

Chapter 41

Hungrily, they took in their new surroundings - a huge artists' studio.

One end of the room was filled with paintings in varying states of completion. Two young men worked at a large canvas, one stirring a pallet of dull colours for the other who thoughtfully dabbed a long thin brush at the robes of a nobleman gazing sternly out of the half finished work.

The central area was crammed with sculptures and models. There were busts of men, women and horses, and life-sized models dressed in a variety of military uniforms. There were large chests with piles of material stacked on them. A huge gilded mirror dominated the other end of the room. A table underneath it was covered in drawings, sketches and rolls of parchment.

One wall was almost completely covered with paintings, and another was a hive of activity, with a young lad sweating profusely from the heat stoking a roaring furnace. Beside him another youth stirred a foul smelling pot over an open fire set in rough red bricks.

The atmosphere was hot and oppressive. Ash clouds hung in the air, and sparks from the furnace and the fire constantly peppered the straw floor.

Dan and Sara drank in the scene. They wore smocks and leggings, and Sara sported a jaunty brown beret.

T.P., dressed as always in his minister's clothing, wandered round inspecting everything closely.

Dan spoke: "This is it! We've done it – it must be Leonardo da Vinci's studio. Just what we wanted."

Nobody noticed them till the boy who was painting put down his brush and turned towards them. He spoke in Italian, but Dan and Sara heard him in fluent English.

"Oh no!" he said, "Not more apprentices. The master's gone mad!"

The others stopped and eyed the newcomers up. The boy stirring the pot said gloomily: "Well, Mattidiorni, there's nothing we can do about it, is there?"

"You would say that wouldn't you, Peromo? Go on, get back to your fish-bones, you idler!"

The tall youth stoking the furnace approached them: "Who are you then? What are you doing here? Who sent you?"

Dan stumbled over his reply: "I'm Dan and this is my friend Sara. We're here to learn. Who are you, and where's Leonardo?"

"Oh you know Leonardo, do you?" said the youth, wiping the sweat from his brow. "Fat lot of good that'll do you in this madhouse! Why d'you want to know who I am then?"

Sara replied: "If we're going to spend time here, it makes sense to know who you all are, surely?"

Mattidiorni, the painter, sniggered: "Impressive speech, lady. Quite the little know it all, eh? What do you think Gerro Tarinto?"

Gerro, the furnace stoker moved a step closer to them: "Why have you come here? There are loads of places you could have gone to. Why here?"

Peromo added: "As if we haven't enough to do without teaching you two the trade."

Suddenly the door burst open and in strode a cheerful chubby man with long dark curled hair tucked tightly under a blue-feathered cap. His shortness of height was made up partly by high-heeled pointed-toe boots. He was wrapped in a flowing blue robe, buttoned to his throat.

"Come! Come!" he shouted, "We're not on holiday yet! Peromo, fuel that fire! Mattidiorni, you've hardly added anything to young Signor Medici's portrait. And Gerro, how can we create molten metal in a cold furnace? Get to it!"

"Yes master", the trio mumbled as they went back to work.

Sara said, "That's a relief. He must be Leonardo. I'd pictured him taller somehow".

The master turned to them and put his hands on his hips: "Well – what have we here? Welcome to my humble studio!"

He gave a deep mocking bow, which T.P., now beside the children, returned.

"I am Andrea del Verrocchio, sculptor and painter supreme, the finest talent in all of Florence. Forgive my petulant apprentices – they know not what they do!"

He roared with laughter at his own humour, and shook his cloak free from his shoulders to reveal a turquoise blue velvet tunic and purple striped hose. He tossed the cloak over one of the models.

"I had an idea we would have company today. Can't think why! But now you're here, you might as well get to work. What are your names?"

"I'm Dan and this is Sara, Signor del Verrocchio," said a puzzled Dan.

Where was Leonardo?

As if on cue, the master shouted: "Leo, rest your palette and show these two the ropes!"

The youth helping Mattidiorni, who had been quiet till now, set his palette down and came over. His searching blue eyes scanned them like a searchlight, interest evident in his striking features. He looked to be in his early twenties, smartly dressed in blue smock and green hose. His golden curly hair shimmered in the dusty haze of the studio. At his waist hung a sheaf of notes held together by a wooden toggle, not unlike the way T.P. carried his sketch maps.

Andrea introduced him: "This is Leonardo di Ser Piero da Vinci, to give him his full credentials. We call him Leo, and he is to be a great artist – if his mates give him the chance that is!" He laughed loudly, slapping his thigh in mirth.

Leo continued to suck his surroundings in through his alert eyes. He bowed slightly, and Dan followed suit. Sara grinned and nodded her head towards Leo. T.P glided up to him and inspected the papers at his waist.

Andrea told him: "Show Dan and Sara the wonders of our palace, Leo, and instruct them in the finer arts of our chemistry".

He picked up his robe, flung it over his shoulders, and left them in the middle of the studio. Just before he went out, he turned round and roared: "Mattidiorni, we must have progress by the end of the week to impress our sponsor. Gerro, you may finish our little clay horse so I may transform it into a miracle of bronze. And Peromo, your smelly bones must be ground to ash, else we can paint no more!"

He clapped his hands and swirled out the door.

The three apprentices joined Dan, Sara and Leo, whilst T.P. continued to inspect the studio. Gerro looked down his nose at Leo, and wiped sweat from his greasy black hair and moist forehead: "How come you get all the easy work? Why can't I get a break from making horses and stoking this furnace?"

Mattidiorni drew himself up and added: "Well, he *is* the master's favourite, aren't you Leo? *And* you leave me in the lurch with my work – no one to fill my palette. Just typical I say!"

Peromo chipped in: "And I've got to do all this basic work when we've got two new juniors. It's so unfair!"

Dan and Sara felt drained by this onslaught of hostility, and looked at Leo for support. He had said nothing so far, but seemed unruffled. When he spoke it was in a clear strong voice, carried by his obvious confidence. "I'm sure our new friends will not be impressed by your whingeing. Master Andrea has given you your tasks, and me mine. Let us do as we have been bid."

The three apprentices grumbled, but went back to their workstations.

"Thanks", Dan said, relieved by the change in atmosphere.

Leo inclined his head slightly to Dan in acknowledgment: "They are jealous," he said. "The studio is busy and we have many commissions to complete so they use any opportunity to complain. Master Andrea knows I will finish any incomplete work, though these three are capable technicians. I will show you our workshop."

As he spoke, they were aware of his dynamism. He moved with grace and confidence, and had the poise of an athlete.

Sara asked: "Where are we exactly, Leo?"

He frowned slightly, and raised an eyebrow: "How can you not know where we are?"

Sara said: "We're not from around here. We've kind of stumbled on the studio, you see----"

Leo looked puzzled: "The bottega of Andrea del Verrocchio is known through all of Italy."

"Yes, I know", Dan intervened, "but we're not from Italy. We're from Scotland, from a village called Mistlees".

Leo drew his breath in sharply, and whistled through his teeth: "From Mistlees. Now I understand!"

Giving them no chance to reply, he strode to a corner of the room where a series of large stained glass panels rested. With a flourish, he picked one up, and twisted it round.

It was the centrepiece of the window from the Mistlees Church, showing baby Jesus in his crib.

Their jaws dropped.

Leo proudly explained: "This is our church commission. We are sworn to secrecy about it, and must talk to no one. Not even the Master knows where it is bound, but I have heard him speak of Mistlees. You are here to see its progress, are you not?"

Dan looked at Sara for confirmation and said hesitantly, "I suppose we are – in a way!"

Leo nodded in satisfaction. He set the panel down carefully and led them to the end of the room dominated by the giant mirror. He cleared a space and unclipped the papers from his waistband. "You must describe what your countryside looks like. I will set the birth of Jesus in your landscape".

He picked up a stick of charcoal, and, looking into the mirror, began to write rapidly and smoothly on one of his papers, his left hand flying down the page.

All the while, his eyes swept round the studio in the mirror, checking what the other apprentices were doing.

Dan nudged Sara: "This is his mirror writing! Look how he does it!"

Sara was hugely intrigued: "Leo, what are you writing? And why write like that?"

Leo stopped and for the first time, looked self-conscious: "I have Master Andrea's studio to watch over, and always there is someone to check, someone to scold, someone to encourage. I write without need to see my work. The words are in my mind, written large, and I copy them, allowing them to flood on to my page. I use the mirror, and my words therefore are hard for these boys to understand, but for me they are the memory of everything I see. My mind is like the surface of this mirror, reflecting truth to the page".

"How on earth did you learn to write so fast?" Quizzed Dan.

Leo shrugged: "With practice comes pace", he replied. "Come! I have written of today's meeting with you. Now tell me about your fields, your hills, your sunshine and your rain!"

His infectious tone encouraged Dan. He described the countryside around Mistlees, the hills and valleys, the fields and their crops, and the weather.

"It's autumn now, and it's getting colder. They say it'll be a really cold winter this year with a lot of snow".

While Dan spoke, Leo sketched constantly, his charcoal flowing effortlessly across page after page of his loose-leaf notebook. He looked up suddenly however, and asked: "Snow? You have snow in Mistlees?"

Sara grinned: "I don't suppose you get much snow around here. Our winters are full of snow".

"I shall add snow to my window", Leo said solemnly,

"And I know how I will sign myself! Master Andrea says we cannot use our true names, but I will borrow yours and add another name".

"Daniel Vico!" said Dan.

Leo's face split into a huge smile: "Yes! Daniel Vico!"

He looked in the mirror at Mattidiorni, Peromo and Gerro whilst doodling with his charcoal. They read in the mirror:

"Study this phenomenon of snow – how it forms and falls, its shape and substance, its relationship with cloud and wind. Talk to Paolo Toscanelli, ask Master Andrea, find where and when I can witness it and draw its gentle fall."

He finished and gathered his papers together, clipping them to his waistband.

"Let me show you our work".

They walked to where Gerro had been stoking the furnace. He sat on the floor working on a model clay horse, one foreleg raised and head held high as if ready to prance. It looked exactly like Nuada's horse, Pan.

"Gerro is coating the model with wax to create a shell. Around this he will wrap a plaster mould, full of little holes. When the work is complete, Master Andrea will heat it, and the wax will melt, running out of the holes. He will replace this lost wax with molten bronze, and when it cools, will break the mould".

Gerro looked up and said aggressively: "And take all the credit for my work!"

Leo ignored this outburst: "We will have produced another exquisite bronze horse which Gerro will smooth and file and polish."

"You make it sound so easy," Sara said.

"As long as we accurately use our eyes to gain an abundant

appreciation of the infinite works of Nature, our science will find ways to mirror her art."

He showed them some of the studio's sculptures. Several were clearly of important men and women, their confidence evident in the lines of their faces.

Leo explained that apprentices were taught how to model in plaster and terracotta before being shown the intricacies of bronze casting.

The most impressive piece was over a metre tall, the bronze of a young man holding a short sword with the head of a heavily bearded man at his feet. The youth's boots, armoured kilt and curly hair were beautifully etched with gold.

It was Leonardo.

He spoke with pride: "Master Andrea says I will conquer the world, so he portrays me as David defeating Goliath."

"It's magnificent," Sara said. "He's captured your expression perfectly."

Dan nodded enthusiastically.

Leo led them to where Mattidiorni painted his noble subject.

"So you've decided to grace me with your presence!" He exclaimed. "At least you can see some quality here!"

His subject was a young nobleman. The expression on his face was a stern thin-lipped smile, but came across more like a sneer. He had gathered his robes round his plump figure as if to impress an audience, but the whole effect made him appear comical.

"Lorenzo di Medici", announced Mattidiorni.

Leo grimaced. "Looks nothing like him – and I've told you so".

He whipped out a sheet of paper, and sketched furiously:

"His brow is narrower, like so; his lips fuller, like so; his nose more refined, like so; his neck narrower, like so."

Within seconds, a face sprang from the paper which bore a resemblance to the painting, but which was more elegant, softer and less arrogant.

"Pah!" blustered Mattidiorni, "You've no idea how to capture his position, his status, and his power!"

Leo looked calmly back, and replied, "But I *can* capture his essence."

Mattidiorni glared at him, and resumed work on the painting, bristling with anger.

"Let's see how Peromo's getting on", said Leo, leading them to the fire on which he stirred a horrible looking mixture, smelling foul and burnt.

"What's he doing?" asked Sara.

Peromo replied, "I always get the worst work. No one values my creative skill. Master Andrea thinks all I can do is boil these bones!"

Leo said: "You're such a pitiful creature. Stop running yourself down, and being such a victim. No one *will* value your work till you stop moaning and start standing up for yourself".

"It's all right for you, Leo. You get to do all the best stuff. Not only do you do that stained glass work, but you're going to be doing some of that Baptism painting."

"Well - get stuck in Peromo, and things will fall to you in time."

Leo turned away from the sulking boy, and told Dan and Sara, "Peromo's doing really valuable work, though it might not look like it. We use the ash from these chicken bones as the base for painting on wood. We take the mixture like this-----." He scooped some of the bones from the pot and dropped them on a wooden board. He picked up a lead hammer, pounded them to a fine ash and ran it through his fingers. He and Peromo spat on the ash to create a thin paste, which he carefully spread on a small square of wood with a palette knife. It quickly dried to form a clear smooth white background.

"That's our practice panel," he said. "We use this to do preliminary work for painting, to test colour and perspective – for all our basic work. If the surface is discoloured we use this ash compound as a cleaning substance".

He picked up a bowl of chalky white dust. "This comes from the village of Vush, where a volcano used to coat the countryside in this pure ash – ash di Vush".

"What about your paints," asked Dan, "Where do you get them from?"

Leo and Peromo looked blankly at him. "Where do we get them from?" echoed Leo. "Why, from here of course – we make them here!"

"Oh" Right!" said Dan, embarrassed. "How?"

Leo replied in a proud tone: "Well, that could take all day to tell. We use earth from the fields; herbs and spices; crush the stems and heads of flowers; and many different stones ground to dust give the pigments for our colours.

For bright blue, we grind that rarest of stones, lapis lazuli, but only for the very best works. For red, we use cinnabar and ---". He paused as the squawking of a chicken interrupted him. In a flurry of feathers, it burst into the middle of the room from the corner where it had been resting. T.P. had scared it, and he stood shifting embarrassedly from foot to foot, his hand over his mouth.

Peromo grunted: "I might have known Luca would wake up about now."

"Why do you keep chickens?" asked Sara.

"You know very little for those who come to inspect our work," said Leo thoughtfully.

Peromo added, "They're just checking we know what we're doing, I suppose."

Leo nodded, continuing: "We now work in oils, so we use egg yolk to bind and egg white to clarify our colours. Mattidiorni is our egg expert."

Sara grinned. "Eggspert," she cracked.

Mattidiorni had joined them during Leo's technical explanations, and he snorted loudly: "It is a fine art we employ to make our colours workable. You will find no other studio in Florence with such brightness of colour, such richness of hue and such long life."

"Oops" said Dan, "That's you told!"

Whilst Sara reddened, she recovered quickly, and retorted: "Well, I'm surprised you can manage to do it then!"

Mattidiorni flushed, and stalked off, fists bunched. Leo cautioned, "He is a dangerous foe. Watch for him".

Sara said, "Well, I'm not going to be bullied by him that's for sure!"

A new look of respect crossed Leo's face: "Let me show you what I am working on with the Master".

He crossed to an easel covered in a blue linen cloth. With a dramatic flourish, he whipped the cover off to reveal an unfinished painting of an ancient baptism. One man poured water over the head of another dressed in a loincloth. The baptised figure had his hands clasped as if in prayer. There was only the barest sketch outline of the rest of the painting.

Sara reeled against Dan: "This is exactly what I saw in my dream!"

Dan, who had realised the studio was from his own dream, felt a ripple of excitement shiver through him, and Sara felt it too as she recovered from the shock of having her dream come true.

Leo saw their reaction, but thinking they were simply impressed by the painting, proudly announced: "The Baptism of Christ!" He stepped forward, and said: "Master Andrea is working on the figures of Christ and John the Baptist, but has told me I may do the background and one of the angels. See!"

He bent underneath the easel and picked up a drawing of the painting, showing two angels on the other side of Christ from John the Baptist.

"I will start work soon to assist the Master."

"That's superb", said Dan, "but does the Master not do all his own painting?"

"This is how we learn. The Master takes a commission from his clients, agrees his fee, and plans the work. Like so." He pointed at the drawing.

"His apprentices prepare the paint and the panel – the surface of the wood. We use many different types – walnut and poplar are common – and then he teaches us how to compose, how to use colour, how to heighten shadow and brighten light. If he trusts enough, he allows us to do small sections of his work."

"I didn't know that", Dan said.

Leo shrugged: "It is a true test for us. I can paint anything I see. My eye recalls every line, every plain, every image, motion and the colour of all I see, but an angel! I have never seen an angel, and this will be difficult, even for me!"

Sara said, "I'm sure you'll manage, Leo."

He nodded thoughtfully. Seeing the other apprentices were still busy at their duties, Leo suggested: "Shall I show you my Florence?"

Dan nodded, and Sara said: "Let's go!"

Chapter 42

Even as they left the studio, they inhaled a foul smell of cooking, burning and washing mingled with the stale stench of unwashed bodies. Sara grimaced and wrinkled her nose. Dan coughed to rid himself of the horrible mix of odours.

Leo saw their reaction, and pointed up the narrow street. "It's the city market", he told them, "the Mercato Vecchio. It always pongs!"

T.P. rubbed his hands in anticipation, unclipped a page from the papers at his waist and began sketching. He glided off up the street.

Leo led them the other way, past tall sandstone buildings, with elegant doors and windows. It was busy with merchants, traders and ordinary men and women, simply dressed. The street opened out to a crossroad, and before them was a wide river, a solid stone bridge the crossing.

"The River Arno," Leo announced, "Florence's lifeblood. It carries silk and wool to the free port of Livorno, from where we trade with the world".

They stood leaning on the stone wall of the bridge. Not far downstream was another bridge, with houses and shops along its length. From both ends of it came a steady stream of people coming and going. They could hear the buzz of conversation, an occasional shout rising above the swell of voices.

"The people love the Ponte Vecchio," Leo said. "It's paradise for those who buy meat and fish."

They stood companionably for a few minutes, Dan and Sara savouring the scene in the heat. The background noise gradually dissolved in the swirl of peal upon peal of bells, ringing round the city, tolling out the midday hour. The river was crowded with cargo boats, jostling for position as they sailed or rowed up and down stream. Impressive stone buildings lined both sides of the lazily flowing river. Church spires crowded upward all round the city, with high towers in the distance and hills behind.

Leo followed their gaze, and said, "Come! I will show you where I walk to clear my head when I need to think."

They followed him through the dusty streets, to the towering city walls with its impressive towers. On the way, Leo stopped at a stall crammed with bread and pastry. He negotiated with the stall owner,. pointing now and again at Dan and Sara, and eventually grunted his approval of the purchase of three good-sized rustic loaves and a hunk of cheese. They ate as they walked to the gates.

As Leo greeted the city guards, clad in striped blue and grey uniforms, it was obvious they knew him. "Come on Prince Leo – how's this for your scrapbook?"

The taller of the two posed with his sword at the throat of his mate who pretended to be mortally wounded, rolling his tongue round his lips and raising his eyes heavenwards.

Leo laughed and said, "Come on Driselo, you'll have to do better than that to achieve immortality through my pen!" He tossed them a piece of his bread.

The guards laughed and waved them through the gates. They walked along a rutted track for a while, till Leo turned off on to a path snaking its way through an olive grove, the trees gnarled and wizened. The path led up a hill lined with cypress trees, like soldiers, marching to the summit.

Since leaving the city behind, Leo had become more animated, his walk more energised, his eyes even more alive, and he chatted non-stop about the landscape. He pointed out small plantations of grapevines, orange groves, trickles of water hardly wide enough to call streams, and little stone houses dotted round the rolling countryside.

He seemed to know every fold in the land, every contour and every view, pointing them out to Dan and Sara with evident pride.

They stopped at a ramshackle well, and Leo wound the bucket down, bringing up cool refreshing water. As Sara drank deeply, Leo sketched her profile, quickly bringing her to life on his paper. She was amazed at the speed with which he captured her expression, and flattered at the pleasing result. She pointed at it and said proudly to Dan: "Well? What do you think of that?"

"It's pretty good, that's for sure. What a likeness, Leo!"

Leo smiled silently, and they resumed their walk, following the cypress trees to the top of the hill. The view was beautiful. They could see for miles in the crystal clear air, the sun shimmering off the endless undulating landscape. Every hill seemed to be topped with a little house or farm. One had a castle perched precariously on its peak, and in the distance, beyond stands of trees, a steep hill had a round tower as its sentry, pointing to the puffy white clouds above.

They sat under the tall cypress tree crowning the hill, and drank in the majesty of Florence. It sprawled across the countryside, ringed by the city wall with its dozens of watchtowers. Church steeples and large high flat-roofed buildings broke the surface of the city, carved from end to end and side to side by narrow streets, and cut through in a gentle broad curve by the River Arno.

Leo called the biggest buildings "palazzi", the mansions where the most important and wealthy citizens live. He pointed at the cathedral

– the Duomo, with its huge spreading dome, and traced with his finger in the air the streets leading to Master Andrea's studio.

It was a glorious viewpoint.

Dan said, "I can see why you come here. The views are amazing."

"Yes, and I draw all I see. One day I will paint these scenes, but I wish no-one to know where this spot is, so I will paint an impression of the hills, the trees, and the land, and none will guess where I paint from."

Dan stood and leant against the bark of the cypress tree. He felt energy course through him, and started back. Leo nodded: "You feel it too! I fill my energies from this old warrior." He patted the tree trunk softly.

Sara slid her arms around the tree, hugging it and feeling its wrinkled bark soft against her face. She too felt the power of the tree's energies recharging her.

Dan looked at her, scrunching his eyes up against the glare of the sun.

"I can see your aura filling up – gently expanding and getting brighter!"

Leo asked: "What is this you see? Her aura? Where? I cannot see anything."

Dan taught him the technique they had learned: "Just kind of squeeze your eyes closed a bit so everything's a bit hazy. Don't look directly at anything – just try to focus on the area round her head. Things should seem a bit fuzzy".

Leo clenched his fists, bunched his shoulders and glared ferociously from under his eyelids. Dan laughed: "No! Not like that Leo! Relax! Start off calmly and don't force it. Gently, gently!"

Leo responded, and Dan nodded. "That's better", he encouraged, and was rewarded when Leo smiled suddenly.

"I see it! It's grey – no, green – no, neither – both!"

He whipped out his paper and sketched rapidly what he saw, pleasure at this newfound knowledge clear. He said: "I am learning anatomy, and can see how our bodies work. I understand how the heart pumps the blood, which feeds every vein and every muscle, but today, I make a new discovery. We have another sense, invisible to most eyes, which shows our energy – a reflection perhaps of our inner strength and nature. How is this propelled? How driven?"

As he spoke, he added note after note to his pad.

"Speak to Antonio Pollaiulo. Is this aura a phenomenon he has encountered? Is it physical? Is it spiritual? How does it grow and change? In what light seen best? How do climate and health and age affect it? What gives it colour? Make this a matter for further study. Compare the aura with the angel's halo – are they the same – or different?"

Dan and Sara were captivated by his eagerness, his will to learn, and could see his aura expand as his enthusiasm grew.

"Leo?" Sara interrupted. "Hadn't we better get back?"

He looked up at the sun, and nodded agreement, tucking his sheaf of papers back on his belt. He led them through the fields and the trees, back to the city.

Chapter 43

Moments after arriving at the studio, the three ill-tempered apprentices, led by Mattidiorni, assailed them: "You'd no right to disappear like that! How dare you leave us working while you wander off? I've been slaving away, having to grind my own colours. You're supposed to help me on this, Leo!"

Peromo added: "My fire nearly went out thanks to you. I had to draw more wood from the cellar, but you've got the key, so I had to find the spare, and that took forever, and then a new batch of cuttlefish arrived, and I had to clean the pan out and start again with that. It's just not fair!"

Gerro walked right up to Leo, and asked, "So where *have* you been then? What have you been up to? Why is it OK for *you* to take time out?"

Mattidiorni interrupted. "He thinks he's king around here! He'll have been up his precious hill again, showing off to these two. Look at them! Grinning like Milanese cats!"

Dan, who had been amused by the quick fire exchange, was annoyed by Mattidiorni's insult. Realising all three were trying to suck energy from Leo, Sara and himself, he coolly squared up to him, although much younger and smaller. In a clear firm voice, he replied: "You've no right to talk to us like that, Mattidiorni! You're entitled to your opinion, but don't ram it down our throats. Have some respect for us please!"

His words hit home quickly, and Mattidiorni coloured up, blustered an apology and backed away.

Meantime, Leo replied to Gerro Tarinto: "Gerro, why are you always asking dumb questions? What's the real problem?

Don't you realise that as senior apprentice here, I have the right to some space and time of my own! Also I chose to show our two guests something of our noble city, so I think our time has been well spent, don't you?"

Gerro, embarrassed, muttered, "I suppose so".

Pressing home his advantage, Leo added: "Not just I suppose so, Gerro – you mean – "of course Leo", don't you?"

"Of course, Leo," Gerro replied.

Peromo shrank away during these exchanges, but Leo followed him back to his fire and told him: "And you're being pathetic again! Take responsibility for your own actions! Stop blaming everyone else for your own shortcomings. You should have planned to have wood to keep the fire going. You know how much it burns in a day. All you had to do was put the chicken bones aside and start boiling the cuttlefish bones. Organise yourself, man!"

Peromo struggled a reluctant "OK", but Leo persisted: "Peromo – what do you say?"

"Yes, I guess you're right. I should have made sure I had the wood, and then I could have dealt with the cuttlefish much better."

"Good!" exclaimed Leo, rubbing his hands. "What now?"

Sara had watched the whole scene in the hazy light of the sun filtering through the windows, backlit by the fire and the furnace.

It had been like watching an energy battle.

At the start, the energy fields of the three apprentices extended towards and around Leo and Dan, whose energies were sucked in by them. As Dan and Leo responded, however, their energy had grown to match their three opponents. At the end of the whole exchange, their individual auras pulsed gently round their own immediate space.

She felt like applauding, but kept quite calm outwardly, though bursting with pride at the way Dan and Leo had stood up to the three lads.

Leo said: "It's the Palio tomorrow, so why don't you finish what you're working on now and we'll see you in a couple of days."

This cheered the three up, and they hurriedly tidied up, took off their working smocks and made off, with almost a cheerful farewell to Leo and the two children.

Sara asked: "You said it's the Palio tomorrow – what's that?"

Leo's face lit up. In a breathless rush, he said: "Our Palio is a mad horseback race through the city. Each gonfaloni has its own horse and rider. They use any means they can to win. They train for a year for the honour of winning – by the sea, on the coast is the best training ground. The last race was won by our deadly rivals, the Drago Verde from San Giovanni, but this year our pride and joy will be Apollo, a beautiful stallion, ridden by Bertruso Festi, our champion in waiting!"

All this was delivered without pause and Dan and Sara were desperate to ask questions. Dan was first: "Hang on Leo, we don't know what this is all about. What did you say at the start about gondolfs or something?"

"Our gonfaloni are our districts. All of Florence is divided into areas, each with its own name, its own proud traditions. There are four major areas – Santo Spirito, Santa Croce, Santa Maria Novella and San Giovanni. They are named after our most important churches. Each of these quarters has four districts or gonfalon, and ours is called Carro, the waggon. We are in the Santa Croce quarter, a small but proud and important part of the city. The major families from here are the Baroncelli, the Ciacchi, the Nardi and my very own family, the Vinci. See – here is our flag!"

He delved into the pile of fabrics on top of the chest and produced a large dark blue flag with an eight-spoked yellow wheel as its centrepiece. There was a light blue corner section housing a red cross and a thin border at the top.

"The other gonfaloni include the black lion, the ox, the red lion, the viper, the unicorn and our fierce rivals, the green dragon – Drago Verde! All the gonfaloni ride this race once each year. We call it the Palio. The Palio is the sacred prize – a beautiful tall banner of crimson and gold. It is treasured by the gonfalon beyond wealth, and tomorrow Carro will win!"

"How can you be so sure?" Sara asked.

"Nothing is sure except what you believe", replied Leo. "Our gonfalon has made agreements with some of the others to help us in our race – to stop the Drago Verde".

"But that's cheating surely?" Dan declared.

"All is fair in the Palio!"

"When does it start?" asked Sara.

"One hour before sunset, but all day there are parades and marches, blessings for the horses, prayers for the riders, and the city will be full. All the people from the villages and farms come to rejoice in the celebrations."

"It sounds fantastic!" Sara enthused. "Can we watch it with you?"

Leo considered this for a moment before replying: "I believe my father would be happy to include you with his guests".

"Your father! I hadn't thought about you having a father!" Blurted Dan. "I – I - I mean, it's just that - I – eh – oh sorry Leo, I hadn't realised your father lived here too!" he stammered.

"The race goes past his offices, which are nearby," said Leo stiffly. "We will watch from his balcony".

"Brilliant," interrupted Sara, trying to lighten the atmosphere, "I'm looking forward to it already! Can we support Apollo and Bertruso with you?"

"I shall be honoured", Leo replied, brightening. "Now!" he said, "We must eat and sleep, for tomorrow will be a great and busy day."

He prepared them a meal of thick vegetable soup and a dish of spaghetti with cheese which Dan and Sara found somewhat dry. They washed it down with water, while Leo enjoyed a glass of red wine from a wickerwork flagon.

It was dark outside, and Leo lit candles, which gave the studio a ghostly feeling. Sara shivered, feeling also the cold, the fire and the furnace now cold embers.

After eating, Leo winked and said, "Let me show you my latest invention!"

He walked to the mirror end of the studio. At a point in the wall there was a thin wire running across just above head height. He bent down and pulled a lever.

There was a clanking sound, like chains unwinding, and, from the floor, up rose a long linen sheet. It ran up the wall to the wire, and unfolded itself along it, suspended from metal hooks, to form a curtain screening the end of the room off from the studio.

"Dan said, "Well, that's one invention I didn't know about!"

Leo looked curiously at him, before saying: "Good, isn't it? However I am unable to get it to go back mechanically. I have to fold it up by hand which is troublesome!"

"Never mind, Leo, it's pretty impressive as it is!" commented Sara.

Leo gave them straw mattresses and some blankets from the chest.

"I'll sleep near the door", he told them, and they wished each other good night.

By candlelight, Dan and Sara reflected on the day.

"I really got confused at the start", said Dan. "I thought Master Verrocchio was Leonardo".

"I did too", Sara replied, "but it's great, because this is before he got really famous. He's learning his craft, isn't he?"

"Yes, and he's pretty good too – did you see the speed he draws at?"

"And his mirror writing –it's unique, isn't it?"

"How did you like your sketch?"

Sara blushed, though Dan didn't see in the dim light: "I –I – liked it. Nobody's ever drawn me before".

"Quite a first then! By Leonardo da Vinci!"

Sara said, "It's brilliant isn't it? You know, we left our parents not believing us, and we'll have to start convincing them all over again when we get back. It's enough to make you weep."

"There were a few times today which could have made us weep. What a nasty lot Leo's mates are!"

"I'm not sure he'd call them mates, but you're right, they were really mean with us – and to him."

"Did you see how he dealt with them?"

"Yes – he stood up to them all, and faced them down – but he didn't do it nastily, did he? He just spoke his mind firmly. Hey! And you did too! You were great standing up to Mattidiorni! Well done you!"

"Thanks Sara, but there's no point in just lying down to a bully like that – he's an older version of Mark, and we know how to deal with him now, don't we?"

"Yes, but it's so pointless – such a waste of energy. You know,

I watched you all going at it tooth and nail, and your energies were all over the place! It was only at the end that everything got back to normal".

Dan reflected for a moment before replying: "I'm not sure I would have stood up to Mattidiorni if he'd been more threatening."

"You mean like if he was going to hit you?"

"Yes – I think it's fine to stand up for yourself in normal circumstances, but if the atmosphere's really bad, I guess you'd have to just walk away."

"----and not do anything to make things worse?"

"Spot on Sara. But I didn't feel that it was going to get violent today. It was just bullying. And I'm beginning to understand something else. You and I were feeling a bit of rivalry about the project, weren't we?"

She grinned. "Yes, you could say that!"

"But we both know that sharing our research and the way we're doing the project will give each of us a better end result – and that's not cheating either, because we've got our own different styles, and we'll present and write things differently."

"That's true" Sara reflected, "And think about how much energy was wasted today by arguing instead of keeping calm."

"You mean if everyone cooperated – shared their energy?"

"Exactly! They're all talented people, but they're wasting their time and energy squabbling instead of working together".

"Will you tell them or will I?" Asked Dan.

They both laughed. Dan thought for a moment: "I wonder how you *do* get the message across to people like that?"

The air rippled, and a familiar figure hovered beside them.

"Metatron!" they chorused.

His deep voice intoned: "I hear you ask the unaskable, question the difficult and seek to learn the impossible!"

"Oh Metatron," said Dan, "that's a bit over the top!"

"An interesting expression, a curious phrase. You were talking about delivering a message, conveying a point, I think."

"Yes", Dan replied, "these apprentices are pretty tough, and we think they should work together much better. How do you get them to do that?"

"A fine point, a good notion, and a difficult idea. Each one will learn different things in different ways at different times. All we can know is what we wish to know. We need to wish to know what we need to know to know better."

Sara guffawed. "That's just gobbledygook! Nonsense! How can we make sense of that?"

"The answer is in my words, the solution there to see. Your friends will learn when they are ready, when their minds are open. Their time is not yet to know it – your time is now and you know it. You wished to know what you needed to know."

Dan said: "My brain hurts, Metatron, we'll need to think about it, because right now it doesn't make much sense to us, and I guess we're tired too, so we'll need to sleep on it."

"I leave you to think, to consider and to weigh the scales of weighty words."

He vanished in a haze.

Unseen by Dan or Sara, the dividing curtain twitched. Leo, disturbed by their conversation, had observed Metatron's arrival and departure, and, jaw dropping with amazement, but excited beyond words, had sketched every detail of the shimmering angel.

Dan yawned, and with a grin, said to Sara: "He's quite a character, isn't he?"

"I like him, but he isn't half hard to follow sometimes. And talking about following, where's T.P. got to, I wonder?"

Dan shrugged and said: "He'll probably still be drawing his maps, like he did in Rome."

He lay down and was about to pull the blankets round him when he felt something in his pocket. He sat up. Excitedly he exclaimed: "Sara! Sara! Look! I'd forgotten! I've got the Rainbow Catcher with me!"

Sara sat up too: "That's fantastic! We must use it to bring back proof of where we are!"

"Brilliant! We can take photos of the studio ---"

"--- and some of Leo's work----"

"---- and the Palio!"

"Then we'll have proof nobody can deny!"

Dan agreed, and added: "Let's check my essay on Leonardo. Remember I did work on his models. I'll have a look and check whether any of them are here!"

Sara said: "Assuming it works in Florence!"

"Oh! Good point! I'll switch on and see!"

He cautiously turned the Rainbow Catcher on and the familiar gentle buzzing sound was clear: "Yes! It works! Right, let's get my Leonardo file."

While he scrolled through his documents and opened the file, an extremely puzzled Leo secretly observed them, and was startled when an image of typing and diagrams appeared on the wall beside the mirror – the first page of Dan's essay.

Dan carried on: "Look – here's his parachute, here's his model machine gun; his winch catapult, and all his diagrams about flight – all the studies of wings, and this – his flying machine!"

"There's nothing like these here, Dan. They must have been done when he was older."

"True, so he must improve his skills sometime then! Hopefully he'll manage to get his curtain going down automatically by then!"

They laughed, and Dan, still excited by having his Rainbow Catcher with him, said: "Let's text dad! Tell him where we are – that'll be proof of a kind won't it?"

"Yes, and attach a couple of photos!"

"Great idea!"

He switched to camera mode, and shot the screening curtain, stood up and photographed the table under the mirror with its documents and rolls of parchments. He saved them to his photo folder, and another thought struck him.

"Let's see what time and date it's showing. It would be terrific if it's today's date in Florence!"

They checked, and were disappointed – the timer was stuck at the exact time and date they had left Mistlees.

"Never mind," consoled Sara, "hopefully the text will work OK".

Dan sent a brief message:

"hi dad in leonardo da vinci studio don't know date fab place photos attacht d & s xx".

He attached the two photos, pressed "send", and after a second, got a reassuring "peep" - **"Message sent".**

"That is *so* good!" Sara said.

Leo, who had furiously sketched everything he'd seen, silently slunk back to bed, his mind in turmoil. Dan and Sara said good night to each other and were soon asleep in the studio's stillness.

Chapter 44

Yawning, Dan and Sara woke up slowly, roused by Leo heaving the curtain along the pole. Dan thought he gave them a grudging look, but quickly dismissed this as imagination.

"Morning, Leo!" he said cheerfully.

"Good day, Dan. Good day Sara," he replied stiffly.

"Everything all right?" Sara asked.

"Yes of course it is, but I was up early, working so the day can be free."

"What were you working on?" enquired Dan.

Wordlessly, he showed them. Sara gasped. He had made a life-sized clay model of her head, laughing, and tilted slightly back as if she had just heard a joke. Leo looked at it appraisingly, saying: "I used my sketch, but changed your posture to capture you as I see you."

"It's stunning!" Said Dan, "It's like you've taken a mould of her face!"

Sara thought it was incredible – first a drawing and now a model of her.

She felt embarrassed, but Leo said reflectively: "The eye – our window to the soul – is how we fully observe and enjoy the beauty of nature and life".

Sara brushed down her smock, and quickly changed the subject while Dan grinned quietly: "What's the plan for today, Leo?"

Leo's expression again puzzled Dan. It was as if he was scoring points, and had recorded another victory: "We will watch some of the gonfaloni marching before going to my father's offices to watch the race. But first, we must eat. I know the very place!"

They walked into the street and a riot of noise and colour.

Flags hung from every window and balcony, and people strolled arm in arm, smiling and laughing. The atmosphere was cheerful but tense. In the air hung the anticipation of the race.

Leo led them through streets filled with the aromas of herbs and spices, to a row of stalls serving food and drink, where the wonderful scents of fresh baked bread and pastries overlaid with the distinctive tang of barbecued meat, assailed their senses. Dan's mouth watered. Leo stopped at a stall and Dan tugged Sara's arm: "Look, it's her again!"

The woman serving them *did* look like Miss Ambrose, but her hair was a much more delicate shade of red, and Sara said: "This is bizarre. How *can* it be her? How did she get here?"

"And is Mark here too?" Questioned Dan looking around.

Leo, slightly more relaxed now, greeted the stall holder: "Good day my beautiful Rossa Bemmis. A brisk day for business, I trust?"

"Indeed, young maestro, a very good day! And what may I tempt your palate, or should I say pallet, with, this fine morning?"

Leo laughed and treated them to skewers of piping hot grilled meat, hunks of Tuscan bread and warm Florentine pastries. A sweet fruity drink washed this feast down. Dan and Sara avoided eye contact with Rossa, and Leo looked puzzled by their reaction.

As they ate, they wandered the streets, thronged with people sporting the colours of their gonfaloni – some carried flags, others wore monstrous hats topped with the emblems of their district. Like large soft toys, green and red dragons, black, gold and red lions, and beautifully fashioned snakes – vipers from the *vipera gonfaloni* – perched impossibly on top of their cushioned hats.

Supporters of each district good-naturedly jeered their rivals.

There was an undercurrent of hostility from some groups, and Leo explained this was because of political ill will between the ruling Medici family and the followers of Luca Pitti – he called them *del poggio* – from the hill.

"We are *del piano* – from the plain. All agree there will be no fighting during the palio, but some would tempt their foes to quarrel."

Leo became his normal self again during the morning, and got excited as they strolled up towards the Piazza della Signoria, a huge open square packed with supporters of every gonfaloni. The atmosphere was electric. Groups of people sang songs praising their districts and cracked jokes about their opponents.

Dan thought it was like being at a football match with sixteen different teams competing.

"This is quite something!" he said, and Sara agreed enthusiastically.

At that, a huge cart pulled by a dozen men pushed its way through the crowd, and Leo pointed excitedly: "It's the Carro – our waggon!"

It was bright yellow with four enormous spoked wheels, at least three metres in diameter, taller than the wooden carriage they propelled. On the waggon a colourfully dressed jockey sat astride a pantomime horse, which nodded its head at the crowd. Much cheering and laughter accompanied the procession, and following it was a band, drums striking out a cheerful marching rhythm, trumpeters blaring a tuneless toot. Everyone waved their Carro flags, totally caught up in the atmosphere of the moment.

Above the noise came the resounding tones of a huge bell.

"The Vacca!" explained Leo, "The cow! It's the bell of the Signoria, sounding the holiday for those at work this morning! Everything stops for the Palio!"

The bell tolled twenty one times, deafening them in the process.

"We'll go to the stable!" Leo shouted, and headed back towards the studio. He stopped at an anonymous looking wooden door in a wall under the arch of a tall building spanning the street, and knocked sharply.

"Password?" rang out a voice.

Leo sang the note: "SO – SO – SO!" and the door squeaked open. They were greeted by two heavily muscled individuals who recognised Leo and let them in. Leo introduced them briefly to the bodyguards whose unsmiling manner was distinctly forbidding.

Inside was a sawdust enclosure smelling of hay and horses, and a handler walked a beautifully elegant black stallion round and round the perimeter.

The horse's coat gleamed, and its bright black eyes flitted around, whinnying softly from time to time, arching its neck and lifting its forelegs in a trotting motion.

Sara was captivated, and couldn't tear her eyes off this magnificent animal. It had no saddle, no harness, and no adornment of any sort except for two yellow spoked wheels, one painted on each flank, and a smaller wheel perfectly etched between its twitching ears.

Leo quickly sketched it, capturing its grace and nervous energy perfectly.

"Apollo! Our champion!" He declared to Dan and Sara.

A small man with bright blue leggings and a shirt like a huge Carro flag greeted Leo: "I thought you'd enough sketches of his lordship!"

Leo grinned: "Bertruso! Good to see you! Are you set to win for us today?"

"As ready as I'll ever be," the rider replied, "and we've stolen a march on Drago Verde – the priest has blessed us already, so Apollo can settle to his job easier."

Dan and Sara looked puzzled, and when Leo introduced them, Dan asked: "Bertruso, what were you saying to Leo about the blessing?"

He replied, "Our priest blesses us in San Mottusha -our chapel - before the race. Every gonfaloni does this. It is to wish us luck in the race. And just as he blessed us, saying: "Go little horse and return a winner!" Apollo made a very big mess on his shining marble floor!"

Leo roared with laughter: "We will definitely win today – it is the very best of omens! If the horse poohs in the church, it means we will win!" he explained to Dan and Sara.

Sara wrinkled her nose, much to Bertruso's amusement. He ruffled her hair fondly, and she noticed how gentle his touch was. He told her:"The horses get very agitated in church. Often it can take hours for them to calm down, but we took Apollo early for the blessing so he will be relaxed for the race".

Just at that, T.P. glided up. In an aside, Dan asked: "Where have you been?"

"Ah, I have captured the streets of the city!" He patted his papers.

Suddenly, Apollo reared up, hooves flailing the air, nostrils flared, and eyes bulging with fear.

"Oh, no!" Groaned Dan. "T.P.'s spooked him!"

Whilst T.P. silently withdrew, Apollo's handler tried to calm him down, but the horse was panicked and bucked furiously. He galloped away from them, almost colliding with a wall, veering off at the last moment. Bertruso ran to him, but the horse swerved to avoid him, knocked the handler over and charged towards the closed gate.

Dan stood aghast, mouth open, when a voice of command cut through the courtyard: "Apollo! Rest easy! Stay!"

It was Sara, standing in the horse's path, arms outstretched.

"Watch out!" yelled Dan, but she didn't move. Instead Apollo reared up, neighing edgily, his hooves poised directly above her head.

She said: "Easy boy, easy," in a softer tone, and Apollo swivelled on his back legs, and his thrashing hooves clumped down on the ground. He stood still, shaking and sweating, and Sara went to his side, gently whispering reassurance, stroking his flank and patting him.

Bertruso shook his head: "Magnificent! What courage!" He took over from Sara, and walked Apollo off round the courtyard.

Dan said: "That was fantastic! Well done!" and Leo softly applauded.

Sara grinned: "Yes it *was* pretty good, wasn't it?"

"I don't suppose I'll hear the end of this for a while!"

Leo said: "I trust Bertruso can calm him down before the race. What a disaster that almost was."

Apollo seemed to have recovered from his fright, Bertruso and the handler taking turns at walking him and drying the sweat from his neck and body.

Bertruso came over to Sara, and said: "I cannot thank you enough, young lady. I do not know what scared him, but without your quick action, Santa Croce would not have raced today!"

Sara blushed: "I just hope he'll be OK for the race. Can you tell us more about it?"

"Of course. We run across the town, from the Porta a Prato to the Porta alla Croce – the two main gates, through the streets and squares, trying not to knock the crowd over----"

"----- and trying not to be knocked off your horse by the other riders!" added Leo.

"Yes", said Bertruso, "especially Gostanzo Landucci!"

"He is the rider for the Drago Verde", explained Leo.

"So what do you do until the race?" Sara enquired.

"We will exercise Apollo gently for a while, keep him calm, and then he will rest until the end of the parade. After that, it will be time to go to the Porto a Prato for the race."

"Aren't you nervous?" Dan asked.

"Nervous? Of course I am nervous! How could I not be when I carry the hopes of our gonfaloni! But I try to be as calm as I can – I am not good at that!"

Dan looked at Sara, and as she nodded slightly, they took deep breaths, and sent him calming energies. He felt their gazes, looked puzzled, but felt the radiant effect of their thoughts and energy, and began to grin: "You are wise children. I feel you are helping me. I must learn to do this for myself!"

Leo felt excluded from this exchange, so began to sketch a close-up of Apollo's head. A stray cat meandered across the yard, and he captured its outline quickly in a few brief strokes of his pen. He rejoined the trio. "We should leave Bertruso to compose himself for the Palio".

"Of course," Dan replied. "Where now then?"

"We will walk the town some more and then go to my father's office."

Sara asked: "Can we get flags to wave, or something to show our support?"

Leo put his hand to his mouth and exclaimed: "Of course! I had forgotten. That is one of the reasons for coming here! Benzoin! We need flags!"

The horse handler patted Apollo's mane, left him with Bertruso, and retrieved three large flags from a pile at the door of the stable. Leo showed them how to hold the strong wooden cane two handed, and wave the flags in a slow criss-cross motion, describing a figure of eight in the air in front of their bodies. This allowed the Carro pattern to be clearly seen as the silken material fluttered gracefully through the air from side to side.

"If we stand in line – like so, –" he demonstrated, putting his body between Dan and Sara's, "we will put on a great show!"

They practised this synchronised flag waving for a few moments, till Leo quickly upended his flag, winding the material around the wooden pole. He hurled it up in the air, and as it spun around above their heads, it gently unfurled. Leo caught it by the handle, immediately resuming the gentle patterned flag waving.

Bertruso and Benzoin applauded, while Sara said: "Brilliant!"

"You still have the flag master's skill!" Bertruso said.

Leo grinned appreciatively: "When I came to Florence first, I was one of the boys leading the Carro parade. My friend Alonzo and I were the flag masters, and we practised for hours to throw our flags like this."

He did it again, and this time the flag seemed to float down, though the pole was clearly difficult to catch as it turned a perfect half circle in the air. Leo caught it and in one sweeping motion, resumed his side-to-side action.

As Bertruso and Benzoin returned to looking after Apollo, Leo, Dan and Sara wished them luck for the race, and the bodyguards let them back into the street.

They soaked up the atmosphere for a while, going to the river to appreciate the scale of the proceedings. Florence was thronged with people, and the scene was vividly colourful, with the gonfaloni flags and costumes bobbing through the streets.

Leo scrounged them a bowl of soup and bread from a friend in a wool maker's workshop, and, suitably refreshed, they made their way to Leo's father's office.

They walked along a number of streets, past workshops - wool, basketwork, glassware, cooking pots and earthenware all evident – before reaching a tall imposing stone building, three stories high with a tower at its height.

"The Palazzo della Podesta!" announced Leo proudly. "This is where our town council meet. It is where our glorious poet Dante met with the Council of the Hundred before his exile from Florence. Look! My father's offices!"

Directly opposite were several ornate doors with elaborate knockers. Leo banged on one shaped like a cloud with a sword and a tree forming the struts to lift it. A tall servant with an elaborate blue uniform opened the door and beckoned them in: "Master Leonardo! Your father awaits. Please go up."

They passed through the open hatch in the impressive wooden counter and up curved mahogany stairs to a large drawing room filled with people talking in raised voices. Most sported Carro costumes or flags.

"Leonardo my boy! At last! Where have you been? And who are your friends?"

Leo's father separated himself from the group he was with, and embraced Leo.

A tall thin man, he wore a pair of narrow glasses perched on the end of his nose, with a thin metal support which he constantly adjusted, giving him the air of an absent minded professor as he peered over the lenses. He had dark curled hair and bushy eyebrows, and sported a greying beard. He wore a shirt like Bertruso's, and his face was flushed with excitement.

Leo emerged from his dad's hug with a rueful grin: "Dan; Sara; my father – Ser Piero da Vinci!"

Piero bowed to Dan, nodded his head and tilted his glasses at Sara who almost giggled at the comical sight.

Leo continued: "Dan and Sara are friends working for a few days at the studio------"

"-----and I trust they have learned a few things too!" burst in a loud voice.

Master Andrea Verrocchio joined them, a full glass of wine tipping awkwardly from his ringed fingers. Piero made room for him in the tight circle, and said: "Another two prodigies, eh Andrea?"

"Indeed, Piero! I trust so!" He looked enquiringly at Leo, who nodded and replied: "I have shown them round the studio, and they were most interested in the *stained glass window* project!"

As Leo accented the words, Andrea drew back and looked carefully at the children. He rubbed his chin with his free hand, slopping wine out of his glass in the other.

Leo said in an aside to Dan: "I think the Master is now confused!" He continued: "Father, I trust it will be in order for Dan and Sara to watch the Palio from the balcony. They have not seen the race before".

"And what a year to watch it too!" Piero replied. "We have not won the Palio for more years than I care to remember – since Leo was a child on the farm – but this year, Apollo and Bertruso are unbeatable!"

They went on to the balcony, a stone structure sweeping along the front of the buildings. Already it was busy with spectators supporting Carro, flags draped down and fluttering in the breeze.

The adults carried on their animated conversations in the drawing room while Leo, Dan and Sara watched the pre-race parade. Dan was thankful there was no sign of T.P.

Representatives from all sixteen gonfaloni marched past, each with its drummers, trumpeters and flag wavers, and all adept at the manoeuvre Leo had demonstrated. It was like a carnival, colourful, cheerful and extremely noisy.

The Carro waggon rolled past, they waved their flags as they had practised and the jockey gave them a cheery grin. The Drago Verde followed, supporting a large green costumed dragon whose head had split, showing the outline of one of the men inside.

Leo joined in a chorus of playful booing, and said to Dan: "Another omen – see! The head has torn loose – a sign that luck is not with them today."

Behind the Drago Verde dragon followed Mattidiorni, Peromo and Gerro Tarinto, each draped in their yellow flag with the proud green dragon emblem. They gave Leo and the children an ironic wave as they passed by.

Dan said: "So *that's* why there's no love lost amongst them!"

Sara replied: "Yes – that makes sense."

After all the marchers had passed by, they could hear the rousing noise of the procession wind its way through the town, and the atmosphere intensified as race time approached. People prayed, sang, chatted and got themselves into position.

It was hot, but the sun was going down, and Leo said: "It will not be long now."

They adjusted their flags on the balcony and leaned on the stone railing.

"What will we see from here, Leo?" Sara asked.

"The race flows past us – it is about half way through the course. You will hear the cheers before they arrive, and after they leave, and then it is in the lap of the gods! Let us hope Apollo has been calmed."

Ten more minutes stretched like an eternity, and then the Vacca tolled three times, resounding through the streets, and they heard a distant roar.

"They're off!" chorused the spectators.

The cheering followed the race through the streets, and intensified as the horses and riders came closer.

Dan nudged Sara. "I've never heard such excitement. Have you?"

"It's like life or death for them, isn't it?"

"Sure is – I hope Carro win, because I wouldn't want to be here if Bertruso loses!"

At that, there was a huge upsurge in noise, and all along the balconies people leaned forward. At the end of the street, three horses appeared, racing flat out, followed by a straggle of other riders.

Cheers of "Bertruso! Carro! Apollo!" rang out, Dan, Sara and Leo joining in, and they saw Bertruso, in the distinctive Carro shirt on the straining Apollo, knees gripping the horse tightly, left hand wound in to the horse's main, right hand poised with whip in hand.

He was sandwiched between a huge grey horse and a smaller white one.

The grey horse's rider wore the colours of Drago Verde,

the other a bright red shirt, the ladder of the Scala gonfaloni emblazoned front and back.

Apollo was narrowly behind the other two. As they passed under the balcony, they clearly saw Gostanzo Landucci, on the Drago Verde horse, push towards Apollo, and simultaneously, the Scala jockey whipped Bertruso's tightly gripped left hand.

Instinctively, he relaxed his grip, and Apollo swerved towards the white horse, pushing it against the sandstone wall. The rider's knee scraped along it, and he lost his grip on the horse, tumbling awkwardly to the ground. The horse carried on its headlong race, but the Drago Verde rider plunged ahead of its two rivals, Landucci making clear space for himself as the chasing pack thundered past in a clattering line, narrowly avoiding the fallen Scala jockey.

It was over in a flash, and the roar of the crowd receded as the race rushed on.

Sara exclaimed: "Oh! I hope he's OK. That was really nasty!"

Dan excitedly replied: "It sure was. Did you see him whip Bertruso?"

"Yes – and they're out the race now!"

Leo butted in: "No! Scala are still in the race – it's the horse that wins, even if the rider falls!"

People scurried from their vantage points to help the fallen jockey, who was shaken but unhurt, dusting himself down ruefully. The cheers from the crowd could still be heard in the distance. Everybody began to talk at once, replaying what they'd seen.

Piero shook his head: "It will be hard for Bertruso to catch up now. We can only hope and pray!"

The mood of the spectators was dampened, and people huddled together, waiting for news of the result.

The Vacca began to toll, and everyone fell silent.

Leo spoke in a low voice: "The bell will tell us who has won. Four peels for Scala, seven for Carro and eight for Drago Verde".

DONG! DONG! DONG! DONG!

Dan and Sara exchanged heart-stopping glances.

DONG! DONG! DONG!

Silence.

The place erupted. Everyone cheered to the rooftops. People jumped up and down, shouting with joy. Dan's back was quickly sore from congratulatory slaps, and Master Andrea lifted Sara up merrily. Leo was ecstatic: "We've won! We've won! Bertruso has done it! What a man! What a ride!"

Dan's face was flushed with excitement: "What an atmosphere! Fantastic! How on earth did he do it?"

Sara, out of breath herself from cheering, said: "I don't know, but he did! Wonderful!"

Over the next half hour, there was much coming and going, and they learned what had happened. The Scala horse, riderless, had taken a wrong turn, and was immediately out of the running, whilst Bertruso continued hard on the heels of Landucci. At a sharp turn by the river, he had taken a calculated inside line and edged level. Landucci, distracted, had tried to push Apollo with the sheer weight of his mount, but had misjudged, and instead had stumbled badly, letting Bertruso through.

Two other horses had surged past Landucci who finished a distant fourth, with Carro a clear winner from the black lion and viper gonfaloni.

Leo tugged Dan's arm, and pointed to the balcony: "Come! See!"

Dan followed him, with Sara just behind, and in the street, they saw the triumphant Carro procession. The two stable bodyguards led a glistening Apollo at the head of a long snaking crowd. Bertruso, his shirt ripped from his back, sat on the shoulders of two supporters, mobbed by his admiring fans. The Carro waggon followed, the pantomime horse and rider replaced by a group of men holding aloft a huge silken banner – the prized Palio. It was purple and blue, fringed with red and yellow, and bore the figure of an angel, its halo golden in the fading light of the sun.

Everybody sang the Carro anthem accompanied by drummers, trumpeters and a host of schoolchildren arm-in-arm.

It was an amazing spectacle.

"The Palio!" said Leo. "It is ours for a year!"

Sara said quietly to Dan: "I think it's time to go."

"Go? Go where?"

"Home Dan – home. I feel it's time to leave."

Dan thought for a moment, and replied: "I guess you're right, Sara – we need to work out how though."

"I'm sure the answer's back at the studio. We can think about it on the way."

"OK! Best tell Leo we want to go back then."

Leo was puzzled they wanted to leave, but respected their decision, and Dan and Sara thanked Piero enthusiastically for his hospitality.

"But you've only just got here", he said. "The celebrations will go on all night!"

"I'm sure they will," replied Dan, "but we need to check things at the studio."

Master Andrea waved farewell, and they pushed through the

throng, down the stairs and onto the street. The light was fading fast as they reached the studio, Leo leading, and Sara asked Dan: "Have you worked out how to get back?"

He grinned. "Yes, but it might be tricky!"

The studio was dim, and Leo looked expectantly at them both: "Well?" he asked, "what do you want to do?"

"It's a bit complicated," Dan answered. "We've had a fantastic time with you, and I know you're going to be very famous. I'm glad we met you, and you've taught us so much. Thank you!"

Leo was puzzled, but Sara said: "Trust us Leo, we just need to move on now". Dan said: "Can you put your curtain up Leo, and give us a moment please?"

In silence, Leo sprung the clanking curtain up into position.

T.P. materialised from the air around them: "Leaving without me?" he said huffily.

Sara put her hand to her mouth: "Oops! No, of course not, T.P.. It's just that so much has happened today. We forgot!"

T.P. folded his arms in disapproval.

Dan shrugged and pulled his Rainbow Catcher from his pocket, switched it on, and flicked through his files. He clicked on a photo of the rug, and beamed it on the floor in front of them. The image crystallised, lighting up the immediate surroundings, and Dan and Sara stepped on to the photo together, Dan holding the Rainbow Catcher to keep the image still. T.P. was a half pace behind.

They felt the floor tremble slightly, and breathed a sigh of relief, until the shimmering air was filled with an all too familiar cackling: *"Thought you'd slip away, did you? Catch them now, Samahazai! Now, when they fall between two worlds!"*

The air was scorched and stank foully, as the two rebel angels stretched out their arms for them. Dan felt his hair begin to scorch, and Sara's skin crawled with the horror of the demons.

"Get away! Get lost!" Dan shouted, but his voice was drowned by T.P.'s booming command: "You will not touch these children! They are in my protection!"

Azazel turned to T.P.: *"We know how to deal with you, interfering preacher!"*

He drew in his breath, grinned a face splitting grimace and spouted a tongue of flame at T.P., who jumped back off the rug. Samahazai raised his arms high above his head and fell on him, while Azazel continued to spout fire at his exposed legs. T.P. thrashed furiously, kicking and struggling, but was losing the battle against the rebel angels.

Dan and Sara, horrified and despairing, were frozen in place on the rug, which intensified its vibration. They started to feel the familiar sensation of returning home, T.P. now smothered by Azazel and Samahazai, when Dan suddenly felt his hand gripped fiercely.

"No! No!" he shouted as Leo pulled the Rainbow Catcher from his grip, like a bullet from a gun.

Chapter 45

Stumbling awkwardly as he landed on the rug, Sara pulled him up. He was still shouting: "No! No!"

Sara said: "Sshhhh Dan! Quiet! Are you all right?"

He dusted himself down: "Yes, yes, I think so! What a nightmare!"

"You're not kidding! That was awful. We nearly got taken by these – these – monsters!"

"If it hadn't been for T.P. we would have been!"

"What were you yelling about?"

"Leo took my Rainbow Catcher! I should have known! I should have remembered my dream! That's what it was – my loss – it was Leo stealing my Rainbow Catcher!"

"Oh no!" chipped in Sara, "What a disaster! How could he do such a thing?"

"Don't know, but he must have seen us using it the other night, and stolen it when we least expected it."

"And what's happened to T.P.? He's not here. The rebel angels have got him! They'll kill him!"

Despite the horror of leaving Florence, Dan couldn't help but smile: "I don't think so. He's a ghost, remember!"

"Oh, of course, but even so, what happens when a ghost fights an angel?"

"Or two angels. I've no idea, but he can't die because he's already dead."

"But will they take him to – to- wherever they go to, wherever they live?"

"The nether world, one of them said before."

Sara shivered: "That was awful. It's put me right off time travelling. It's too dangerous."

Dan looked at her for a moment: "It's really important that we carry on. There's nobody else who can get to Peter. Nigel told us we'd be safe."

"Safe! Safe! You call what happened safe? I don't think so."

She shook her head: "I know we need to carry on, Dan, but we must find a way of protecting ourselves. These rebel angels have had a go at us three times, and they're not likely to give up, are they?"

"No, I don't suppose so. We need some of that energy you used to stop Apollo."

"The same energy you used to get out of the lion's cage."

"Yes! We must practise focussing our energy so we can – can – blow them away!"

"Or get the good angels behind us."

"That's a good idea. Right! Next time we travel, we should try to call them up and ask how to keep away from them."

"OK, I'll buy that."

They sat quietly for a few moments before Sara began to cheer up: "Remember, Dan, you sent your dad a text and photos."

"So I did! Let's think this through. I sent the text ---- but ---- he won't have received it yet, will he, because we always come back without missing any time in Mistlees."

"Oh, we didn't think of that when we were in Florence. We presumed he'd get the text while we were there---"

"-----and so much for dad wondering if we could keep in touch while we're away. It won't work because there's no gap here in time!"

"So what do we do now?"

"Well, we'll have to move quickly, because that text will be arriving anytime now------."

He tailed off as the cellar door slammed open. Hugh shouted: "Dan! Sara! What's this? What's happened?" He waved his Rainbow Catcher.

"We're coming up dad. It happened. We went to Leonardo da Vinci's studio!"

Hugh gaped in astonishment, and Bruce appeared in the doorframe behind him, grinning: "Pretty nifty photos guys – how did you do that so fast? We just sat down".

Dan and Sara climbed the stairs, and the four of them joined Liz and Diana who sat, eyebrows raised expectantly. "Well?" Liz asked.

"Well mum, nothing happened when you were with us, but the moment you left, the rug glowed and we stepped on it, and we've been to Florence to the time of Leonardo da Vinci".

"---- and we met him ----"

"-----and his father -----"

"----- and the Mona Lisa?" asked Bruce.

"No! We were there when he was still an apprentice!" retorted Sara.

"Oops! Well shut my mouth!"

"Yes – do!" glared Diana. "Slow down kids, and talk to us. Tell us what happened".

They took it in turns to tell the story of their last two days in Florence, and in the main were met by silence, Diana more receptive than the others to their tale.

It was the detail that began to convince Liz and Hugh, Bruce occasionally stifling a pretended yawn with the back of his hand, his scar showing livid on his cheek.

Sara scratched her cheek, and with a start, Dan saw her face was red, and the small scratch had lengthened.

Hugh sat forward when Dan told them Leonardo had stolen his Rainbow Catcher: "What!" he exclaimed.

"Calm down dear," said Liz, "it's only a toy."

"Only a toy!" he shrieked, red-faced.

"Hugh! Keep your voice down – you'll wake Tim."

Immediately she spoke, the door yawned open, and in came Tim, rubbing his eyes sleepily, two of his soft toys clutched in one arm. "What's all the noise?" he asked, and when greeted with a bemused silence, he jumped up and down.

"Yes! Yes! You've been away in time again, haven't you? Where to? Where to? Tell me! Tell me!"

He tugged Dan's arm, and everyone had to laugh, puncturing the tense atmosphere.

"Right Dan, you'd better tell Tim, hadn't you?" Liz said.

Dan's heart hammered. He realised his mum and Diana were beginning to truly believe, and Tim's arrival was helping them, clearly taking their time travels in his stride. Hugh spoke, but Dan didn't hear his words, lost in thought about what to say, knowing he and Sara must get the adults to believe them.

"Sorry, dad – what did you say?"

"I said: "That Rainbow Catcher's one of only a very few. How am I to explain that it's gone?"

Liz asked: "Explain to whom, Hugh? You're the boss!"

"Yes, I know I'm the boss, but – but – but –."

"What's a rain-bow-cat thing?" asked Tim. "Where's it gone?"

"Oh this is all too much," said Hugh, putting his head in his hands.

"It's OK dad", comforted Tim, giving him his two soft toys.

Bruce sang softly: "Two little boys had two little toys and----," he silenced at a warning glare from Diana, who suggested cups of tea all round.

Hugh said: "I think this deserves something a bit stronger", and promptly poured four whiskies, topping them up with water. Dan explained to Tim about the Rainbow Catcher, and his eyes shone with excitement.

"Dad's got one too, Tim."

"Let me see dad – let me see!"

"Later, Tim, later. I need to talk to Dan and Sara."

Tim sat on the couch hugging his soft toys, and listened wide-eyed to the conversation. Diana led the questions, and when they heard the depth of the replies and their absolute conviction and sincerity, they all began to believe in the possibility of the unbelievable.

Again it was Diana who spoke their thoughts out loud: "So you think you're following in Peter Friis's footsteps?"

"Yes, Mrs Christie," Dan said. " Nigel told us Peter had been time travelling, but he got lost somewhere, and he's predicted we would travel three more times----"

"-----two more, now," interrupted Sara.

"Yes, twice more now, and we need to find him."

Hugh added: "And the codex."

"How can you do that?" Liz asked. "Do you have any idea where he is? Any clues?"

"If we could understand the table downstairs, we might have some ideas-------"

"-------but even then, Dan we're not a hundred per cent certain how to get to exactly where and when we want to, are we?"

"Well – we did both dream about Leonardo's studio."

"----and ancient Rome was because of Tim's play----"

"-----and I dreamed about the dinosaurs – and the Mayans-----"

"----- and we both dreamed about Tara-----"

Hugh nodded. "So there is a pattern then?"

"Yes, dad."

"So where do you think you'll go now?" chipped in Bruce: "Outer space, I suppose!" He laughed, but nobody else did, and Dan said: "I think that might be it. That exhibition Nigel took us to was maybe a signal."

Hugh thought for a second: "You know, if you do travel through time, you need to make a record of it. I'll get you another Rainbow Catcher!"

Dan's jaw dropped: "That's fantastic! Thanks dad!" He hugged Hugh, who backed away, embarrassed. Liz and Diana exchanged a knowing look, and Bruce applauded sarcastically, Tim joining in.

"Right!" Liz declared, "That's enough for one day. Bed, Tim! And you too Dan!"

Diana took Sara's hand, and said, "Yes. Quite right. Time to go."

The Christies left, and the two boys went off to bed, Dan's head spinning with excitement.

Before sleep, Tim said: "I hope you go to the moon, Dan!"

Dan grinned and said: "I'm not sure about the moon, Timmy, but I can't wait to find out where we go!"

"Neither can I!"

Chapter 46

The mysterious trapdoor and its many unanswered questions beckoned.

On Saturday, Dan and Sara took torches, and went to buy a packed lunch from The Deli. As they entered the shop, Brad Maipeson quickly hid something he was studying behind the counter. He bent down and carefully put it in a drawer. He came round the counter, rubbing his hands together, with a slight flush on his pale cheeks: "Well, well, the two wanderers! Have you managed to find anything else interesting?"

Puzzled, Dan asked: "How do you mean, anything *else?*"

Embarrassed, Brad stammered: "I mean – well- last time I saw you, you said you found Mr Dewbury very helpful. What I meant was, have you found anything interesting for your project?"

Sara replied coolly: "Not really, Mr Maipeson. Can we have two cheese sandwiches and two cartons of orange juice please?"

"Yes. Yes, of course," he replied and scurried back round his counter to collect the sandwiches: "So where are you off to today? Anyplace exciting?"

"No," said Dan, "Just off for a walk."

"Well, good day for one, that's for sure. Where are you walking to?"

Sara bunched her fists, gritted her teeth and said: "Round the village."

In an undertone she added: "Not that it's any of your business."

"Pardon?" Brad asked.

Sara smiled sweetly and said: "Nothing, Mr Maipeson."

He frowned, the lines on his forehead making his wrinkled

face look almost comical: "Must be a long walk if you're taking sandwiches then."

Dan ignored him and paid for the lunch: "Thank you, Mr Maipeson. Goodbye for now!"

They left, and Sara turned round after a few paces to see him watching them from his doorway. She shivered: "What a creep! Why's he so interested in what we're doing?"

"He's just nosey. I wonder what he was hiding when we came in."

"Do you know, for one split second, I thought it was the codex!"

"No way! How could *he* know about the codex?"

"He's always snooping around." She stopped suddenly and put her hand to her mouth: "Maybe *he's* working with Miss Ambrose!"

"Oh no, surely not!"

"Well, someone is. It could be him."

"But what about Mark?"

"Oh, I don't know, Dan. It could be either of them."

"How can we find out?"

"Maybe we should talk to Nigel again."

"Yes. I agree. What a turn up if it *was* him".

"Horrible man!" Sara concluded.

They walked slowly on to the church. Sara said: "I told mum and Bruce we were spending the day on the project."

"So did I!"

"Well, it's true!" Sara said. "We are, aren't we?"

Dan laughed. "You've got a nerve!"

" I suppose so! Last night went well, didn't it?"

"It sure did, and I think part of that is all our positive thinking---"

"------And cooperating instead of competing".

"Do you think that's part of it too?"

"Yes, I do. We acted as one, and it worked – even Bruce didn't crack too many bad jokes!"

Dan chuckled, remembering Bruce's comment about outer space. He looked at Sara's cheek: "I see your cut's getting bigger. Did you scratch it or something?"

"Not that I remember, but mum mentioned it too, and – and – well----," she tailed off lamely.

"Well what?"

"When Bruce goes on about things, my cheek acts up!"

"Really?"

"Yes, and I don't understand why."

"Are you sure?"

"Pretty sure, and each time it happens I feel a bit dizzy."

"I don't understand that either," replied Dan.

They carried on walking. "Sara, do you think we'll go into space?"

"Why not – it's in our minds pretty firmly now, isn't it?"

"Yes, but it would be good to know in advance. We must have a closer look at the table to see if we can pick up any clues."

"OK – that's a deal! Oh! We're here already", she said as they arrived at the church.

"I'd like to look at that window again," Dan declared, and they opened the door to the empty building. The beautiful stain glass window shone in the sunshine, reflecting prisms of light on the pews. The group of wise men with Mary and Joseph around the crib had attentive expressions, and Dan's face lit up in a broad grin: "Look at the wise men, Sara – recognise anyone?"

She gasped: "That's Leo's dad – and Master Verrocchio!"

"And Bertruso!"

"What a joker Leo is!"

"Was, you mean".

"Ah! Yes, I suppose *was* is right. The snow's there because of us, you know."

"I think that's brilliant – and the name, Daniel Vico came from us too."

They grinned in satisfaction and Dan said: "We'd better get a move on."

They went outside and uncovered the trapdoor with its crossed bones. Dan shone his torch down the old wooden ladder. He pushed to the back of his mind his fear of heights, and led the way.

He carefully swung his leg down to bridge the gap in the rungs, and reached the foot safely. Sara followed, helped by Dan shining his torch.

The rocky walls glistened in the torchlight. They were covered in moss, which gave off the moist mouldy smell they recognised from their first visit. Away from them stretched a tunnel, carved roughly into the rock, about two metres in height.

"Shall we go for it?" asked Dan.

"Yes, I'm ready this time!" replied Sara.

The ground sloped gently downwards, and for the first thirty metres the tunnel was straight, but it began to curve gently as they walked, first one way and then the other. The walls glistened lightly with moisture, but underfoot it was barely damp.

After a few minutes, the tunnel began to widen and the roof got higher.

"Who made this tunnel?" Dan asked reflectively.

"Don't know, but it must go *some*place."

They stopped to drink some juice. Sara shivered.

"Are you cold?" asked Dan.

"No, not really, I'm just a bit spooked by this place. It's obviously been used for something, and by someone, but why don't people in the village know about it?"

"Hmm, I don't know, but nobody can have been down here for years. We came across the entrance by accident, and it took us all our strength to lift it."

"Well, I hope it doesn't collapse while we're down here!"

"Hey! You mustn't think like that. Come on, let's keep going."

They walked on for around ten minutes, and Sara said: "We must have walked a fair old distance by now – and it's still widening."

Occasionally the sound of their feet began to echo.

Dan stopped and said: "If our footsteps are echoing, we need to be careful, because something's different up ahead."

"Yes, the sound's like when you're under a bridge. When you shout, your voice comes back to you."

"Let's try!"

He yodelled, and Sara laughed nervously at the funny sound. The yodel and her laugh rang around the tunnel, making a hollow sound ahead. Cautiously, they walked on, linking arms for reassurance, shining their torches off the ever-widening passage.

Suddenly, it opened out into a huge cavern. Phosphorescence lit the enormous space, and it took them a while to refocus and take in their surroundings. Dan gasped with amazement and clutched Sara's arm. He pointed to the middle of the cavern.

A large bell sat on top of a huge jumbled pile of stones from which poked shattered wooden benches. The rubble spread across the floor of the vaulted space.

"Oh my goodness!" Sara exclaimed, "It's the old church!"

They walked round the ruins. Massive iron girders, twisted and rusting, were scattered through the heaps of stone blocks, and the old wooden benches were shattered, jagged edges sticking out, pointing like accusing fingers.

"This is incredible!" declared Sara, as they picked their way carefully round.

She stopped suddenly: "Oh, Dan, what about the villagers?"

Dan nodded silently. Instinctively, he looked towards the soaring walls of the cavern, and spotted several wooden stakes in a neat row. He walked over to them.

They were graves, each forming a shallow mound, and marked with simple wooden crosses. Old spades, shovels and three large ancient wheelbarrows sat to one side. The middle cross had a faded inscription carved on its face.

"WE WILL MINE NO MORE".

They puzzled over this strange message, until Dan said: "This must have been a mine. That's why the church collapsed – it was built on top of the old mine workings. Look! They were digging here!"

Beyond the neglected graves was a pile of stones, glittering with spangles of bright light. Dan picked up a few of the shining chips, and examined them. He passed them to Sara: "I think this is gold!"

"No way – gold! Here! In Mistlees?"

"That book dad got me talked about gold mining in the hills. The prospectors used to travel for miles looking for likely sites, living off the land. Some made fortunes, but there were never any seams which yielded much return. They mainly dredged the rivers and streams."

"----But here? Underground?"

"They must have done it secretly---"

"---until the church collapsed----"

"-----and they had to stop!"

Dan thought for a moment: "That's why the trapdoor's got the crossed bones. It was the miners' sign – their mark telling the graves are here!"

Sara sat down on the heap of rubble near the bell, examining the tiny specks of gold: "What should we do now?"

"Good question! This is an incredible discovery. Mr Dewbury will be amazed."

"And what a scoop for our project!"

"---- and there'll be no problem convincing anyone this time, because it's right here in the village!"

They ate their lunch in companionable silence, sinking in to the quiet atmosphere of the place.

"We'd best get back", said Sara.

"I know. Isn't it strange that this place has been here for centuries, and nobody's been here since the miners left?"

"It's a hidden treasure."

"Oh – good joke!"

"I didn't mean it like that, Dan, but it *was* a good joke!"

They switched on their torches again and made their way back along the tunnel to the wooden steps, back to daylight through the hatch.

Chapter 47

Excitement spread around Mistlees like wildfire, and Saturday afternoon saw a procession of visitors to Dan's house, including Mr Dewbury, who, amazingly, did not seem very happy: "Well, children – apart from the question of whether you should have gone down that tunnel without an adult like me, this changes our village history. Hardly satisfactory at all."

Dan flushed, and Liz squeezed his hand. She said sharply: "That's pretty unfair, Mr Dewbury. Just because it wasn't *you* who made the discovery, doesn't take anything away from it. I'm very proud of them both!"

Dan and Sara were delighted by her words. She had spoken their thoughts.

The minister shifted uncomfortably in his seat. He coughed: "Well, be that as it may, I've had a look at the ruins, and it's plain to see what happened. The miners had quarried away the supporting earth, so all those support beams and girders under the church were no use at all. They were right over a huge empty space – not an underground lake at all!"

Liz asked: "What about the graves, Mr Dewbury?"

"Well, PC Ian Vengell and the Fire Brigade from Perth are there now, but I'm sure those are the graves of the congregation – and of course Reverend Deayton – buried by the miners."

Sara spoke after a brief silence: "Mr Dewbury, what will happen now?"

"They'll want to make sure the site is safe. I hope they'll seal it off, and leave it as a memorial for these lost souls. We'll put up a plaque in the church commemorating those who died".

Dan asked: "What about the gold mine? There was lots of it spread round the cavern".

"Well, of course that's Church property. Fred Wingsole, the jeweller, will examine the stones you brought back at the beginning of the week, but for now, you must keep quiet about that. The last thing we want is a rush of people trying to get their hands on gold in a hallowed place".

"That's true," reflected Dan, "that would be a disaster".

Mr Dewbury rubbed his hands together: "Well Mrs Goodwin, I'd better get back. I've tomorrow's sermon to prepare for."

They said goodbye, and Mr Dewbury left.

"He didn't even thank us!" Dan declared.

Sara added: "He's jealous he didn't find the old mine."

Liz said: "Well, I do find him a strange character. You would think he'd be delighted to find out the truth about the old church. Anyway. I need to get on too, and get dinner ready."

Sara and Dan went to his room and tried to play a game on his PC, but neither could concentrate. Dan checked his e-mails, which he hadn't done since he got the Rainbow Catcher.

There was one message in his inbox.

"My dear Daniel, I am so sorry I took your machine, but it is an amazing invention. I will use it wisely. As you left, there was a disturbance in the air, and on my mirror are the words: T.P. WILL RETURN. I heard Sara say that name so this may mean something to you. I hope The Mistlees window provides much pleasure.
Fond regards, Leo.

"Oh my goodness!" gasped Dan, "He's found out how to use it!"

"What have we done? He can find out anything from our time!"

"Including this e-mail address!"

Sara said: "Dan, you have to give him credit! No wonder he was an amazing inventor. He just needs to search the Internet!"

"That's mind boggling! And what about the message on the mirror? Does that mean T.P.'s OK?"

"It must do, but how's he going to get back without us and the rug?"

"I've no idea, but he says he'll return, so he must have a plan."

"I hope that means he finished off the rebel angels."

"Hmm, I wouldn't be so sure about that."

"No, maybe not. Oh no! Look at the time!" said Sara, "I'd better get going."

"OK Sara, I'll see you on Monday".

His mind still buzzing, he kept thinking about the mine and the gold; and Leo and his lost Rainbow Catcher. He went on the Internet, keying "Leonardo da Vinci" into the Search Engine. Up came thousands of references, and he searched through the first few sites. He clicked on one about his paintings, and looked at The Baptism of Christ - the unfinished painting they'd seen in the studio.

The painting was not by Leonardo but by his tutor Verrocchio. Most of it had been done in egg tempura, but the angel on the left had been painted with oils, and X-rays showed this part of the work was different from the rest, leading scholars to conclude that Leonardo had painted the angel.

Dan knew this was true, as Leo had told them he had to paint the angel, but was worried about it, as he hadn't painted one before. His eyes opened wide as he saw the angel was Metatron.

"How did Leo do that?" he exclaimed.

Metatron's face and his curly flowing hair had been perfectly captured by Leo. Dan read on to discover that Verrocchio had been so impressed by the quality of Leonardo's work that he had seldom painted again.

Dan's eye skimmed down the list of Leo's paintings, and he was instinctively drawn to the "Virgin of the Rocks". When he clicked on the name, the picture took a moment to appear, and Dan gazed at it open-mouthed. The girl on the right of the painting, described as an angel, was Sara!

Her face was quite clear, in remarkable detail though her hair was long and curly, and she was pointing in exactly the same way as she had after Leo sketched her when they climbed the hill overlooking Florence.

Leo had used his sketchpad as the basis for Sara's face in this dark and forbidding painting.

Fascinated, Dan remembered how Leo had told them he was studying anatomy. He switched to a website describing his studies. There was page after page of incredibly detailed drawings of every part of the human body, showing veins, muscles and arteries, and describing how the heart pumps blood around the body.

The website said the drawings were so accurate and so far ahead of their time that they were still used by medical students today as a reference point.

Dan grinned broadly: "The crafty so and so," he muttered. "He found out how to use the Internet and copied them from there!"

Using this as a thought, he studied more and more websites, many of which declared Leonardo's work as centuries ahead of its time. He was repeatedly described as a genius.

His machine designs, sketches of aeroplanes, parachutes, siege engines, canal workings, water wheels and drills were all brilliantly captured, but Dan knew that Leo had used twenty-first century pictures and photographs, and translated them into his drawings, making them fit the materials and environment he lived in and understood.

No wonder he was described as a man ahead of his time.

He sat back and stretched. Leo had indeed been brilliant, but it was the Rainbow Catcher that had made him a genius!

Chapter 48

Reflecting on the way to school, he told Sara about searching the Internet, and she listened, amazed, at the start of a very busy Monday. "So I'm in one of his paintings?"

"Clear as you like. Remember how quickly he drew you that day, and how you pointed at his sketch?"

"Yes, I do."

"Well that's what he's painted in the Virgin on the Rocks, except he's changed your hair to make it dark, long and curly".

"And Metatron. How did he manage to paint him?"

"Not sure, but he must have spotted him that night without us noticing".

"That would explain how he knew about the Rainbow Catcher!"

"And why he seemed a bit strange the next morning. He said he was tired because he'd been up making that bust of your face, but he must have seen what the Rainbow Catcher could do -------"

"--------- and been thinking how he could get his hands on it-------"

"---------- to satisfy his thirst for knowledge".

"Incredible!" they said together, and laughed.

Dan said thoughtfully: "If he saw Metatron, how did he not see the rebel angels and T.P.? Remember he said in his text there was a disturbance in the air. He obviously couldn't see them."

"Maybe it was to do with the light?"

"Hm, don't know," replied Dan.

In school, they were very much the centre of attention. Miss Ambrose asked Dan to tell the class what they had seen in the cavern, and he described everything except finding the gold.

When Mark asked where the tunnel entrance was, she interrupted: "I think it's best that remains a secret for now, Mark. The Police and Fire Brigade need to make sure the site's safe, and they won't want people traipsing around."

As they went for morning break, she said to Dan in an aside: "I've wanted that discovery to be made for a long time. Everything's coming together very well".

She nodded, grinned at Sara, and collected her folder from the desk before Dan could ask her what she meant.

They couldn't get peace at break because of all the questions everyone asked.

"How many graves were there?" "What tools did they use?" "Did you find anything else from the old church?"

Mark walked past, and in a loud aside, said: "We knew it was there all along!"

This provoked a silence, followed by cries of: "No way!" "Rubbish!" and "Chancer!"

Dan looked at him. Surely he wasn't taller than last week? He shook his head but he could see Mark's shirt was far too small for him and he walked as if his shoes were pinching his toes.

Had he travelled to Florence and stayed longer? What else could explain it?

After break, they handed in their essays on Leonardo da Vinci. It was hard to settle down to work, and football practice was almost a relief for Dan – at least till it started. Graham "Pele" Esson got them to warm up with some practice shots at goal, and Mark's team scored time after time. There was no doubt Mark himself was playing better. He seemed stronger, more balanced and his shots had real power in them.

For some reason, Dan couldn't raise the positive energy he needed, and this affected his teammates who struggled to get the ball past Will.

The match afterwards followed the pattern of their first game, Mark's big mates brushing past Dan's team to put four goals past Struan. Dan couldn't shake his depression at the thought of not being captain in the inter school tournament. His mood lifted however when Graham got them all together for one of his "team talks".

"Right boys! We've got a star line up for the tournament, and the good news is that we're allowed two teams so Dan – your lot can come too. You won't do well as you're not as physical as Mark's team, but at least you can support them when you've been knocked out!"

Shane bristled, but Dan put a hand on his arm and said: "We'll show them, don't you worry!"

Once again, Graham finished the session by boring them, this time with details of all the superb goals he'd scored in his professional days.

Iain asked: "Which teams exactly did you play for?"

"Boys, in a long and glorious career, you go to the best clubs, get treated like royalty, the fans love you, and the goals come naturally, especially to someone with my talent".

"But who did you play for?" persisted Iain.

Graham winked at him behind his steamed up glasses: "I don't want to put you off, boy, by blowing my own trumpet. Suffice it to say that many great teams benefited from having me in their squad." He clapped his hands, and said: "Right lads! Not long before we head off to Glasgow for the tournament, so keep fit, keep practising and I'll see you next week!"

Dan's team sat for a few moments as Mark, Liam, Eddie, Sandy and Will walked past. Mark said to Dan in a deep tone: "That's it, second raters – best to have a cosy chat – that'll be all you'll be able to do when we come back with the trophy!"

Dan looked coolly back at him, and Mark flushed and turned on his heel.

Instead of deflating him, Mark's comments filled him with confidence, and he said to his team: "We all know we can play better football than them, but we're not organised properly. Graham's knocked us off balance, so we need to find a way of working together to beat them."

Shane said: "Graham's a phoney! I bet he hasn't played for any decent teams!"

Hamish agreed. "You're right, otherwise he'd have told us who he scored all those goals for."

Dan said: "I know, but we've got to get our act together, and we've only got a couple of weeks to do it."

"So what's the plan?" asked Struan, still annoyed at himself for not saving more goals.

"Why don't we have our own practice, and work out some tactics?"

They all agreed, and arranged to meet after school on Wednesday.

When Dan got home, Liz said: "Oh Dan! That's good timing. Mr Wingsole, the jeweller's here. He's had a look at the gold you found!"

"Oh good! Where is he?"

"He's waiting in the lounge."

Fred Wingsole was a weedy man, with a bulbous nose and bald head. His shirt collar was too big for him and his grey eyes had a shifty quality Dan was uncomfortable with. He stood up as they came in.

"Hello Dan, I'm Fred Wingsole from the jeweller's. You've certainly put the cat among the pigeons, haven't you?" he said with a twisted smile.

"How do you mean, Mr Wingsole?" Dan asked.

Mr Wingsole's face fell, and he muttered: "Well, what with you finding the gold and all", he replied.

"Oh, I see! Well, yes, I suppose so. What did you make of it?"

Mr Wingsole dug into his pocket and produced the grains of gold: "Fool's Gold, Dan – Fool's Gold. That's what you've found."

"What's Fool's Gold?"

"Many people mistake it for gold, because at first sight, it looks the same, but it's a brassier yellow than real gold, and has little value."

Liz took Dan's hand at his disappointment.

Mr Wingsole continued: "It's just iron pyrites. They're found in cubic crystal. The word pyrites comes from the Greek word for fire, because it sparks when you strike it with a piece of steel."

"So it's not gold then?"

"No, I'm afraid not, Dan. The miners weren't getting rich, and that's probably why they abandoned the old mine. There was no money in it for them."

"But why all the secrecy then? Why didn't they let the village know about the church collapsing into the mine?"

Liz said: "They maybe felt guilty their work loosened the foundations of the church, and didn't want to be blamed for it collapsing."

"That's awful! It's so sad, mum".

"I know, darling, but at least we know now about the gold."

Mr. Wingsole stood up, and made to leave, but Dan asked: "Can I have the gold we found, anyway, please?"

"Oh! Of course you can. Here!"

He reluctantly handed the small pieces of crystal back to Dan, who studied them before tucking them into his pocket. As he left, Nigel drew up in his car.

"Hello, Dan. Hello Mrs Goodwin!" he beamed.

"Come in Nigel," said Liz, "Have you heard all the excitement?"

"Indeed I have! Isn't it remarkable? You've done well Dan – what an incredible discovery."

In the lounge, Dan told how he and Sara had found the old mine. Nigel's eyes lit up when he described finding the graves, and then the gold. "Why, that's amazing!"

"Well, yes, Nigel, but the jeweller's just been here, and says all we've found is Fool's Gold."

"Iron pyrites, eh?" replied Nigel. "Well that's not so bad is it?"

"Mr Wingsole didn't seem to think so. He says there's no value in it."

"Hmmm. Perhaps not great commercial value, but iron pyrites are an excellent protective stone. They defend you from all sorts of negative energy. They have a unique power, you know. People used to carry them when they were doing dangerous work - as a sort of talisman – a charm, if you like. It was used as treatment for fevers, and for reducing swelling. Miners used it to prevent lung disease, and to help them sleep."

"Oh, so is that why they were digging it out?"

"I think that's highly likely, Dan. They say it helps you remember good things, like the warmth of the sun, and friendships – and love."

Liz patted Dan's hand: "So it's not so worthless after all, then."

"No, and there's still a market for iron pyrites, I believe."

Dan thought for a moment before replying: "So why did Mr Wingsole tell us there's no value in it?"

"I don't really know. Certainly there's nothing like the value of real gold, but in reasonable quantities, your find is certainly worth something. You know, Peter must have known about this because he used to wear a ring which looked like gold, but he always made a joke of it, saying it was appropriate for an old fool like him!"

They laughed, and Nigel said, "Well, how are the timetrippers?"

Dan looked hesitantly at Liz, who replied: "Well, I think they're fine, Nigel. They say they've been to Leonardo da Vinci's studio---"

"------It was Master Verrocchio's studio, mum."

"Sorry, Dan but you know what I mean".

"So there are two more trips to make – and I'm sure you'll find him."

"You mean Peter?" clarified Dan.

"Yes, of course – Peter. You know, I really miss him. I wish he was back here."

Liz looked doubtfully at Nigel: "How can you be sure he's out there someplace – what did you say, lost in time?"

"How can drops of water form a river? The pattern is there, Mrs Goodwin. We must part the waters to find the drops."

This left Dan and Liz silent, and Nigel stood up and said: "Right, I must be off. Good luck, Dan, and we'll be in touch."

Dan showed Nigel out, and said: "Nigel, we're really worried ------"

"-----about Mark and Mr Maipeson?"

"Yes, but how did you know?"

"You must leave things to me just now, Dan. We must tread very carefully."

Dan made to say something else, but Nigel looked deep into

his eyes and he couldn't think what it was he'd wanted to say.

Nigel left with a wave.

Shortly afterwards, Hugh returned from work, a smile playing round the corners of his mouth: "Well, Dan, here it is!" He handed him a new Rainbow Catcher.

"Oh dad – thanks! That's brilliant. I'll take care of it – I promise!"

"You'd better, my lad. This is real state of the art."

Dan looked at it, and spotted some new buttons.

"Let me show you", said Hugh, "We've made one or two refinements. This button is a motion detector. If you want to test whether anyone's near you – say, in the dark, or if you think someone's broken into the house, you press the button and it picks up any movement within a twenty metre radius. It converts that movement into an image giving you its size and location."

He demonstrated it, asking Liz and Dan to be still, and on to the screen came a fuzzy image of a shape moving backwards and forwards. An arrow pointed towards the kitchen.

"Oh, Hugh, there's someone in the kitchen!" Exclaimed Liz.

The shape moved and the arrow grew larger.

"It's getting closer!" She exclaimed in alarm.

The door opened and in came Tim, a glass of orange in his hand. Dan and Hugh burst out laughing, Liz blushed, and Tim said: "What's so funny?"

Hugh explained, and Tim said: "Let me try!"

Hugh said: "OK, Tim, but you must keep quite still, else it'll pick up your own movements."

Nothing registered on the screen for a second, but suddenly a shape formed, and the arrow pointed outside the house.

"I don't believe this!" Liz said.

The shape stopped moving, and the doorbell rang. It was Sara.

Dan said: "You didn't half give mum a fright!"

Liz shook her head and went to make tea, while Hugh showed them the other additions to the Rainbow Catcher: "We've extended the infra-red capability to allow you to take photos in the dark. The sensor operates when you click this button, and the motion detector picks up whatever goes past the sensor and photographs it digitally. Wild life photographers use this technology to record nighttime activities of birds, insects and animals. And talking of technology, here's something for you."

He keyed a code, and the Rainbow Catcher projected on the wall. "Watch this", he said, and turned on the TV. A cartoon appeared, but before they could see it clearly, it moved and danced in the air above the machine. The characters chased each other round and round in a perfect circle, bounded by a thin bubble shape. The colours were sharp, the definition of the action clear, and the characters' voices came straight from their lips in the air above the machine. The children's jaws dropped, and Tim especially was fascinated. He walked round and round the cartoon. Dan said: "It's a hologram! This is fantastic! I've seen some of these in TV ads, but this is much better."

Hugh replied: "Yes, I think you could say we're quite proud of our holographic projections".

"This is great, dad. I can't wait to try it out!"

"Hang on! Hang on! I'm not finished yet. Because of what happened when you lost the original Rainbow Catcher, I got the technicians to install a personalised alarm, so if someone takes it from you, it does this!"

He pushed another button, and it let out a piercing high-pitched wail. They covered their ears from the noise, and Liz came rushing in: "What's happened? What's that noise?"

Embarrassed, Hugh switched it off, and said: "Sorry, dear, just testing the new alarm system".

She snorted and returned to the kitchen, much to the children's amusement.

Hugh said: "I need to programme it to your body characteristics, so the machine can register you as its owner."

He pointed the scanner at Dan, and clicked a series of buttons on the keypad.

"There! That's it now – it's all yours, but beware! If it's out of your possession for over a minute when the alarm's on, it'll howl like a banshee!"

"What's a banshee?" asked Tim.

Sara replied: "It's a screeching ghost!"

"Like on Scooby Doo on the hologram?"

"Just like on Scooby Doo on the hologram!"

Satisfied, he went to join Liz, and Hugh followed.

Dan sighed: "It's been a heck of a day, Sara! I don't know whether I'm coming or going!"

"Why? What's happened?"

Dan updated her, and she said: "No wonder you feel like that. How's your energy?"

"Not bad, considering, but I'm a bit washed out!"

Sara focussed on him for a few moments in silence, projecting her energies, and Dan felt his spirits lift, her efforts recharging him. He said: "You know, Mark's getting taller again. He's much bigger than everyone now."

"He was big enough to start with."

"I know, and his football gear's far too small now."

Sara replied: "So maybe we're right. He's timetripping like us and always stays longer."

"But we never see him."

"No, that's true, but what else could make him grow so quickly?"

"I don't know, but it's a huge growth spurt he's going through."

She said: "I wanted to see that stuff you saw on the Internet – Leo's paintings and things".

"You mean you wanted to see how you looked in the Virgin on the Rocks?"

"Well, all right, smarty! Yes, I did actually."

With a grin, Dan said: "Well, let's do it on the Rainbow Catcher then."

He switched on the machine's PC, and they scrolled the Leonardo websites, projected on the wall. He found the painting and said: "There! That's you!"

Sara studied the image. It was definitely her, and she shivered.

"It's really weird to see my face in an old painting. I can't get over it!"

"Here - I'll show you Metatron. Look! It's him, isn't it?"

"It is too. Leo's so good. Every detail of his face is as clear as crystal".

Sara continued to browse, and clicked on "The Madonna of the Snow".

The article described how an ancient festival celebrated a miraculous fall of snow on a hillside in the summer. One of Leonardo's first recorded drawings was of a view from a hillside, but scholars couldn't decide exactly where the hillside was. Leo had written on a corner of the drawing: "*Di di santa Maria della neve addi 5 daghossto 1473"* ("On the day of the Madonna of the Snow, 5th August 1473").

Dan commented: "He said he'd find out all about snow. He must have found out about this old festival!"

"Yes, I'm sure he did – and look at the drawing!"

"Why – that's the view we saw – look – there's the hills around it -----"

"-------and the castle in the distance."

"-------- and the woods, and the tower on the hill!"

They looked at each other, grinning.

"Well, WE know where it is!" Dan exclaimed.

"And we've been there!"

They carried on reading, and Sara pointed at another Italian phrase.

"Io morando dant sono chontento."

This had been written on the other side of the paper from the hillside drawing, and the article said it wasn't clear what the phrase meant exactly. One scholar thought that *"dant"* was an abbreviation for d'Antonio, Leo's stepfather, and that the phrase meant: *"I, staying with Antonio, am happy".*

Sara clapped her hands in delight. "They've got it all wrong – it's you! It's not dant or d'Antonio, it's *Dan!* He was saying he was happy staying with you!"

"Hey, that's neat! Good old Leo – and I wondered whether he'd really liked me!"

"Well, there's your answer – written on the back of the hillside view!"

They switched off the Rainbow Catcher, and Dan said: "I think we should have another look at the table. Let's see if we can work out the etchings."

"Good idea! I haven't got long before tea, but if we're quick we can do it now."

They went down to the cellar and were struck by the aroma of spices and orange.

"I still don't understand these smells," puzzled Dan.

Sara shrugged, and they looked at the table.

"Let's examine the bits we recognise", she suggested.

The segment with the dinosaurs showed some of the animals they'd seen when with Phaelar and Jafyre, and the image of Phaelar pointing his stick was plain. The letters in the middle read: TERC.

"What's TERC?" asked Sara.

"I don't know. Let's look at this bit."

The neighbouring segment was obviously Rome – figures in togas, lions and a chariot were the main etchings. The letters read: EMOR. Dan said it slowly: "E –M – O – R. What's EMOR?"

Sara nudged him excitedly: "It's not EMOR – it's ROME – EMOR backwards!"

Dan smacked the palm of his hand against his forehead: "Of course it is – how obvious! Why didn't I see that?"

Sara grinned: "It's just my natural genius you know!"

"OK! OK! I give in! So what's TERC then?"

"Well, if it's backwards too, it's C-R-E-T, not TERC."

"What does CRET mean then?"

"I've no idea, but let's try the dictionary on the Rainbow Catcher."

Dan switched it on and skimmed through the dictionary. He

used the hologram display so the words swirled in the air in front of them. There were only four words starting with C-R-E-T, and Dan's eyes scanned them upwards: "*cretonne – a strong printed cotton fabric; cretin – colloquial idiom for idiot; Cretan – a native of Crete; and cretaceous – composed of or like chalk---.*"

"That's it!" yelled Sara, "It's *cretaceous* – look! – the second definition - *relating to the last period of the Mesozoic era (between the Jurassic and Tertiary periods, about 146 to 65 million years ago) at the end of which dinosaurs and many other organisms died out*".

"That's it! Well spotted! That's exactly what it means. That's where we were in time – in the cretaceous period, when the dinosaurs died out. So Peter wrote the names backwards."

"Or at least the first four letters, because they've all got four letters."

"Right! Let's crack on with the rest of the table."

The next segment they looked at was obvious. The figure of Nuada gave it away even as they read: A-R-A-T.

"Tara!" they chorused.

The neighbouring segment, with an artist's easel, painting and sculpture was also easy. The lettering read: N-O-E-L.

"Well, it's not Noel, like Christmas, it's L-E-O-N – for Leonardo", Sara said.

"Yes! Next!"

Before they could look at the next segment, the Rainbow Catcher beeped. It was a message from Leo, but there were no words, just an attachment.

Dan clicked to open it, and let out a yell as T.P. poured himself out of the Rainbow Catcher. Sara shrieked, and then they both laughed with relief as he made a show of dusting himself down: "Did you think you'd lost me then?"

Suddenly, the cellar door opened, and Liz shouted: "Are you all right? What's the noise?"

"Eh, it's OK mum, I just dropped something and got a fright!"

"Well, tea's ready anyway. Come on up!"

She went back to the kitchen, and Sara said: "T.P., It's good to see you! What happened? You were grabbed by these two monsters!"

He replied gravely: "They failed to recognise the power of good against evil. For now, they are gone, but they are becoming bolder, and stronger too. You must beware."

Dan said: "We've talked about that. We need to get our angel friends to help us."

"Yes. I cannot help you where you travel next."

"Why not?" Sara asked.

"I am bound to the present and the past and to this Earth."

The children looked at each other: "So we're travelling into space after all!" Dan exclaimed.

Sara said: "That's another piece of our jigsaw then. I'd better go and let you have your tea. When can we follow up?"

"I can't make Wednesday – we're having a football practice. It'll have to be the weekend. How's Friday for you?"

"That's fine – after tea?"

"Yes. Good".

Over tea, the family talked about the new Rainbow Catcher. Hugh was obviously proud of it, and told them: "We'd actually been working on holograms for some time, but the compression techniques simply demanded too much chip space, so we miniaturised the chip itself. It lost us some picture definition, but we got round that by using centrifugal colour washing."

"Hugh, I'm sure it's fascinating for you, but I don't know the half of what you're talking about!" declared Liz.

"Yes, of course. Sorry! Anyway, we finalised the new developments last week, but when Dan had his model pinched, I added the security alarm, and that's it now!"

"Can I watch it before bed, dad?" pleaded Tim.

Liz said: "Yes, but you can't stay up late, Tim – school tomorrow, remember."

The boys went to Dan's room, he found the machine's replay facility, and they watched the rest of the Scooby Doo cartoon on holographic TV.

Dan went to bed not long after Tim.

Monday had been a very busy day, too busy by far.

Chapter 49

"You should see Mark's eye! He can hardly see out of it!" Said Sara on Wednesday morning. Dan glanced at Mark standing on his own in the playground looking sorry for himself. His right eye was purple and swollen, the eyelids puffed and angry looking. Everyone was staring at him.

"Are you all right?" Dan asked.

"Nothing for you to bother about Danny boy. Just a war wound!"

"How did it happen?"

"Mind your own business!" He snorted and stomped off, limping.

Dan shrugged at Sara: "It's like he's been in a fight".

"That wouldn't surprise me at all," she replied.

School was hectic, with Miss Ambrose putting them through a series of Arithmetic and English tests. Dan, Sara and Shane all had full marks in Arithmetic, and Miss Ambrose arched her eyebrows at Sara: "You've improved considerably, Sara – well done! Have you any tips for your classmates?" She looked at Ali and Asha.

Sara flushed: "Eh, not really, Miss. I think I've just been concentrating more this term".

"You've been much more confident and positive too. Good work!"

She read out the results of the Leonardo da Vinci project, and Sara and Dan had the top marks. She congratulated them: "The detail of your work is first class, almost as if you had inside information on his work. It's just the sort of standard I've been looking for – very well done!"

Dan was really uncomfortable. He couldn't stop thinking about her having the codex and what secrets it contained. He knew he had to wait till they found Peter, but he really felt like challenging her. He bit his tongue in frustration.

She also handed back their essays - on subjects of their own choice – and said: "The standard of work was very high, children. You've shown a great deal of imagination, and put a lot of thought into your essays. That's what this school has always prided itself on. We aim to teach you about life, not just about individual subjects, and you've fulfilled that spirit very well indeed.

Iain, I'm really proud of you. Your essay on "Historical Agriculture" was a treat to read. You must have put a good deal of research into it. We'll work on your technique a bit more, but it was a very interesting essay.

Mark, I'm not sure "Goals I've Scored" was quite the sort of subject I had in mind, but it was a fairly decent effort. Scoring six goals against Dan's team was a marvellous feat. Well done!"

Mark blushed furiously, his black eye almost shut, while Dan and his teammates looked at him in disbelief.

Miss Ambrose turned to Sara: "Your essay on "The Mayan Civilisation" had a very authentic ring to it – almost as if you'd been there yourself!" she said with a smile, which lingered after the class's laughter died down.

"Yes, a very good essay, Sara. You didn't mention it, but there's very little written record left of the Mayans. Their codices were nearly all destroyed – at least all but a few."

She beamed, and Dan and Sara could hardly believe the obvious satisfaction in her tone. She continued: "The best effort though was Dan's. Your essay about the battle in mythical Ireland was one of the finest essays I've seen from Primary 6 pupils – an excellent piece of work. It too has that atmosphere which is so hard to recreate unless you've actually been there. Excellent!"

She gave Dan his essay back amid ironic cheers from the class. Miss Ambrose ignored them, and said quietly to him: "The clock tower was interesting, wasn't it?"

Dan was stunned. How did she know about the clock tower? He hadn't mentioned it in his essay. Was she Sorbema after all?

At lunchtime, he shared his puzzlement with Sara: "That proves it! She always seems to know what's going on with our time travels."

"Maybe we're reading too much into it, Dan. Even if she travels too, she can't know *everything* about our trips."

"Well, her comment about the codex settles it. She's got it and she's boasting about it!"

"I agree, but we have to remember she's working with someone else. Is it Brad Maipeson or is it Mark?"

There was no answer. It was another mystery.

On their way back to class, they saw Mark leave Mrs Braid's office, a smile on his lips. As he passed them, he smirked, his face lopsided. The swelling had spread under his eye and looked very painful: "Top marks, eh? That's not everything you know. There's a bit more to life than that!" He laughed at his own joke.

Dan replied: "Well, you're certainly proving that today. What a shiner!"

"All in a good cause," Mark retorted over his shoulder.

At football, Hamish told Dan: "You've been hanging back a lot, trying to look after Struan. You're our goal scorer, so you need to be up in attack all the time, ready to pick up through balls".

"Fair enough, but Struan, you've struggled in goal these last two weeks. What's been wrong?"

"Well, to be honest, it's been you. You're always hanging about my goal, like I can't do it myself, so I've lost my confidence."

"Oh, I'm sorry – right, I've got the point. I'll stay up in attack. You're a good goalie, Struan – I'll keep out your way. What else do we need to do?"

Hamish said: "Well, when I was captain, I always made sure everyone knew their main positions, and what to do in attack and defence".

"I haven't done that, have I?" said Dan.

The others shook their heads. After a bit more discussion, they practised some set pieces – throw-ins, free kicks and corners, and Dan sensed their confidence. He realised how self-centred he'd been. His improvement at the game had been all about himself, and he hadn't thought properly about how he should act as a captain, and consider all the skills and abilities of his friends. He vowed not to make that mistake again, and gritted his teeth silently. He was determined to show Graham "Pele" Esson how wrong he was.

Over the next couple of days, the children were busy and had little time to think about the cellar, but after tea on Friday, Tim went to bed, and when Sara arrived, they went downstairs. T.P. greeted them, drifting easily from side to side. They grinned when they saw the lines of models were almost completely broken up. In their place were five groups, each representing a trip. The newest had the artist's easel, a beautiful black horse and the statue of Leo in miniature.

The table gleamed in the bright light, and Sara asked: "I wonder if we'll go someplace tonight."

"I don't know Sara, but I'm really keen to check out the rest of the segments."

There were three left to examine. T.P. looked over their shoulders, occasionally shape-shifting through the table itself. Working out the fifth segment was easy.

The thatched house, the pyramids and the snake were the clues. The lettering read: A-Y-A-M, and Dan immediately said: "Maya! It's the Mayans!"

This left two segments. The sixth showed a flying saucer and a bubble shaped car with wheels and stilt-like legs.

Sara said: "These are the models!"

"Yes, they are! The flying saucer must be to do with space."

As they spoke, the rug's violet circle began to glow. It changed from a dull muddy blue to become a lovely bluish purple colour, exactly like the deep shade in a rainbow.

They looked at each other. Dan said: "You know, our adventures started in the middle of the colours with the green circle - the dinosaurs ----"

"-----the Cretaceous period!"

"------ moving outwards with yellow for the Mayans, orange for Tara, red for Caesar and Rome-----"

"-----to the outside edge."

"And when we went to Leonardo's time, we were on the blue circle, inside the green."

"So the two left are the inner colours – violet ---"

"----- and indigo in the middle."

"So what's violet then?"

They read the letters on the table together: A-M-O-F, and Sara said: "so it's

F-O-M-A! What's FOMA?"

They said: "Fomalhaut" together, the rug pulsed strongly, and they stepped on to its violet ring. T.P. shouted: "I can't come with you!" and they were sucked into space.

Chapter 50

Surprisingly, they were still on the rug, T.P.'s voice ringing in their ears. He had disappeared. The violet circle stopped pulsing and all was silent – for just a second. The first sounds they heard were shouts of: "Yes! Well done, Andy! Great work Gribol! What a hoover!"

Confused, they looked around and found themselves in the centre of a group of children, all about their own age, dressed from head to toe in skin hugging violet clothes. They wore the same outfits, and Dan couldn't help smiling at the cheerful greeting: "Welcome aboard! Great to see you!"

Sara blinked rapidly, and asked:"Where are we? Who are you?"

A thin boy with short blond hair stepped forward with a brown haired girl. Both grinned broadly. "Hi!" said the boy, "I'm Andy."

"And I'm Gribol," added the girl.

Andy said: "If we got it right, *you're* Dan and Sara."

Gribol said: "If we got it wrong, *we're* in trouble!"

The rest of the children laughed.

Dan frowned: "What's going on? Where are we? Who are you?"

"Questions!" said Andy.

"Questions!" said Gribol.

"Right, team, back to your stations," Andy announced.

"While we brief them," added Gribol without pause.

They sounded like one person with different voices, so smoothly did one follow the other.

For the first time, they took in their surroundings. They were on a small platform in the middle of a brightly lit circular room, like a huge upturned metal goldfish bowl. Large screens glowed all around, some displaying graphs and diagrams, others relaying pictures. One was of a bustling town, another showed rolling countryside and on a third, waves crashed on a rocky coastline.

The remaining children, in pairs, attended the screens, while another boy and girl sat at an open table examining an inset display which sparkled and glowed, reflecting on their intent faces.

"Right!" Andy said, clapping his hands, "Let's get to it!"

Dan interrupted: "This is a space ship, isn't it?"

"Right in one" said Gribol.

Dan and Sara looked at each other meaningfully.

Andy said: "We've been practising with our new fine-tune hoover, and you're our first ever pick-ups."

Gribol went on: "We've used it in practice, but often live trials can be a problem. We even got the rug perfectly with no loss of matter at all."

"We're on our second mission from home, exploring and collecting."

"Hang on! Hang on!" Dan said, "What do you mean exploring and collecting? You're talking like we're some kind of specimen!"

Andy and Gribol looked at each other before replying. "Let's go back a stage," led Andy.

"Start from home," Gribol followed. "We're from what you call the Piscis Austrinus constellation - The Southern Fish."

"Actually from Fomalhaut."

"Well – nearby anyway."

Sara said: "We know about Fomalhaut."

Dan added: "We've been talking about it too."

"We know," said Andy, "That's why we picked you up. We felt your mind waves, and the hoover did the rest. Clean as a whistle."

"What's the hoover?" Dan asked.

"It's a device we use for scanning things, analysing them in detail, assessing them, and collecting them"

"How?" Sara asked.

Gribol replied: "It breaks the target down into subatomic particles, and converts them to what your scientists call strings."

"Strings are the atom's building blocks. We call them micro –strings."

"---- pulls them through its relativity converter, and reassembles them."

"Just like we did with you!" they both finished.

Dan shook his head: "Hold on. How come we're one minute in Mistlees, and the next here?"

"And dressed differently too," added Sara.

"Oh! We thought you were used to that," said Andy, "With your time travels."

"What happened to time? It must take time." Dan queried.

"Oh, that's what the relativity converter does," Gribol replied, "It stops time, reverses it, or moves it on a bit."

"And the particle analyser mixes the various strings, or atoms, needed to make your new clothes."

"Easy!" They chorused.

"Come and meet the gang!" said Andy.

Gribol led them to the table. "This is Lisa, and this is Gary," she announced.

Lisa looked up, smiled and said:"Hi, I'm Lisa Greenly----"

"----- and I'm Gary Ellisen", her companion said.

"I'm Dan – and this is Sara. Pleased to meet you. We're trying to understand where we are, and what's happening."

"Why, so are we!" said Lisa.

"Well, not really," said Gary.

"That's what *you* say."

"I know, but it's just because the polarity reverses in space-time due to the neutrinos----"

"----- they just slide through, don't they?"

Sara stopped them: "Excuse me, what *are* you talking about?"

"Sorry," Lisa said, "Just got carried away".

They spoke in the same way as Andy and Gribol, one following the other as if they were one voice.

"Please tell us what you're doing!" asked Dan.

"We're the flight duo who get us from A to B and back again."

"Well, usually."

"I've told you, control the quantum effect by magnifying the wave transmission."

"OK! OK! I'm on it."

Gary pressed a series of small buttons, and the displays on the table's screen lit up with a fluorescent whoosh. At the left side was Earth, and on the right, gigantic in comparison, was a purple planet surrounded by a huge series of rings. "Right, we've got it then!"

Good. Let's check everyone's ready."

Dan asked: "Is that Fomalhaut?"

"Sure is," Lisa and Gary said together.

Andy said: "Let's show Dan and Sara around before we go back."

The first screen showed a town. The small fidgety boy at the controls introduced himself as Denis.

"And I'm Lutous," spoke the tall elegant girl, whose short white hair was startling against her black skin.

"What's this?" Asked Sara.

Denis answered first: "We're examining the pollution levels in London."

"To see what change there's been in the last five years."

"How can you tell the difference?" Dan asked.

"Oh, the machine stores all the readings-----"

"-----interprets them and displays the results."

A series of tables flickered on to the screen, replacing the panoramic view of central London. They read:

air pollution:	**+ 2.9%**
acid precipitation:	**+ 4.5%**
water pollution:	**– 3.2%**
land pollution:	**+ 1.0%**
photochemical smog:	**+ 8.4%**
particulate matter:	**+ 11.1%**

Sara asked: "What are the last two things?"

Denis scratched his ear and said: "Good question!"

Lutous added: "Very good! Do we know?"

"We know! Photochemical smog's the stuff your cars chuck out. It's full of carbon monoxide and the like; and particulate matter is what used to give you "pea soup" smogs."

"Right, and that's the heavy muck - particles of rubber, tarmac, unburned bits of coal, oil, wood, and lead."

"And they're hard to control, and hang around for a long time!"

"But London's been working at water pollution."

"Let's have a look."

Denis cracked his fingers, waggled them and switched the screen to a view of the city, zooming in on the River Thames. The camera briefly showed the surface of the water, and then plunged underneath.

"Bring it up!" Denis said, and Lutous magnified the image, and turned it to show the scene under the surface. Fish swam past, and Denis clicked a switch that labelled them.

"Salmon. Dogfish. Skates"

"Brilliant! Let's see the water pipes."

Denis clicked buttons rapidly, and the camera pulled free of the water. The single image split into eight, each of which swiftly tracked to the buildings on either side of the river. The walls appeared to dissolve as the camera view cut through and displayed eight pipes, all with water running through.

"Analysis?" asked Lutous, and Denis scratched his leg and flicked a micro switch. In the centre of the screen, up popped a chart, showing rapidly changing figures.

He told them: "That's the amount of water being used for drinking, cooking, cleaning, washing, and so on, and the proportion of additives - well down on last time."

"----- and there's why."

Lutous pointed at a line of figures:

"Sewage sludge: –8%; bio-digestion: +15%; treated waste water: +4.9%.

This rapid snapshot of London's water fascinated the children, but Andy and Gribol moved them on to the next screen, which was unmanned.

"Wildlife, trees and plants," explained Andy.

"What are you looking for?" Sara asked.

Gribol said: "Checking out your animal and insect life - and birds -

"------ and soil---"

"----and seeing how your vegetation's doing."

Dan found this rat-a-tat-tat form of speech they all used

amusing, and he suppressed a smile as he asked: "What's the verdict then?"

"Verdict?" queried Andy.

"There's no verdict", added Gribol.

"Soil pollution's getting a bit worse, and affecting your crops, and tree and plant life ----"

"------- and insects are multiplying ------"

"------- though that's the warmer weather-----"

" True, and there are more foxes, and rabbits of course ------"

"---- and rodents like rats and mice -----"

" ---- and voles and moles."

"Are moles rodents?" asked Sara.

"Good question!" Andy said.

Gribol clicked the screen and the view of the rolling woodlands changed to a huge photo of a mole. Underneath, it read: "*There are 27 species of mole (Talpidae family), all in the Northern hemisphere on Earth, though remains of Golden Moles have been found underground on Mars. They belong to the seven families of insectivores (shrews, moles and hedgehogs) comprising 375 species of mammal.*"

She said: "Right! They're mammals OK, like rodents are, but Insectivores-----"

"------ not rodents?" Andy added.

"Not rodents."

Sara said: "Did I read that correctly? I thought it said there are moles on Mars!"

"*Were* moles on Mars," replied Andy.

"Like there were lots of things on Mars," added Gribol, "And not just *things*. Animals, plants, insects, trees------"

"------ I know, I know, but they're gone now, and it's our fault, you know."

"How's it our fault?"

"Didn't you know we used their water?"

"Hoovered it?"

"Hoovered it!"

Dan stopped them: "Hang on! Did you say you took the water from Mars?"

"Well, yes," replied Andy, "but we needed it more than Mars did."

Gribol said: "I remember now. We did it just before they had a big burn out----"

"----- freeze out actually."

"Same thing really – everything died pretty quick in the cold."

"But we got the water!"

"We got the water."

"Your scientists are just starting work there, aren't they?" asked Andy.

Dan replied: "Well, I know there have been a few probes sent there."

Gribol said: "I saw that in the Other Planet Newscape – they found hematite and geothite"

"What are they," Sara asked.

"They're what are left after you take water away."

"Hematite's an iron oxide, and geothite's an iron mineral----"

"----- and they're often left lying around where there's been lots of water."

"What about jarosite?" Gribol asked.

"Yes, they found that too."

"That'll tell them the water went pretty fast."

Sara asked: "Jarosite?"

Andy replied: "It's a mineral that proves an acid environment, and if it's there they can tell that wet times came to a quick end----."

"Did we really take it all?" Gribol was asking as the couple led them to the screen showing water crashing on rocks.

"We left a bit at the poles, but it's all frozen up now."

They reached the next screen.

"This is Mike and this is Stolwind", announced Andy.

The duo turned as if in slow motion.

Gribol said: "They've been working on water levels and their effect on your climate."

"Oh that's interesting. What effect do they have?" Sara asked enthusiastically.

Stolwind was a long limbed girl who looked Asian. Her hair shone beautifully in the bright light, but it was hard not to notice her eyes. They were deep black, contrasting sharply with the whites of her irises, and when she looked directly at Sara, her eyes seemed to cut right through her. Sara found she couldn't hold her gaze.

Dan found the same with Mike, whose sharp blue eyes had a similar effect.

They felt really uncomfortable. Stolwind looked carefully at Mike who, after a frozen second, nodded. She spoke in a carefully measured deep tone: "As Earth heats up, your Poles are melting, and your water levels are rising."

She softly clicked each of her four fingers with the thumb on her right hand, and the picture behind her changed to show four different scenes, all of floods.

One showed a river crashing through a narrow gorge, sweeping trees and bridges away with its thundering speed.

The second highlighted a family perched on the roof of a wooden shack, with floodwater rising rapidly all around.

The third appeared to show a tiny island, with waves sweeping over it, but as they adjusted to the scale, they saw it was a small village, engulfed with water.

The final image was startling. It showed a tidal wave rushing up a river, swamping the countryside in its path, houses, roads and woods disappearing under its relentless progress. It swallowed up a high road bridge, and Dan shouted: "Hang on, that's the River Tay – it's come past Dundee, and it's heading for Perth!"

Mike clicked his fingers, and replaced the image with one of a tidal wave engulfing a beautiful sandy beach. He said slowly: "That one has yet to happen."

Dan shivered, and told Sara: "I don't want to see this stuff. It's horrible."

Mike and Stolwind turned back carefully to their screen, and the children heard them say together: "Soon!"

Andy cheerfully spoke: "Sorry about that!"

Gribol added: "So on we go!"

The neighbouring boy and girl were intent on their screen, and Dan and Sara watched for a second before Sara said: "They're playing chess!"

The screen was a three dimensional chessboard, crammed with pieces. There were four armies, two attacking side to side and two up and down. As if by magic, a pawn dressed as an ancient Egyptian, stripped to the waist and carrying a small dagger, attacked a Darth Vader clad bishop whose back was turned. The struggle only lasted seconds, and the bishop dissolved into thin air.

Moments later, the Egyptian was attacked from above by a

knight, a cowboy on horseback with a bandana wrapped round his mouth. He coolly shot the Egyptian, blew the smoke from his barrel and took the vacant space. With a yell, a ninja warrior rook leapt along the screen and shredded the cowboy and his horse with a series of quick-fire blows.

The fourth army was the Danaans, complete with Coegloamer pawns, Nuada and Sorbema as king and queen, and the Vashad Thains as the other support pieces.

Andy said: "That's typical of Ginnay and the other Andy-----"

"------ showing off as usual!"

Andy and Ginnay turned round dramatically. One moment they were facing the screen, and the next, without visible movement, they faced the children.

"Hi!" they chorused, "We're playing chess."

"I'm the cowboys and the Danaans," said Andy.

"And I'm the Egyptians and the ninjas", said Ginnay.

"How do you move the pieces?" Dan asked.

Andy replied: "We influence them. I'll think through play options, the players analyse them and then make up their own minds".

Ginnay continued: "The problem is that all of them hate losing, and they sometimes develop minds of their own".

As they spoke, a voice rang out: "Charge!"

Startled, they looked at the screen to see the Coegloamers charge across the screen as one, skittling the Egyptians into oblivion. The Vashad Thains moved up and down screen, in perfect rhythm, and within thirty seconds the board was clear of all opposition. Three Coegloamers rode up to Nuada, one dragging an Egyptian pharaoh, another a sheriff, and the third the heavily armed leader of the ninjas.

Andy groaned: "No, not again!"

The first Andy said: "Let's leave these guys and meet the last team."

Ginnay protested: "They don't always behave like this you know!"

They walked further round the spaceship, leaving Andy and Ginnay arguing playfully. They reached a massive hologram of the solar system, like the one in the Museum. The sun was orbited anti-clockwise by its eight planets - Mercury, Venus, Earth, Mars, Jupiter, Saturn, Uranus, and Neptune, but there were thousands of smaller bodies evident on the screen.

Andy told them they were mapping asteroid movement.

Dan asked: "Is that what all the small things are?"

He answered: "Well, yes----"

"----and no!" said Gribol.

Dan and Sara looked confused, so they explained, Andy leading: "You're looking at asteroids, planets and all your moons."

"You've got 75 of those, but only discovered 63 so far."

"Right, but we're following all those asteroids."

Sara asked: "Why are you watching the asteroids?"

"To stop them bumping into you of course!"

"How do you do that?"

"Hoover them!"

"You hoover them?"

"Yes! Not many of them are very big, but they make a fair old dent in a planet if they collide-----"

"----- so we hoover them up to stop them-----."

Sara said: "What do you do with them?"

Andy tapped his nose with his index finger: "Ah! That's the smart part! We dump them ---"

"------- in black holes------."

Dan said: "You hoover stray asteroids and put them in black holes?"

"That's what I said, didn't I?" replied Andy.

"Sure did!" answered Gribol.

Andy continued: "There are millions of these guys, though only a million or so are over a kilometre in diameter."

"They're made of stone and metal - mainly iron-----"

"----- but there's carbon in there too-----"

"------ so we break them down in the hoover to their component parts, and flush them down the nearest black hole."

Dan said: "I've always wondered what a black hole is."

"In simple terms?"

"In simple terms!"

Andy explained, with Gribol's help.

"When a high mass star-----"

"----- that's a huge guy-----"

"------ reaches the end of its life, it explodes - collapses in on itself----"

"----- and when the core of the star collapses, it continues to collapse on itself---"

"----- forever---"

"----- forever----"

"--- and nothing escapes the gravitational field it produces----"

"----- nothing----"

"---- not even light ----"

"----- which is why it's called a black hole---."

"So we dump the asteroids there."

Dan wasn't sure he properly understood, but it made some kind of sense.

Andy said: "Think of it this way. If Earth was squished down to the size of a football, by something like a giant car crusher-----"

"------- planet cracker----"

"---- OK – planet cracker----"

"----- but still had the same amount of matter in it, then it would take more speed than the speed of light -----"

"------ to escape its surface-----"

"---- because everything's held so tight together----"

"---- that would make it a black hole!"

They swapped a high five at this conclusion.

Andy added: "It's all energy you know. E= mc squared."

"That was your Einstein guy, wasn't it?"

Dan said "Yes, I think so." He added: "It sounds like you're watching over us."

"You and all the rest!"

"Well, only this system."

"Yes, all right, only the solar system-----"

"---- for now-----"

" -----until we can graduate to some bigger systems----"

"---- and bigger equipment----."

Andy rubbed his hands together: "Yes - bigger and better equipment!"

They led Dan and Sara back to the table where Lisa and Gary waited patiently.

"Ready? Asked Lisa.

"Ready!" replied Andy and Gribol.

Lisa looked at Dan and Sara, and said: "OK! We're going home, so best get yourselves ready."

Gary continued: "Find a place to sit where you're not touching anyone else and put your hoods on"

Lisa demonstrated by pulling over her head and face a snug fitting mask she produced from a pocket in her outfit. Gary pulled his sleeves over his hands and they formed gloves round his fingers.

"Why are we doing this?" Sara asked.

"We're going to whiz through space------"

"----- and time---"

"------ and we don't want any bits to come loose-----"

"---- and don't touch anyone else---"

"----- so you don't get all mixed up!"

Dan and Sara obeyed, as did the others. When they were ready, they were completely cocooned in their violet coveralls, with no flesh exposed. They could still see through the thin material, and chose a spot to sit near Andy and Gribol.

Lisa shouted: "Ready?"

Everyone chorused: "Ready!"

Gary leant over the glowing screen, held the palm of his hand directly above Earth, and swiftly moved it to above Fomalhaut.

"Go!" He said.

Chapter 51

Eerily, Dan and Sara felt the air round them crumble, and felt weightless.

There was a strong smell of burning, and a vivid flash lit up the spaceship.

Dan could see Sara but she shimmered all over, and he realised he could see straight through her to where Andy sat. He could see through him too, and his mind absorbed the fact he could see through *everything.*

The Earth hung in front of him, but in an instant it was gone in a trail of sparks, and he felt cold, then hot, and suddenly solid again.

The firm shape of the spaceship was there as before, and the children removed their hoods and rolled back their gloved sleeves.

"Not so bad, was it?" asked Andy with a grin.

"Hope they've steered OK – you know what Gary can be like." Gribol added.

Lisa and Gary shouted: "Spot on! Centre target!"

Cheers rang out from the other children, and Dan followed Sara in removing his hood and glove coverings. Lisa said: "Open up!" and Gary waved his hand at the curved section of wall beside him. The metal shimmered and disappeared and again they could see directly outside through clear glass.

Hanging in the dense blackness of space was a giant version of the plane from the cellar. Sara clutched Dan's arm wordlessly. It was the size of a jumbo jet, its shiny surface dotted with small dart-like pairs of wings. The underside was one long deep window through which children wearing violet costumes peered, waving at them.

"How's that for accuracy?" asked Gary.

"Pretty good for a beginner!" grinned Lisa.

Dan was astonished. He turned to Andy and asked: "Andy, all this is moving so fast. Please stop for a moment and tell us what's going on!" Sara nodded firmly in agreement.

"Ah yes, of course!"

Gribol said: "That's our short trip plane. We use it for nipping in and out of Sahasrara."

Sara asked:" What's that?"

"Sahasrara is our home planet," replied Andy.

Dan said: "But I thought you were from Fomalhaut."

"Well we are, but on Earth, you haven't discovered Sahasrara-----"

"------ because we've kept it hidden from you so far."

"How can you keep a planet hidden?" Dan asked.

"Oh, dust clouds, and comets, and so on ---"

"-----but I think your scientists are getting close to finding us now, though they're only guessing we're there right now!"

"They know something's causing the dust clouds, but you don't have the equipment to work it out."

"You'll get there in due course, so for now, think of us as Fomalhaut's little sister----"

"----- or brother!" finished Andy.

"Let's show you!" they both said, and they crossed to Lisa and Gary's table.

They spoke quickly to Gary who nodded, and he clicked several buttons on his screen. Up popped a huge bright blue planet with hazy rings, like muddy clouds, circling round it.

"That's Fomalhaut!" explained Gary.

"And that's Sahasrara!" showed Lisa pointing to a bulge in the rings.

They could see a round red planet nestling in the folds of the swirling clouds.

Dan shook his head in amazement: "So many things we don't know," he said.

Right!" said Andy, "Next thing's to get there! Are we ready, Lisa?"

"Ready!" She replied.

Gary waved to the waiting plane, and two pairs of its wings began to rotate. It glided alongside, and an enclosed platform slid from its body, connected to the spaceship, and Gary said: "We have transport!"

They all walked through the connecting tunnel to the plane, and were greeted enthusiastically by a small group of other children. A boy and girl stepped forward, and exchanged greetings with the spaceship team.

Lisa and Gary introduced Dan and Sara.

"I'm Alf," said the stocky black haired boy.

"And I'm Melamee," his slim red haired companion added. She looked a bit like a teenage version of Miss Ambrose, her face covered with freckles, her hair tied in two pigtails. Sara and Dan exchanged a look.

"We pilot the plane", they announced.

"What do we have to do?" asked Dan.

"Do?" replied Alf.

"Nothing!" finished Melamee, with a grin.

Andy said: "This time, we just sit and enjoy the ride."

Melamee showed them to a row of deep reclining chairs, demonstrated the seatbelts, and left them sitting opposite Andy and Gribol. The others spread round the remaining seats.

They heard a humming sound, and were pushed back deep into their chairs as the craft set off for Sahasrara.

Dan said to Sara: "This is some trip. I feel a bit out of my depth! And it's Miss Ambrose who's piloting us!"

"I know. It's all a bit weird. How come they're so young, all of them?"

As if they'd heard them, Andy and Gribol replied. They were more relaxed than on the spaceship, and conversation flowed easier.

Andy said: "We age in a different way from you, though we look the same physically. Years on Earth go past extremely quickly – about five times quicker than ours. It means we live a lot longer than you, and so we have much more time to learn and get experience."

"So how old are you, Andy?"

Gribol answered: "In your years, Andy's fifty eight, and I'm fifty nine."

Dan gulped: "How long do you live for?"

Andy replied: "Our average life expectancy – in your years – is about four hundred."

"Four hundred!" exclaimed Dan, "That's some age!"

Gribol said: "I suppose it must seem that way, but for us, it's quite normal. We're only now getting our early experience of real space travel, but our parents and their ancestors have been doing it for thousands of years."

"So how come you haven't made contact with Earth?"

"Oh, we have, but you don't seem to believe it."

"How do you mean?"

"Well, we've picked up hundreds of people from Earth and taken them aboard our spaceships, but when they return to Earth, nobody believes them. We get upset, because your newspapers call them "alien abductions", when all we're trying to do is say hello, and help your planet develop."

"Really?" quizzed Sara.

"Yes, really" she replied.

Andy added: "But we don't help our cause sometimes, do we?"

Gribol looked at him and after a moment said: "Oh, you mean the fireballs and stuff?"

"Yes, and their Bermuda Triangle."

"Ah, but that's different – we're saving people there!"

"I suppose so, but they don't know that, do they?"

Dan interrupted: "What's all this about fireballs and the Bermuda Triangle – I've heard of that."

Sara said; "That's the place where boats and planes keep disappearing, isn't it?"

Andy agreed: "That's right. It's all about weather to start with. There's a huge stretch of the Atlantic Ocean near Bermuda which gets really violent storms, which come from nowhere, and cause planes to crash and boats to sink."

"It's like the other place, near Japan, called "the Devil's Sea", where compass readings go all wrong, so people get confused."

"So when there's a sudden storm and your compass gives wrong readings----"

"----it's no wonder there are accidents."

Dan asked: "So where do you come in?"

"Well," replied Andy, "when the plane's about to crash, or the boat's about to sink, we-----"

"-------hoover them?" quickly interjected Dan.

"Hey, smart!" exclaimed Gribol. "Right! We hoover them!"

"And what happens to them then – you don't flush them down a black hole do you?"

"Hey!" said Andy, "What kind of people do you think we are? We take them home with us."

"We save them!" Gribol added.

"Incredible!" muttered Dan.

"You mentioned fireballs," Sara said. "We saw one in Rome, but it was a couple of thousand years ago!"

"Wow! And you talk about us having long lives!" laughed Andy.

Before Sara could say anything, Gribol held up her hand: "We know! You're the timetrippers! Getting yourselves quite a reputation."

"Eh? How?" asked Dan.

Andy winked: "You could say we heard you coming!"

Gribol cautioned: "Enough, enough. Tell them about fireballs!"

Andy continued: "Well, it's a bit silly really-----"

"----- and embarrassing!"

"Right! As we grow up, we learn all about Weather."

Dan asked: "You learn Weather as a subject at school?"

"No – we don't have schools like you do. Pretty much everything is learned – how do they call it, Gribol?"

"On-line!"

"Yes, on-line, except we don't need the machines you use because everyone's implanted with a chip at birth."

"What do you mean?" Sara asked.

Andy answered: "It's easy really – we all have chips in our forearms – you can't see them because the skin grows over them – which are like your computers, but more powerful."

"Yes, about a million times more powerful!"

"That's unbelievable!" Dan exclaimed.

"Well, you think so now, but you soon won't!"

Gribol interrupted: "Get on with it, Andy!"

"OK. Anyway, we learn about Weather, and have to experience every type of weather condition so we can learn to control it."

There was silence as this sank in. "You control the weather?" Dan asked.

"We *can* control it, but only when we're there, and that's only a small fraction of the time----"

"----once every few years."

"One part of our training is projecting lightning flashes, and sheet lightning, but sometimes the beginners get it wrong and roll the lightning up instead of stretching it out----"

"---- so you get our fireballs!"

Dan burst out laughing, and Sara joined him.

"So the fireball we saw in Rome came from you guys?"

"Well yes actually – sorry about that!"

"That's brilliant!" Dan declared.

Sara thought for a moment and said to Gribol: "There's something I'm really curious about. I'm confused about your names. All the boys have short names that we know ------"

"------ like Andy, Gary, Denis, Mike, and – who's the pilot of the plane?"

"Alf." Answered Andy.

"Yes," Sara continued, "but the girls have really unusual names – ones I've never heard of, except for Lisa. Lutous, Melamee, Ginnay, and you, Gribol. Why's that?"

Gribol grinned: "Ah, that's our nature. We kind of beg, borrow and steal things from all round the universes, and names are a speciality. The boys have names from Earth, but most of the girls' names are from Pluto. It used to be one of your planets."

"From Pluto!" exclaimed Dan, "but people surely can't live there – it's too far away from the sun".

"Not on the surface, they don't!" Replied Andy, "But it's really warm in the middle, you know."

"Like the opposite of our place," said Gribol.

Andy leant forward: "Quite right! It's far too hot for anyone to survive on our planet's surface, so we live deep inside where it's cooler."

Gribol grinned: "Quite cosy in fact - once you get used to it."

Dan was puzzled: "If it's too hot on the surface, how do you get inside to where you live?"

"Good question!" Andy and Gribol replied.

Alf shouted: "One minute!"

Andy said: "You're about to find out! Watch this!"

He turned on a screen above them showing an outside view of the plane.

The screen split into two sections, the lower one showing what was directly underneath them.

It was a seething roaring furnace.

The surface of Sahasrara was ablaze with flames soaring thousands of metres high above its surface. It was a fantastic frightening extravaganza of yellow, red, orange and blue, licking furiously up towards them.

Suddenly, on the upper screen, the outside of the plane burst into flames, huge tendrils of fire scorching along towards the camera. The plane dived into the roasting cauldron, and Sara screamed and screamed.

Chapter 52

Engulfed by the searing flames, the accelerating plane plummeted, and Dan gripped Sara's arm firmly.

Melamee saw their fear, and shouted: "It's OK! This is normal!"

Dan, who couldn't see how this was in any way normal, heard a loud "Ti Ti Ti Ti" sound, and felt a surge of energy through the plane. The top of his head vibrated as the plane burst through the firestorm, and they entered Sahasrara.

The fires disappeared, and the cameras showed a huge bowl-shaped landscape. For as far as the eye could see were hills, fields, towns, villages, and cities, all basking in glorious sunshine. It was such a beautiful peaceful scene that Sara gasped: "This is glorious!" she exclaimed, "But how did we get through the flames?"

Andy said: "That was Alf and Melamee showing off a bit. All we do is fire up the plane to match the heat on the planet's surface, use the hoover to zap a gap for us, slide through and the hoover reshapes everything behind us!"

"Dan asked: "How come the plane doesn't melt?"

Andy and Gribol said: "Good question!" and Gribol answered: "It's made of an unbreakable substance with a melting temperature several thousands of degrees hotter than the planet's surface."

"How hot's that?" asked Sara.

Andy said airily: "Oh, about 10,000 degrees centigrade."

"Right!" said Dan thoughtfully.

As they talked, the plane landed softly, and Alf and Melamee opened the front double doors. The Fomalhaut children exited cheerfully, and headed towards a row of bubble-like cars with stilt legs.

Sara pointed, a huge grin on her face: "That's our model!"

Dan nodded, and replied: "It's weird, isn't it? We come all this way, but there's always something familiar."

"Thank goodness!"

The cars sped off silently, each carrying two children.

Dan asked Andy: "What are the stilts for?" but before he could reply, a car stopped at a tall concrete building that looked like a multi-storey car park.

"That's our headquarters," Gribol told them, "where we meet before we go on a mission, and store our stuff---"

" ------and check out the places we're going to."

As they spoke, the car's stilts operated. They lifted the car straight up in the air like a giant car jack, extending effortlessly upwards till the car reached the fourth level. A doorway opened, a ramp appeared, the stilt legs telescoped into the car's body and it drove smoothly inside.

"Fantastic!" Dan said.

Gribol asked them: "Would you like a tour of our home?"

Sara nodded enthusiastically, but said: "I don't know about you Dan, but I'm starving!"

"Yes, me too – it seems an age since we ate!"

Andy and Gribol walked them across to a bubble car; they all climbed in, and drove to the children's headquarters. Sara's tummy lurched as the car shot up to the fourth floor, and she said: "It feels like a roller coaster!"

They drove on to the ramp, and parked beside the other car. They were in a huge open space, brightly lit, though they couldn't see any lights. At one end sat a group of children watching a screen displaying a green and blue planet revolving majestically, three moons gliding around its orbit.

They watched for a few moments, fascinated. Andy told them: "We call that guy Mayan Fujimout."

Gribol continued: "The Mayans, as you know, were amazing astronomers. They charted the planets and stars in incredible detail, and though their viewing equipment was primitive ------"

"------ extremely primitive!-----"

"-----they discovered Fujimout, which is somewhat unique!"

"It used to be part of your solar system, but – a bit like Pluto – it has a very odd orbit, like a giant rugby ball-----"

"-----and at the same time as the Mayans disappeared, so did Fujimout!"

"What happened to it?" Dan asked.

"It was right at one end of its orbit, and it just kept going!"

"It's now pretty near us in fact----"

"---- and that's where our friends are going next!"

Andy led them to a table where Lisa and Gary sat eating. They looked up and grinned. "Beat you to it!" they both said.

"Sure did!" Andy and Gribol chorused.

Andy rubbed his hands together: "Right, what would you like?"

"What is there?" Sara asked.

"Well, anything you want really," Gribol replied, "As long as it's in the machine's programme, you can have it!"

She pointed at a small square metal box. Beside it sat a pile of plates.

Andy said: "I'll show you!" He thought for a moment and said: "Pasta!"

The machine vibrated gently and said, in a smooth deep tone: "What type please?"

"Em, I think I'll have lasagne."

"Meat or vegetarian?" asked the machine.

"Vegetarian!"

There was a soft humming sound, Andy slid a plate under the raised side of the box, waited a few moments and pulled out a steaming hot plate of lasagne.

It smelt delicious, and Sara felt her mouth water. "Can I try next?" she asked.

"Sure!" said Gribol.

Sara said: "Haggis!"

Andy and Gribol looked at each other, and the machine was silent for a second before replying: "Is that maggots?"

Sara laughed, and replied: "No – haggis – h-a-g-g-i-s!"

The machine gurgled, and said: "No known correlation for haggis."

Dan said: "Good try, Sara – you beat it!"

Andy said: "We don't know what haggis is, but if you tell us how it's made, we can programme it."

"I don't think you'll want to know!" Joked Dan. "Come on Sara, try something simpler."

"Beans on toast!" She said.

"Wholemeal, white or brown toast," answered the machine.

"Brown!"

After a few seconds, she had a huge plateful of beans on toast. Dan was next and ordered steak and chips – "well done steak", he replied to the machine's question. Gribol had a vegetarian salad, and they ate companionably, washing the meal down with water from a small fountain.

"This place is amazing," Dan said. "It's quite beyond anything we've seen before."

"Glad you like it." Andy said.

After their meal, they set off to tour Sahasrara. As they drove, Dan had the feeling he'd been here before, and said so to Sara.

"I know – I feel the same. Why is that?"

Andy explained: "You *should* feel at home. This is the Scottish countryside."

"How can it be Scottish?" Dan asked.

"We change the countryside quite often, and knowing you were coming, we thought you'd like to see your own fields, moors and hills."

Gribol explained: "Our hoover has what you would call a giant photocopier which scans images of the land and reproduces them here!"

"You mean you copy things and change the look of your planet?" Sara asked.

"Yes," Andy replied, "Neat isn't it?"

"It's fantastic!" said Dan.

"Wait till you see Inanna then!" Gribol smiled.

"Inanna's our main town," clarified Andy.

They drove past fields of wheat and barley, through valleys flanked by heather- clad hillsides, passing herds of sheep, which scattered at their approach. After a while, Dan realised there was something odd. There was no road, yet the car drove smoothly through the countryside.

Before he could frame the question, Andy said: "Yes, that's right. The car glides above the surface – we don't need roads in the country!"

"What are the wheels for then?" Sara asked.

"We like the wheels, don't we, Gribol?"

"We sure do – they give such a nice feeling of balance and security."

Dan shook his head in wonder. He suddenly remembered his Rainbow Catcher, and took it out. Andy and Gribol were curious, so he explained, and they encouraged him to try it out. He took a few photos of the countryside and videoed a herd of nearby cows. Soon they saw a town emerge in front of them.

"Inanna," Pointed Andy.

It was the strangest place they'd ever seen. Soaring above the buildings were two huge structures, side by side. Sara couldn't believe it: "The Eiffel Tower and the Empire State Building!" she exclaimed.

"Right!" echoed Andy and Gribol.

"We really like them and thought they'd look good here," Andy explained.

Dan laughed: "So you hoovered them?"

"Well," said Gribol, "Copied them!"

The town was made up of buildings, statues, streets and monuments, copied from Earth. They drove along Princes Street, with Edinburgh Castle on one side, but the Houses of Parliament on the other. Big Ben was planted at the head of part of the Great Wall of China, and standing beside the Leaning Tower of Pisa was Nelson's Column.

Sara said: "I can't believe we're seeing this!"

Dan kept taking pictures as they drove through this unreal town. "Why are there no people in the streets?" he asked.

"Oh, nobody lives here," said Andy, "It's just for show!"

"So where do people live?" asked Sara.

"We'll show you!" Gribol replied.

They drove over the Golden Gates Bridge from San Francisco, which soared over the canals of Venice, and out of town. Just beyond stood a plain square building, made of purple plastic.

"This is one of our homes," said Andy.

Gribol continued: "It's like first base for us. Because we move around so much, we don't really stay anyplace for long, so all we need is a basic crash pad."

So it proved, as the Fomalhaut duo showed Dan and Sara round. The house was communal, and rows of cubicles, like office workstations, lined the central corridor. These doubled as sleeping quarters and relaxation spaces, each with their own bed and a bewildering array of screens and gadgetry.

There was an eating bay half way along, with several of the incredible food machines and fountains dispensing water and - as Sara discovered when she tasted it – fresh strawberry juice.

Andy said: "You can change that to whatever taste you want."

Gribol said: "You know - it's probably about time to sleep."

Andy agreed and found Dan and Sara adjoining cubicles.

Dan asked: "Why's nobody here? The place is empty"

Gribol replied: "There are a few expeditions on, so most folk are away. That's good as we have the run of the place."

Sara said: "How do you know what time it is here? The daylight always seems to have the same brightness, and I haven't seen any clocks."

Andy said: "No, we're not big clock fans. We just kind of sleep when we're ready - the same with eating."

"What about daylight then," Dan asked. "When does it get dark?"

"It doesn't!" they chorused.

Andy explained: "The surface of the planet's so hot, it gives us heat and light."

"Yes, it's pretty clever really. What we've done is drill millions of small holes in the surface of Sahasrara, every few metres, and they let the warmth and the light through, so it's always daylight and always warm."

"But what about rain and snow, and different weather?" Sara asked.

Dan butted in: "That's why you pinched the water from Mars!"

"Yes – afraid so!" They both replied.

They left Dan and Sara, and the pair sat on Dan's bed to catch up on the day's events. Dan started: "This place is unreal! There's nothing here that's their own. They seem to have pinched things from all over the place to make it home!"

"I know, but you have to admit it's incredible!"

"Oh, yes, but it lacks something."

"Like what?"

"The real feel of a home. Look at this place – it's soulless – bare floors, no decoration, cubicles that are identical – there's no life in it."

Sara reflected: "You're right, but I feel fine – in fact, my energy's been great all day."

"So's mine – why's that?"

"I think it's because everyone's really in tune with each other. We've seen the way the pairs talk – they're all like two peas in a pod. Each seems to know what the other's thinking all the time."

"You're right – they're all working for and with each other."

"Just like us. What's the point in competing when working together gets you the benefit of both people's views?"

"Yes, and they seem to energise each other, which is what we do -----"

"----- so we're pretty much in tune with them----"

"--- but they're much older than us-----"

"-----though they look and talk like children our age!"

They sensed a change in the atmosphere – a subtle softening of the air around them, and a soft clear voice said: "You have wisdom beyond your years."

In front of them hovered a dazzling angel.

It sparkled like thousands of diamonds reflecting light all round the cubicle, so bright they blinked hard to refocus in its brilliance. A violet flame shimmered round its head, and they could see through its softly glittering wings to the wall beyond.

Dan and Sara were speechless for a few moments, stunned by the power and energy of the angel. It spoke again: "Wherever you travel, we watch over you. I am Kamiel, archangel of light, power and energy."

Dan replied: "How come you're here, on Sahasrara?"

"We are not bound by space and time. Our concerns are limitless. Fomalhaut, its planets and moons, and especially Sahasrara have a vital role in Earth's passage."

Sara asked: "What do you mean, Kamiel?"

"Fomalhaut is one of the four key stars in the heavens, called archangel stars. They watch over other stars, like Sahasrara, which will influence Earth's development. You have been chosen to see mankind's potential."

"That sounds scary!" Dan replied.

"It is only what you wish it to be," Kamiel said softly. "Your friend Peter works with us, as does Nigel."

Dan was flabbergasted: "Nigel! Peter! Do you mean Peter Friis?"

"You will find him soon. He and Nigel are lightworkers."

"What on earth are lightworkers?" Sara spluttered.

"Those who move along their chosen path to help mankind," Kamiel said carefully.

"But what does that mean? I've never heard of lightworkers?" she asked.

"They work tirelessly to help the health of your Earth – in body, mind and spirit. They strive to reduce fear, to curb anger and promote peace and well being."

Dan said: "We need lots of that, for sure!"

"Lightworkers are all around you. You will know them by their actions."

"And Peter's one of them? You say we'll meet him? Where? When?" asked Dan.

"Your questions will be answered. Keep on your chosen path, and you will find him."

Sara broke the silence that followed: "Kamiel, we've had lots of help from other angels, you know – Metatron, Vohumanah and Zuphlas. Are you like them?"

"Like, but not like. They are of the Third Sphere, the closest to mankind. I am of the Second Sphere – of dominions, virtues and powers. My role is to keep balance in the angelic realms and to watch over other angels."

"Like a boss!" Dan said.

"We know no boss as you call one who rules. We work from within – what you see in me is an external figure for what lies within us all. You must seek to find yourself, and be thankful for all you discover."

Dan thought for a second before saying: "Kamiel, if you watch over other angels, you'll know we're having trouble with two rebel angels."

"Azazel and Samahazai."

"Yes, and so far we've been lucky. We've had some help from a friendly ghost, but T.P. can't travel away from Earth, so we need your help."

"What do you wish for?"

Sara replied: "We don't want to see them ever again, but if we do, how do we get rid of them?"

Kamiel said: "You use your energy fields wisely and well, but now you must learn to project them. Your auras will shield you. Be not afraid."

There was a brief flash of purple flame, the atmosphere thickened for a second, and Kamiel disappeared. The children looked at each other. "Oh heck!" Dan began, "What do you make of that?"

Sara shivered: "I'm not sure – he said our auras will shield us, but how? How do we project our energy?"

"We have to think about it, Sara, but remember I said we needed more of the kind of energy we used when I escaped from the lion, and when you calmed Apollo down? I'm sure that's what he means."

"But how do we practise that? We both acted on instinct. I'm not sure I could have practised what I did in Florence."

"Well, maybe that's it. I agree. I don't think I could have practised it either. We'll have to react on instinct if we meet them. We'll both have to remember to use our energy fields."

"OK, I'll go with that! What did you make of Kamiel? I didn't follow all he said to us, but he's like a super-angel, isn't he?"

Dan laughed: "That's a neat way of putting it – a super angel!"

"Kamiel" said Dan, "He said we'd meet Peter – that's terrific!"

"Hmm – Peter and Nigel – lightworkers. Working to make things better. Maybe they'll help us against the rebel angels then."

"If they're around at the time! But Kamiel said we had to find ourselves."

"Working from within – that's right!"

"I think we'll need to sleep on this. My head's buzzing!"

"Me too. Let's let it sink in a bit more, and see what happens tomorrow!"

"Hm! With no night here, how will we know when tomorrow comes?"

"Oh, I'm sure we'll know. Andy and Gribol said they sleep and eat when they feel like it, so when we wake up it'll be tomorrow."

"Ah, but then it'll be today!"

"OK Smartie! You know what I mean!"

"I do, I do!" Dan dodged her mock punch.

She went to her own cubicle, and they were soon fast asleep, Sara thinking she should give the food machine the recipe to make haggis like the Deli.

Chapter 53

Dan stirred and looked round, woken by a clatter. He peered out from his cubicle to see Sara doing the same.

"What was that?" she asked. "Did you hear the noise?"

"Yes, I did!" Yawned Dan, still bleary eyed.

They wandered towards the eating area, drawn by the sound of voices.

"----- and they don't need air to breathe either," said a deep male voice.

A high-pitched female voice replied: "No, they're quite extraordinary. They absorb ozone through their skin, and store it in their equivalent of lungs, which convert it to pure oxygen---"

"And their two hearts -----"

"TWO hearts!" they heard Andy say as they reached the voices.

"Ah!" said Gribol, "Welcome! We're just catching up with Ted and Inndumis. Come and join us!"

Ted and Inndumis were much older than the others. Ted looked in his fifties, thought Dan. He was grey haired, small and dark, in complete contrast to Inndumis who was extremely large and very pale skinned. She was older than Ted with a shock of white curly hair standing almost straight up from her head.

Andy introduced them, and Gribol asked what they wanted to eat.

They both opted for cornflakes, dutifully produced by the food machine, and Andy asked one of the fountains to give them milk.

"Full cream organic, semi-skimmed, skimmed or soya?" asked the fountain in a thin watery voice, causing Dan and Sara to burst out laughing.

"We must reprogramme that voice!" declared Andy.

Sara said: "Full cream organic for us both please," and the machine obliged.

Gribol told them that Ted and Inndumis were just back from Saturn where they'd met the locals.

Dan said: "I thought there was no life on Saturn."

Ted laughed: "I suppose it depends on what you mean by life!"

Inndumis continued: "Yes, they're rather strange – take a bit of getting used to."

Ted said:"There's not so much gravity as here, and the planet's not very dense-----"

"------ so they've adapted to that, and built anti-gravity cells near the rocky core which blend in beautifully with their surroundings."

"So what do they look like – the people I mean?" Dan asked.

"Hmmm, not sure you'd call them people - more like plants really----"

"------ yes, they're like water lilies---"

"Egyptian lotus, I think!"

Sara said: "Are you saying they're plants – I mean like real plants in a garden?"

"Well, it's not a garden down there, and technically they don't live in water---"

"-----but it's like water."

Andy said: "Let's see them then instead of talking about them."

Ted gently slapped his wrist and said "Saturnians!"

Above the table, an image beamed from the chip in his wrist. It was amazing - a swirling sphere of flowers appeared – tall blue-petalled, with yellow irises, and broad flat leaves. The main stems of the plants split in three near the base and the Saturnian lotus plants walked across a yellow lake. Their heads inclined towards each other and they spoke in indistinct syrupy voices.

The quality of the holographic image was stunning – it had depth, clarity and a true three-dimensional look, far superior to Dan's Rainbow Catcher.

Sara said: "Are these really the people who live on Saturn?"

There was silence for a moment until Gribol began to laugh. Andy, Ted and Inndumis joined in. Andy said: "Sorry guys, but Ted and Inndumis are the jokers in our pack – they thought it'd be fun to wind you up!"

Hesitantly, Dan and Sara joined in. Sara said: "I didn't think these things could possibly be people!"

Ted replied: "OK – fair enough, but did you like the animation?"

Dan said: "Brilliant – how do you do that?"

Inndumis said: "We think of an image, focus clearly, and our microchips translate it into pictures."

"They nearly had you going though, didn't they?" Andy asked.

Sara said: "Well, maybe Dan, but not me!"

Gribol said: "You can fool the body but never the soul!"

"What are we up to today?" Dan asked.

"We thought we'd take you to a mountain climbing contest."

"A what?"

Andy explained. "A mountain climbing contest. We have them regularly to keep in shape. It's a great way of tuning up minds and bodies."

Dan and Sara looked at each other, and Sara voiced their thought: "Is this another wind-up?"

Gribol assured them it wasn't, and after finishing their cornflakes, they left in the bubble car, saying farewell to Ted and Inndumis, still chuckling at their Saturnian lotus flower joke.

They drove through the countryside, which had changed. It was hillier and covered in snow, purple and yellow flowers peeping through. The snow didn't affect the car, which glided smoothly towards a distant peak.

Andy told them they'd changed the countryside from Scottish to Swiss for the competition, Gribol adding they had switched off the heat and warmth from the surface to keep the snow from melting.

Andy said: "We change the mountain every year. This year it's a mixture of several different ones, because everyone knows the Himalayas---"

"----- and the Alps." Added Gribol.

Dan was really quiet during the trip, and Sara quizzed him.

"Well, to be honest Sara, I'm feeling a bit nervous – I've never been great with heights, and I suppose that's in my mind. I'm worried we might have to climb."

Sara reassured him: "Don't worry – it'll be all right. I'm sure they'll not put us in danger."

As they drove, bubble cars and small planes whizzed past. When they arrived at the base of the mountain, several hundred people had gathered. Andy and Gribol waved cheerily to other children, and they found seats in the centre of a large semicircular row in a huge outdoor theatre.

The mountain climbing contest was being held on the cliffs in front. Dan paled as his eyes climbed them. A sheer rock face stretched hundreds of metres vertically up, in places leaning outwards. Then the cliff became icy, its smooth gleaming surface winking in the light. The snow-covered peak was so high, it was almost out of vision.

Dan and Sara could see no handholds on the smooth cliff.

"How on earth does anyone climb that?" Wondered Sara.

Andy replied: "You'll be amazed! Today you'll see four of our best climbers tackling it. This is finals day."

"We had several heats a few days ago, which we missed because we were on Earth-----"

"------ or near it anyway!"

Dan was quiet and Sara explained why to Andy and Gribol.

"Really?" Queried Gribol. "We can fix that, you know!"

Sara asked, "What, fix his fear of heights?"

"Absolutely!" Andy declared, "We'll do it after the competition."

Dan's heart sank, and even though Sara tried hard to re-energise him, he still felt nervous.

The four contestants were introduced to huge cheers from the enthusiastic crowd. Teresa was tall, slim and moved like a ballet dancer; Thelma was slightly smaller and stocky, and made a show of flexing her muscles; Dhureen was extremely petite and seemed hardly tall enough to be able to climb the rock face.

The only boy in the competition was Winkles, a tall stringy character with a slouch and a permanent smile. He winked at the crowd.

"That's why we call him Winkles," said Andy in an aside.

All of them were clad in the familiar violet body suits, but wore thin climbing shoes studded on top and on the soles with short spikes, curved like tiny claws. These gleaming spikes studded fronts and backs of their gloves, and pads on knees and elbows.

Gribol said: "The diamonds help their grip on the climb!"

"Diamonds!" Exclaimed Sara. "These are diamonds?"

Andy replied: "Yes, they need something pretty tough to hold their weight."

Before Sara could ask the question, Gribol said:"We get the

diamonds from Ganymede, one of Jupiter's moons, where your scientists think there's a layer of ice under the surface------"

"-----but it's not ice, it's diamonds-----."

Sara said: "And you hoover them?"

They laughed: "We hoover them!"

The starter lined the four climbers up at the base of the cliff, and Sara wondered: "Don't they have any other equipment?"

Gribol puzzled: "Other equipment? What other equipment would they need?"

"Well – to climb that cliff. Surely they need something to hang on to and pull themselves up?"

"No, that's the point really, this is mind over matter."

Sara looked doubtful, and Dan withdrew further into himself. She nudged him: "Come on Dan, this isn't like you! Snap out of it!"

"I can't! I'm feeling ill at the thought of the height of that rock face. Look at it!"

As they looked up, the starter blew a small horn, and the blast let loose a huge whoop from the crowd.

What happened next was unbelievable. Teresa walked up to the cliff, sized up the sheer climb and stood very close to the rock. She stretched her arms high over her head, gripped the wall with her diamond spiked hands, and began to clamber, her fingers, elbows, feet and knees a blur as they pulled her body upwards at an amazing pace.

Thelma crackled her knuckles as she approached the cliff, and calmly jumped upwards. She caught a near invisible handhold, swung her body round in a circle and hurled herself up, swinging through 360 degrees. She briefly anchored herself with her diamond studs and repeated the same movement, again and again.

The tiny figure of Dhureen meanwhile began to climb sideways, like a crab, using fronts and backs of her hands, together with the soles and tops of her shoes. She moved so fast, her hands and feet merged into one.

Winkles, watching all this with an amused grin, turned to the crowd who cheered him loud and long. He winked and turned back to the cliff. He walked forward, put his right foot up high in front of him, and began to run up the cliff, feet pumping furiously, hands swinging effortlessly by his side. He occasionally straightened his rapid climb with a touch on the rocks with left or right hand.

Sara gasped: "I don't believe I'm seeing this – it's totally impossible!"

Andy said: "Nothing is impossible if your focus is right."

Gribol continued: "This is what these guys do! Their training is geared to the climb – it's all they think about and their energy carries them up as much as all the physical skills."

"Mind over matter!" They chorused.

As they spoke, the four contestants reached the long stretch of ice. Teresa and Thelma were virtually together in the lead, and Winkles was about to pass Dhureen. The figures above them were almost too small to make out, and Sara was scrunching her eyes to see better when a gigantic screen beamed a hologram of the action directly in front of them.

The crowd cheered the close-up of the four climbers.

Suddenly, Thelma slipped as she swung herself on to the ice face. They saw her lose her grip and she began to plummet downwards. Teresa shot a hand out to catch her but missed.

At that second, Winkles caught Dhureen up, and they stopped, linked arms and smoothly broke Thelma's fall, Winkles swinging her back up the ice face.

The crowd roared their approval, and the race went on. They made slower progress on the ice, and the four chose different routes.

Teresa kept moving up in a straight line, her slim body hugging the cliff face even closer. Thelma, recovered from her fall, changed technique. She bunched her body up tight on the ice, hands close to feet, and sprang upwards like a jumping frog. She moved to Teresa's left to avoid bumping into her.

Dhureen's crab-like climb slowed, like the others. She made fewer movements, but stretched her leading left leg and arm in longer motions. She moved to Teresa's right.

Winkles was amazing. He stopped dead at the end of the rock climb, digging in the tops of his feet and his palms, absolutely tight against the surface.

The crowd held their breath while he casually scanned the icy expanse ahead.

He stretched into a star shape for perfect balance, bent his knees, and pushed straight up, running again, arms and legs widespread.

The crowd roared again as he passed both Thelma and Dhureen, catching Teresa up directly above him. He moved slightly to her left to overtake, and the huge screen clearly showed her grin as she matched his move, blocking his advance.

"This'll be fun!" Andy declared.

Winkles sidestepped to his right and Teresa followed. He moved swiftly further right and again she blocked him. He ran on the spot for a second, and suddenly burst upwards, diagonally left, too fast for her to respond.

However, while this private duel played out, both Thelma and

Dhureen caught up, and they reached the final snowy section in a line abreast.

Gribol jumped up and down in her seat, and Sara was riveted by the action.

It was strange, but nobody now cheered any individual. Applause was for the skill of the climb, not the climbers. So when Dhureen's sideways movements thrust her ahead of the others, she was cheered loudly, as was Teresa when she caught her up.

Thelma now changed technique to the same style as Winkles, arms and legs pumping through the deep snow. This acted like a signal for Dhureen and Teresa, and suddenly all four were sprinting towards the summit, side by side.

Incredibly, they ran in perfect harmony – left right left right left right left right, each step pushing them through the cascading snow at terrific speed.

The snow they disturbed fell like a white waterfall.

Teresa's height seemed to be helping her, and the hologram showed her inch slightly ahead, but Dhureen, sensing this, increased her rhythm, breaking the perfect timing they had achieved, to catch her. Thelma's face reddened with effort as she too stepped up her stride length to keep pace, and all of this began to leave Winkles behind.

The hologram showed they had about a hundred metres left to climb, and for the first time, Sara could see the finish line, a ribbon coloured exactly like a rainbow, fluttering at the top of the snowy slope.

The three girls, now dead level, increased speed together, and Winkles was a clear ten metres behind. The camera focussed on him momentarily, and his arms and legs pumped furiously in a blur, his face calm and relaxed, a slight grin playing round the corner of his mouth. He caught the girls up in seconds, slowed to their pace, and all four crossed the finish line together.

The slow motion replay showed them automatically adjusting to their different heights as they crested the line so that the crowns of their heads broke the tape together. As they did so, it dissolved, leaving the four competitors alone, catching their breath on the flat snowy summit.

The crowd went wild, cheering and clapping each other on the back.

"Best race we've had for years!" Shouted Andy.

"Fantastic finish!" Exclaimed Gribol.

Sara, face flushed, and sore from all the backslapping, hugged Dan in her excitement, and he too joined in the celebrations, though hesitantly.

He said: "They deliberately dead-heated!"

Sara nodded: "I know! I know! What a great way to end the race!"

The atmosphere was electric, and they played replay after replay of the final hundred metres. Over the final few metres, the four moved as one, perfectly in tune with each other at the most pressured, competitive and tiring part of the race.

Sara shook her head in amazement, and Andy said: "Yes, that's what's possible when you work as one."

Gribol turned to Dan: "We'd like you to tell us what you're afraid of-----"

"------so we can help you free yourself from your fear," added Andy.

Dan thought for a moment and said: "I don't know if I can say what I'm frightened of. I just know I'm afraid of really high places, and --- looking down makes me dizzy, and – and—I think I'm going to fall."

"OK!" Andy replied, "First I'm going to talk to you for a moment, and then I'm going to link you up with Winkles, and we'll help you feel the fear-----"

"------face the fear----"

"-----and free yourself!"

Andy started: "Dan, what is it you're afraid of?"

"I'm scared of really high heights."

"How does that make you feel inside?"

"Very scared – dizzy - almost like panic."

"How does your tummy feel?"

"Churning round and round, starting to make me feel sick."

"And your head?"

"Like I said – dizzy, confused – I can't think straight. Everything starts to blur, and I don't feel in control of my body."

"And your energy?"

"It just drains from me – disappears - and I can't seem to get it back till I'm away from the height."

"But you know all about positive thinking and how important it is to keep your energy high and your thoughts focussed in, don't you?"

"Yes, but my brain seizes up, and all of that gets forgotten."

Gribol interrupted: "Right, Andy, enough! Dan's uncomfortable. Let's get a hold of Winkles."

Dan and Sara looked around. Everyone looked up. The four climbers were hang-gliding down the cliff – at least that's what it seemed, but they had no equipment. Teresa, Thelma, Dhureen and Winkles spread themselves wide like starfish, and webbed material between their arms, bodies and legs acted like parachutes, allowing them to glide to the foot of the mountain. They landed to a rousing cheer and long and loud congratulations, till slowly the crowd began to make their way home.

Andy spoke to Winkles who sized Dan up and nodded. He strolled over, rolling his left shoulder: "Hi Dan, just stretched the joint a bit much in that last little rush!"

Dan shook his outstretched hand, and Sara pushed her way in to do the same.

"That was a brilliant climb!" She said, "What a race! I could hardly believe it!"

"Well," grinned Winkles in a cheerful lopsided way, " Thanks for that! We practise a bit, and we know each other pretty well, but it's not about the result, but how we apply what we know and how we focus!"

He turned to Dan and said: "Right Dan, we need to climb!"

"Oh no, I can't – I really can't!"

"Do you think *I* can climb?"

"Of course you can!"

"So trust me – put your arms round my shoulders and hook your legs round my waist."

"Like a piggy back?"

Winkles chuckled: "Like a piggy back!"

Dan did as he was told, and Winkles began to climb the vertical rock face.

Sara gasped and Dan shut his eyes tightly. Within seconds, they were twenty metres off the ground.

Winkles stopped: "Open your eyes, Dan," he said softly, "and see the beautiful view to your right."

Dan hesitantly peered from under half-shut eyes, and saw the snow covered fields rolling towards the horizon.

"Don't do anything else except enjoy that view."

Dan, too scared to look down, absorbed all the details of what he could see.

"OK - close your eyes again – we're going up!"

Winkles climbed another hundred metres, stopped and said: "Right, open up and this time look left."

Dan did, and despite his fear, gasped at the scene. He could see much further, and the fields looked smaller. The hills were snow crested, but beneath the peaks, the earth formed impressive lines of brown and grey dappled with the white of drifting snow. The scale of the landscape was incredible. He noticed movement and focussing on this, realised he was watching a line of bubble cars gliding through the fields.

"Pretty, isn't it?" asked Winkles.

"Yes - it is," Dan muttered.

"Right – close your eyes again, and up we go!"

Dan continued to see, inside his eyelids, pictures of the countryside, and the time flashed by until Winkles stopped again and said: "Open your eyes Dan, and look all around."

To his bewilderment, they were at the very top of the mountain, and he instinctively gripped Winkles tighter. Winkles let him down on the snow, and Dan shivered with cold and fear.

"This is the worst it can get - cold and scared, and two thousand metres up. Look around you."

He did and saw the most magnificent panorama. Tiny white fields, stretches of woodland, miniature herds of cows, winding rivers, and beyond, the town of Inanna with its strange architecture.

"How does that make you feel?" asked Winkles.

"It's beautiful – I feel good – really good, but-----," he hesitated, "I'm starting to feel nervous."

"OK – hold my arm and close your eyes."

Dan did so.

"Think about the beauty of the view. Remember the rolling country, the snowy fields, Inanna in the distance, and think how lucky we are to be able to see it all."

Dan felt his energy level rise.

"Now hold tight, open your eyes and look down, but remember how good you feel".

Dan obeyed and for a horrifying giddy moment felt he would faint, but Winkles held him steady.

"Think beautiful country, think how lucky we are, and focus on a section of the cliff. Look carefully at it and tell me what you see."

Dan's mind was in turmoil, but he tried desperately hard to do as Winkles said.

His eyes focussed on the join between snow and ice. Slowly and haltingly he said: "I'm looking at the snowy cliff, and see the snow get shallow where it turns to ice."

"Tell me about the colours you see."

Dan frowned, seeing only white, but as he thought about it, noticed the snow was a clear sparkling white, but the ice had duller black undertones. He noticed more: "I can see the ice reflect colours – like a prism – you know, one of these pyramid type shapes which reflect colour. I can see bits of yellow – green – red – like rainbow colours, but they come and go as the light catches the ice."

"What else?" Winkles asked.

"Well, the ice looks glassy smooth, but when you look closer, you can actually see little cracks running through it, and there-----!" He pointed down.

"------you can see where one of you made a path to the snow!"

"Can you trace that path?" asked Winkles.

Dan's eyes carefully scanned the ice face, and excitedly said: "Yes! Look! Little dents in the ice! You can tell someone's climbed from way down there at the rocks to the snow line ----- and then on to the top!"

Winkles gently let Dan's arm go and said: "That's excellent, Dan – even I struggled to see it so clearly to start with."

Dan realised he'd been looking down for several minutes without fear, and, for a second panicked. Quickly though he shook his head to clear the feeling, and began to grin: "Hey, that was good! How did you do that?"

Winkles winked: "You did it all yourself! You have to feel the fear and do it anyway! Break it down in your mind to little things you *can* focus on, think of all the positives, and for every positive thought you have – there's no room for a negative one!"

"Thank you so much, Winkles!" Dan said sincerely, exchanging a high five.

"Fancy a ride?" asked Winkles, and next moment Dan, arms round Winkle's neck, legs gripping his waist, was gliding down. He whooped in exhilaration: "Fantastic! What a feeling! It's like a fairground ride in the sky! Look at that view!"

At the foot of the cliff, Sara watched in amazement as they floated gracefully to the ground below.

Chapter 54

When he landed, Dan was jubilant: "Did you see me, Sara? I can't believe I just did that! It was fantastic! Amazing! Brilliant!"

Sara couldn't help but share his excitement: "When I saw you go up, my heart was in my mouth, but seeing you fly down was out of this world!"

"Literally!" Joked Andy, as he and Gribol slapped Dan on the back.

"How's that fear of heights now?" Gribol asked.

"Oh, just so good! I never imagined I'd be able to do that – ever!"

"What did he say to you?" Asked Sara.

"He was so calm and confident – he got me to take things easy – just to look around slowly, take things in, and then I realised I was looking down, talking and not afraid!"

Winkles, grinning quietly in the background, said: "You did it yourself, Dan. It's just about the way you think about things, the way you focus, and using the positive energy you have. You did a great job!"

"Thanks again, Winkles – I'm over the moon!"

They all laughed at his unintended joke.

On the way back to base, Andy and Gribol told them they would soon have to leave for Mistlees.

"Is there anything you'd like to see or do first?" asked Andy.

Sara replied: "I'd love to see what the sky looks like from here. I know you're under the planet's surface, but you must have a way of seeing through to space".

"No problem!" Gribol answered, "Dan? Anything you'd like before going home?"

Dan thought for a moment and said: "Well, something's puzzled me since we arrived – it's probably because it's so light all the time, but I can't see anyone's aura – you know, your energy field."

Andy said: "I think we can more than satisfy that one, don't you, Gribol?"

"Without a doubt!"

When they arrived at the Sahasrara headquarters, they sat at the eating station table. They had toasted cheese sandwiches washed down with orange juice.

Gribol rubbed her hands: "Right Dan! You asked about our energy fields. Well, you're right about the brightness here – it does make it difficult to see our auras, but we certainly don't lack in that department!"

Andy flicked his wrist, and said: "Half darkness!"

Immediately, he was bathed in a cloud of grey, a covering extending about a metre from his head and body. They could still see him, but his features were softened by the darkness produced by his chip implant. Through the haze, they saw his aura extending round his head and shoulders. It was a wonderful cascade of colour – rings of yellow, purple, blue and green shimmered, expanding and contracting gently as he moved his head.

Gribol said: "OK – enough of the light show!" and Andy flicked his wrist making the darkness and the colours disappear.

Dan said: "Andy, that was superb! The colours were so clear – so bright!"

"Well, we've had a while to develop, I suppose!"

Sara said: "The colours must mean something. When we see our auras, they're kind of grey and green and all fuzzy."

Gribol replied: "As you develop, so will your energy field. Purple's a spiritual colour, and it shows Andy really understands himself well. Blue and green tell you he's a really balanced guy with healing ability, and yellow shows you he can teach people - lead them through life."

Dan spoke first: "We know you're pretty advanced people – will we develop like you?"

Gribol replied: "We see the people on Earth coming along nicely, but it'll be great when all the troubles stop."

"Like wars and things, you mean?" asked Sara.

"Right!" Andy continued, "and it *will* happen - soon - when the way you run things changes."

"How do you mean?" Dan asked.

Gribol said: "Put it this way - we're one planet - one people - one mind----"

"-----and one mission----"

"----two actually----"

"-----yes, I suppose so----"

"----- to develop ourselves-----"

"-----and others!-----"

"------like your Mayan friends did!"

"But what can we do?" Dan and Sara asked together.

"Exactly what you're doing now! Listen, learn and put it into practice!" Andy and Gribol chorused. Andy said: "It's all in the mind. It's such an amazing powerhouse, and you need to keep on developing it."

Dan spoke quietly: "The powerhouse of the mind. I'll remember that!"

Andy said: "Right – let's show you our night sky!"

Gribol swept her arm overhead, and projected from her wrist a huge dome of light. It shaped into a dark sky studded with glowing stars and planets. They could see, in incredible detail, meteorite showers, bands of twinkling radiance, and several shapes much larger and brighter than the rest.

The children gasped.

"Spectacular, isn't it?" Andy nodded.

Sara studied the sky intently: "I think it's *so* beautiful! Is this what you see from Sahasrara?"

"Fomalhaut actually, but there's not much difference," Gribol replied.

Andy guided them through the skies: "That really bright one in the middle is Canopus – it's pure white because it's so hot – about 2,000 degrees hotter than your sun."

Dan remarked: "Amazing! Where is our sun? Can you see it from here?"

Gribol pointed high up, and said: "That's it there – the yellow one, and near it you can see Regulus and Sirius"

Sara said: "But why's it yellow – surely it's white?"

Andy answered: "Because you're quite close to it on Earth, its dazzling brilliance makes you see it as white, but it's classed as a yellow star. That's the beauty of seeing from this distance – you see its real colour."

Gribol continued: "That band of stars is the Milky Way, and there is Rigel – you can see it's slightly pink. As it ages it'll be a red star like Antares and Betelgeux."

Dan and Sara burst out laughing, much to Andy and Gribol's puzzlement, so Sara explained how she had mixed up Betelgeux and Zaphod Beeblebrox in the Museum.

After a few more minutes studying the incredible sky tapestry, Gribol swept her arm again, and the stars and planets disappeared.

There was silence for a moment, and it dawned on Dan and Sara that their trip was nearly over.

As if she'd heard them speak, Gribol said: "Don't be sad----"

"-----you'll be home soon----"

"------and be able to climb those mountains!" Laughed Gribol playfully, punching Dan's arm.

They set off for the plane, and met Gary, Lisa, Andy and Ginnay, who gave them a thumbs-up and a wink. Denis and Lutous both looked mournful, and Mike and Stolwind gazed silently. Alf and Melamee piloted them through the planet's atmosphere, and this time Dan and Sara were able to appreciate the wonderful spectacle of sliding through the furnace of flames to black space beyond.

They stopped to board their spacecraft home, and Dan said: "Sara, we never really looked at the flying saucer. It's the model from the cellar, isn't it?"

Sara nodded, taking in the huge smooth shape of the craft. Windowless, with bright shiny surfaces, it hung motionless, like a giant spinning top.

Before they knew it, they were through the boarding ramp, and Gary shouted "Ready!"

They all chorused: "Ready!" and shot through space in the shape altering way that had taken them to Fomalhaut. When they stopped, hovering above Earth, Andy and Lisa produced the rug, and after thanking everyone for their fantastic adventure, Dan and Sara stood on the violet circle again.

It pulsed, and Andy and Lisa shouted: "Hoover!"

Chapter 55

In a flash, the spacecraft disappeared and thin air whistled around them, but something was wrong. The rug seemed suspended in space, lit only by the light of the stars twinkling all around them.

Sara gripped Dan's arm: "What's happened? What's going on?"

"I don't know! We've stopped moving! This is all wrong!"

They were surrounded by a clear bubble, which extended in a circle round the rug. Through the bubble oozed a grey slime, and Sara drew back in horror. Dan gasped, and the slime coiled on the surface of the rug, piling itself higher and higher.

Sara shrieked: "What is it? What is that stuff? Help!"

The pile quickly grew taller than them, and they cowered at the far edge of the rug. It wobbled and trembled, and gradually took on shape and form, splitting into two figures, hazy at first but more solid by the second.

"Oh no!" yelled Sara as the rebel angels took full shape.

"Well, well, children. Caught you in mid-trip have we?" cackled Samahazai.

Casually he breathed a puff of flame that scorched the air in front of Dan and Sara.

Azazel's glowing eyes pierced the grey atmosphere: "No T.P. and no angels here, my little friends!"

Samahazai continued, his voice rasping in his throat: "Nothing to stop us this time. You will enjoy your new world, I'm sure! No family, no friends!"

"No ghosts, no angels! Nobody but us for company!"

They lifted their arms menacingly, and moved closer.

The bubble's air was running out, and it was desperately hard to breathe. The rebel angels seemed unconcerned.

Dan yelled to Sara: "This is it! This is where we must fight back. Our energies! Our auras! Focus, focus, focus!"

They quickly regrouped, standing tall right beside each other. Dan felt real fear, but his will to live coursed through his veins like rocket fuel.

He suddenly felt brave and strong, and Sara felt his energy surge.

She took a deep breath, terrified by the angels who were right upon them, and felt a massive burst of power flow from her very core.

They sensed and then saw their energy fields grow and strengthen, and Dan forced himself to think of their expanded auras as a shield as Kamiel had told them. Sara picked the thought up immediately, and as Azazel breathed a jet of fire straight at them, it hit their combined energy field and bounced back at him. It surged on past as if from a flamethrower and hit the side of the bubble, bursting through it.

Both rebel angels shrieked horrifyingly as they were sucked through the hole like water whirlpooling down a sink.

Azazel screeched: "*You will not stop us next time---!!*"

The bubble sealed itself, and the rug flew through space and time again.

They landed in the cellar, looking around unbelievingly. The rug pulsed reassuringly under their feet.

Sara burst into tears: "Oh, Dan, that was horrific! They were so close!"

"I know, I know!" he said softly. "But we won! We did it! They're gone now. We're all right". He sat on the floor.

"*You* might be all right, but I'm not."

He put his arm round her shoulder: "I'm not exactly a hundred percent, but we're safe now!"

"Phew!" said a voice from behind them.

It was T.P., and as he glided in front of them, they couldn't help but feel their spirits lifted by his comic appearance. He wore angel wings and had a large wobbly halo hovering above his head: "I thought this would help if the rebel angels got past your defences."

"Well, they didn't, T.P., but you look ridiculous!"

He wiggled and the wings and halo disappeared: "You were delayed in your return, I believe."

Sara told him what had happened, and he bristled with indignation: "They try to rise above their station. You have dealt wisely with them children."

"Yes, thank you, T.P., but otherwise we had a fantastic time! What an experience. It was amazing."

Dan added: "I agree. I still can't believe Winkles got me to lose my fear of heights."

"Hey, he said you did that yourself."

"I guess that's right. We must keep thinking positive thoughts."

Sara nodded: "If we do that, will it help us develop, like they said?"

"Well, it can't do us any harm, can it? Now we're back, what about mum and dad – and your mum and Bruce? What will we tell them? T.P.?"

He drew himself up to his full height and pronounced: "In life – and beyond – the truth is always the answer."

Sara said: "Well, we've got the photos to show them – that'll help, won't it?"

"Yes – great! Are you up for it?" asked Dan.

Sara gave herself a mental shake and nodded: "Yes, but let's leave out the rebel angels, shall we?"

"OK, let's go!"

Liz and Hugh were watching television as they burst into the lounge. Hugh turned the volume down: "What's happened? Are you all right?"

"Yes, dad – fine - we've been to outer space – to Fomalhaut, a huge planet-----."

Sara interrupted: "Actually to Sahasrara – it's close to Fomalhaut!"

Liz smiled: "Calm down, calm down. Start at the beginning – tell us what happened."

They did, and Liz and Hugh asked careful searching questions, keen to check the children were telling the truth. Their excitement was infectious, and Dan noticed mum and dad were sitting on the edge of the couch.

He said proudly: "*And* I took some photos so you can see for yourself."

Hugh rubbed his hands together: "Excellent! Let's see them. Put them on holographic mode, Dan."

Dan searched the Rainbow Catcher's memory, found the Sahasrara photos, and beamed the first one up. Hugh and Liz were silent as they saw a field of cows grazing in what looked exactly like the Perthshire countryside. Hugh said: "At least they're a normal size!" The next photo showed rolling countryside, then a herd of sheep appeared, and Dan realised they were looking at Scotland.

"Em, Dan, are you sure about this?" Hugh asked.

"Oh, dad – I know what this looks like, but they copied the look of things from all over, and to make us feel at home, they copied our countryside."

"Right," said Hugh thoughtfully.

His heart sinking, Dan clicked on the next photo, and his spirits leapt as an image of Andy and Gribol standing beside their bubble car appeared.

"See!" he yelled. "That's Andy and Gribol – and their car – like our model!"

Liz smiled in relief, and then frowned. She pointed to the area around their heads: "What's that? What are all these colours?"

Dan gasped: "Their auras! We've taken their auras!"

Hugh gulped, shook his head and said: "I didn't think it would work. This is unbelievable."

Liz asked: "What are you talking about? What didn't you think would work?"

They looked expectantly at Hugh, and he reddened: "I – I – just didn't expect this! It's the first time I've seen it work!"

Liz raised her voice: "Darling, would you please talk some sense. What are you saying?"

Hugh spread his hands outwards and shrugged: "We've been working for a while to integrate every type of available photography to the Rainbow Catchers – that's why we added the infra-red capability, but this – but this--."

Dan said: "Dad! What's the problem? You can see the photos are from Sahasrara. Look at the car! Look at their auras!"

"That's what I mean. Normal cameras can't photograph people's auras – and I'm not sure I believed people have auras anyway, but Iain at work's been on at me to use Kirlian photography."

"What's that? Asked Liz.

"In simple terms?"

"In simple terms!"

"Kirlian photography takes pictures of energy fields. They say that everything has a unique kind of force field surrounding it, and by using high voltage frequencies and electron-----."

"Simple terms, dear!"

"Yes, of course – sorry! Well, we had to experiment with some new techniques, but we've made Kirlian photography safe to use in normal photography and Dan's Rainbow Catcher is the first to use it."

"So it can photograph auras?" Liz asked.

"Yes – just like those two! The quality's amazing, even if I say so myself"

Dan and Sara grinned at each other and Sara began to wonder how she would tell her mum and Bruce about their trip.

The doorbell rang, and as Liz answered it, they heard her say: "That's good timing – come in! Come in!"

She led Bruce and Diana in, and Sara gave her mum a hug. Bruce waved a hand mysteriously in the air: "We were just thinking about time! How it slips away when you least expect it! How can you stop it passing you by? How can you turn back the clock?"

"That's enough, Bruce!" Diana said, "Stop being silly! We just wanted to catch up with you all!"

Bruce looked irritated, made a mock bow and sat down, his eyes fixed on Sara, his scar gleaming in the light. Instantly, she felt her cheek burn and before Bruce could look away, she saw the glint of satisfaction in his eyes. Diana saw none of this exchange, and Sara suddenly felt very alone.

Liz said: "I'll make tea while you tell them what's happened, Hugh."

Hugh said: "I think the kids will make a better job of it than me," so Dan and Sara told them about Sahasrara. Bruce roared with laughter at the first of the photos: "That's just up the road! Did you ask Farmer Giles if you could take pictures of his cows? You've even managed to shrink them!"

"Ha ha! Bruce – just wait a second," said Hugh, and even Bruce was silenced by the photo of Andy and Gribol – but not for long: "Bright characters, those two, eh? Can't see the rain for the rainbows!"

Even Sara laughed, but at least they were able to finish their story feeling the adults had a fair measure of belief.

But, she thought, what was Bruce trying to do?

Chapter 56

Leaving for school on Monday, a huge friendly Alsatian followed them, wagging its tail eagerly. Sara paled and gripped Dan's arm: "Dan, Dan, don't let it near me!"

"Why? What's wrong? Look at him – he's beautiful!"

Tim bent down to stroke the brown and black animal, but it brushed past and sat in front of them, in the middle of the bridge over the burn.

" Dan, I can't go near it," said Sara, her voice trembling. "It terrifies me!"

"OK, OK! I know you're afraid, but look at him – isn't he great?"

The Alsatian sat patiently on the bridge, looking from one to the other, panting gently, its tongue lolling from side to side.

"I can see it's a nice looking dog, but look at its teeth! It was an Alsatian that bit Bruce!"

"I know, but it can't be the same one! Sara, think about all you've been through!

Look at him, he's obviously well looked after – do you really think he'll bite you? Why do you think he'll bite? Focus on him! Tell us what you see."

She hesitated, while Tim bent down, patted the dog and started to stroke it. He grinned up at Sara.

She said: "Well, I can see he's OK with Tim – at least it looks like it."

"Go on!" encouraged Dan.

"He's got a collar with a tag on it, so he belongs to someone."

Dan walked forward to read the tag, and said: "He's called Canponi! He belongs to the Italian family on Tondee Farm!"

"I know them!" Sara said: "They're nice people. I wonder what their dog's doing in the village."

Dan stroked Canponi: "Feel how soft he is. He's quite harmless. See! He's begging you!"

Canponi lifted his paw towards Sara, and it hung loosely in the air, drooping slightly. He looked comical, and, despite herself, she couldn't help laughing.

"Well, if you're sure," she said, and walked slowly the few steps to the dog.

Canponi stood up, wagging his tail so hard his whole body shook. In alarm, Sara backed away, but Dan said: "Come on – you can do this! Think positive!"

She took two deep breaths, felt her energy flood back, and cautiously patted the dog's back: "Oh, he does feel smooth – and soft – and lovely and warm!"

She bent down carefully, stroking Canponi who nuzzled against her. He licked her hand as she put it under his nose. Behind them came a big cheerful voice: "There you are, you naughty boy! Where have you been?"

"Hello, Mrs Capaldi," Sara smiled, "We've just met Canponi."

Mrs Capaldi was a very large eccentric lady. She wore a thick tweed coat, woollen hat, gloves and Wellington boots, despite the warmth of the day.

"Oh, you know his name! That's the beauty of these tag things. He just loves children. That's probably why he's here. Come on boy, back to the car!"

She waved vaguely over her shoulder. Canponi again wagged his tail furiously, looked at Tim, then Dan and finally Sara, giving her another lick before trotting off with his owner.

Sara realised what she had done: "Hey, I did it! I actually petted a dog! How's that for bravery!"

Tim was not impressed, but Dan grinned and punched her arm lightly: "Well done! Very well done! Feel the fear and do it anyway!"

Tim gave them a puzzled look and ran on ahead, leaving Sara flushed with excitement being tugged along by Dan. Her cheek pulsed.

"Come on, we'll be late!"

The day passed quickly, Miss Ambrose reminding them this was the last week for the project: "I'd like it handed in sharp next Monday morning!" she said, directing her gaze at Mark, Ali and Asha. As Dan and Sara left class for lunch, she asked how their projects were progressing.

They looked at each other: "Well," Dan said reluctantly: "We need to visit the graveyard and the Community Centre this week, write about them----"

"------and then tidy up everything------."

"Good! Right then – off you go, and don't forget to look carefully at the old headstones. I'm sure you'll find some curious ones. Sometimes, as in books, there are codes hidden there, buried deep". She laughed, and as usual, left them wondering what she meant.

Over lunch, they agreed to finish their village tour the next day. Dan said: "Sara, I've been thinking. I wonder what the future will hold."

"What do you mean?"

"Well, we learned so much in Sahasrara, and it made me realise we've got so much more to learn. As time goes on, will we get to be like them?"

"You mean like Andy, Gribol and the others?"

"Yes, if we lived in the future what would it be like?"

Sara laughed: "I've no idea, but I suppose I wonder about it sometimes. As long as it's free from rebel angels!"

"You can say that again!"

"As long as it's free from rebel angels!"

"Ha ha! Very funny!"

After school, at football practice, Graham kept the two teams separate, spending his time with Mark, still sporting his black eye, and his side. Mark wore new kit that fitted his huge frame. Dan, Shane, Iain, Hamish and Struan practised taking corners, free kicks and throw-ins, and Dan came up with a brilliant set-piece move from a kick-off, involving the whole team.

After a while, Graham blew his whistle, and got everyone together: "Right, lads, I'm happy with Mark and his team. What about you lot?" He asked Dan.

Dan looked coolly back and said: "We'll be ready OK."

"You'll be ready? You mean you're not ready yet? What have you been doing, boy? *We've* practised move after move to perfection. You should try doing that too – mind you, if it means accurate passing, you'll have no chance!"

He roared with laughter, and Mark, Liam, Eddie, Sandy and Will joined in.

Dan's team kept calm and Dan's steady strong gaze and positive smile gave his friends confidence. Mark's team felt it and their laughter stopped.

Graham carried on laughing, stopped in his own time, lifted his huge glasses to rub the tears from his eyes, and said: "OK! That's it for now – see you all next week!"

Dan stayed behind with his team: "We should think of

codenames for the moves we've practised, so nobody knows what we're going to do."

Iain thought this was a great idea, and the others agreed.

"OK then, think up some names and we'll talk about them next week."

Struan asked: "Is next Monday our last practice?"

"Yes," Shane told him, "and then it's off to Glasgow for the tournament. I can't wait to thrash Mark and his crowd!"

Dan said: "Hey – easy now – we mustn't be over confident."

"I know, but they're so full of themselves – they deserve to be taken down a peg."

"Just be thankful we've got a good team, and if we play as we know we can, the results will take care of themselves."

The boys left football practice feeling good about their game.

Chapter 57

Later that night, Dan revised his project. He felt very proud of what he had written, and was especially pleased with some of his drawings – the Sunken Chapel and the Tower in particular.

His photos of the stained glass window and the Cradle of Scotland Church were very clear and striking, and he pasted them carefully into his workbook.

Satisfied, he drank a glass of orange juice and went to bed.

He dreamed.

He stood with Sara in Edinburgh's Princes Street, but the castle was facing the wrong way. In the gardens between the castle and the street ran a beautiful river flowing in and out of a small loch.

They stretched their hands out and were immediately in Mistlees, but it was different.

The Tower still stood, the two churches were clearly visible, but most of the houses sat on platforms turning slowly in the sunshine.

Again they stretched out their hands, and they were on a golden sandy beach. The sea moved in different directions. In one place there were high waves and surfers balanced bravely in the surf. In another, it was calm and people swam in gentle waters.

A mermaid swam gracefully past and a dodo waddled along the beach, its plump body ungainly on two skinny legs.

They looked at the ground and each of them had two shadows in the sunshine.

They drank a cup of tea with a friendly old man.

He woke up, startled by the power of his dream, so strong in his mind's eye.

Chapter 58

In the evening, Sara revised her project. She felt immensely proud of what she had written, and was especially pleased with some of her drawings – both churches in particular.

She rewrote the section on the history of the village, putting in the full story of the collapse of the Sunken Chapel.

Satisfied, she drank a glass of milk and went to bed.

She dreamed.

She stood with Dan in Edinburgh's Princes Street, but the castle was facing the wrong way. In the gardens between the castle and the street ran a beautiful river flowing in and out of a small loch.

They stretched their hands out and were immediately in Mistlees, but it was different.

The Tower still stood, the two churches were clearly visible, but most of the houses sat on platforms turning slowly in the sunshine.

Again they stretched out their hands, and they were on a golden sandy beach. The sea moved in different directions. In one place there were high waves and surfers balanced bravely in the surf. In another, it was calm and people swam in gentle waters.

A mermaid swam gracefully past and a dodo waddled along the beach, its plump body ungainly on two skinny legs.

They looked at the ground and each of them had two shadows in the sunshine.

They drank a cup of tea with a friendly old man.

She woke up, startled by her dream's power.

Chapter 59

Talking excitedly, Sara told mum and Bruce her exhilarating dream.

Diana listened carefully, but as usual, Bruce kept interrupting: "A mermaid? They don't exist! And dodos have been extinct for centuries!"

"A bit like you," Diana replied.

"Ho ho ho! Very funny," said Bruce, but he quickly came back with another quip: "How come you had *two* shadows? One not good enough for you, or were there two suns?"

Sara flushed, her cheek stinging: "I don't know Bruce, I'm only telling you what I dreamed."

Diana told her to ignore him: "What do you think the dream was about, dear?"

"I'm sure it was about the future, mum. The places all seemed from a time we haven't seen. The buildings, Princes Street, even the way people looked – it was kind of futuristic."

"Well, I'll be interested to know what Dan makes of it – he's the expert on dreams."

On their way to school, Sara told him, and he listened in silence. He stopped at the burn, looked at her and said: "The sea *was* strange, wasn't it. Like there were different sections, all doing their own thing."

"Yes, and people surfing and ----." She tailed off. "How did you know there were different sections? That's just what it felt like."

"I had exactly the same dream!"

"No way! The same dream?"

"Yes – *exactly* the same dream!"

Sara paled and shivered with excitement: "Dan, what does it mean?"

"It must mean that's our seventh time trip – to the future! Sara, your cheek – your scar's got bigger again!"

"Oh no, has it? I felt it again this morning when I was talking to mum and Bruce. Every time he makes me feel small, my cheek suffers. It's like he's determined I get the same scar as him."

"But you can't transfer a scar, can you?"

"It's dragging me down a bit, Dan – you know, draining me, and I don't know what to do about it."

Dan thought for a moment, and said: "Whether he's doing it deliberately or not, it's happening, so why don't you use some of your positive energy back on him?"

"Like standing up to him?"

"Yes. Focus on him. Don't let him intimidate you, and see what happens."

"Right," she said decisively, "I will! Mum's worried about it too, but I haven't told her what I've told you about Bruce."

They finished the walk to school in silence, but both found it hard to concentrate, so much so that Miss Ambrose held them back while everyone else went to lunch: "I know it's difficult, and there's a lot going on outside school, but you must keep your wits about you. We don't want anyone else finding out about our secret, do we?"

Dan stammered: "How do you mean, *our* secret, Miss Ambrose?"

"That's what it must remain – at least for now! So off you go and enjoy your lunch."

She left them with a smile. Dan and Sara looked at each other, and Dan said: "She's got a cheek. It's like she's daring us to say something about the codex."

"I know, but Nigel said not to do anything. He's supposed to be doing something about it."

"Well, it's about time he did, because I'm fed up with all these smart comments."

After school, they dropped off their bags, took their project folders and walked into the village, buying crisps and juice at The Deli. Brad Maipeson smirked at them: "Well, well, here come the essay king and queen!"

"What do you mean, Mr Maipeson?" asked Dan.

"I hear you've written the best essays. Experts on Leonardo, eh?"

"Who told you that?" Demanded Sara.

"Ah ha! Must have been a little bird!" He chuckled to himself.

While serving them, he kept asking questions: "So where are we off to today then? Long walks again?"

Dan and Sara ignored him, paid for their snack and walked off up Main Street.

Sara turned round quickly in time to see him watching them. She stopped and he went back into The Deli.

"What a nosey man! Yeuk!"

Dan laughed.

The Community Centre, with its older sign: "VILLAGE HALL", was a plain stone building. In the entrance hall was a huge notice board, with all the local events and activities advertised on posters and typed sheets.

Dan hadn't realised Mistlees had so much to offer. There was a bridge evening on Wednesdays, cookery classes on Thursdays, country dancing on Fridays, and a dance every Saturday night.

The band for the following Saturday was The Mistlees Fliers. Sara nudged Dan: "That's us – the Mistlees Fliers!"

There was a martial arts class every second Tuesday night, and Sara said: "That's the class Bruce takes."

"Oh yes. What does he teach?"

"Well, he's a black belt in Karate, so he does that, and Aikido."

"What's that?"

"I think it's fighting with swords and things, but they use wooden sticks to be safe."

"A bit like the Vashad Thains then?"

She laughed: "Yeah, right!"

Also on Tuesdays was a class called "Decadent Cooking."

"What on earth is that?" Sara asked.

Dan shrugged and they picked up a leaflet:

"Mrs Braid will help you rediscover the art of cooking ancient dinner table favourites. Enjoy suckling pig, jugged hare, mock hedgehog and carpetbag steaks, cooked in the old style. 8pm till late."

"Yeuk!" Said Dan.

"Mrs Braid!" Exclaimed Sara.

"How weird!" They chorused.

"Just like her," Dan added.

They grinned, and explored. There was a nursery in the main hall, with a rabble of children running round chasing each other. A large lady was trying to restore order – it was Mrs Capaldi, wearing two sweaters and a scarf, and very red in the face: "Children! What will your mothers say! Stop! Stop! It's time to go home!"

The children ignored her. Sara wondered where Canponi was, and felt a wet tongue licking her hand. There he stood, tail wagging happily, and Sara found herself stroking him with no trace of fear.

In the hall was a hand carved wooden plaque, dedicated to the men and women of the village who had died in the two World Wars. Underneath their names, it read: "**ANGELS ALL**". There were nine names from the First War, and seven from the Second. Dan jotted them in his notebook, and said: "I wonder if any of them are buried in the graveyard."

Sara said: "Yes, we should check, but would they not be buried where they fought?"

"I don't know Sara, but we'll find out."

The tour of the Centre only took half an hour, and on their way out, Dan picked up the Mistlees Post.

"WITCHCRAFT'S KILLING MY COWS!"

Farmer Giles, talking to Jenny Morrison, our local reporter, says he has lost four cows to the mysterious disease affecting his herd.

"I'm at my wits end. I've tried everything, but they keep getting bigger and bigger. They're locked up at night and nobody can get at them. They've stopped producing milk and are tired all the time.

There's no natural explanation for this. The vet's done all the tests but he's baffled too. I think it's witchcraft. Someone's put a spell on them!"

"How horrible!" Sara said.

"Isn't it" Agreed Dan.

They walked to the south of the village to the graveyard. Neither had been there before, and Dan photographed it with his Rainbow Catcher. It sat peacefully outside the edge of the village, enclosed by a dry stane dyke. The air was completely still, and the atmosphere thickened as they approached. Dan shivered, looked round and said: "Thank goodness we've not been followed recently."

"Yes. Since Miss Ambrose got the codex, I guess she doesn't need to".

"I'm surprised Mr Dewbury's not here. He usually pops up when we're looking at things to do with the church."

At that, a figure stooped over a small grave straightened up, arched his back to get rid of stiffness, wiped his hands, turned round and greeted them with a grunt: "Well - finished the project yet?"

Sara replied: "No, this is our last piece of research, Mr Dewbury."

"Ah! A fitting place to end!" He smiled at his own joke.

"What can you tell us about the graveyard?" asked Dan.

As if reluctant to tell them anything, he slipped into the monotone of a guide telling a familiar story: "In olden days, they always buried people outside the village to cut down the risk of disease spreading. It's not known when the first soul was buried here, but it's been the resting place for Mistlees families for centuries. Even those who leave the village and live all their lives elsewhere seem to want to be laid to rest in this spot. I'll show you the earliest gravestone."

He led them to a worn headstone in a corner. It was small and rectangular, and made of grey sandstone. The carved inscription was worn away, and all they could make out was several rows of faded lettering.

Dan ran his finger across what appeared to be the dates, but couldn't make them out. Mr Dewbury appeared to lose interest and walked away without further comment.

Dan realised they weren't normal numbers: "Look, Sara – the date's are in Roman numerals!"

He traced them carefully, his finger gently pulling away their soft covering of moss: "The first one's an M – then a D – then there's two C's – and then three X's – and a V!"

Sara thought for a moment and said: "That's 1735!"

"How do you know that?"

She blushed and said: "I've been studying! Is there another date? That will tell us when this poor soul passed away"

Dan traced along the line, and read again: "It starts with an M – then a D – then 2 C's - then – I think it feels like an L."

"Yes, yes, an L would make sense – that stands for 50!"

"And then there's some X's – one, two, three X's, and that's all."

"1780!" Declared Sara proudly, "1735 till 1780. 45 years old. Can you make out the person's name?"

Dan tried, but the rest of the wording on the stone had disintegrated badly. He felt from top to bottom, until he almost gave up, but the lettering on the very last line was in a better state of repair.

"I think I can feel some of the letters here," he said. "It starts with an S!

S – E – E – K–T – H – E – P – A – T – H – W- I –T – H – I – N."

Sara exclaimed: "Seek the path within!"

Dan wiped his hands free of moss: "Well, that was good! What a pity we couldn't find out their name."

"Never mind – you did well – let's look around a bit."

The graves were in neat rows, the oldest at the back. The earliest gravestone they could read clearly was

JAMES G DONNACHAIDH
15TH MARCH 1812 – 10TH MAY 1904
REST IN PEACE
DEAR FATHER
AND DEARLY LOVED HUSBAND OF HELEN
19TH OCTOBER 1813 – 1ST DECEMBER 1894

Dan calculated: "He was 92! That's some age! How do you pronounce that name though?"

"I think it's Donnachy – it's maybe Gaelic or something."

"Yes, you're probably right – and his wife was 81. What a great old couple!"

"Brilliant! I like that. It's really nice to see a couple living to that age – especially in these days."

Dan looked again at the headstone: "Look, he was born on the Ides of March, the anniversary of Julius Caesar's death!"

"So he was! That's interesting."

"Right. Let's find the war graves."

Dan checked the list he had made and they moved along the rows. Sara spotted one of the names first: "Look! There's one!"

SERGEANT BRUCE MACLEOD
1886 – 1915
KILLED IN ACTION
IN DEFENCE OF HIS BELOVED COUNTRY

Next to this headstone was another made of pink granite.

AMELIA AMBROSE
SPINSTER
1845 – 1915
DEAR SISTER OF ANNA
TEACHER OF OUR PARISH
LIVING WITH US ALWAYS

Dan and Sara looked at each other in amazement. Dan said: "Anna! That can't be her ---"

"----- Miss Ambrose----"

"-----but it says she's a teacher here---"

"------but that would make her-----"

"-----far too old to still be alive!"

"There must be some mistake----"

"----or it's someone else in their family."

"How odd!"

They found several other gravestones marking those who had died in the World Wars, and Dan checked them off carefully. He said: "It looks like most of them were buried here after all---"

"------ though there's a few not here, so probably buried in France ----"

"-----or wherever else they died."

Satisfied with their trip they walked home slowly, puzzling over the thoughts Amelia Ambrose's strange headstone had set off.

Chapter 60

Dan and Sara sat companionably in Dan's lounge that night, writing up their project notes. Sara did a sketch of the graveyard, and copied the wording from the headstones for Amelia Ambrose and Sergeant Bruce Macleod.

Liz and Hugh came in. "Hello Sara," said Liz, "It's good to see you. How's the project going?"

"Oh, very well I think, Mrs Goodwin. We're nearly finished. I've just got to read it all through and make sure I haven't missed anything."

"And I'm the same, mum – I think you and dad will enjoy reading it."

"Oh, I'm sure we will. Sara, Dan tells me you both had the same dream last night."

"Yes, I know – and we think it means we're going into the future."

Hugh rubbed his hands together: "If you do, you need to bring back some ideas for developing the Rainbow Catcher!"

Liz gave him a look.

"OK, OK, but you can't blame me for trying!"

Liz said: "I get so worked up when I think about you travelling through time. When will you go?"

Dan and Sara looked at each other, and together said: "Friday night!"

They worked on the project as the week wore on, and by the end of school on Friday, were finished, leaving the weekend clear. They were excited by the prospect of Friday night, and after tea, the four adults, and Tim, knowing what the evening might hold, were in the Goodwin's lounge. Bruce had put on an old T-shirt, which read: "BACK TO THE FUTURE".

"Very funny!" laughed Liz.

Bruce replied: "And that's not all!"

From his pocket he produced a toy space rocket: "I just need to miniaturise myself, jump aboard and I'll be joining you!"

"Oh Bruce, stop being so silly! Anyway, they're not going into space."

"Oh no, neither they are – I'm always a step behind!"

Hugh was more serious: "Now, are you both sure about this, children? I know everything's gone smoothly so far, but this may be very dangerous."

"Dad, I'm sure we're going to be all right. We've always felt as if there's someone watching over us."

At that point, the doorbell rang, and Liz ushered Nigel in, beaming his broad smile: "Hello everyone! Well, this is the big night!"

Sara asked: "How did you know we're going to time trip tonight?"

Nigel replied: "The time is now. The way is clear. We must all seek the path within."

Dan and Sara looked at each other, Nigel's words echoing those on the old gravestone, but before they could say anything, Tim, face flushed with the excitement of the evening, burst out: "Mum! Dad! Look!" He pointed at Nigel.

Around his head and shoulders was a beautiful swirling halo of colour – purple, green, blue and yellow.

There was a stunned silence, which Nigel himself broke in a soft voice: "When there seems nothing to say, worry not about there being nothing to say."

His aura gently pulsed and faded.

Bruce sang: "Rainbows keep falling from my head", and everybody groaned.

Hugh said quietly: "It feels like the time has come."

Dan and Sara nodded.

Diana said: "How do you do this?"

Dan said: "Well, if you remember ----"

"-----what happened when we went to the time of Leonardo---"

"------ the rug didn't work when you were all in the cellar-----"

"----so we think-----"

"-----you should all stay here!" they chorused.

"Wow!" Bruce said, gazing at Sara: "Quite the little double act!" His scar glowed and Sara again felt her cheek painful. She looked steadily back at Bruce, who was clearly surprised. He suddenly scratched his cheek and Sara's pain disappeared.

"Yes!" She thought.

"Well then", said Hugh, "I hope all goes well."

"It will", said Nigel, "In the end!"

Diana and Liz gave him an odd look, and they hugged the children before they left the room. Nigel came into the hall, and gripped each of them gently by the arm: "I'm sure you'll come through and find Peter."

Dan said: "Nigel, during the week, Miss Ambrose told us we had to stay quiet about what she called "our little secret"! We could hardly believe it".

Sara continued in a rush: "And she told Mr Maipeson all about our essays, so we think they may be in it together. And Mark too! He's growing so fast he could be spending lots of time in the places we've been going to!"

Nigel held up his hand: "Slow down, slow down! Dan has told me what you believe, but all may not be as it seems," he replied, "Talk to Peter when you find him. He'll know what to do"

Sara said: "Yes, we need to! It's so infuriating. Why can't you just go and demand they give it back? I'm sure the codex is in the Deli. Mr Maipeson's probably trying to decode it."

"There are forces at work we should not interfere with, children. If it was straightforward all would be well, but I fear there are dangers ahead and we must be cautious."

Dan looked at Sara, shrugged his shoulders and said: "All right Nigel, we'll see what Peter says if we find him."

They went down to the cellar, Nigel wishing them good luck before rejoining the others in the lounge.

Liz said: "The way they say this works is that they travel through time, but come back as if no time here had passed."

Diana agreed: "So we'll know very soon what happens."

But this time, there was a very different turn of events.

Chapter 61

Entering the cellar, Sara said elatedly: "Wasn't Nigel's aura fantastic?"

"I know – it was like Andy's – so bright and clear."

"I thought we'd *never* get away – it was like a party with everyone in the room!"

"Well, we're on our own now, so let's see if we can go and find Peter. Nigel's pretty determined we do that first."

"And then get the codex back safely."

The cellar smelt of tea and toast.

"That smell's so good it makes my mouth water," Sara exclaimed.

"I know, but we still don't know where it's coming from."

They went to the rug, which lay peacefully beside the table. T.P. was lying on it, and made a show of yawning and stretching as they approached. He was obviously pleased with something, and Dan saw what it was. All the models were in groups – seven of them.

T.P. glided around them: "How do you like that then?"

"Very good T.P.", replied Sara, "You've been busy."

"Not much else to do round here," he grumped. "No trips, nothing to map, nobody to talk to!"

"Oh, you poor soul," Sara said, "Are you coming with us now? We think we're going into the future."

T.P. replied: "I cannot go to the future. As I have told you, I am bound to the present and the past and to this Earth. I trust you are pleased with my work?"

There were two new groups, one containing models from

Fomalhaut, with the spaceship, the flying saucer, the Eiffel Tower and a miniature Golden Gates Bridge.

The other group had a number of futuristic buildings in it together with the bubble car. Dan scratched his head: "That car's in the wrong group," he said.

T.P. huffed: "You will find it is in the correct position, young man."

Dan said: "Oops, sorry! So we're definitely off to the future. If we are, we should see that on the last section of the table."

"Let's look."

The final segment of the table was intricately carved. The highlight was a classic looking building, rectangular, with carved figures looking out from along its length.

Dan frowned: "That's the museum in Princes Street!"

"But it can't be if we're going to the future."

"Maybe we're wrong then."

"Oh, I hope not!"

There were houses surrounding the museum building, with sweeping curves and smooth surfaces. Sara said: "They're lovely aren't they?"

"Yes, very – very – elegant, I think, is the word."

There was a symbol close to the centre of the table.

Sara said: "What is that?"

As Dan shrugged his shoulders, the air in the cellar changed and became fresher. The smell of tea and toast was replaced with the lovely aroma of flowers.

In front of them shimmered Metatron and Vohumanah.

"You wish answers, and need to know solutions. I can provide knowledge, speak to you of facts, and tell you what you want to know!" Metatron announced.

They laughed, delighted by the arrival of the angels. T.P. bowed deeply.

"OK Metatron, tell us what this symbol means then".

"This sign has been used and chosen to mean over many years and through time a symbol, a sign for new beginnings. It represents a successful outcome, a good result, as you might or would say."

Vohumanah shimmered brightly, and his voice seemed to reach deep into their minds: "When you believe and follow that belief, you sow the seeds of your future. That sign is that future. It is ING".

"ING?" asked Dan.

Metatron replied: "ING is the name for the sign, for that representation of the seeds of the future. It is a good sign, a fine sign."

Vohumanah added: "You may make of it what you will, build the future you desire, create your own destiny."

"So we can make it a really good future?" Dan asked.

Vohumanah replied: "The future is yours to do with as you will."

"Well," said Dan, "I want us to be OK----"

"-----and we want to find Peter----"

"---and find out how to get the codex back -----"

"-----and come back safe without the rebel angels getting in the road!" Finished Sara.

The angels glowed briefly, and dissolved into thin air. T.P. was nodding his head: "Wise angels indeed," he intoned.

Dan rubbed his hands: "OK Sara, are you ready?"

"I think so!"

"Let's go then!"

"Hang on, hang on, we don't know where we're going!"

"But the rug does! Look!"

The centre circle of the rug had begun to pulse softly, its deep indigo blue lighting up the rest of the rug.

"Wait!" said Dan, "We didn't figure out what the numbers on the table mean!"

They read them out loud: "1 – 9 – 2 – 2 ! 1922."

Dan said: "That can't be right, that's going backwards in time!"

"We need to *read* them backwards", Sara said.

The rug was warm and welcoming. They left T.P. looking mournful, and crossed the other colours to the centre circle, their gateway to the future – 2291– hand in hand.

Chapter 62

Over the next moments, they felt the whistling rush of air as they were sucked through time, the whooshing sounds of their passage ringing in their ears.

The noise and the feeling of being in two places at one time died away.

They were still standing on the rug.

Still standing in the cellar.

The table and the racking stood in their normal places.

The smell of tea and toast was back.

As they adjusted to the shock, a cheerful voice said: "Cup of tea, anyone?"

They looked round in astonishment to see an elderly man with straggly curly white hair sticking out in all directions. He wore faded blue dungarees and an old red cardigan. Outsize glasses, very smudged and with silver rims, perched on his nose, and magnified laughter lines round his huge brown eyes. His bushy black eyebrows arched mischievously at them. Standing slightly stooped, he waved a familiar old kettle.

"Peter!" Exclaimed Sara.

"Sara!" Replied the man.

"Peter?" asked Dan.

"Yes, Dan – Peter!" He confirmed.

Dan said: "But I don't understand. How come you're here in the cellar? You weren't here a moment ago!"

"Look around, Dan."

They did - it was the same cellar, but different. The table was exactly the same as the one they knew, but beside it was another, much larger, and carved into many more segments. The racking overflowed with models – more than double the number Dan and Sara had neatly organised only a few weeks previously, only for T.P. to continually reorganise them.

There was no fluorescent lighting. In fact, there was no visible lighting at all, but the cellar was as bright as before though less harshly lit.

"Yes", said Peter, "It *is* the same cellar, but it's changed a bit in the last two hundred odd years, hasn't it?"

"Oh my goodness. We were right then!" said Dan.

Sara continued: "Is this two thousand two hundred and ninety one?"

"The very same, my dear! Now, shall we have some tea and toast and a little chat to catch up?"

Dan and Sara relaxed and agreed. They wore the same clothes as when they set off, and Dan patted his pocket to check his Rainbow Catcher. As Peter poured tea, the children felt a flood of questions.

Peter seemed to realise this, and asked, with a grin: "Well, who's first?"

Dan said: "Peter, it's amazing to meet you! Everyone thinks you're dead, you know – except for Nigel, of course. He said we'd find you – that you were lost in time."

Peter laughed. His laughter was like his speech, husky and slightly rasping. His whole face lit up and his glasses almost wobbled off his nose: "Good old Nigel – he's such a fusspot. I'm not lost at all. I know exactly where I am!"

Sara said: "Yes, *you* do, Peter, but you just disappeared, and nobody knew what happened."

"Well, I suppose that *was* a bit naughty, but there was a lot happening in Mistlees – not all of it good –and an old man sometimes needs his own space – and time," he said, his soft brown eyes twinkling.

"But what happened? Was it to do with the codex?" Asked Dan.

"Well, yes, in a way, but Nigel and I had a disagreement."

"Really?" said Sara. "He didn't say anything about that."

"No, I don't suppose he would. Always the soul of discretion is our Nigel."

"He said you'd help us to get the codex back. Miss Ambrose and Mark, or Brad Maipeson, stole it from Nigel in the museum!" Sara blurted out. Peter looked surprised as Dan added: "And she keeps making comments about it. We know there are secrets and codes hidden in it. What are they, Peter? How do we get it back?"

"Why can't we just tell the police?"

Peter held up a hand: "Hold on! So many questions! You need to give me time to tell you what I know!"

Dan and Sara quietened down and Peter said: "Right! Let's go back a bit. I've always been convinced we could travel through time, and when I found Mistlees, it was the perfect spot. Nigel and I, with a little help, discovered how to do it, and at the beginning, it was so exhilarating! Nigel never wanted to come with us, said it was better he stayed at home".

Dan frowned: "You said "us". Who else was with you?"

Peter said: "In a moment, Dan, in a moment. We went together to the Cretaceous period, and then to see the Mayans, but both times, things went horribly wrong, and I carried on travelling on my own. I refused to have anything more to do with her!"

"You mean Miss Ambrose?" asked Sara.

Peter paused: "Miss Ambrose? No, it was Mrs Braid who came with me!"

"What!" They exclaimed together.

"Mrs Braid."

Dan said: "I can't believe that! What about Miss Ambrose?"

"No, she never came with us."

Sara asked: "Why Mrs Braid?"

"She was very interested in my work. Nigel warned me to keep her at arm's length, but I thought she would help, especially given her knowledge and her great interest in antiquity. How could I have been so wrong?" He shook his head sadly.

"What happened?" Dan asked.

"Phaelar and Jafyre didn't trust her, and, as it turned out, with good reason, but the crunch came when we were with the Mayans. I didn't know it then, but Mrs Braid had heard about this long-lost codex, full of the most hidden secrets of the Mayans. She was desperate to find it, and bring it back, but Parimanu sensed this and got Kaimi to keep it hidden. When Ramona found out, it was all we could do to get home alive, I can tell you.

I told her that was enough, she would never travel with me again, but I know she's been desperate to get her hands on that codex."

"But why, Peter? What's in it?" Sara asked.

"Well, it appears to be the story of The Mayans' life, but when you put together certain patterns of hieroglyphs and images, they form a secret code."

"But what does Mrs Braid want it for?"

"She's always wanted to understand the secrets of the ancients, always delving into the past, but the codex is more than that for her. She wants it for her own ends, and that's not good."

"I see", Said Dan thoughtfully, "So if Miss Ambrose with Brad or Mark, have the codex, there may be four of them working on it!"

"I'd be surprised if they're all working together," Peter replied, rubbing his chin.

"But they must be! We know Miss Ambrose drove the getaway car, and we're pretty sure it was Mark or Brad Maipeson who's the thief, the one we saw jumping into her car. It was probably Mark, and Brad's trying to decipher it in the Deli. And from what you say, Mrs Braid masterminded it all. And that fits too, because we've seen Mark go in and out of her office."

"Are you *sure* they're all working together?" Peter asked.

Dan said: "They *must* be! We were being followed round the village, but when the codex was stolen all that stopped."

Sara continued: "Yes, you're right, and Mr Maipeson hid it that day we walked in the shop."

"And Miss Ambrose had obviously spoken to him about our essays."

"Which proves how close they are!"

"But we didn't know about Mrs Braid! No wonder she's been so cool towards me."

"So, the question is, if they've got the codex, what are they going to do with it?"

Peter hesitated before replying: "I'm afraid you won't like this, children, but that depends on you!"

"On us?" They chorused.

"Yes, on you. Parimanu trusted me enough to tell me that only those who travel through time will have the rightful power to own the codex, and the knowledge to unravel its secrets!"

"Why do we need power, Peter?" Sara asked.

"Because there will be great danger in getting the codex back."

"But why? What dangers could there possibly be?"

Peter hesitated for a moment: "Mrs Braid is a witch!"

"A witch!" They both exclaimed.

"Yes, a witch and the worst kind too. She looks to ancient ways to develop her power which is why the codex means so much to her."

"But we haven't seen her do anything a witch might do," Dan said, but as he thought, he said: "Oh no! The cows!"

"What cows?" Asked Peter.

Sara explained and Peter said: "Oh dear, she's experimenting already."

Dan said: "Why would she experiment with cows?"

Peter shook his head: "You won't believe me, but I can guess."

Sara looked puzzled: "Well?"

"I told you things went wrong with the Mayans, but I didn't tell you exactly what happened with Phaelar and Jafyre."

Dan asked: "What do you mean?"

"Mrs Braid stole Dion's son and brought him back."

"What!" They chorused.

"I'm afraid so. Dion's son is Mark."

There was a stunned silence.

"Oh my goodness!" Dan said, reeling with the shock.

Peter continued: "Is Mark getting bigger?"

Dan and Sara looked at each other: "Yes, he is," Sara replied, "How did you know?"

Peter nodded thoughtfully: "It's the effect of bringing him through time so quickly. His system is reacting against the twenty first century. Mrs Braid thinks the codex will give her a formula for controlling his growth."

Sara shuddered: "How awful!"

Dan said: "You mean *stopping* his growth."

"I'm afraid not, Dan. She wants to create a monster! But she must have control."

Sara said: "This is horrible, Peter."

"Is this why you disappeared?" Dan asked, incredulous.

"Well, in part, yes, but I didn't know then that you'd follow in my footsteps".

Sara queried: "Is that what's happened? Have we followed in your footsteps? – to the same times and places as you?"

"Yes, pretty much so, Sara. That old rug's very persuasive, isn't it?"

They looked at the rug, which rippled slightly and pulsed in a comfortable way.

The children nodded thoughtfully. Dan asked: "So what happened with Nigel?"

"Ah, yes, Nigel. Well, after the bother with Mrs Braid, I travelled on my own. After I'd been to Sahasrara, I planned to travel to the future so I could see what I could learn that could influence things, but Nigel wasn't happy about that."

"Why not?" they both asked.

"He said we'd be interfering with the space time continuum. He was worried I'd come back with ideas from the future and put them into practice, even though it might have helped."

Dan flushed, and Sara grinned: "That's what your dad wants you to do!"

"And what Leo's done too!" Dan replied.

Peter chuckled: "Ah, it's an eternal problem – what comes first, the chicken or the egg! Well, I thought, I wanted to come here, was determined to come in fact, and when I got here and saw how things are in the future, I just decided to stay."

Sara asked: " But what about your family and your friends----?"

"-----and Nigel!" finished Dan.

"Humph! My family never much liked me anyway – always thought I was a bit loony – and as for friends – no time for them – too much to do. And I thought Nigel deserved to stew for a while."

"But that's so unfair!" Sara exclaimed.

"Do you really think so?" Peter asked.

"Yes!" They chorused.

Peter looked crestfallen, and sipped his tea: "The only thing I hadn't thought about was the codex actually being found – and by two so young. But for a while, I've sensed you close in my tracks. Am I right in saying that your travels have given you heightened powers?"

"Yes, they have," Dan agreed.

"Well, the more you travel through time, the more powers you will gain."

The children exchanged a glance, and Sara asked: "What kind of powers?"

"I think it's best you find that out yourselves, but that's what you'll need to get it back."

"What?" Dan asked.

"To get the codex back will need the power you're gathering. Mrs Braid is very dangerous and will do anything to stop you. She will also be frustrated as she doesn't yet have the knowledge to unravel its secrets. And to decode it *you'll* need the knowledge you gain from your travels."

"Does Miss Ambrose have that power and knowledge?" Sara asked.

"Or anyone else?" Dan added.

"Not yet."

"So how can she and Mrs Braid decode it? How can they do it without us? After all, we're hardly likely to help them. Why can't we just go to the police?"

"And tell them what?"

Sara replied: "That they stole the codex of course!"

Peter asked in a serious tone: "And what will you tell them about where it came from? How you got a hold of it? And why you didn't call the police at the museum? Will you tell them the local headmistress is a witch?"

The children were silent as they absorbed this.

Peter brightened quickly, and said: "Well, what's done is done! We need to talk about the steps to take when you return, but at the very least, you can tell Nigel I'm all right."

Dan questioned: "When *we* return? What about you?"

"I'll stay put. Nothing to come back for. You're living in Opportunity House, my family are happy with the money from the sale of the house, and I'm sure Nigel will understand."

Sara said reflectively: "He misses you, you know."

"I suppose I miss him too from time to time," Peter admitted reluctantly. "Anyway, before we do anything else, let me show you this magnificent future. What would you like to see? What would you like to know about this splendid year?"

Chapter 63

Still bursting with questions, Dan asked Peter to tell them about the cellar.

Peter explained: "Opportunity House is in an extremely powerful site."

Sara said: "You mean, with the ley lines in the middle?"

"Ah, good! You know about them! Well, with a bit of work and help from an old mapmaker----."

"Timothy Pont!" Interrupted Dan.

"Very impressive!" Nodded Peter, "I can see you two are sharp – very sharp. Yes, with Timothy's map and some intuition, I found Opportunity House, and its wonderful cellar, and everything moved on from there."

"You know Timothy's ghost still haunts the cellar?" Sara asked.

"Really!" Exclaimed Peter.

"Yes, he's been with us on most of our trips. We call him T.P."

"Well I never. How extraordinary. Has he been there all the time?"

"I suppose so. Did you never see him?"

"No I didn't my dear, but it does explain some odd things!"

Dan said: "I see a big new table, and lots of new models. It looks like you're still travelling through time, Peter."

"Yes, I am!"

"Tell us where you've been!" said Dan.

Peter shook his head: "No, Dan, I'm sorry. With these things you have to work it out yourself – just like you've been doing."

"I understand, but can we have a look at the new table and your models?"

Again, Peter shook his head: "That's for *your* future."

He put his cup down, brushed the toast crumbs from his fingers, and said: "Let me show you Mistlees."

As they went upstairs, Dan and Sara couldn't help but notice some of the models. There were pyramids, palaces, temples, bridges, space ships, a penny-farthing bicycle, and dozens of tiny figures, amongst them exotic animals and fish, sailors, dancers and an ancient king sitting on a miniature gilded throne.

"Now!" Cautioned Peter. "Eyes off!"

Dan grinned with the excitement of this feast created from Peter's travels.

The house had changed inside. It was painted white and grey, and the rooms had basket woven tables and chairs, and beds that slid in to the walls. Models, machines, and boxes lay everywhere.

"Amazing how it accumulates," remarked Peter.

Dan's room was almost empty, containing nothing but a blue plastic table and chair and two slide-away beds.

"For visitors," Peter explained.

Sara said: "There's no television, Peter, and no computer or anything."

Peter winked, and pointed his wrist at the ceiling: "News!" he said, and above them appeared a hologram of a woman pacing up and down. She had very short black hair, and wore a one-piece red suit. She said: "The Earth economy continues to grow, and trade with other universes has seen yet another dramatic rise, fuelled by shortages of raw materials. Our ability to recreate these using claytronics and nanotechnology has led to a huge upsurge in the space ship industry as transport supply continues to be stretched to the limit."

Dan and Sara were bewildered, but Peter motioned them to be

quiet for a moment. The news person continued: "And now the weather where you are."

The hologram changed to show a small black man with a cheerful grin. He too wore a one-piece suit, blue in colour: "Hi!" he said engagingly in an unmistakable Scottish accent. "I guess you'll know what's coming, but here goes anyway. Our run of unbroken sunshine - now 125 days – is set to continue for another week. Farmers are delighted by the incredible grape harvest, and this year will be another for superb wines.

Climatologists are ready however to give us two days of controlled rainfall, to refill reservoirs and give a bit of rest to all you non-sun worshippers. Temperatures will remain steady at around 30 degrees, and blue skies will continue till ten o'clock tonight. That's it for now, and I'll be back at the same time tomorrow."

The children looked at Peter: "Yes, global warming turns out not so bad after all. It just took a while to develop the technology to make our own rain."

"How on earth do you do that?" Asked Dan.

"Oh, I'll show you," Replied Peter. "We'll take a trip to the coast tomorrow."

Sara asked: "What was she saying about clay something or another and nanotechnology?"

"Ah, very clever stuff. Nanotechnology is like miniature science. Research on it began before you were born, but only moved ahead properly last century. Scientists use amazing microscopes to make things much smaller than atoms, and claytronics uses them to make anything you want out of a piece of material."

Dan was lost: "Peter, I don't understand."

Peter said: "Let me show you then." He picked up a piece of

what looked like grey plasticine, pointed a beam of energy from his wrist at it and said: "Rugby Ball – size 3."

The clay quickly shaped itself into a small rugby ball. Peter tossed it to Dan. It was exactly like a rugby ball. It *was* a rugby ball. Dan handed it to Sara: "That's fantastic!" He exclaimed.

Peter took the ball from Sara and again pointed the energy beam at it.

"Block of pine wood," he said, and the rugby ball changed shape to become a square piece of light coloured wood. Dan handled it cautiously.

"It won't bite!" Peter reassured, "This is claytronics in action!"

He explained that the substance could take the shape of anything in its memory cells.

"How?" Sara asked.

"Well, I've got one of these rather neat chips you saw in Fomalhaut. Got it fitted when I arrived. I use its memory to list useful things, beam into the material all the details of what everything's made of and how it looks, and bingo! Off we go! That's what the newsreader was saying. We use it to convert into coal, steel, brick, wood and all sorts of raw materials other civilisations need. Good, isn't it?"

"It's brilliant!" Sara said, "Can you change it into a new pair of track shoes? My feet are sore because these are worn out!"

Sara was joking, but Peter used a beam from his wrist chip to scan her feet, beamed this to the clay, and said: "Track shoes. Colour?" He asked Sara.

"Blue and white!" She said, and the clay changed shape into two brand new track shoes. They fitted her perfectly, and she said: "Oh, what a relief! Thank you, Peter!"

"My pleasure. They should help you walk round the village".

The first shock hit them as they opened the front door.

Sara's house had gone.

She gasped and clutched Dan's arm: "Mum! Dad"! She cried.

Peter put his arm round her: "I'm sorry, Sara – I should have warned you. Just didn't think. No, you mustn't worry about your mum and dad. Remember you're a long way into the future."

"Oh, of course! I forgot for a moment. How stupid of me! But what happened to our house?"

"Well, unfortunately, the subsidence you know about from the old mine under the church spread to this part of the village, and your house was pulled down about a hundred years ago!"

As they absorbed this, Peter winked: "But I tell you what. They found something very interesting buried in the garden. Come and I'll show you."

They walked through the village, and on the way, had their second shock. Peter had two shadows. One, cast by the sun, was normal, a black outline of his body shape, reflected on the pavement. The other formed a ring round him, spreading outwards from his feet for about a metre.

It was green.

Where they crossed, his body shadow covered the green one. The children gaped, and Sara said: "This is what we dreamed about!"

Peter stopped: "Did you really dream about this? How interesting!"

"What is it?" asked Dan.

"People here spend a lot of time developing their minds, just like people used to do before we had computers and televisions and all the modern technology we use. Well, now technology works for us, not the other way around, so there's time to contemplate, to meditate, to think about what we're all here for, and to develop spiritually.

We were never very good at using the full power of our brains, but that's all changed, and part of that is this well-being shadow. If it's green, like mine, it means I'm in good health and good spirits".

"What if you're ill?" asked Dan.

"Well, if I'm off colour or out of balance, the shadow will be grey or black or purple, depending on what's wrong".

Sara puzzled: "What's the point of all that though?"

"Well, we don't have doctors or hospitals any more. Everyone uses the powerhouse of their mind to cure simple ailments, and if someone's not quite a hundred percent, their well-being shadow tells us what's wrong, and we use healing energy to sort them out. We all work to help each other, so it's not like the world you're used to."

"That seems very – very- well – terrific really," struggled Sara. Dan was quiet.

"What's up Dan?" She asked.

"The expression Peter used – "the powerhouse of the mind". That's what Andy said too."

"It *is* a powerhouse, Dan. Andy was right," Peter replied.

They were delighted to see the main village landmarks still there. The old tower, the two churches and the graveyard looked, from a distance, exactly the same, basking in the hot sunshine. They squinted as they came into the main street. Amazingly, it looked just as they knew it, but all the shop frontages were painted in dazzling bright colours – red, yellow, green and orange abounded. People strolled up and down, just like a normal Saturday morning, with only two differences.

The first was clothing – in the heat, most people wore shorts and loose fitting tops, and some wore the type of bright coloured one-piece suit they'd seen on holographic television.

The second was the phenomenon of the second shadow. Virtually all were green, but they passed an old man, head bent and walking with difficulty. His well-being shadow was a murky grey. A middle-aged lady stopped and spoke to him. They couldn't hear what she said, but saw the effect. The man straightened up a bit, looked calmer and more cheerful, and his shadow changed colour to green.

"That's what I meant by healing energy," Peter told them.

They looked in shop windows, and every one sold decorative products. One stocked candles and ornaments, another a huge variety of coloured paper, and a third was filled with books.

Dan asked: "What's all this, Peter? Where are the food shops? Where's The Deli? And what are these shops selling?"

"Yes, I suppose that must be a bit strange for you. Do you remember the food making machines you saw in Sahasrara?"

They nodded.

"Well, all our food comes from them now, so we don't need food shops.

Everything is automated, so people have endless leisure time, and these are our antique shops."

"Antique shops! They can't be antique shops – everything's new!" Exclaimed Sara.

"New to your eyes perhaps, but remember you're in the future and these things are interesting to people today."

Peter led them into a shop selling glass and mirrors, all beautifully decorated and etched.

"Nice aren't they?" said the lady tending the shop. "We've got some new ones taking shape over there." She pointed at two square mirrors resting on a shelf. Carved dark wood frames on both slowly formed as they watched, and an intricate pattern etched itself into the bottom corners, looking like a delicate tracing of frost on the surface.

"Claytronics!" Peter told them.

"It's amazing!" Dan said.

Peter took them to the Community Centre, which was little changed except for a bright new entranceway. They were pleased to see the tribute to those who had lost their lives in the World Wars still there, if a little worn with the passage of time. There were no cries or shouts from children. Instead, the main hall was a museum.

"This was my idea," said Peter. "I thought it would be nice to have a record of Mistlees through the ages."

The museum was fascinating. As they looked round, a man entered.

He was the strangest looking person Dan and Sara had ever seen, so much so, that Dan had to stifle a laugh. Sara punched his arm: "Dan!" She cautioned.

"Sorry – can't help it!" He chuckled.

The reason for Dan's amusement was immediately obvious. The man was about two metres tall, dressed in a one-piece black suit. His head was bizarre.

Dan whispered: "It's Mr Potato Head!"

Sara too began to giggle, but fortunately the man didn't seem to notice. He was studying a display cabinet at the other side of the museum. He had one long strand of hair wrapped round his head, like a pile of anchor rope. One ear was enormous, sticking out from the side of his head, whilst the other tilted backwards.

His nose was long, with a deep curve in towards his mouth. His lips were the wrong way round. One eye was wide and staring, the other small and half-closed, his eyebrows were arched like an upside down V, and his whole face had an awful lopsided look.

"Oh, Dan – it *is* Mr Potato Head! How terrible for him!"

Peter watched them with evident amusement: "He's one of the early claytronics robots," he explained. "When they started to make them, they weren't sure how easy it would be for them to make their own shape, and they got a good few wrong before they perfected the technique."

Dan breathed a sigh of relief: "Thank goodness he's a robot. I feel bad about laughing, but I couldn't help it!"

Peter nodded: "Yes, they use the early ones for work like this – looking after the museum. They do a good job, you know."

The robot tidied the display and walked out.

In the museum were photographs of the village stretching back to Dan and Sara's time. One showed the school with Mrs Braid and Miss Ambrose smiling at the camera. Another captured the old church against a lovely red sunset.

In one cabinet were remnants from the collapsed church – pieces of the old wooden seats and a cross from the pulpit.

There was a separate case devoted to the fool's gold, and they were excited to see their names quoted as discovering the mine. Dan's jaw dropped as he read on. "Look!" He pointed.

The caption read:

"DAN GOODWIN AND SARA CHRISTIE DISCOVERED THE FOOLS GOLD AND, BELIEVING IT TO BE REAL, CONSULTED THE LOCAL JEWELLER OF THE TIME, A GENTLEMAN NAMED FRED WINGSOLE.

HIS ADVICE WAS THAT THEIR DISCOVERY WAS WORTHLESS.

SEVERAL WEEKS LATER, THE LOCAL POLICE FOUND HIM EXCAVATING LARGE QUANTITIES OF THE MINERAL TO SELL ABROAD. HE WAS CAUGHT REDHANDED IN THE MINE.

HE SERVED THREE MONTHS OF A SIX MONTH PRISON SENTENCE."

Dan exclaimed: "I *knew* there was something fishy about him!"

Sara just laughed.

Peter said: "Over here, children. This is what I wanted to show you."

The sign read:

TIME CAPSULE

WHEN A HOUSE IN DIRSETT AVENUE WAS DEMOLISHED IN 2187, A TIME CAPSULE WAS FOUND BURIED IN THE GARDEN.

LEFT BY ONE OF THE HOUSE'S PREVIOUS OCCUPANTS – SARA CHRISTIE AND HER FRIEND DAN GOODWIN - THE CONTENTS PROVIDE INVALUABLE EVIDENCE OF WHAT LIFE WAS LIKE IN MISTLEES LONG AGO.

Sara clapped her hands in excitement: "Dan, look! This is something we must have done! Look what we've put into it!"

Displayed in the glass case were a whole series of familiar items. Dan's Playstation and some of his games sat beside Sara's schoolbooks, one open at the last page of her Mistlees project. They read what Miss Ambrose had written in her spidery hand: *"Congratulations on one of the finest pieces of work I've had the pleasure of reading".*

Sara nudged Dan: "Told you I'd have the best project!"

In the display case also were the flying saucer and plane models; a pair of Sara's old trainers ("those are the ones giving me sore feet!" She said); a cup from Dan's kitchen; their museum tickets; a local newspaper with the story of the find of the old church remains; a copy of Tim's swimming certificate; and a photograph of them in front of Opportunity House.

Dan shook his head in wonder: "It's incredible!" He said. "Now we've seen this, we know exactly what we need to do."

"Yes," Peter agreed, "But what comes first, the chicken or the egg?"

Dan nodded: "Just like Leonardo. What came first – his original work or my Rainbow Catcher as his inspiration?"

An empty display case puzzled Dan: "Why's this empty, Peter? It looks as if something's been torn out of it. There are bits of old paper lying around. Look!" He pointed to the corner of the cabinet. The fragment of paper read: **MISTLEES POST.**

"I took that paper out when I sensed you were coming. That's what happens in the end."

"What happens, Peter? You must tell us", said Sara

"No I can't. That's not right. This is too important for you to be influenced."

Dan nodded: "I understand."

They left the Community Centre, and Peter took them back to Opportunity House. They took a detour to look at Elfsite Reach Primary School, and found it looking as it always did, but it was now a Centre for Global Education. Pupils of all ages stood in little groups having a break. Children as young as four or five mixed freely with adults, and Peter told them how traditional school subjects were taught: "The wrist chips we have are programmed to feed the brain all the basics of Arithmetic, English and three foreign languages – French, Mandarin and Spanish."

"Why Mandarin?" Asked Sara.

"The Chinese economy became the world's biggest a long time ago so it was natural everyone should learn a major language from their culture. Since then however, we have moved away from individual countries and the world is one large community."

"Does that mean people aren't proud of being Scottish or English?" Asked Dan.

"Funnily enough, it doesn't. Everyone has what you would call dual nationality – Earth first and Scottish second, for example. You can still study the works of Robert Burns or Hugh MacDiarmid if you want."

They stepped inside the door of the school, and Peter pointed his wrist at a blank screen: "Scottish subjects," he said, and a list of subjects appeared before them.

Agriculture
Customs
Industry
Language
Literature – pre 1500
- 1500 – 1900
- 1900 – 2100
- 2100 – PRESENT DAY
Politics
Sport

"You can study these here or at home, using our technology", Peter told them.

"It sounds really good," Sara said, "But if the world's one big place now, what about things like politics and Government?"

"Oh, that's much easier now," replied Peter. "We don't have political parties or country governments now. Everyone's consulted about issues big and small, and can vote for or against whatever they are interested in. Every morning, we download a list of things that may affect us, with discussion papers giving enough information to allow us to make decisions, and we vote online. It's all run from Room 1103."

"I'm not sure I follow that," Dan said, puzzled. "What's Room 1103, and what kind of things do you vote on?"

"Well, this morning, I was asked if I wanted to vote on Mistlees getting a new church – the old one's reached the end of its life unfortunately. There was also a vote on whether to extend Earth's partnership agreement with our friends in Sahasrara, and another one on expanding our DNA programme."

"DNA programme?" Sara asked.

"Yes, we use DNA technology for very specific purposes now. After it helped us eliminate heart disease, cancer and all the other horrible diseases we used to suffer from, we turned its use to some very interesting subjects."

"Like what?" They both asked.

"Aha! I'll show you tomorrow," Peter replied mysteriously.

"OK, fair enough, but what's Room 1103?"

"That's the place where the issues we vote on are put together. It's run by groups of volunteers, who do all the work, preparing the downloads and suchlike, and the voting, and they organise the resources they need to do whatever needs to be done."

"What an incredible system!" Dan announced.

"Yes, it works really well, and people have a great sense of involvement at every stage of every issue."

As they turned to walk away, a small lady with sharp freckled features, startling red hair tied back from her face and smiling blue eyes, went past them. She wore a yellow one-piece suit, and said brightly in a soft low voice: "Hello Peter, hello Dan, hello Sara. Another lovely day!"

Dan and Sara were speechless.

It was Miss Ambrose.

"But – but- it can't be!" Said Dan.

She turned, winked and walked on. Peter chuckled: "Parallel universes take a while to understand!"

"What do you mean? Asked Sara.

"There's another world out there if you know how to look for it."

In silence, they strolled back to Opportunity House. In the kitchen, Peter offered them a meal, and Sara said to Dan: "Shall I try again?"

Go for it!" Dan agreed.

"Haggis!" She said to the machine.

Back came a cheerful metallic voice: "With neaps and tatties?"

"Oh, yes!" Exclaimed Sara.

The glorious rich smell of the steaming plate of haggis wafted round them as it arrived accompanied by mashed turnip and potato, and Sara licked her lips in anticipation. Dan got a plate of pork chops, with new potatoes and peas, while Peter had mince pie.

The meal was delicious, and during it they discussed the next day. Dan said: "You told us you'd show us how you make rain-----"

"----- and how you use DNA", Sara added.

"Hmm! Yes I did, didn't I?" Peter said slowly. "Let me think now.

If we start early enough, you can have a quick look at Edinburgh, then I'd like to show you our Travel Academy, and then on to the coast to show you what I promised! Quite a day, quite a day!"

Dan asked: "What's the Travel Academy, Peter?"

"Well, I don't want to spoil the fun – you'll see tomorrow! Now, time for bed, so let's have a good night's sleep."

They tidied up, and the children went to Dan's room, where Peter showed them how to control sliding the beds in and out of the wall. He triggered a release switch, and the children roared with laughter as a screen, like those surrounding hospital beds, appeared and split the room in two.

"What's so funny?" Peter asked.

Dan replied: "Leonardo da Vinci would love to see this. I bet this slides back again without a fuss!"

"Of course it does," Peter said and clicked the switch for the screen to slide smoothly back into the wall.

"Goodnight, children. I'll see you in the morning."

"Goodnight, Peter," they said together. They sat on Sara's bed.

"Dan, there's lots today that's been hard to take in, but I can't believe we saw Miss Ambrose again. And this time, it *was* her. It seems impossible!"

"I know, I know, but we *did,* so how come?"

"Well, every place we've been, there's been someone who looks like her, so it's either as we thought, that she somehow travels through time like us, or it's someone who looks exactly like her----"

"------ like a relative, you mean?"

"Yes! What would that make her here? - a great great great great great granddaughter!"

"Or-----," Dan said carefully, "She's some kind of time lord-----"

"-----like in Dr Who?"

"Exactly!"

"Hm, I'm not sure about that. Peter said something about parallel universes. What does that mean?"

"I don't know either, but my head hurts with it, so we maybe just have to accept what we've seen, and sometime we'll find out how it happened."

"And how she knows all about our timetrips."

A thought struck Dan: "If she's somehow travelling through time like us, she must be gathering knowledge to decode the codex - for Mrs Braid."

"I can't believe she's a witch."

"Well, I've been thinking about that. The first time I met her she was sweeping the playground with an old broom."

"You never told me that!"

"It didn't seem important then," Dan said defensively. He continued: "And that Decadent Cooking course would be right up her street. Making ancient recipes!"

Sara grinned: "Like Witches Brew!"

Dan laughed: "Cooked in a cauldron!"

"The Cauldron of Dagda!"

They roared with laughter, releasing the tension they felt.

Dan asked: "What did you think about the rest of the day?"

"It's amazing! It feels like a great place, but – but – empty."

"That's it! Empty! Everyone we saw seemed very nice, very pleasant, but there wasn't much life about them."

"I wonder why?"

"Is it something to do with the way things have moved on? Peter said everything's automated, so people have lots of time on their hands -----"

"----- to develop, and grow their minds."

"But what do they *play* at? Even the guys on Sahasrara had loads of fun about them, but we've not seen any of that-----"

"----yet anyway," finished Sara.

"Well, let's see what happens tomorrow, shall we?"

"Yes, good idea!"

Dan took out his Rainbow Catcher: "I haven't taken any photos yet. Remind me tomorrow, would you?"

"Sure, but why don't you try out that infra-red camera? You could set it up at the window, and see if it takes anything."

"OK," Agreed Dan, and placed the Rainbow Catcher on the windowsill, set it to infrared, and tucked himself into bed. It felt so strange going to bed in his own room in his own house in his own village, but knowing none of it was his in this future time.

Sara's thoughts were similar, with mixed emotions about her house which had gone so many years ago.

Chapter 64

In the morning, it was hot, as the forecaster had predicted.

They felt it through the window, and stirred early. Peter knocked on the door to wake them, and they showered and dressed, Sara going first. The shower impressed her. It was a walk-in cubicle, and instantly dozens of jets above and around her sprayed hot water. After a minute or so, a polite voice asked: "Shampoo?"

"Oh, yes please!" She said, and the shower obliged.

"Conditioner?" She was asked and again she said: "Yes."

Next she was bathed in soap, washed off with more hot water, and finally the water turned to warm air, which dried her in moments. She hadn't lifted a finger.

"Fantastic!" She smiled, putting on her clothes.

Dan too enjoyed the experience. Breakfast was a bowl of porridge from the machine, and before they knew it, it was time to go.

Peter said: "Right! Let's get the car out!"

Dan said: "That's strange! We haven't seen any cars yet."

"No, we don't use them much round the village. People prefer to walk, and of course many go high-speed anyway."

"Sorry?" Queried Sara. "High speed? What's that?"

"Ah! Gave the game away a bit there! Never mind, you'll see later on at the Travel Academy. We really only use cars for slowmo trips."

"Peter," said Dan, "What on earth is slowmo?"

"Ah, sorry, yes, slowmo – that's slow motion."

"Slow motion!" said Sara. "We're surely not going to Edinburgh in slow motion?"

"No, of course not, it's only slow in comparison with – with high-speed."

Dan and Sara gave each other a look, and Sara arched her eyebrows.

"Right!" She said, "Are we ready to go?"

Dan nodded, and patted his pockets: "Oops! Forgot my Rainbow Catcher. Hang on a tick!" He went back to his room and collected it. "Right! Ready!"

Outside there was no car.

"Peter, where's the car? In fact, what kind of car *do* you have?"

Dan's question was soon answered. Peter opened the garage, and inside sat a small round blue object, about twice the size of a football. He rolled it into the driveway, winked at them and said: "You'll like this!"

He pointed his wrist chip at it and said: "Blow bubble blow!"

Sara burst out laughing, but Dan's eyes opened wider and wider as the shape began to grow – and grow – and grow – until it turned into a bubble car, just like those from Sahasrara, but without legs. It had four large tyres, and a very inviting interior.

Peter flicked his wrist and one large segment swung open for them to enter.

"We copied this from our friends in space", Peter told them calmly, "But we've improved the design. To save space, we use miniaturisation to store it, and we don't need the legs any more."

"Why not?" Dan asked.

"Well, they always seemed a bit of an added extra, so we got the same result by using the tyres."

"How do you mean?" Quizzed Sara.

"Watch!" Peter said.

He said to the car: "Four metres up!" Immediately, the car's tyres blew up to a huge size, taking the body of the car high above them. The children laughed, Peter got the car back to normal size, in they got, and set off.

The countryside was little changed, but Dan noticed there were no pylons or cables anyplace.

"No, that's right," Peter told them. "All our energy comes from wind and wave power, and we catch the wind with windmills that look like trees".

He pointed at a small wood of tall pine trees, their branches turning easily in the breeze: "That's our wind power. It's a bit more countryside friendly than two hundred feet high windmills."

The road was quiet, though every so often they heard a whizzing noise, and the car rocked gently.

"What *is* that?" Dan asked.

"Later!" Said Peter, "You'll find out later!"

They reached the River Forth, north of Edinburgh, and to the children's surprise, there was no Road Bridge and no Rail Bridge, the two dramatic landmarks they were used to.

"Don't need them now," Peter said.

"But how do we cross the river?" Puzzled Sara.

Peter spoke to the car: "Water crossing." The car stopped at the edge of the river, and the four tyres gently expanded out and round them to form a shape like a giant dodgem car. Peter drove into the river and they sailed comfortably across.

"This is fantastic!" Dan said.

"Yes, it's handy having the option of floating over, isn't it?"

Edinburgh was the same city, but different in many respects. As they passed through the suburbs, they saw the houses were like those on the table in the cellar – low sweeping shapes, curved and with mirrored glass all round.

"You can see out from inside, but we can't see in," Peter told them.

All were mounted on platforms, and, astonished, they saw one house gently and smoothly swing round on its axis until it faced the opposite way. They gaped at this spectacle, much to Peter's amusement: "I forgot to mention that houses now can follow the sun – or keep it out if you want. All you do is pull a lever, and adjust the house's view to suit you."

The New Town with its solid stone-built flats looked intact, and when they reached Princes Street, the first thing they noticed was the castle facing the wrong way, exactly as in their dream.

"That was a great engineering feat, " Peter told them. "It's mounted on a turntable and spins round to catch the light during the day."

The Gardens were beautifully green, with trees, shrubs and flowers planted in neat patterns, but the highlight was the river which flowed in one end of a small lake and meandered away through the trees, east towards the coast.

"Oh, it looks lovely!" Exclaimed Sara, "And it's exactly like my dream!"

"And mine!" Added Dan.

"Yes, it *is* pretty. Since we stopped using the railway, it seemed a good idea to channel some of the Water of Leith through the old railway tracks, and bring back the lake that was here centuries ago – the Nor' Loch".

People sat beside the water, and strolled through the Gardens in the morning sun. Princes Street itself had a new frontage opposite the Castle. All the ugly old buildings had been replaced with a two-storey brick and glass structure, stretching the full length of the street, broken only by entry to the roads that cut through arches at ground level.

"All of it is a living museum, art gallery and a storehouse of our national treasures," Peter explained.

"It's stunning!" Exclaimed Dan.

There was a reasonable amount of traffic flowing through the Street, mainly bubble cars, but some larger vehicles, made of clear glass and shaped like arrowheads, piloted smoothly along, packed with tourists.

"A bit better than the old buses!" Peter said.

The children's eyes were wide with wonder. The scene was punctuated with whizzing and zooming sounds, and Dan asked: "What *are* these noises?"

"Patience, Dan, patience!" Peter said.

Dan pointed: "Look – the old art gallery!"

There it stood with its carved figures looking sedately over its pillared walls.

"Yes," said Peter. "Some things last for ever."

While they drove on towards the coast, Sara asked Dan if he'd checked his Rainbow Catcher.

"Oh no, let's see."

He switched it on, and found the infrared camera light winking. "It's taken something!" He said. He scrolled through, and set the holographic beam. Up came an image of a huge black cat, snarling at the camera, its teeth bared and eyes yellow. They instinctively shrunk away from the picture.

"I think it's a puma!" Dan exclaimed.

"That's quite likely," Peter said. "We get all sorts of interesting animals now in Mistlees. Pumas, cougars, wild boar, and even the odd grizzly bear!"

"Really!" Said Sara, "It must be very dangerous."

"Not if you're careful," Replied Peter. "We use our energy fields to calm them down and send them on their way. They're used to us anyway – tend to keep themselves to themselves."

"It still sounds scary to me!"

They reached a long low windowless brick building, and Peter parked up. The sign above the door showed a face looking down at them, with a third eye in the middle of its forehead. Underneath it read: **AJNA.**

"This is the Travel Academy", Peter announced. They walked through sliding doors to an open rectangular space, like a huge football pitch. It was brightly lit from some invisible source and filled with whizzing noises, and they blinked at what they saw.

People stood at one end of the pitch, hands outstretched. They then disappeared to reappear instantly at the far end, making the zooming sounds they had heard all morning.

"What on earth is going on?" Sara queried.

"Fascinating, isn't it?" Smiled Peter. "Let's see if we can get you a bit of coaching!"

A slim man came over to them, his green well-being shadow positively glowing.

"Hello Peter," he said in a cheery voice, "Back for some more tuition?"

"No, Father, not for me this time. I've brought along two young friends who don't know anything about high-speed travel. Can you spare them a few minutes?"

"Of course! I'd be delighted!"

He introduced himself as Father Stan Masset.

"Are you a minister?" Sara asked.

He laughed: "No, I don't think you could call me that. They call me Father because I invented the technique I'll show you – like a founding father, not a religious one, but please call me Stan – everyone does!"

He led them to the end of the open space: "First I'll need to give you a brush up on energy fields. You know about them, don't you?"

Dan replied: "Well, yes, a little bit."

"Right then! We all have an energy field surrounding us, and so does every object and living thing."

"Oh!" Said Sara, "I thought it was just people who had them."

"Well, it's most obvious with us, but plants, trees, birds and animals all have their own energy field, and so do buildings, cars, spaceships, and even your everyday items like cups and plates."

"Are you serious?" Dan asked.

"Very much so. We discovered this by using a special type of photography."

"Kirlian photography?" Dan said.

Father Stan looked impressed: "Very good – yes, Kirlian photography. It picks out the field and identifies its strength. High-speed travel uses our energy field and that of the place we want to go to. Let me show you."

He raised his hand, turned his palm towards the wall at the far end of the pitch, and in a flash, he was there, a whizzing noise the only trace of his passage.

He turned round, and performed the same action to stand on the spot he'd left a few seconds before.

"How did you do that?" Dan asked.

"I focus my entire energy field through the palm of my hand and project it at the place I want to reach. It joins with the energy field of that place and immediately connects us."

"Is that what all the whizzing noises are?"

"Oh, I would think so. People love high-speed travel. It's energising and fun, and gets you where you want to go immediately."

"But what happens to you when you're travelling?" Sara asked. "Scientists say we become pure energy for the fractions of a second involved. Good, isn't it?"

"Good! It's brilliant! Can we try?" Asked Dan.

"Of course. Here, stand beside me".

They stood facing the far end of the pitch. All around them people whizzed up and down. Stan got them to think about what they wanted to do: "It starts in the mind, that powerhouse of yours. You need hugely positive energy to do this. Focus on getting from here to the other end, and find the exact spot you want to travel to".

When they did this, they realised the other end was not a solid wall, but a series of wooden posts, closely set side by side.

"Pick one of the posts out. Now imagine your energy field moving from all around you to the very centre of your palm. Feel it gather there, and then get your mind to hurl it all the way to the post you've chosen, and let the combined energy take you there."

Stan whizzed to the other end immediately.

Dan screwed up his concentration, trying to follow Stan's instructions, but nothing happened. He heard a screech from Sara, which started right beside him, but finished at a post at the far end where she stood.

"I did it! I did it! Did you see me Dan?" She screamed. "Oh, let's see if I can get back!"

Dan watched her line herself up slowly and carefully, and felt her concentration as she focused her energies through the palm of her hand. She disappeared for a split second to stand beside him again.

"That was absolutely brilliant!" She exclaimed, "What an amazing power. I felt it ripple through me as I shot here!"

Poor Dan could not get the right focus, and could only watch as Sara went whizzing from end to end. Peter joined them, and said: "Sara, that was extremely good. It took me about four sessions with Father Stan before I got the hang of it. Don't worry, Dan, you'll master it some other time. We need to get to North Berwick now."

The children thanked Stan who was delighted with Sara's success: "Stick at it, Dan, and come back when you get the time!"

"Thanks Stan!" They chorused.

They completed the journey to North Berwick and the coast, passing intriguing holographic signposts: **"MUSEUM OF SPACE AND FLIGHT; MOTOR MUSEUM; SKI SLOPE."**

Sara asked: "How can you ski in all this heat?"

Peter pointed ahead at an impressive conical hill, covered in snow.

"That's North Berwick Law – it's been a local landmark for centuries. It was converted to a ski slope for beginners some time ago. The snow's artificial, and it's protected from the sun by an energy field, which keeps it at a constant temperature. The kids love it for a short fast run and it acts as a springboard for more advanced skiing in the Pentland Hills".

All down the coast ran a succession of golf courses. They stopped at one to watch for a moment, and saw two ladies, dressed smartly in red and blue. They carried one club each, and as they reached their balls, the first lady said something to the club and it shortened. The head of the club changed to a steeper angle, and she struck the ball smoothly towards the green.

"Claytronics again!" Peter informed them.

On the left, before North Berwick, was a lovely old ruined castle.

"That's Dirleton Castle. It's a great trip for the family. People used to come here mainly on Sundays, but now most days are leisure days, so more people can appreciate the beauty of our countryside and its history."

They had been following the course of the River Forth at a slight distance, but now the sea came fully into view. It looked calm and peaceful, twinkling in the sunshine. There were a few little islands dotted along the coast, the biggest being, Peter told them, the Bass Rock.

The road in to North Berwick was tree-lined, a beautiful green avenue leading them through the outskirts of the town. Large houses, one or two idly turning, basked in the sun, and the streets were quiet as they approached the golden sandy beach. They parked the car, and Peter miniaturised it, rolling it into a little line of other deflated cars.

The smell was very familiar – seaweed and salt air combined to give the feel of being on holiday. The sea close to shore was amazing. It was split into sections, and in each, different activities were in progress. Closest to shore, in gentle surf, children splashed happily in and out of the waves.

Further out, the shape of the sea changed completely and

body-surfers competed with windsurfers in high rolling waves that washed on to the soft sandbank barrier separating the two areas. In the distance, the sea was again calm, and yachts with enormous soaring sails scudded swiftly across the surface.

The children were puzzled. Dan said: "Peter, we actually dreamed about this, but how come the sea's calm far out, then really choppy where the surfers are, but at the shore, there are only tiny waves?"

Peter told them: "We always had problems with the good weather. There were no waves for the surfers and even sometimes for the yachts, so we put turbines under the sea driving these waves. They're adjustable of course, so we can have waves as high as you like. In fact, a few months ago, they held the world body surfing championships and the waves were forty metres high. It was a marvellous spectacle. At all four sides of the area are restraining engines which control the water and stop the waves from coming outside its boundaries."

"What a great idea!" Sara said.

As they spoke a huge fat bird waddled past, its outsize beak snapping noisily.

It was light blue with grey tufted tail, and short stubby wings with yellow feathers.

Dan exclaimed: "That's a dodo. We dreamed about that too, but it's supposed to be extinct!"

Peter replied: "Oh, it *was,* but that's how we use DNA technology now – to save endangered species and bring back some of those that were extinct. Isn't he cute?"

They couldn't help but laugh as the ungainly flightless bird waddled along the beach snapping its beak. Two pink-breasted pigeons swooped past it on their way to long grass at the edge of the beach.

Peter said: "That's another example of our DNA work. Those two look like ordinary pigeons but they're actually passenger pigeons, hunted to extinction at the start of the Twentieth Century."

They wandered along the beach to a little peninsula where a small building nestled into rocks.

SEALIFE CENTRE

Peter said: "This is an interesting place. Let's pop in."

Screens round the wall displayed dozens of different species of birds and fish, and one told the history of the Bass Rock, from early days when it was a sailing landmark to the time when a lighthouse, long abandoned, was built. Excavations in the twenty second century had revealed a rich vein of quartz, and traces of the very rare blue sapphire had also been found.

The showpiece of the Centre however, was a series of holograms beamed directly from the Bass Rock. They were fantastic. The island was high with sheer cliffs falling away on all sides, and its surface was crammed with bird and animal life. Nesting seabirds jostled beside huge tortoises, while hosts of beautiful butterflies shimmered above them. Penguins and seals launched off a man-made ring of rocks at the foot of the cliffs, and mermaids swam sedately through the water.

"Mermaids!" Exclaimed Sara.

"Like our dream again!" Added Dan.

"Yes," said Peter. "This used to be a wildlife sanctuary, but we don't need those any more because life of any sort nowadays is sacred. Nobody harms anybody else, and wildlife is safe everywhere. However, the Bass Rock has always attracted birds, and with a little encouragement, we now have a whole host of different species living here."

Dan persisted: "But mermaids?"

"Well, there are actually mermen too, but I can't see any today – they're very shy, you know. They were introduced about forty years ago, and there's a big family of them now. That was a fascinating example of how good technology is today, because when scientists considered using DNA to bring back extinct animals and fish, they found some DNA they couldn't identify on an island called St. Kilda in the Atlantic, and what you see is the result."

He pointed at the large trundling tortoise dominating one of the holograms: "He's a character and a half! He's a descendant of Lonesome George, you know."

Sara asked the obvious: "Who is Lonesome George, Peter?"

"Was, my dear, was! Well, the Abingdon Island Giant Tortoise from the Galapagos Islands was about to become extinct during your time. There was only one left, so they called him Lonesome George, but some far-seeing scientist took a sample of his DNA, and now we've got quite a little colony."

A bright golden toad suddenly appeared right beside the tortoise and its long tongue flashed into the air, catching a purple moth that promptly disappeared down the toad's throat. Off it hopped.

"That's another unusual one – two unusual ones actually when you count the moth. The guzzler is a golden toad. They had virtually all gone because of the mess people were making of the tropical rainforests, but now we've got a good-sized collection here. You might even recognise the moth from your trip to the Mayans. It's the Mayan Insulania Moth, a very interesting specimen. It's supposed to have amazing vision, seeing everything for miles around it."

Dan laughed: "It didn't do very well today then, did it?"

"No, you're right! Maybe it's not all it's cracked up to be."

Peter continued: "The climate here is a great help too. Scotland is now like the Mediterranean used to be. Everyone comes here on holiday, and with no government and red tape to get in the way, small businesses abound so tourists are very well catered for."

"It's incredible to hear about all the changes," Dan said, "And to see some of these birds and animals is brilliant----"

"------but," continued Sara, "It all feels a bit unreal still."

"Not surprising!" Peter agreed. "I'd be astonished if this felt real straight away. It took me ages to get used to it. I've got an idea though to help make it a bit more real for you."

With a twinkle in his eye, he led them to the main street of the town, to a brightly coloured shop. Outside hung a huge red banner proclaiming: **"ROGER'S."**

Peter said: "If this doesn't make you feel at home, I don't know what will!"

Outside the door, a sleek golden Labrador welcomed them, its tail wagging furiously. Sara, feeling much more confident about dogs, patted it, and it looked up adoringly, panting in the heat.

The shop felt warm and cosy, and a slim handsome young man, all smiles, greeted them: "Hello!" he said cheerily in a voice that immediately made them feel welcome, "I'm Roger! I hope you don't mind Pip greeting you. He's a frisky little rascal. Where would you like to sit?"

He led them past the front of the shop, which sold a dazzling array of colourful exotic flowers, to an open area surrounded by bookshelves crammed with interesting looking titles.

The shop was busy, but he found them a table underneath a glass canopy through which streamed the sun.

"Another lovely day!" Roger announced, "But you do know there's rain planned later?"

Peter replied: "Yes, thanks, so we heard. What do you recommend today, Roger?"

"Well, Vera's just finished another batch of her cracking scones which we could serve with home made strawberry jam and clotted cream from our farm in Dorset, or---."

Before he could say any more, Sara said: "That sounds great! I'll have a scone!"

"Good stuff!" said Roger. "Also we've got some still warm Scottish Pastries with Cranberry Jelly, or how about some East Lothian sourdough – that's a local speciality bread, by the way, served with home made butter and a little marmalade I made just the other week."

Peter said: "It all sounds lovely. I'll have some of the sourdough thanks."

Dan added: "And I'll try a Scottish Pastry."

"Jolly good choices," Roger said. "Something to drink? I've got a whole range of different coffees, most of them from coffee beans grown locally, or some tea from our plantation down the coast. Or perhaps – for the children at least – some good old lemonade – home made naturally, and we flavour it with Star Anise, a rather nice touch of the exotic!"

"Lemonade please!" Chorused the children, and Peter, smiling, asked for a cup of tea. Roger sailed off, a huge smile on his face, and the children had a look at the bookshelves. Many of the titles looked new, but there were also some books they recognised, though with different covers. They spotted Treasure Island, The Jungle Book, the Harry Potter books, and right beside them, a title which made Dan's jaw drop: The Timetrippers.

Peter came up behind them and said: "I don't think you should read that one just yet, but it *was* one of the best selling books of all time, you know. They say there's a secret code hidden inside, but nobody's found it yet."

They returned to their table to be served by a lovely young lady who smiled constantly: "I'm Vera, Roger's wife, and I'm so pleased you've chosen to be our guests today. The scones are delicious, even if I say so myself, and this batch of sourdough is real top drawer. As for you young man, with that Scottish Pastry, I'm jealous myself!"

She unloaded the serving tray and went off with a swing in her step.

"What lovely people!" Sara said.

Dan said: "I didn't like to ask, Peter, but they said everything's home-made. Is that in these food machines?"

"Oh good gracious no – not in a place like this. Here, they've kept up all the old traditions, but sadly, this type of place is slowly dying out. Roger and Vera are quite an institution in North Berwick".

The food and drink were delicious, and afterwards, Roger and Vera thanked them profusely for their visit and wished them a joyful day. Pip's tail wagged happily as they walked away.

Dan said: "Peter, they didn't ask for any money. Why not?"

"That's a bit of an old tradition. First time visitors to Roger's don't need to pay."

As they walked back to the car, Dan said: "You said you were going to show us how you make rain."

"So I did, so I did! Thank you for reminding me." He looked up at the sky: "Yes, it's just about time anyway. Let's go down to the front to watch".

They strolled down to a beach beside a golf course at the far end of town. Above it was a covered promenade and already a small crowd of people were gathered under its shelter. They joined them and Peter pointed out to sea: "There are our rainmakers!" He said.

A small fleet of large yachts sailed slowly into view. As their colourful sails drew level with the town, the sails went down and in their place up went spinning vertical cylinders, like giant corkscrews. They heard a low whine, starting softly and growing rapidly to a crescendo, and at the peak of noise, jets of water poured upwards from the cylinders, vaporising as they reached the sky. In their place, dark clouds formed and it immediately began to rain, the drops pelting down on the surface of the sea,

From behind the yachts rose gigantic outspread fans, waving backwards and forwards, sweeping the clouds towards shore. The first droplets pattered on the roof of the promenade, and soon it was raining hard.

Peter explained: "They suck in seawater, whisk out the salt, and blow it into the air at a temperature which makes it vaporise, and form rain clouds. Clever, don't you think?"

The children were fascinated. They turned to watch the clouds move slowly across the town and inland. What happened next was completely unexpected. Puddles formed on the road, and under their surface, they saw shapeless blobs. These quickly grew tentacles, which expanded to fill the puddles, reached out, cleared the road of sand and leaves, and scrubbed the road surface. They disappeared as quickly as they had appeared.

"What on earth was that?" Dan asked.

"Oh, that's our road sweeping crew. They're there all the time, the blobs, but they're tiny. The rain makes them expand, and they're programmed to – to – wash and brush up!" He joked.

Dan and Sara shook their heads in amazement. After a few minutes watching the rainfall, they walked quickly to the car. They were drenched, and after Peter blew the car up, they climbed in, and he pressed a button to draft air round, drying them like a hairdryer.

The drive back to Mistlees was uneventful, though the rain followed them all the way. Sara sang quietly to herself to the tune of Scotland the Brave: "La la la la la la la! La la la la la la la! La la la la la la la – la la la la!"

Dan rolled his eyes in mock despair, but the song energised them both.

After a hearty dinner of steak, chips and peas from the machine, Dan and Sara were ready for bed and bade Peter goodnight.

"We'll need to get you home tomorrow, children, but there's much to talk about first!"

They were too tired to complain and soon were fast asleep, their energy low.

Chapter 65

Lying in bed later than usual, they woke to the sustained patter of rain on the roof. Dan stretched, and spoke quietly: "I dreamed about the future, Sara."

She groaned: "Oh, no, Dan! Not more! Let's get home first please."

"I know, but we go through some kind of time shift when we travel home. It wasn't clear what it was, but we get delayed."

"Were you frightened?"

He thought for a moment: "Yes, I was – for some of the time, but most of it was OK, and that's the thing about it here – I've been feeling great since we arrived – I mean, positive and really focussed."

"Apart from your feeble attempts at high-speed travel you mean!" Joked Sara.

"Ha ha! I'm just a slower starter than you. Wait till I get going, and we'll see who's good at high-speed."

"The way Stan taught us was great, wasn't it?"

"Yes, and I think it's the same basic thing Gary did to fly the spaceship."

"I hadn't thought about that, but right enough, he held his palm over the screen, and moved it from Earth to Fomalhaut-----"

"----and we whizzed there."

Dan thought for a moment: "Maybe that's one of the powers we need to get the codex."

"Well, you'd better hurry up and master it then!"

"OK, OK! But I wonder if that's how we've been travelling through time?"

"How do you mean?"

"Well, every time we've gone someplace, we've had something

quite clearly in our minds either through dreams or thinking about where we might go---"

"----- so is it our thoughts which project us there?"

"Why not? Joining the energy of our thoughts to the place we want to be."

"Well, it does seem to fit."

Sara thought for a moment and chuckled: "I'll tell you someone else who travels the way Stan taught us!"

"Who?"

"Superman! When he flies through the air, he puts his arm out and off he goes!"

"Brilliant – and so does Spiderman!"

"Yes, but he cheats – he uses that spider web stuff."

Peter knocked on their door: "Good morning Dan. Morning Sara! It's another wet day. Just the thing for a bit of time travel!"

Over breakfast, Sara asked: "Peter, what about the codex? How do we get it back?"

"Well, I think I'll need Nigel's help to do that."

"Nigel? But you said he wouldn't travel with you," Sara said.

"I think when he knows what's at stake, he'll change his mind. We need to work out where and when you can gain the powers you'll need to get it back and the knowledge it'll require to decode it. If you try to take it back without protective powers, you will be in grave danger!"

"But how will it help if Nigel's in the future with you?" asked Dan.

"We'll be able to map out your travels and ensure you get to the places and times to give you the tools you'll need."

Sara's face fell: "So you mean we'll have more trips through time? It's been bad enough, battling the rebel angels -----."

"You've met the rebel angels?" Interrupted Peter sharply.

"Yes, of course," she replied, "Didn't you know?"

"No, and that means things are even more serious than I thought."

"How?" Dan asked.

Peter stroked his chin before replying, and Dan noticed his ring made of Fools Gold: "There is an ancient prophecy which says that if the fallen angels take from our world a child of the earth, mankind's future will be for ever changed."

"What!" Sara exclaimed, "How come?"

"The prophecy foretells that if they capture a human being, they open up a rift in the space-time continuum that can never be repaired. The rift will widen with terrible consequences. Time will go backwards as well as forwards. It will be disastrous for mankind".

"That sounds horrific!" Dan said.

"Yes, it is, so you *must* get the codex back. In the wrong hands, our future will be very bleak, very bleak indeed. The secrets of the codex can prevent that happening."

Dan and Sara were stunned into silence. After a while, Dan said: "That's why the rebel angels have been attacking us."

Sara added: "They want to destroy everyone!" She set her jaw firmly, and reddened slightly, her scar glowing. She said: "Well, we'd better get on with it then!"

"What?" exclaimed Dan.

"Remember what Parimanu told us? He said we'd been chosen to save their knowledge and to help mankind. He knew! This is what it's all been about. We've got to get that codex back, get the secrets from it, stop Mrs Braid and her crew from their horrible plans, and sort out the rebel angels!"

Dan, trailing in her wake slightly, said: "Are you sure?"

"Sure? Of course I'm sure. Who else is going to do it? Right. Peter, what do we have to do next?"

A somewhat bewildered Peter replied: "Well, the first thing is to get you home safely. Then you must persuade Nigel to join me here. We'll plan your next moves."

Dan remarked: "If we're going home today, what will we tell people about you, Peter?"

"Yes, I thought you might ask me that. Well, I think the least said the better, don't you?"

"Yes that's fair enough, but we'll have to tell our parents. They know we're looking for you," Sara said.

"But will they tell anyone else?" Peter asked.

Dan replied: "It's hard enough getting them to believe us, so I don't think they'll be saying too much about time travel!"

"Good, and you'd better keep the search for the codex quiet too. I feel they'll try to stop you because it's so dangerous."

Dan said: "We need someone to help us then. Someone in Mistlees."

"Who?" Sara asked.

"I don't know", puzzled Dan, "Someone we can trust. Mr Dewbury's the obvious one, but he always seems so remote."

"OK, we need to give that some more thought," Sara said.

"What do we need to watch out for in Mistlees, Peter?" asked Dan.

"I think for now, just be careful - trust no one and say as little as possible."

"How will we communicate?" Dan asked.

"Through your Rainbow Catcher. I can use my chip implant's Message Sender."

"Will we be able to reply?" Sara asked.

"I hope so, young lady, I sincerely hope so. Now, we must think about getting you on your way. Is there anything else you want to know ?"

They thought, and Dan said: "The smells, Peter, tell us about the smells. There's always an aroma of something in the cellar and we can't work out how that happens."

Peter laughed: "Oh, that's my little joke. I discovered that smells travel through time too, but they use a slightly different channel from us, and I use that to filter through some of the scents from my trips!"

"So it's been you all along?" Sara queried.

"Yes. I knew somebody sometime would want to investigate, and I thought it might give them a clue that all was not as it might seem."

"Well, it certainly puzzled us!" Dan replied.

In the cellar, the rug sat solidly between the two tables. This made Dan think, and he asked: "Peter, if we use the rug to travel, how do *you* do it, because the rug's always with us?"

"Well, the rug's only programmed with seven destinations – one for each colour – so it's a bit limited really. When I got here, and had my chip put in, I used its time travel memory to send the rug back to Mistlees."

"You mean you can travel without it?" Sara asked.

"Oh, yes. My microchip is like a very advanced Rainbow Catcher. I programme it to specific times and places."

"How amazing!" Dan said.

"Yes, this chip," He patted his wrist, "Is a great companion. I'll let you into a little secret. I call mine Isis."

"Why Isis?" Sara asked.

"Isis was the Egyptian mother goddess. She had a bit of a tough time, because her husband, Osiris, was killed and cut up into pieces and his body scattered over the land. Isis went on an epic journey to find all the pieces and built temples over each fragment she found. You'll see her on ancient carvings, and her outstretched wings and her turbulent travels seemed good symbols for my travels, so *my* chip is Isis!"

"How strange is that?" Sara declared.

Dan said: "Peter, my dad was keen for me to get some ideas from the future to help him develop the Rainbow Catcher. Can you help?"

Peter looked doubtful: "Hm, I'm not sure Dan. As I told you, that was the main reason Nigel worried about me travelling to the future. He didn't want me to bring back future technology. I'll tell you what though – if you tell him what you've seen, maybe that in itself will help."

Dan replied: "That's fair enough, thanks."

"Now, let's get you home!" Peter said, pointing his wrist at the rug: "Home!" He said, and the rug's centre circle glowed and pulsed, its indigo blue gleaming in the light.

They stepped on to it, holding hands, and with a loud swooshing sound, they were off.

Peter smiled to himself and checked his wrist chip.

"Oh no!" he said, "I've sent them slowmo! What a terrible mistake!"

Chapter 66

By that time, Dan and Sara had heard the familiar wheezing whoosh, and felt a rush of air through their hair, but then everything changed.

The cellar and the walls of the house dissolved, the air rippled round them and they were suddenly suspended above the village. Their feet were locked to the glowing rug under their feet, but it was as if they stood on a flying carpet. The outer edges of the rug flapped briskly in a breeze, but they stayed still, though everything slowly changed shape beneath them.

For a fraction of a second it was pitch black, then bright daylight, then dark as night, and back to light. Sara clutched Dan's arm, but the stroboscopic light effect made her movements appear jerky and unnatural. "Dan!" She shrieked, "What's happening!"

Dan held her tightly. He too had to shout above the wind: "I don't know, but it's not supposed to be like this! Look! We're right over the middle of Mistlees!"

They looked down, and through the rapid switches from day to night, saw things change. A new building at the edge of the village quickly demolished itself before their eyes, leaving a bare patch of earth that immediately grew grass and trees.

The shops in the main street changed colour rapidly. The surface of the street changed in seconds from black to grey. In the countryside, fields changed from green to brown, to green and brown in an endless rhythm, rippling in the light and dark.

Dan said: "Everything's changing. The village is going backwards in time. Look!"

He pointed at a farm outbuilding, swiftly collapsing to a

skeleton frame, which disappeared, replaced by a green field.

Sara shrieked: "Dan, what's happening to us?"

Dan stayed calm, and tried to think logically: "Hang on, Sara! I'm going to try something!"

He pulled out his Rainbow Catcher, and switched it on. He clicked to the date/ time menu. It was a blur of numbers, and for a few moments he couldn't make anything out. As his eyes adjusted to the speed, he saw the date changing.

He couldn't see the days, but the year changed from 2287 to 2286. A minute later, it changed to 2285.

"Sara, we're going back in time, but slowly!" He shouted.

"It doesn't feel slow to me!" She shouted back.

"No, you're right! Something's gone wrong and we're seeing the years fall away. It's 2283 now!"

Sara squeezed his arm: "What can we do?"

"I don't know! If it keeps going like this, it'll take hours to get back home again!"

"What if it doesn't stop and we keep going back and back even further?"

"Surely that won't happen! We need to keep calm. We mustn't panic!"

"I'm already panicking!" Replied Sara, but something in Dan's confident tone calmed her down. She breathed deeply, and began to think more positively. As she did so, a luminous glow spread all round the rug, persisting through all the rapid changes of light.

Dan gasped. Their four angel friends appeared, surrounding them, hovering just beyond the fringes of the rug.

Sara gasped: "Are we glad to see you!"

Vohumanah spoke first, his tone and words reassuring:

"You do well to think good thoughts. Your journey has been set in a dimension difficult to change. You will watch the world unravel to your own time."

Dan shouted above the turmoil: "Will we get home OK?"

"Continue to focus your energy. Your passage may not be smooth, but your thoughts are your key to safety."

His words seemed to fall around them like a protecting veil, encouraging them both.

Metatron continued: "When time moves quickly through, and days and years flow by, but backwards from the future, here to reach your past, then keep your hearts and minds inspired, your thoughts in tune with time. Keep pace with time and time keeps pace with you."

Despite their precarious position, Dan and Sara smiled at his strange speech.

Zuphlas spoke softly through the rushing flow of months and years: "When you watch all round you transform, be reassured you stay the same. The seasons change, the climate changes, and ever time rolls back. Closer and closer to home you reach, our protection near at hand."

Kamiel, the violet flame round his head unaffected by the air speeding past, completed the angels' words: "Peter has called on us to guide you. It was he who set you on this path, he who wishes you safely through. Our mission is clear. We watch over you. Be secure."

Before the children could reply, all four angels melted into the wind. Dan and Sara were speechless for a few moments, absorbing their words.

Dan said: "Wow! That was powerful!"

Sara nodded, her head bobbing strangely in the ever-changing light. "I feel better though," she shouted.

"Me too!"

They were quiet for a while until Dan started to chuckle.

"What's up?" Sara asked, "What's so funny!"

"I was just thinking in the silence. That's the longest I've ever heard you keep quiet. For years in fact!"

"Ho ho, very funny. I wish I could say the passing of time made you funnier, but I can't!"

"Very good Sara! Right, let's work this out. I reckon a year passes about every minute, judging by the Rainbow Catcher. I'm going to see if we can work out how long getting home will take."

Whilst the seasons flew past in Mistlees, he set the calculator: "Right, it's now 2270. Oops! No, it's 2269 already. Right, at a minute a year----"

"-----we'll be home in just over four hours!" Completed Sara.

"That's right! Well calculated!"

"You didn't need the calculator for that!"

Underneath them, the shops changed colour again, and a row of houses on the edge of town crumbled, replaced by familiar cottages.

Sara exclaimed: "That's where Iain and Shane live!"

"Or used to!"

For a while, they watched the fascinating pattern of changing seasons.

Dan suddenly exclaimed: "Sara! If we're travelling in real time – I mean our own real time, not time travel time----"

"-----it's OK, I know what you mean!"

"That must mean that we're not back home when we should have been".

Sara put her hand to her mouth: "Oh, no, everyone's going to be worried about us! They'll think we're lost!"

"Like Peter!"

Excitedly, Dan said: "But that must mean we can text them!"

"Yes! Brilliant! Let's do it!"

"Hang on then, what's the date?"

He checked, and the flashing figures told him: 2250.

"What will we say?" asked Dan.

Before he could reply, a ghostly hand reached from above and the Rainbow Catcher was torn from his grip.

"Oh no! It's gone! Someone's stolen it!"

"How! How! This can't happen! We're in a time tunnel. There can't be anyone else around. You must have dropped it !"

"I didn't! I didn't! A hand appeared from no place and grabbed it!"

In despair, they looked up, down and all around. They saw nothing apart from the changing colours beneath.

Suddenly, the air was pierced by a loud screech.

Dan exclaimed: "That's my alarm! It's set to go off if it's away from my body!"

The noise grew louder and louder, surrounding them and reaching a deafening crescendo. They both saw an arm reach casually over the edge of the rug at their feet. It was pale and skeletal, and they could see right through it. Sara shrieked and Dan bent to grab it, but couldn't reach, and couldn't move his feet either.

As the arm withdrew, it dropped the Rainbow Catcher on the rug. Abruptly, the alarm stopped, and it beeped as Dan stooped to pick it up.

"What on *earth* was that!" Sara exclaimed.

Dan said: "I don't think it was *anything* on earth!"

"I bet it was something sent by the rebel angels!"

"Well, at least it's gone!"

"Why's it beeping?" asked Sara.

Excitedly, Dan said: "We must have a message!"

He clicked through the menu. There was one text waiting.

It read: "just curious - doppelganger dan".

Dan shivered. He read the text to Sara.

"What's a doppelganger?"

"I've no idea, but whoever or whatever that thing was, it left the message!"

"Oh, this is weird!" Sara said.

"I'm going to look up that word," replied Dan. After a few moments, even in the ever-changing shades of dark and light, Sara saw him go pale: "What is it Dan? What's it say!"

Silently, he passed the Rainbow Catcher over, and she read from its dictionary:

"Doppelganger (pronounced dop'l-geng'ar), noun – a ghostly double of a human being, a wraith, an apparition."

"I wish we were out of here!" She shouted.

Dan regained his composure: "We need to get that text done! But first we'd better not get caught out again! I'm putting the motion detector on!"

He started to text while the years flowed past, and Mistlees ever so slowly began to return to normal on the ground beneath.

Chapter 67

Every passing minute carried them closer to their own time as the years whipped past. Dan sent his text:

Travlin home all ok be back for midnight d & s x

Occasionally, the arrow on the Motion Detector span, but no images registered.

Sara asked: "What time is it – I mean, what *year* is it now?"

"It's – oh, it's the turn of the century! 2200 – and now 2199!"

"Well, we're making progress!" Sara shouted.

The village continued to change shape as houses appeared and disappeared.

Sara exclaimed: "Look!"

Below them, the bare patch opposite Opportunity House was quickly replaced by the familiar shape of Sara's house. She said: "That makes me feel so good! We're definitely on the way!"

The Rainbow Catcher beeped. It was a reply from Hugh:

Glad all wel v worried here wot hapnd? Dad

They exchanged texts for a few minutes.

found peter he ok timetrip in slowmo

great news re peter wots slowmo?

Slow motion

Ok how u no when u get home?

Travlin 1 yr in 1 min

Wot yr peter in?

2291

so u in 2150?

2145 now

tel us if any probs

k

There was something reassuring about this exchange, and for the first time, Dan and Sara settled to enjoy the ride. Neither was tired despite the fact they'd stood stock still for two and a half hours.

"Maybe this is one of the powers we're developing," joked Sara, "The stamina to stay on our feet for hours!"

They were used to the constant light change, and could click their fingers in time to the colours marking the changing seasons. As the century again changed and the Rainbow Catcher registered 2099, Dan punched the air: "Yes, not too long now!"

Suddenly, the air darkened, and just beyond the edge of the rug they saw the rebel angels, so faint they looked like shadows. Sara gripped Dan's arm, and stood forward aggressively: "I'm not having any of this!" She exclaimed.

Before she could do anything, however, they heard the two demons cackle like a cracked old gramophone record. Azazel said: *"This time you may be safe, but beware when next you venture through our realms!"*

Samahazai, his shape flickering wildly, added: *"It will be soon – very very soon!"*

They dissolved into the atmosphere.

"Thank goodness for that!" exclaimed Dan, "They can't be able to get at us travelling like this!"

Sara replied grimly: "Yes, but they'll be back!"

They discussed what they would tell the adults on return. Sara said: "I think we just need to talk about finding Peter, and what the future was like. Any more, and I'll never hear the end of it from Bruce!"

"Right! No mention of the angels, nothing about Mrs Braid, and we won't talk about the doppelganger either. But what about the codex? What will we say about that?"

"Peter said the less we say the better. Let's just say he doesn't know where it is, but we've to keep our eyes and ears open."

"That sounds good! Agreed!"

As the years flicked past, the daylight seemed less bright. Dan said: "That must be all the pollution. In the future, the weather's better----"

"-----and there's less muck around!"

Dan pointed silently beneath them. Opportunity House began to glow.

"We must be nearly home," said Sara. "What happens then? I mean, how do we get back in the cellar?"

At the stroke of midnight, they felt the rug wobble slightly, they sideslipped through the air, the house dissolved, reformed round them, and they were back in the cellar with a gentle whoosh.

The air suddenly was filled with noise and in a circle round them, stood Hugh, Liz, Diana and Nigel cheering loudly. They were engulfed with hugs and pats on the back. Bruce was last to join in, and Sara felt her cheek sting, but ignored it.

T.P. stood behind Liz, a broad grin on his face. He bowed as Dan grinned at him, and glided round the cellar in a triumphant swoosh.

"Thank goodness, thank goodness," Liz kept repeating.

Dan and Sara grinned excitedly at each other. They felt like returning heroes.

Back in the lounge, they started to tell their story. Tim, carried off to bed earlier, rushed in: "Dan! Dan! Sara! Where have you been!"

Dan picked him up and swung him round: "We found Peter!" He said with a huge grin.

The children fascinated the adults with their trip to the future.

Diana and Bruce were shocked to learn how their house would eventually disappear.

"We'd better sell it quickly!" Bruce said.

"North Berwick sounds like the place to buy then!" Said Hugh.

Diana asked: "What about the codex? What did Peter tell you?"

Sara replied: "Oh, nothing much, unfortunately, mum. He just told us to keep our eyes and ears open around the village."

"That's a bit disappointing, isn't it?"

"Yes, but it somehow doesn't seem so important now."

Nigel looked thoughtful at this exchange, but said nothing.

"How is Peter," he eventually asked, "I've been worried about him."

"He loves living in the future, Nigel-----," Dan said.

"------ and he'd like you to join him!" Sara added.

Nigel was unusually quiet.

Liz put her hand on his arm: "Are you all right?"

"Oh, yes, thank you! I'm so pleased the children are safe, and Peter is well. I knew in my heart he was, and that the children would find him, but sometimes thinking you know and knowing are not the same thing."

"What will you do?" Hugh asked him.

Nigel grinned: "It sounds like he may need someone to keep him on the straight and narrow."

Bruce said: "It'll be a busy old rug then. I thought I'd drop in on myself ten years on from now so I can see if I'm rich enough to retire!"

Diana punched his arm.

"Ouch!" he complained, "What's wrong with a bit of forward planning?"

Hugh asked: "Did you manage to get some ideas for the Rainbow Catcher?"

Dan replied: "Peter said it would be enough to know how things are in the future and that you could work out what to do from that."

Hugh nodded: "I guess I knew that would be the right thing. We can't play around too much with time, can we?"

The other adults nodded agreement, but Dan and Sara weren't so sure about that.

Chapter 68

They slept soundly after their adventure.

Liz took Tim shopping, and Hugh left Dan till he woke just after 11 o'clock.

He came sleepily into the kitchen, yawning. Hugh greeted him cheerily: "Morning, Dan! Good to see you up and about at last!"

"Oh, I know, I was shattered last night. What's the plan for today?"

"No plans – just a day to rest and recover!"

"That's good! I need to get my energy back."

Sara came over for lunch, Liz and Tim returned and Dan and Sara went to the cellar. "At last!" Sara said, "Some space to ourselves!"

"I know! That was quite a trip yesterday----"

"----- and good to meet Peter!"

T.P. drifted round the shelving: "I am indeed pleased you have returned. May I join your conversation?"

"Of course, T.P.," said Dan, "Feel free."

"Free is not what I feel, young man. Very much not free, in fact."

"Oh, I'm sorry, I wasn't thinking. Maybe we'll find a way to set you free."

"I would forever be in your debt."

"Well, if you can help us work out what we should do, that would be a start."

T.P. listened attentively, sometimes leaning an elbow on his knee, sometimes drifting slowly backwards and forwards as if in deep thought.

Dan continued: "We've got loads on our plate, Sara. How do you feel about it?"

"You know, the minute Peter described that old prophecy, I was struck by a stab of real certainty."

"What do you mean?"

"I just *knew* that this is what we have to do!"

"You mean, get the codex back?"

"Yes, and work out its secrets. I'm in the mood for a fight!"

Dan held up his fists in mock anger: "OK, come on then! Hit me!"

"Ha, ha! I tell you what though, I feel I'm battling against Bruce too. I really think he resents me and the attention I get."

"Do you think so?"

"Yes, and no one, not Bruce, Mrs Braid, Mark, the rebel angels or anyone else is going to beat me."

"Right! Let's get up and at 'em! What do we need to do?"

"Well, I think we should sound out Mr Dewbury. Have a chat with him and see if we think he could help us."

"Yes, it would be good to have another minister on our side!" Dan said with a grin at T.P.

"What about Nigel?" asked Sara.

"He said he would join Peter, so that was easier than I thought it might be."

"I think that was because of what we said about the codex. He knew there was more to it than we said."

"Yes, you may be right."

T.P. had been quiet listening to their exchange, but leant forward at this point: "I may be able to help with the codex."

"Really?" asked Sara.

"Mapmakers work with symbols and abbreviations all the time. We are able to look at things and find what others cannot, and see patterns where order is hard to discern."

"That's brilliant!" said Dan, "All we have to do then is find it and bring it to you!"

"I look forward to that day," T.P. replied.

Sara said: "What should we do about the gang of four?"

"What's the gang of four?"

"Miss Ambrose, Mrs Braid, Mark and Brad Maipeson?"

"Oh, very witty!" A thought struck him: "I'm sure now Mark *was* the thief."

"How?"

"Well, we didn't know that Mark had come back with Mrs Braid, and if she's trying to control his growth, it's likely he *was* the one."

"But he doesn't get on with Miss Ambrose."

"Well, that's what it looks like, but Nigel said that all may not be as it seems."

Sara reflected: "So maybe Brad Maipeson's not involved at all. After all, we didn't actually see him with the codex."

"Oh dear, what a tangled web!"

"Hmm. Well, Peter said to keep our eyes and ears open."

"What if we watch them all and see where they meet. That way we might find out and see where they've got the codex hidden."

"That's a good plan. And then wait for Peter and Nigel to get to work!"

T.P. asked: "Will Nigel be leaving us?"

"Yes, T.P.", said Sara: "He's going to help Peter work out where we need to go to help us get the codex back."

"We have not met, but I have seen him many times with Peter. They work as one."

"We gather they're both lightworkers," Dan said.

"Yes, and this earth needs them. He will be missed."

"Maybe we could get him to map Mistlees in the future for you?" Sara suggested.

"That would be most gratifying!"

"OK, Sara," resumed Dan, "Seems like we've got a plan."

"Good! You know, we never even talked about where Peter's living."

"Yes, it's an amazing place."

"But would you like to live there?"

"No! Definitely not! I don't think we're ready for that kind of life, do you?"

"No, it seemed so – so –"

"----- adult?"

"Yes, that's the word! The children are already programmed with all our school stuff, so how do they grow up?"

"I don't know, but I'm happy here, in our own time!"

"So am I, but what about Nigel? Will he be happy there?"

"Well, for our sakes, I hope so. He disappeared pretty quickly last night. I guess he'll want to join Peter soon."

"How will he manage that?" asked Sara.

Dan nodded at the rug: "I'm sure our magic carpet will work that out!"

"That was spooky, the hand we saw!"

Dan shivered: "I think I'm quite happy to forget that!"

"But it shows there's lots of strange things we don't know anything about. Scary!"

They were quiet for a moment. Dan asked: "Sara, how are you feeling?"

"How am I feeling? I'm fine – why?"

"I mean, how's your energy? What are you feeling deep down?"

"Actually, I'm feeling really confident. It must be something to do with learning so much so quickly."

"That's true. I've learned a huge amount about myself – and about dealing with other people too."

"When I think back to just a few weeks ago, before you arrived here, I know I've changed----."

"Yes – you've got new trainers!"

"Oh, I know! I realised this morning I've still got them. But where are my old ones?"

"Well, we saw them in the museum----"

"----in the time capsule we leave----"

"-----but how can you leave them when you haven't got them?"

Sara felt goose bumps prickle across her scalp. She pointed. Sitting neatly under the table were her old trainers. Dan shivered too: "How on earth did *they* get here?"

Sara shrugged: "Well, I don't know, but at least I *do* know where they're going!"

Dan said: "I've come back from the future feeling I know how to keep my energy high----"

"----me too. I feel better able to focus, and recognise my own feelings, getting rid of any doubts really quickly, and energising myself - and you---"

"---yes - working together to be stronger than we are as individuals!"

"If we've learned that, why can't other people?"

"I suppose everyone learns in their own way, and in their own time."

"For us, time has been accelerated."

"Except when we came home----"

"-----in slowmo!" They chorused, laughing at their trip the previous night.

Chapter 69

At school on Monday morning, the children handed in the Mistlees project.

They couldn't help looking at Mark. He looked fearsome, his new height and breadth setting him head and shoulders taller than Miss Ambrose. His black eye still shone, but both eyes actually seemed smaller and sunken, overhung with thickened eyebrows. He wore new clothes, but already they seemed on the small side, his shirt bulging over his trousers. A faint moustache showed on his upper lip.

"Something wrong?" He growled at Sara under his breath. Embarrassed she looked away.

Dan and Sara avoided eye contact with Miss Ambrose, unsure how to react to seeing her in 2291. She told the class: "I'll give you some free time this week, so I can mark this and give you the results on Friday".

She grinned at Dan and Sara: "Well, children, what does the future hold, I wonder?" After half a heartbeat, she added: "Good marks, I hope!"

Dan didn't know what to say. How could he ask her what she was doing nearly three hundred years in the future? How could this be the same person who had the codex? How incredibly two-faced she was! He shook his head.

At break, Mark swaggered over to them, edging Sara out of the little circle they formed with Iain and Shane. She gently edged herself back in, smiling sweetly at him. Somewhat unnerved, he looked at Dan and blustered: "Well, little one, are you ready for your last practice?"

Dan smiled nervously: "Well, hello Mark. Good to see you too! Yes, I would say we're ready, aren't we, lads?"

Iain and Shane said together: "Oh, we're ready!" giving Dan a moment to recover his poise. Mark withdrew with a throwaway: "Right then! See you on the battlefield!"

Ali and Asha felt a change in the class atmosphere. Sara's position had strengthened, and all the girls wanted to include her in their conversations.

Ali and Asha stood in her way as she returned to class. "Hey, teacher's pet!" Said Ali sarcastically; "Going to get good marks for your little project then?"

Sara smiled confidently: "Hi Ali! Hi Asha! Well, I hope so! What about you?"

"Never mind about us, smarty," retorted Asha, "You'll crash and burn for sure!"

Sara thought for a second, looked steadily at Asha, then at Ali, and replied: "I don't think for a moment I'll crash or burn. The real question is - will you? I hope not!"

The A-bomb duo was deflated. In silence, they followed her in to class.

At the last football practice before the weekend's tournament, Graham gathered the two teams together: "Right, lads, we've got the draw for Saturday. The format is a round robin. That means, for those who don't know," he said, looking at Dan, "That each team plays the three others in their group, and then the top two teams from each league go into the semi-final. Mark! Just as well your boys are fit – you'll likely have five matches to play. Dan! Don't worry, you'll be out quickly, so you can support them!"

Dan coolly shook his head: "I don't think so," he replied, to a loud snort from Mark.

After training, Graham told them: "Meet outside the school at eight o'clock sharp on Saturday. Don't be late – the tournament starts at ten thirty, and we want time to get settled first."

On their way home, Dan and his teammates agreed to stage an extra practice session on Wednesday.

Dan received an e-mail from Nigel that night:

Hello Dan,
I owe you and Sara a huge debt of thanks. You've found my good old friend, and I'm going to join him – I think you'll be needing some help with the codex, and working with Peter, I'm sure we'll be able to influence events. I'd like to travel on Sunday. May I use your cellar – and the rug?
Nigel.

Dan e-mailed back:

Hi Nigel,
Good to hear from you, and I'm glad you want to join Peter. He's missed you! We will too, but we know you'll both be helping. Of course you can use the cellar and the rug. See you after lunch on Sunday.
Cheers,
Dan.

Over tea, he told mum and dad Nigel would travel on Sunday.

"I'm not surprised," Hugh said. "Poor Nigel must have been lonely. This gives him a chance to rejoin his co-conspirator.

You wonder what trouble they'll get up to in the future!"

Dan and his squad had a great session on Wednesday. They rehearsed Dan's set-piece move from kick-off, and agreed code names for all their moves, grinning at the simplicity of their invention.

During the week, Mrs Braid went round school to get support for the tournament. She gave Dan a real scowl, and he recoiled as if he'd been struck. She muttered something under her breath. It was the first time he had seen her really angry, and he wondered what had prompted it, realising he didn't have the power or the confidence yet to tackle her. As he looked at her, he wondered how he hadn't noticed how much like a witch she actually looked. Her pointed nose, long thin fingers with curved nails, her straggly grey hair, crinkly olive skin and her large black skirts completely gave it away. She frowned at him and he quickly looked away, suppressing a shudder.

By Thursday, it was clear there would be a double-decker bus full of supporters to travel with the two teams. Sara said to Dan: "That's terrific – the school have never had such huge support for anything!"

"It's great, isn't it? But you should have seen the look I got from Mrs Braid. If looks could kill, I wouldn't be here."

Sara felt a chill deep inside: "Her looks probably *can* kill! Don't say that!"

"I didn't mean it quite like that."

"Oh, I know, but why was she so grouchy?"

"I bet she's frustrated because she can't work out what's in the codex."

Sara nodded: "That could be spot on you know. They've had a few weeks to crack it, but maybe it's beyond them."

"That's good for us, but also dangerous. What if they find a way to use us?"

"How?"

"I don't know – kidnap us, torture us?"

"Oh, Dan, that's silly. No way!"

"I know, I know!"

The week passed quickly, and as they walked to school on Friday, Dan said: "We get our marks back today. How do you think we'll do?"

She grinned: "I've always said I'd have the best project, and win the prize!"

"So what do you think now?"

Sara replied: "I hope we *share* the prize!"

Dan stopped, and, in mock surprise, said: "You hope we *share* the prize?"

She grinned: "Yes, that's what I said!"

"Well, let's see!"

Miss Ambrose greeted the class cheerily: "Well, I must say that marking this year's project has been a real treat. In all the years I've been here---," she smiled, and coughed behind her hand, "-----I've not seen such a high standard."

The class felt proud. They looked round at each other, sharing little smiles and nods. When they settled down, she continued: "So, I'll hand out the results now. I've graded them from A to E – A is the highest, and we've never had an A yet. And remember – you've all done very well!"

The children shuffled expectantly in their seats.

"Mark," she said, "It's a pretty good effort. I liked your description of the main street, and the village activities. You certainly seem to know all the secret hiding places in Mistlees! I've given you a C."

Mark smiled smugly: "Thank you miss!" while Dan and Sara looked thoughtful.

"Ali and Asha, it looks to me as if you worked together – perhaps a bit too closely – but I've given you C's as well, Ali a C +"

They breathed a sigh of relief.

Most of the class were graded C, but Iain was delighted to get a B.

"The thought you put into agriculture and how the village has developed was first class. Very good work!"

Iain blushed, and several of the children tapped their desks in approval.

Shane matched Iain's grade, much to his satisfaction, Miss Ambrose commenting on his attention to detail on village architecture.

Dan and Sara realised theirs were the only two projects left, and shared a nervous look. Miss Ambrose smiled warmly: "Sara, your project was excellent! I loved the care you've put into it. I hadn't realised how interesting the graveyard is, and what a treasure trove of history lies in the headstones. I'm not sure how you know there's a historical connection with Leonardo da Vinci in the church, but if it's true, it's fascinating!"

She set the project carefully down on Sara's desk: "Great work – very well done - A +!"

Sara gasped, and the class were quiet for a moment before everyone cheered and banged their desks. She reddened in embarrassment, and said quietly: "Thank you, Miss!"

When the class quietened down, Miss Ambrose continued: "I said there would be a prize for the best project, and this year is the first time I've awarded an A, never mind an A+. I was delighted with Sara's work, and so that leaves Dan."

The class listened in expectant silence.

"When you consider he has only lived here a few weeks, Dan has had more to learn than anyone about Mistlees, and I believe he's captured the spirit of the village beautifully! The descriptions of the churches and the tower are excellent, and of course your discovery, with Sara, of the fate of the Sunken Chapel really is the icing on the cake. In joint first place, Dan – well done indeed – an A+!"

The class erupted, even Ali and Asha lending support to the cheers. Mark glowered under raised eyebrows.

Dan was thrilled, despite his feelings about Miss Ambrose, though he couldn't help but wonder briefly if she was deliberately praising them to enlist their support in decoding the codex. He looked at Sara who mouthed: "Told you we'd win!"

Miss Ambrose walked to her desk, and collected two yellow boxes: "I hope you'll remember this project for a long time!" She said, handing them their prizes. Amidst much excitement, they opened the boxes to reveal two silver clocks, engraved:

MISTLEES PROJECT – FIRST PRIZE

They were the centre of attention for the rest of the day, both delighted by their efforts.

On the way home, they shared for the first time their excitement.

"I am *so* pleased!" Sara exclaimed.

"Me too!" Dan replied, grinning from ear to ear.

That night, the Goodwins made dinner for the Christies, a celebration for the children's work, and the parents were able to read, for the first time, their projects in full.

Hugh said: "I'm very proud of you both. I've learned more about Mistlees in the last couple of hours than in the previous three months! Well, done, you two!"

Bruce couldn't resist adding: "Yes, it was so hard to choose a winner that even the clocks have stopped together!"

They looked at the clocks, sitting side-by-side on the table, and laughed.

Both had stopped at exactly the same time. Only Dan and Sara realised the significance. Both had stopped at exactly 2.29 with the second hand just past the hour.

2291.

They looked at each other and shivered.

On Saturday morning, the two teams and their supporters made a cheerful crowd on the bus. Spirits were high with the excitement of the day to come.

The bus was full at eight o'clock, but there was no sign of Graham.

He rushed up twenty minutes late, puffing and panting, glasses askew and his baggy tracksuit rumpled out of shape.

"Sorry about that!" He gasped, "Must have slept in! Right, let's go!"

Mrs Braid tutted, and the bus set off. Fortunately, there were no hold ups, and they arrived at the Oldhome pitches in Glasgow at ten o'clock.

Mark's team, Mistlees Firsts, were in a league with Glasgow Royals, Coptly Spartans and Mount Redcate, while Dan's team - Mistlees Seconds, were matched with Edinburgh College, Grumbey Gate School and Nescine Road.

Mistlees Firsts took the field against Coptly Spartans, and quickly got into their stride, with Liam and Eddie scoring early goals. Coptly Spartans did not seem to have much ability, and

Mark's team ran out easy winners, scoring five goals without reply.

On the other pitch, Glasgow Royals beat Mount Redcate 6 – 0.

Suddenly, it was the turn of Dan's team, drawn against Edinburgh College. Straight from the kick-off, the opposition made a neat attacking move pay off with a right-footed strike from their captain. Struan had no chance of making the save.

Dan called their planned kick-off move, passing to Iain who put a through ball straight to Shane, who side-footed it to Hamish. Dan came through on his outside to stroke a low ball under the goalkeeper's despairing dive.

1 – 1.

Struan made some amazing saves as the College team attacked time after time.

The match was very close, but the College team edged in front in the last minute with a ball lobbed over Struan's head. On the touchline, the Mistlees support was disappointed. Graham shook his head, and muttered: "No hopers!"

Dan was disappointed, but felt his team had played well.

Grumbey Gate School played a kick and rush game to defeat Nescine Road 2 – 0.

The second matches resulted in Mistlees Firsts comfortably beating Mount Redcate 3 - 1, while Glasgow Royals put eight goals past the luckless Coptly Spartans' keeper.

In Dan's section, Edinburgh College demolished Nescine Road 7 – 0, and Grumbey Gate School were no match for Dan and his teammates, getting into a rhythm, winning 5 – 0.

The last match in Section 1 saw Mark's team go down, surprisingly, 1 – 0 to Glasgow Royals, whilst Coptly Spartans and Mount Redcate fought out a goalless draw.

Dan and his team took the field against Nescine Road. It was an easy victory for Mistlees Seconds, by the equal biggest margin of the tournament - 8 – 0.

In the other match, Edinburgh College cruised to a 4 – 1 win against Grumbey Gate School.

The league tables were pinned up at lunchtime in the Oldhome pavilion.

LEAGUE 1

	W	D	L	F	A	Pts
Glasgow Royals	3	0	0	15	0	9
Mistlees Firsts	2	0	1	8	2	6
Mount Redcate	0	1	2	1	9	1
Coptly Spartans	0	1	2	0	13	1

LEAGUE 2

	W	D	L	F	A	Pts
Edinburgh College	3	0	0	13	2	9
Mistlees Seconds	2	0	1	14	2	6
Grumbey Gate School	1	0	2	3	9	3
Nescine Road	0	0	3	0	17	0

2.30pm First Semi-Final

Edinburgh College v Mistlees Firsts

3.00pm Second Semi-Final

Glasgow Royals v Mistlees Seconds

3.45pm Third Place Play –off

4.15pm Grand Final

Over lunch, there was huge anticipation of the matches to come.

The Mistlees supporters were thrilled both teams had got through to the semi-final.

Graham, amazed by Dan's team qualifying ("Don't believe those other teams have ever played before"), sat with Mark's team, flushed with the excitement of the competition.

Sara sat with Dan and friends, calm and composed. Dan said: "We just have to go out and enjoy ourselves. We've done really well so far, and anything else is a bonus!"

Iain added: "Wouldn't it be great to beat the Glasgow lot and play Mark in the final?"

The first semi-final was a tough match. Edinburgh College, who had won all three matches, were clearly confident, but knocked off stride by the bigger Mistlees boys. Mark shoulder charged the Edinburgh captain in the first minute, took the ball from him, passed to Eddie in open space, and crossed to Liam who headed home. The Mistlees supporters cheered, clapping each other on the back.

Edinburgh hit back, however, and at half time it was 1 – 1, a shot ricocheting off the post past Will.

In the second half with less than a minute to go, Sandy picked up the ball from defence and sent a long through pass to Mark, who stabbed the ball into the corner of the net.

2 – 1.

Ali and Asha led the cheers, Dan, Sara and the rest of the team joining in.

Graham was delighted, and could be heard saying in a loud voice: "Great coaching! Spot on! Great execution of my plans!"

Before they knew it, Dan and team were lining up against Glasgow Royals, the only side not to concede a goal. The Glasgow team swung smoothly into action, their attacking duo combining neatly to outsmart Iain and Hamish. A cracking left foot drive saw them one up within a minute.

Before the Mistlees boys could recover, they were two down to a beautifully headed cross from the corner flag.

Dan steadied his nerves, and they fought back with two goals from Iain.

Sara led the Mistlees support, out-cheering a noisy Glasgow crowd.

2 – 2.

The excitement reached fever pitch as play surged back and forwards, neither side able to take an advantage. Struan was immense in goals, giving the whole team confidence.

Late in the game, Glasgow conceded a throw-in in their own half. The Mistlees team had practised this set move many times, and it worked a treat. Shane threw the ball in to Dan who one-touched it back to him. Dan ran into the goal area for Shane to cross. Dan headed the ball down to Iain's feet, and he steered it past the keeper.

Both Mistlees teams were in the final.

As they walked off, Graham emerged from his team talk with Mark's team: "Well, what did you lose by?" He asked.

Dan grinned, and replied: "Winners don't lose, Graham."

He left the astonished coach gaping on the touchline.

The third place play off was a thriller, both teams playing superbly, but Glasgow Royals had the edge on Edinburgh College, and ended up winning by the odd goal in three.

It was time for the final.

Aware of the rivalry between the two Mistlees teams, the local supporters stayed to watch, and the atmosphere was electric as

Dan led his squad on ahead of the Firsts.

Dan won the toss, and elected to play against the breeze. Straight from kick off, the larger boys dominated, Liam and Eddie quickly combining to sweep a goal past a diving Struan.

Mark roughly shouldered past Iain to steal the ball from Shane's feet and toe-ended it up field to a waiting Liam. He elbowed his way round Dan and cracked the ball into the top of the net. The referee did not spot the foul.

Graham shouted instructions from the sideline and beamed at his team's success. At kick-off, Dan prepared the side for their set piece move, and shouted the codename: "Mark!"

Hearing his name, Mark stopped, in time to see Dan pass to Iain. He put a carefully steered ball to Shane, who side-footed it to Hamish. Dan came through on his right to push a low ball into the left corner of the net.

Mark complained bitterly to the referee he'd been put off by his name being shouted, but the referee said: "Son, it may be your name, but it's also the word for someone covering someone else. Play on!"

With a minute to go before half time, Sandy used the following wind to loft a long hanging ball into the Seconds' goalmouth. Dan jumped to head it, but Mark's superior height won, and the ball glanced off his forehead into the net.

3 – 1 at half time.

Graham was on the pitch immediately, waving his arms around and issuing a string of commands to Mark's team, while Dan gathered Shane, Iain, Hamish and Struan into a tight circle. They were breathing heavily, hands on knees.

Dan was upbeat: "It's only 3 – 1, and we've got the wind behind us, so let's give it our best shot!"

In the first minute of the second half, Mark tried to brush past Dan, who neatly whisked the ball from his feet, and dribbled past Liam and Eddie. Iain shouted support, and Dan dummied a pass to him. Sandy fell for it, leaving the path open for Dan to take the ball in to goal.

He swerved left and shot right, and Will's dive was too late. The Mistlees crowd, helped now by the locals, roared their approval.

3 – 2.

Graham was looking anxious, getting very red in the face His glasses were steamed up and his tracksuit even more crumpled than at the start of the day.

Dan's team had a spell of pressure, and several times came close to scoring. Will made a good save from a hard volley by Hamish, and the referee awarded the corner. Dan shouted the corner code: "Will!"

In goal, Will looked confused as Iain's high sweeping corner went to the edge of the penalty area where a waiting Shane trapped it. He tapped it past Eddie to an onrushing Hamish who thundered the ball past Will.

3 – 3.

The ball went into touch and Dan found himself on his own beside Mark who looked quickly round and Karate chopped him in the stomach. Winded, Dan went down, gasping for breath. Mark ran away immediately, and startled, Dan saw Mrs Braid grinning broadly, nodding her approval at Mark.

Dan was incensed and got up, breathing deeply. Sara saw him and he felt her positive energy flow through him.

The ball was ten yards from the Mistlees First's goal.

Dan held out his hand, focussed hard on it and felt a

supercharged rush of power flow through him and he flew the length of the pitch in a flash.

Startled, Liam and Sandy stood open mouthed as Dan took the ball in his stride, with only Will standing between him and a glorious victory.

Will edged out towards him, and Dan dummied to the left. Will covered him, but Dan sidestepped right. Will slipped, and the goal was open.

Dan grinned, turned away from goal, and deliberately pushed the ball over the goal line past the post.

The referee blew his whistle for full time.

The crowd were stunned to silence by Dan's deliberate miss, until they realised he had sacrificed victory to make the final score a draw.

An unbelieving Mark, followed by his teammates, lined up to shake hands with the Mistlees Seconds, while Shane, Iain, Hamish and Struan came to terms with Dan's action.

He simply explained: "A draw's a fair result".

After a few moments, this sunk in and Iain said: "You know, I think you're right!"

Hamish and Struan, the most improved player in the team, nodded thoughtfully and Shane summed up their feelings: "I really wanted to win this game – really wanted to beat them, but I think our codes were a bit unfair on them, and after all, we *know* we could have won!"

Dan said: "That's the way I feel too!"

They walked in a line past Mark's team, shaking hands and clapping each other on the back, amidst loud and long cheers from the crowd.

Mark squeezed Dan's hand painfully, looked him straight in the eye and said: "I wanted to thrash you lot and I thought we would. You cheated to get the draw, but we'll win in the end!"

Dan frowned, but shrugged, feeling renewed energy surge through him as he passed down the line, shaking hands with the others.

Graham puffed across to Dan. In a loud voice he said: "Well done, lad – I knew you had it in you. Just as well the Firsts gave you a chance!"

Dan simply shook his head.

At the prize giving, Dan and Mark jointly collected the cup, Mark avoiding eye contact.

The atmosphere on the bus home to Mistlees was cheerful, but Dan felt Mark's brooding presence all the way. As they got off at the school, Mark shoved in front of him, and a piece of paper fluttered from his pocket to the floor.

Dan picked it up to give back, but Mark was gone. He tucked it in his pocket.

At home that night, Dan proudly told Hugh and Liz about the football, and the Goodwins hosted the Christies, enjoying a takeaway meal, courtesy of the Deli, and delivered by Brad Maipeson who insisted on bringing it in to the house. His eyes were everywhere as he set it on the kitchen table: "Well, I hear Dan sneaked a draw today. That was a stroke of luck, wasn't it?"

Liz replied: "I don't think it was luck, Mr Maipeson. Dan's team are a pretty good side, you know!"

"If you say so," he replied, collecting the money for the meal greedily.

"Thanks mum," Dan said quietly, wondering whether he was the thief after all.

"Well, I hope you enjoy the meal. Having a little get together are we?"

"Yes", replied Liz frostily, "We are actually, so thank you for bringing the meal and I'll see you to the door."

"Fine. fine – no problem. Big crowd coming? The meal's for six. If you need more just give me a phone."

"That will be all we'll need, thank you. Good night!"

"Good night then – have a great evening."

Liz closed the door and leant against it: "Phew, what an awful man!"

She and Dan rejoined the others and Bruce said to him, with a mock bow: "Hail the conquering hero comes! Today Mistlees Firsts, tomorrow the world!"

Dan asked innocently: "Did you ever win a football tournament, Mr Christie?"

"Win one? Win only one? Dan, my boy, I cut my teeth on football trophies. I remember when I was your age----."

"Bruce!" Interrupted Diana, "I know you're sporty, with your clever Karate and all that, but I didn't think you played football at school."

"Ah! But I *thought* a good game, dear!"

He quickly changed the subject: "So how's the Rainbow Catching world then, Hugh?"

As Hugh replied, Dan and Sara went to the cellar, leaving the adults at the table.

T.P. listened as Sara said: "Brilliant! You did it! You travelled high speed!"

"I know! Good, wasn't it? Mark floored me. I felt you helping me, but when I saw Mrs Braid grinning that was it! It gave me the energy I needed. It felt fantastic!"

T.P. said: "Child's play", and Sara laughed: "Jealous, T.P.?"

"Hardly, young lady!"

Dan said: "Tomorrow's Nigel's day."

"Will it work, Dan?"

"You mean - will the rug take him?"

"Yes! Remember it's just been used to taking *us* to different places and times."

"Excuse me!" T.P. said.

"Sorry T.P., I didn't mean to forget you. Of course it's used to you too!"

"Indeed," T.P. replied with a bow.

"But how will it react to Nigel?" Sara continued.

"If he's been thinking positively about it, I'm sure it'll be OK."

"I hope so, but remember the trouble we had when we came back from seeing Peter?"

"Yes", said Dan, "but Nigel's strong. I'm sure he'll be able to deal with anything that crops up!"

"I hope so!" shivered Sara, "What if the rebel angels grab him?"

"Surely not! It's us they're after!"

"Well, that doesn't make me feel any better!"

"No, no – I mean – I think they'll leave Nigel alone. I'm sure they're after us because we're only children."

"So we need to get some more protection! T.P. – you've been a great help and so have the angels, but we must talk to Mr Dewbury soon!"

"Let's hope Nigel gets away safely and then we'll go and see him."

Sara thought for a second and said: "I wish the rebel angels would have a go at Mark!"

"I agree", chuckled Dan. "Oh, that reminds me," he said , pulling from his pocket the piece of paper Mark had dropped.

It was slightly crumpled. He straightened it out.

"What on earth is it?" Sara exclaimed.

Dan scratched his head: "I've no idea."

"Maybe it's part of the codex," Sara said excitedly.

"You're right. It could be. It's like a copy of something pretty old."

"What should we do?"

Dan thought for a moment: "Maybe we should send it to Peter to see what he makes of it."

"Good idea – and how about Leo too? He must know about ancient symbols and hieroglyphics and things."

"Even if he doesn't, he can use the internet."

Sara laughed: "Well, let's do it and see what they both think."

Dan scanned the script into his Rainbow Catcher, and sent it as an attachment to Peter and Leo with an e-mail:

Hi Peter and Leo, we found this today and think it might be part of the codex we're looking for. What do you think? Dan and Sara.

"Right," said Dan, "Let's see what they make of that!"

"It's exciting, isn't it? I hope they'll be able to translate."

But the replies to their e-mail were to come as a huge surprise.

Chapter 70

Excited by Nigel's imminent trip, and the mysterious paper Mark had dropped, neither Dan nor Sara slept well.

Dan's mind was full of dreams.

The Vashad Thains soared up high snowy mountains and jumped pyramids. They walked and crawled through a tunnel hidden deep in the rocks lit only by rush lamps. As they reached a cold but bright daylight, they fought furiously, Dan with them. He moved with speed and accuracy and felt poised and balanced.

An ancient man kept appearing and disappearing, and he was trying to tell Dan something but his words kept spiralling into thin air. A man in uniform was cranking a machine and taking notes, and the codex kept appearing and disappearing. Nobody could make sense of it, but Dan knew he could if he could hold on to it. It was grabbed by the doppelganger, then by the rebel angels. Vohumanah had it for a moment and then Brad Maipeson whisked it away. He was crawling along another tunnel with little room for movement and the air was suffocating him. Someone was punching and kicking him and he fought back desperately till he woke, realising Liz was shaking his shoulder.

"Hey!" She complained, "I'm not attacking you. I'm only waking you up! You were buried in the blankets!"

"Oh, sorry mum, I was dreaming!"

She raised her eyebrows: "Nothing serious I hope!" She said teasingly.

"Well, it was an awful jumble. I'm a bit nervous about today."

"You mean Nigel's trip?"

"Yes. It's been on my mind all night."

"I'm not surprised. It's been on our minds too, but Nigel's confident, isn't he?"

Dan gazed into the middle distance, remembering more and more of his dream: "I think so, mum."

Sara's sleep was filled with a succession of horrors.

She was on the rug with Dan and they were travelling through time, but she landed alone and couldn't find her way home. Everything was shadowy and dark, until she discovered she could switch the light on. She realised that she had been wrong about something vital but could see what she had to do to put it right and get home. Peter and Nigel helped her up but somebody knocked her over. The codex kept appearing and disappearing, grasped by Nigel, and then by Miss Ambrose. Mrs Braid, dressed all in black with a long pointy hat, pulled it away and a giant sized Mark knocked Dan out. The codex was consumed by fire and the rebel angels loomed over her and grabbed her by the shoulders.

"No! No!" She screamed: "You'll never get me!"

"Calm down! It's all right! It's only me! You're having a nightmare!"

"Oh, mum"! She sobbed, as she woke, gripping Diana tightly. "That was awful! Everyone was grabbing the codex and I couldn't get it, but I knew how to get home, and -----."

"It's all right, darling. It was only a dream!"

"I know, I know, and it was all mixed up and it was a bit scary."

She calmed down and was quiet as she remembered more of her dream.

After Sunday lunch, she joined Dan and they shared their dreams. Dan thought for a moment and said: "Well, the one thing that's sure is that everyone wants the codex!"

"Yes," Sara said determinedly, "So *we* need to find it!"

After lunch, a beaming Nigel joined them. Liz and Hugh welcomed him: "Come in, Nigel! It's good to see you!" said Liz.

"Thank you Mrs Goodwin, and it's good to see you too."

"Bruce and Diana wish you luck. They felt it would be a bit much, all of us here again."

"I understand. That is absolutely fine. I don't believe I'll be here for long anyway."

"No, no, of course not," Hugh said.

Tim broke up this awkward conversation, bursting in with the flying saucer in one hand, the plane in the other: "I'm flying today too!" He cried, roaming round the lounge, arms out wide, tilting and circling the models.

Liz said: "Right, well I don't suppose you'll need us now. Hugh, let's take Tim and make some tablet." Tim's eyes lit up.

"I hope everything works out for you," Liz said.

Hugh added: "And for Peter too. Bon voyage!"

Tim wrapped his arms round Nigel, then rushed off to the kitchen with mum and dad. Nigel looked at Dan and Sara, who led him down to the cellar.

The rug sat waiting, T.P. standing on it as if on guard, his hands stiffly by his sides. He bowed and looked surprised when Nigel bowed back.

"You must be T.P.," Nigel said, smiling.

"You know about me? You can see me?" T.P. replied.

"I only had to open my eyes."

"Well, I am happy that you have. I believe you go to meet your old friend?"

"I think he has been on his own for long enough."

"Yes, quite, but not on his own for as long as some", T.P. said dismally.

Sara interrupted: "T.P., stop feeling sorry for yourself. Nigel's going to help us, and so are you. We've got a big task ahead of us, and we need you both to be really focussed."

Nigel grinned at her confidence, and T.P. looked ashamed, muttering to himself.

Nigel was relaxed. He said: "Remember you know more than you think you know. You have learned much. Keep focussed on all that is positive and we will win through."

Dan said: "Yes, I understand."

"Keep clear of Mrs Braid. Wait for Peter and me to prepare you for the challenge."

"Are you ready?" Sara asked.

"Oh yes, I have been ready for a long time."

Sara said: "Tell Peter we're thinking about him ----"

"-----and we'll see you both again------"

"-----soon!"

Nigel focused on the rug and the centre circle began to pulse, its pale indigo strengthening in colour.

"I'll not say goodbye," he said, and stepped on to the rug.

Then came a magical moment. As T.P. drifted absent-mindedly round the cellar, Nigel and the rug began to pulse and fade in rhythm, Sara and Dan moved together, and around them a rainbow of colours formed. Their movements slow and graceful, their features blurred and merged and the two children seemed to become one for a split second.

They converged, and in a glittering haze of stardust, became themselves once more.

The air around Nigel softly glittered, sparkling like diamonds. A violet flame shimmered round his head. Dan and Sara were speechless as he disappeared with a loud whoosh.

The rug vanished with him.

But not for long.

With a roar of rushing air, it was back.

But not as before.

To their astonishment, they saw it was bigger – and white.

Then black.

Then white again, with a kaleidoscope of colours rippling all over its surface.

Red, orange, yellow, green, blue, indigo and violet circles, each the size of a football, pulsed with energy and power as the cellar fell silent.

Before they could say anything, Dan's Rainbow Catcher beeped.

He opened an e-mail. It was from Leo. They read it together.

My dear Dan and Sara,
Your message fills me with dread. What you have stumbled across is written in Theban Script. Also termed the Runes of Honorius this is the chosen language of witches. Alas, I cannot yet translate the message, but I believe it is a letter.
Be very careful.
Fond regards, Leo.

Sara gasped and Dan went pale.

The Rainbow Catcher beeped again.

They read:

Dear Dan and Sara,
This confirms my worst fear.
The paper you have found is not part of the codex.
It is a letter from a witch.
Here is what it says:
"Mark,
We are finding the codex harder to crack than we thought.
D and S are a real threat but I will deal with them. Be patient. Mrs B"

You must keep clear of her! Halloween is close, and her powers will then be at their height. Nigel is with me now, and we will be in touch soon.
Take great care,

Peter.

"Oh, Dan!" exclaimed Sara. "Mrs Braid's after us! What will we do?" She gripped Dan's arm, an icy chill of fear sweeping through her.

Dan felt Sara's terror and shivered.

Grimly, he said: "Well, now we know for sure. She and Mark have the codex. And she says *"we"* are finding it hard to crack, so they're not alone!"

"Dan, how can we fight a witch? And Mark? And Miss Ambrose?"

"And probably Brad Maipeson too," Dan added.

"I feel so alone", Sara said, close to tears.

"Sara, we must be strong. We're *not* alone. We've got Peter and Nigel on our side".

"And me!" said TP, from the centre of the new rug.

"Thanks, T.P." said Dan, "And we have the angels on our side, so that seems good odds to me!"

"But Halloween's not long away. What will she do?"

"I don't know Sara, but we must get Mr Dewbury on our side. He'll know what's best."

They clasped hands for reassurance.

Dan felt very scared, but a surge of inner strength coursed through him: "This is what we're here to do. We have to fight! We'll wait for Nigel and Peter to get back to us, but for now, let's remember all we've learned. We must be strong and positive. I'm not going to let Mark and the others beat us. Together we'll win."

With a determined grin forming on his lips, he said: "It's not everyday you get to battle a witch!"

Sara felt his energy power through her, and gave herself a shake: "Right! Let's do it! We won't give up without a fight, and if there's one thing I can do it's fight!"

Dan playfully punched her arm, T.P. wrapped his arms round them both and the cellar crackled with energy.

They were about to face the test of their lives.

oOo

Acknowledgements

So many influences have shaped The Timetrippers that it's hard to know where to begin – but I do, so I will.

Without Joan Charles, psychic and clairvoyant, this book wouldn't have got off the ground. She coached me to develop my intuition, a great skill, which led me on to learn more about loads of stuff, including reading the series of James Redfield books which start with The Celestine Prophecy. He is happy for me to use his concepts, which if you look under the surface, you'll find in spades.

If you haven't read them, even if you're only 10, take 100 lines and start now! The Celestine Prophecy was the inspiration for writing what I hoped would be like a children's version of the grown-up stuff. Thank you, James.

When I started to write The Timetrippers, I got terrific help from Minnie Grey who's a super author – read her too as soon as you like – and from Julie Steele, at that time doing her editing stint in London.

The moulding influence who transformed the book from a spiritual journey for children to a racing chasing roller-coaster ride is Wendy Rimmington, my very lovely Agent, from the Scottish Literary Agency, who saw something in what I'd written that she felt could be very good indeed if I tried harder and added some things -which I did.

She's a very good grown up minder who would be pretty hard to beat in a trip round the publishing world.

I had some willing (nearly) helpers too who helped fine-tune the final version you're either reading now, or about to start reading (or maybe reading again?) and they are Struan, my 13 year old son, who's now a professional critic; Victoria, at age 10, the first person to read it outside these four walls; her mum, Julie and my oldest son, Dale, all of whose comments and suggestions meant a lot. My big brother Rae and my second son, Scott, astonished me by finishing their reads in record time and with timely input too.

In case you hadn't guessed, all of the above paragraph are Robertsons, but there are some non-Robertsons too who really helped shape the final version, especially Louis Rimmington, who deserves to be a top notch editor.

Special thanks too to Rick Anderson from Ooko for his brilliant cover design and the Mistlees map, and to Dale Porteous and Alan Seath from Refresh Design who created my fabulous website – www.thetimetrippers.co.uk .
Without Chris Elvery, a good friend from Call2Action who put me in touch with these wizards, and who steered me through the technological minefields I encountered, the book would have fallen far short in these areas.

Abune them a' however, is my lovely wife, Shirley, who cajoled, encouraged, applauded, critiqued and loved all I wrote; who reassured, sympathised, steered, was patient beyond words, listened, advised, and also paid all the bills. Her love pulled me through.

On a more practical level, I used a complete multitude of reference sources not the least of which was Encyclopaedia Britannica Online. I read around 40 books and referenced many more, and maybe when I'm rich and famous I'll catalogue them too.

As my memory's not fantastic and if I've forgotten anyone, then I hope I'm forgiven. If you know who else influenced me, let me know, and if I've not thanked anyone properly, please scold me with the thought police, or maybe e-mail me and I'll fix it quicker than a rainbow coloured rug.

hamish@thetimetrippers.co.uk